CARNAGE

NATE TEMPLE SERIES BOOK 14

SHAYNE SILVERS

ARGENTO
PUBLISHING

CONTENTS

Shayne Silvers

Carnage

Nate Temple Series Book 14

A TempleVerse Series

Formerly published as The Temple Chronicles Series

ISBN: 978-1-947709-62-1

© 2020, Shayne Silvers / Argento Publishing, LLC

info@shaynesilvers.com

THE NATE TEMPLE SERIES—A WARNING

Nate Temple starts out with everything most people could ever wish for—money, magic, and notoriety. He's a local celebrity in St. Louis, Missouri—even if the fact that he's a wizard is still a secret to the world at large.

Nate is also a bit of a...well, let's call a spade a spade. He can be a mouthy, smart-assed jerk. Like the infamous Sherlock Holmes, I specifically chose to give Nate glaring character flaws to overcome rather than making him a chivalrous Good Samaritan. He's a black hat wizard, an anti-hero—and you are now his partner in crime. He is going to make a *ton* of mistakes. And like a buddy cop movie, you are more than welcome to yell, laugh and curse at your new partner as you ride along together through the deadly streets of St. Louis.

Despite Nate's flaws, there's also something *endearing* about him...You soon catch whispers of a firm moral code buried deep under all his snark and arrogance. A diamond waiting to be polished. And you, the esteemed reader, will soon find yourself laughing at things you really shouldn't be laughing at. It's part of Nate's charm. Call it his magic...

So don't take yourself, or any of the characters in my world, too seriously. Life is too short for that nonsense.

Get ready to cringe, cackle, cry, curse, and—ultimately—*cheer* on this snarky wizard as he battles or befriends angels, demons, myths, gods, shifters, vampires and many other flavors of dangerous supernatural beings.

DON'T FORGET!

VIP's get early access to all sorts of book goodies, including signed copies, private giveaways, and advance notice of future projects. AND A FREE NOVELLA! Click the image or join here:
www.shaynesilvers.com/l/219800

FOLLOW AND LIKE:
Shayne's FACEBOOK PAGE:
www.shaynesilvers.com/l/38602
I try to respond to all messages, so don't hesitate to drop me a line. Not interacting with readers is the biggest travesty that most authors can make. Let me fix that.

Bloodcurdling screams and ragged, panting hisses echoed off the walls, piercing my eardrums with each reverberation. Screams of agony, not cries of terror. Because we no longer cried about fear.

We'd become dear friends with the sensation. Embraced it with open arms. Devoted ourselves to it like loyal, steadfast lovers. It had been the only way to stay sane. So we screamed when it hurt, and smiled the moment it stopped.

The source of the screams sagged limply, sucking in a deep breath. And then he began to laugh raucously. "That was better than awake water," he admitted dryly. By *awake water*, Carl probably meant coffee. Our mental agility had hit a few speed bumps after a week of being tortured four times a day—more often than we had been fed and watered—so we frequently caught ourselves phrasing things in unique ways rather than wasting the energy needed to remember terms that had once seemed so important. Which was why I could remember coffee; nothing was more important than coffee, except maybe alcohol. Each night we had a rollicking good laugh about that day's new additions to urban slang.

It was the simple things that kept us going.

Anyone listening in on our evening conversations might have declared us quite mad. But I wasn't a brain fixer, so I reserved judgment. I frowned, tasting the phrase on my tongue. *Not brain fixer. Therapist*, I chided myself. I chuckled under my breath, cherishing the small joke so that I didn't forget to tell Carl later. He would laugh and laugh and laugh.

The only thing keeping Carl upright were the chains extending from the thick metal manacles around his wrists to an empty spot on the ceiling. Magic of some sort held them there. The manacles matched my own, and they glowed with faint red runes, like tiny night lights.

I stared at the maestro of our morning's misery with a cold, flat, emotionless look, ignoring the stiff feel to my skin caused by the dried blood caked across my face. I'd already taken my turn, after all. Well, my first turn.

It was early yet.

And our Olympian jailers were nothing if not workhorses. I had at least three more sessions in store over the course of the rest of the day. I'd have to save my brain fixer joke for after that.

The bastard with the knife glanced over his shoulder at me with an expectant smile.

I stared back at him, waiting, my face giving away nothing. "You finished yet, or do you need to take a break?"

The pale, bloody lizard behind him began to laugh in a low, rasping wheeze, lifting his head despite his agony. Blood dripped from his nostrils and ridged mouth—where humans had lips.

"Your mother hits harder than that," Carl wheezed. Then he managed to thrust his hips lewdly. "And I hit Hera last night." His impersonation of Elvis Presley's loose hips made it abundantly clear that he'd had an entirely different definition for the word *hit*.

I let a slow, malevolent smile stretch across my lips as I stared at the god currently in charge of making us more...agreeable. "She also made Carl bleed more," I said. "You know, when she was raking her fingernails into his back as he plowed her. I hardly slept a wink—"

Ares backhanded me, sending my weakened body tumbling. Unfortunately, my own chains were affixed to a ring in the center of the room's floor, which prevented me from reaching the wall. As they snapped tight with a metallic clanking sound, my momentum stopped cold as my manacles—and the wicked thorns lining the interior of the metal cuffs—bit deeply into my already scabbed, bloody wrists, reopening old wounds. As I sat back up, I risked a look down to make sure Ares hadn't dislocated or severed them.

Not that it would have really mattered, anyway. Our jailers had an elixir they forced down our throats if they went too far and accidentally killed or fatally wounded us. Ambrosia had brought me back from the brink of death more times than I could count.

I spat blood out, tonguing the tooth Ares had just loosened with his backhanded blow.

"Don't kill the messenger," I muttered. "It's not my fault if Zeus' power-grid had a blackout and Hera wanted to take a walk on the wild side." I grinned. "It's my turn tonight. I'm going to make that piglet squeal, son."

He stormed my way, his eyes flickering with crimson light, and he lifted his massive boot, preparing to stomp my face.

I didn't shy away. Instead, I stared up at him with a sinister smile on my face. He hesitated, studying my lack of fear with a flicker of unease. He slowly lowered his boot.

"Sooie!" I crowed, taunting him. Carl echoed the sound, cackling hard enough to send him into a coughing, choking fit.

Ares' face contorted into a purple knot of rage and he lifted his boot again.

The door burst open and a large, older man immediately tackled Ares into the wall—right as Ares' boot was flying for my face—and the two of them hit hard enough to make dust fall from the ceiling.

Zeus grabbed his son's face like he was palming a basketball and slammed the back of his head into the wall. Stone crunched, crumbling to the floor. Ares' eyes momentarily rolled into the back of his head before he regained focus, staring at his father with an incredulous look.

"He said he was going to—"

"I don't care what he said!" Zeus thundered, his fists crackling with fingers of lightning around his knuckles, zapping his son's face on contact, and causing his entire body to momentarily spasm. "He's chained up. If I wanted him dead, I would have killed him days ago. You keep this up, and I will lock *you* in here. You've gone through a *gallon* of Ambrosia. Do you have any idea how much those ingredients cost?"

Ares' eyes smoldered with stubborn defiance. "Hermes can make more," he grumbled.

Zeus leaned his head back and closed his eyes, muttering a curse under his breath. He wore a plain white toga with a dark leather belt, and leather sandals, but he radiated authority despite the apparent loungewear. He was a buff, older man with long gray hair and a prominent tan, looking like a wealthy, powerful man in the prime of his life. In short, he looked like a swell guy who owned a dozen successful companies and donated a lot to charities.

In my opinion, he was a sociopathic asshole.

"You shouldn't *need* Ambrosia," Zeus thundered. "What good is repeatedly killing him and then bringing him back? What does he have to fear if he knows he'll wake up after, no matter what you do to him?" Ares frowned as if his father had spoken a prophecy. "And I don't trust Hermes being in charge of anything they consume, not after he tried to help them with his damned coins. It is not his job to clean up your messes."

I'd seen Hermes from a distance a time or two during my captivity, but he hadn't been permitted to see us in private due to the whole coin thing. In my opinion, *help* was overstating it. He'd given me a coin to fight some dragons a few years ago, and then another coin that I'd recently used to break us free of our previous set of Olympian chains after Zeus had strung us up beside Prometheus. Hermes' *help* had landed us here.

Ares clenched his jaw, glaring back at Zeus. "If you're going to neuter me whenever I'm getting anywhere useful, I'm finished trying. *Father*." He stormed past Zeus and left the room.

I sat down on my rear with a tired sigh, eyeing the Father of the Olympians.

The Cloudgatherer.

The God of Lightning.

"Premium stock you got there," I said, jerking my chin towards the cell door and Ares' abrupt departure. "No wonder you fuck animals in your spare time. You're a real goat-getter. Anything to spice up the gene pool, am I right?"

I knew I was wildly twisting the myths, but let's be honest; there was no positive way to spin a story involving an animal and a woman having nonconsensual sex. The fact that you were the animal in the story didn't make it any better.

Case in point, Zeus clenched his jaw so hard his thick beard rose up and down.

Zeus didn't rise to my bait, unfortunately. He glanced over his shoulder at the bleeding Elder. He took a reflexive step back to find Carl flashing him a coldblooded, lizardly grin. Then Carl blew Zeus a wet kiss, flicking his tongue out at him. I chuckled.

Zeus snapped his fingers and Carl's chains fell from the ceiling. The Elder collapsed to the ground with a wet splat, landing in a pool of his own blood. His chains suddenly attached to the other metal ring in the center of the room. There was enough slack in them for us to move about the room, but not enough for us to reach any of the walls.

I settled my hands in my lap, absently glancing at the glowing crimson runes on the chains and manacles. Those on the manacles seemed different—older—than those on the chains, but both were unbreakable. The runes prevented me from using my power, trapping us in this cursed cell on this cursed mountain high above the clouds.

Carl promptly—but painfully—propped himself up into a sitting position, obviously not trusting his legs to support his weight. He assessed his injuries in an idle manner, as if the warden wasn't looming over us.

Two dirty, threadbare, lumpy cots rested near the extent of our leashes. We'd placed the refuse bucket as far away as possible from our beds. That was pretty much it. Well, my satchel and the puffer jacket Carl had borrowed from Chateau Falco—apparently, Ashley's favorite coat—hung on the far wall, out of our reach. The once-pink jacket was now filthy and sleeveless, and needed to be destroyed—and secretly replaced—before Ashley learned of it.

Zeus must have noticed me eyeing my satchel, because he calmly walked up to it, studying it thoughtfully. It hung on the wall, unmolested.

Mainly because they couldn't figure out how to get anything out of it. Not for lack of trying. I'd watched as they'd spent hours reaching inside; in hopes that they might grab hold of one of my magical toys. They'd also thrown every imaginable magic at their disposal at it—all to no avail. So, it hung on the wall, silently mocking their impotence.

If I had been a betting man, I would have gambled that this was the reason for their torture—to try and get me to open it for them. They hadn't even come close to breaking me. Because there was absolutely no chance I would give them what they wanted. I had too many dangerous things in there. My Horseman's Mask, for one. Something about my manacles prevented me from accessing it. Another item out of our reach was Gungnir—Odin's legendary spear, which also featured a Devourer. It was the blade prophesied to kill Fenrir, the giant wolf I had just saved from his own prison cell.

Loki's son.

But I'd taped a Sensate to the spear so that Odin couldn't sense it. Other than that, I wasn't sure what they might want. And, to be clear, I had no idea if that was even the reason for the torture. They could have been trying to sell us a timeshare. Those guys were persistent.

Zeus turned back to us with an annoyed frown, watching us pensively as if considering his next steps. Carl and I were both beaten to hell, bloody, and covered in burns and cuts. Ares had a very hands-on approach to his visits.

Apollo had preferred extreme tanning, chaining us up outside to weather the elements. Carl—being an Elder—had fared that experience much better than me. But his realm had a sun that could boil the flesh from human bones, so Apollo's best efforts probably felt more like a heat-lamp in a lizard aquarium.

On the other hand, I was fairly certain I had some second-degree burns.

I glanced at Carl since Zeus seemed to have zoned out. He looked rough, but he'd looked worse in the last few days. He didn't seem to need any Ambrosia. I almost gagged, imagining the thick, syrupy, strangely savory drink. I'd heard it called the nectar of the gods, and I was very leery about reading the ingredients label.

I hadn't seen any other gods, monsters, demigods, or even pretty architecture of the fabled Mount Olympus. I was betting this Alcatraz-like prison was on its own mountain, and far removed from the paved streets of their capital city.

Olympatraz.

It seemed fairly obvious Zeus didn't want anyone knowing we were here. At least five times in the last few days, our torture sessions had abruptly ended in the middle of the fun parts, and any participating gods had disappeared with panicked looks on their faces.

Zeus had even stormed into the cell one time, looking frantic, and grabbed Apollo by the hair before they'd disappeared.

That had actually been the worst, because Zeus had left our prison cell door open. Carl and I had both strained against our chains, clawing for the opening, but too far away to do anything other than stare helplessly at freedom. Carl had even tried breaking his wrist to slip through the manacles.

He'd quickly fallen to the floor in a puddle of his own blood. Minutes later, Zeus had returned with an annoyed look on his face, muttering about nosy children. He'd taken one look at Carl, gasped in alarm, and then poured an entire vial of Ambrosia down Carl's throat before the Elder succeeded in bleeding out.

As we'd waited for the unconscious Carl to recover, Zeus had lectured me on how the manacles worked. Titan Thorns, he'd called them. The thorn feature was the reason Carl had failed to rip his hand free of the cuffs without almost killing himself. The stronger we pulled, the deeper the thorns would dig into our flesh. The thorns were even angled so that any attempt at such a motion stabbed into the wrist in the opposite direction.

Basically, it was like slowly pressing your palm onto the tip of six blades and pushing towards them so that you were willingly impaling yourself.

We had also learned that it was impossible to purposely harm ourselves in any manner imaginable—which was comical since the gods spent as much time as possible harming us in *every* manner imaginable. Carl had vocally warned them that he would eat through his own wrists to get out of the Titan Thorns.

Turned out, he couldn't.

Every time he'd tried, his teeth had clamped shut just shy of his flesh. From my perspective, it had been eerie to watch—to see him holding his wrist inside his gaping jaws, only to watch him bite down and find his wrist magically out of harm's way.

So, after a few days of creative suicide and self-mutilation attempts, we'd actually found ourselves looking forward to the torture sessions with Apollo and Ares.

At first, the very real concern of permanent danger had held me back. What kind of wizard would I be if I broke out of here as a crippled wreck?

The handi-capable Horsemen of Hope didn't have the same ring to it. But I'd passed the point of despair rather quickly. I looked forward to taunting my jailers, of course, but there was something more to it.

Knowing that they wouldn't—at least for now—let me permanently injure myself, had allowed me to embrace the pain, much like an endurance runner added on another mile to their jog every day. Pushing to see how far they could go. It was all I had to look forward to. How much pain could I handle?

How long could I smile?

How close to insanity could I get without breaking?

How defiant could I be?

I soon learned that I was alarmingly talented at my newest venture—much to the frustration of Ares and Apollo.

Without a word, Zeus spun on his heel and exited our cell, slamming the door shut behind him.

Just like that, he was gone.

I turned to Carl, smiling. "I've got a new one. Brain fixer instead of therapist."

Carl smiled faintly, but I could tell his heart wasn't in it. That was not a good sign, but I kept the thought to myself.

2

It had been a few hours since Zeus and Ares had stormed out of our cell. No one else had returned. Even Apollo had skipped his afternoon torture session with us. So, Carl and I had gotten to work.

I swept my eyes across the crimson runes on my chains. Most of the symbols were strange perversions of the Greek alphabet, but I saw some that resembled Enochian script, hieroglyphics, Kanji, and several other historical alphabets. Judging by the odd modifications to the familiar Greek symbols, I was assuming the others were similarly unique. As I focused upon a new rune, I quickly felt an arctic chill whisper across my forearms. I absently brushed the frost away from my skin, refusing to blink as I studied the rune more intently.

"Ice," I murmured aloud.

"Which one?" Carl asked in a dry whisper.

"The one that looks like a nipple."

Our prison cell was quiet for a few moments. Then I felt Carl lean forward to look over my shoulder. "What kind of nipple?"

I slowly turned to look at him, arching an eyebrow. "Is that really relevant?"

Carl indicated another rune that resembled a chalice with no base.

"That resembles an udder, which is a cow's nipple. There is a vast spectrum of nipples, and all should be considered. My nipples, for example—"

I averted my gaze and lifted my palm to ward him off. "No more nipples. I'm talking about the one that looks like a circle with a peak in the middle."

"Ah," Carl said in a knowing tone. "Like your nipples. I know those well."

Thankfully, he didn't comment further on his familiarity with my nipples and he didn't continue his efforts to show off his own. Instead, he remained firmly in my personal space and narrowed his eyes to slits, committing the symbol and its associated power to memory. We'd both decided to mentally catalog the symbols, hoping to find a way to overpower them or to at least understand them, in case we were released for bad behavior. Because I had a sneaking suspicion that Zeus had a big ask coming our way since his efforts both at breaking us and getting into my satchel had epically failed. I wasn't sure if escaping this godforsaken place would be worth the price he was going to demand.

I eyed my threadbare clothes. They were hardly fit for shop rags in the garage. My wrists were scabbed and bleeding, and dozens of other cuts and sores dotted my skin. Some of my sunburns closely resembled dark, purplish bruises—or maybe I had bruises beneath my sunburns.

In summation, it hurt to exist. And it hurt worse when no one was torturing me, because my defiance in the face of active cruelty was an armor of sorts. Sitting alone brought on a sense of hopelessness—having someone to fight allowed me to momentarily forget about the reality of my impotence.

Carl didn't look much better. Since he was basically immune to sunlight, Apollo and Ares had set to him with blades and, with his exceedingly tough scales, they had to put some real elbow grease into it. Still, he looked tough as nails, ignoring the obviously debilitating wounds since there was nothing to be done for them.

"Say it, Carl," I said, shaking off the thoughts of an eternity spent here. Elders lived a long time, and now that I was a godkiller, my time on Earth might have received an extended lease.

He looked up at me. "Again?"

I nodded firmly. "It helps."

He shrugged, the words meaning absolutely nothing to him since he didn't understand pop culture. "Lara Croft has nothing on you, Master Temple."

"Damn right," I growled, turning back to the symbols. If the Tomb Raider could solve mysterious prehistoric and supernatural puzzles, how could a wizard of my caliber fail?

I turned back to the Nate's nipple symbol and narrowed my eyes as I let my mind wander. Despite not understanding how staring at the symbol had made actual frost cover my skin, I had grown accustomed to the strange reactions by now. I hastily skipped the next symbol—that one had been fire, and it had burned a patch of hair from my forearm before I had managed to swat it out.

Each rune gave off a different pulse of energy. One of them had even felt like a vacuum—not a physical sensation, but as if it had been attempting to gobble up my life force. Carl had dubbed that one the Devourer, and it had even resembled a cut gemstone in the shape of a heart.

As I focused my undivided attention on each new symbol, it would momentarily grow brighter until its associated magical sensation lashed out at me—oftentimes in a hostile manner, like a dog snapping its teeth. This collection of symbols somehow amalgamated into what was blocking me from using my magic. A spell of some kind. Even though it hurt me to study, it was as close as I could currently get to feeling magic.

I couldn't even sense my wizard's magic anymore.

None of my various other powers were accessible, as if I'd only imagined ever having them.

The harder I focused on the newest symbol, the dizzier I became. I let out a measured breath, my eyes watering as I forced myself to continue staring at the hourglass on its side. It almost looked like a Norse rune. Despite the dizziness, I could feel...something emanating from it. Something I almost understood. It almost sounded like a song—

I blinked. No. It *was* a song. I spun and shot Carl a dark glare. He was humming *Do-Re-Mi* from The Sound of Music—his favorite movie ever. To be fair, it might have also been the only movie he'd watched through to the end. He had his eyes closed and he was bobbing his head up and down absently as he hummed. "Carl. Stop."

He opened his eyes and cocked his head. "It helps me relax."

I sighed, lifting a hand to brush my hair out of my eyes. The heavy chains clinked against my Titan Thorns at the motion. I dismissed the symbols decorating the manacles, having already inspected them thoroughly. They had been the first symbols we studied. Strangely enough, they were absolutely identical to the ones on Carl's manacles. I'd assumed they would be different since he was an Elder and I was a wizard. Were they one size traps all?

"Alucard," Carl murmured, not needing to elaborate. The only power seemingly uninhibited by the Titan Thorns was that Carl still had a mental connection with Alucard—able to talk to him through a mind-meld of sorts.

I shook my head firmly. "He would bring everyone up here—if he could even find us, that is—and they would all get themselves killed. This is Mount Olympus and none of my friends are gods. An invasion would only serve to unite the other Olympian gods against a common enemy."

"You are friends with some gods. You are also friends with a fellow godkiller."

I shuddered at the thought of Fenrir coming to Mount Olympus. As far as I knew, he still had his collar, which would limit his abilities. I hadn't saved him only to get him killed or captured again. And I wasn't sure if friends was an accurate definition of our relationship. "Not yet. We need to find our own way out of this."

Carl nodded obediently. He'd suggested it a few times already. "As you wish, Master Temple."

He crossed his legs, and closed his eyes. I watched the holes of his nostrils contract as he took a slow, deep breath, and then they expanded as he let out an even slower exhale.

Carl was an Elder—a human-sized lizard man who scared gods, monsters, and pretty much every supernatural faction I had ever encountered. Carl's white scales were dusty and looked dry—as if he was a snake approaching the season to shed his skin.

Which was something Carl did, on occasion. I was definitely not looking forward to sharing his cell for that experience. The almost erotic sounds he made while peeling off his old skin had been forever burned into my memories from his time living at Chateau Falco, but at least I'd had an escape option there.

I still wondered why, exactly, Carl had chosen to latch onto me when Zeus had taken the form of an eagle and abducted me after we'd rescued Fenrir from captivity. It had seemed more than a reflexive action. Almost as if he had instantly known what was happening the moment the eagle first appeared.

I sat down in front of Carl, mirroring his pose. He cracked open an eye. "What are you doing?" I asked.

"Meditating. Envisioning our escape. Visualizing the fountains of ichor we will soon spill across the steps of Mount Olympus. Relishing in the symphony of screams we will orchestrate. Savoring the tantalizing scents of burning flesh and hot, godly blood as we raze this place to the ground." He flicked his long tongue out as if he could already taste it.

"Oh. I thought you were just napping or something."

He smirked. "I am wakefully dreaming," he said. "I do not seek hope, Master Temple," he said slowly. "I seek guidance for how violent we should be when we do break out."

Okay. I was arrogantly confident on the best of days, but Carl was obviously delusional. "We are slightly outnumbered. We're talking about a whole pantheon full of gods against a shackled wizard and Elder."

He blinked with his transparent, inner eyelid, utterly unimpressed. "The gods are merely playthings to the Elders. The Olympians are more frightened than we are. Can you not taste it on their breath? They hold the leashes to *meteors*. Do not be so impressed by gods." He spat a bloody glob on the floor. "Oh, look!" he exclaimed, pointing at the bloody glob. "One of my baby teeth! I just became a man!"

I stared at him, suppressing an eerie shudder at his dismissive god comments and pretending I hadn't heard—or seen—anything regarding the long, bloody tooth by my foot. "I hope you have an idea about how to get us out of this mess, then."

He nodded pensively. "We will do what we must, Master Temple."

I sighed, not knowing if I liked that vague, fortune cookie answer. "Until I understand what's going on here, I am hesitant to borrow trouble by asking for help from others. Maybe that is what Zeus really wants. To frighten me enough that I lure the new Horsemen—or any of my other allies—here for a rescue mission that is a trap."

Carl had his eyes closed again. "You should meditate on it, like the many-armed godlings once taught you."

I stared at him. Many-armed godlings? I opened my mouth to pepper him with questions, but the answer hit me almost immediately. Shiva. He had taught me astral projection—the ability to let my soul wander the world while my body remained stationary.

That thought tickled my memory for another reason. This wasn't the first time I'd been trapped in an impenetrable prison. I had once been locked up in Hell with Mordred...

Ruin—the baby Beast of Chateau Falco and my own Beast, Kai—had found me. He'd been searching for his father, not knowing he was dead, and had found me instead, having followed the Temple Crest branded into my palm.

I stared down at my palm now, feeling the surge of hope flicker and die as I considered the fact that Zeus might be able to take Ruin for himself. His current form was a storm cloud, after all. I shuddered at the mental image of giving Zeus a Beast of his own.

And if I did see Ruin on the astral fields, he might decide to do something heroic despite my warnings. Bumping into him could be just as bad as contacting Alucard, kicking off a doomed rescue mission. Maybe...I could spy on them, though. Get a feel for what was happening in the world in my absence. That couldn't hurt.

I closed my eyes and began to meditate, clearing my mind of my injuries and aches, squashing my fears and pretending I didn't feel fresh blood leaking from the wound over my ribs. Oddly enough, I hadn't noticed it until I was consciously trying to wall off all physical pain. I must have managed to shut off my pain receptors without trying up until now.

Or I was just numb to it.

As my thoughts faded away, my soul slipped out of my body and I immediately found myself surrounded by thick darkness. I'd succeeded, despite my Titan Thorns. My body might be a prisoner, but my mind was free and at peace—

I heard a crack of thunder that sounded like a glacier calving beneath me, and spotted a spiderweb of crimson lightning in the distance, the only source of light in my dark universe.

It looked like the astral fields were expecting a storm. I stepped forward —even though there was no ground to speak of—wondering if I was the harbinger of the storm or a victim. Then I chuckled. "I'm the Catalyst."

The black skies screamed around me, and the lightning storm bloomed with life.

3

More tendrils of red lightning rapidly crackled across the darkness, bathing me in crimson light. I glanced down at my clothes and scowled. I changed my appearance—since I was astral projecting, and nothing about me was currently real anyway—so that I wore a tailored blazer over a tight-fitting dress shirt that sat dark against a pair of acid washed jeans. Next, I imagined a pair of brown leather loafers. Because loafers were comfy.

I somehow fed power into the red lightning around me and the infinite blackness shattered like a broken, stained-glass window.

As the darkness fell, the scenery changed as drastically as if it had been concealed by a theater curtain or an opera house.

The screams and wails of the dead were almost as high-pitched and vibrant as an opera singer, but nowhere near as skilled.

I was in Hell, surrounded by a writhing mass of boiling lava. Apparently, I'd booked a cruise on the world's shittiest boat.

I slowly turned to find my old friend, Charon—the Boatman—seated before me. He wore his usual dark, threadbare, hooded robe, and his lips were sewn up with thick, filthy, knotted twine. He clutched a can of beer in either hand, and was holding one of them out to me. His oar—a strangely ancient blade-like shape—was wedged into a holder on the side of the boat, and a dented, scuffed cooler sat near his feet. I knew it would be brimming with cheap beer or his mysterious home brew—made with water from the infamous River Styx.

"You can see me?" I asked, reaching for the beer. Typically, the whole point of astral projecting was to see but not interact.

He gave me a flat stare. "Dude. It's my *only* job—to catch wandering spirits." He didn't necessarily *speak*, but his words filled my mind nonetheless.

I grunted. "Right." I took the can, popped the tab, and took a long drink. It felt...amazing. After receiving nothing but tepid sips of water over the last week, it was the most refreshing drink I'd ever had.

"Thanks," he said, smiling at my obvious reaction to his beer. His smile tugged at the twine over his lips, but he had never seemed to care much about the gruesome effect.

"I didn't mean to come here, to be honest," I admitted. I had been thinking about my prison in Hell, though. I must have gotten my wires crossed. And how had I been able to use my power to affect that crimson lightning? I glanced down to see that I still wore my Titan Thorns, and that the similarly crimson runes were glowing. Had I somehow tapped into their power?

I fidgeted uncomfortably under Charon's scrutiny. It had been so long since I'd casually sat with anyone other than Carl, that I felt like a savage animal invited to a dinner party. The only other living people I'd encountered had been torturing me to death. Punishing the monster, Nate Temple, for unspecified reasons. To be fair, I couldn't necessarily blame them.

I'd done some pretty monstrous things in recent years. I hadn't been such a nice—

"You're pretty much the nicest person in the world," Charon mused, sweeping his gaze over the roiling lava as if making sure we didn't have any witnesses. "You know that, right?"

I jolted, wondering if he'd read my mind. "Pardon?"

He nodded. "I know the look," he said, gesturing with his beer towards my face. "Everyone is so scared of the Boatman. Granted, I'm a scary motherfucker. Much scarier than even the rumors lead them to believe. Imagine how scared they would be if they knew the truth—"

He cut off abruptly, and then attempted to mask his faux pas by dumping some beer on his face. Sidenote: with his lips sewn shut, Charon couldn't really drink. He absorbed his beer through osmosis, opting to dump it on his face. I let him have his secret, allowing the silence to stretch between us as I thought on his words. My story was much the same. People were terrified of me. And they only knew the half of it.

"Why do you think I am nice?" I finally asked.

"You invited me to St. Louis. You included me in your legend."

I frowned at him. "Legend?"

"The Legend of the Catalyst," he intoned, officiously. "It's an incredible story. You should read it," he said with a smile again tugging at the twine binding his mouth. "Although the ending blows. Kind of."

I gave him a puzzled frown. "That doesn't make any sense. The story isn't over yet."

He swept his gaze across the lava surrounding us. "Well, this sure looked like a pity party to me. Pouting in the privacy of your own mind. Maybe I was mistaken."

I stared at him very intently, not entirely sure if he was joking or not. "So, the story isn't over yet. Unless I *let* it be over…"

"The version I read was more like one of those 'choose your own adventure types.'" He shot me a flat look. "There were better endings than this one." He leaned back in his seat, resting one arm over the lip of the boat as he regarded me. "That's what typically happens when you're writing an autobiography, though. Unless, of course, someone else cuts the story short for you." He drew a finger across his throat in a dramatic gesture.

I tipped my beer back, surprised to find that I'd polished it off, as I contemplated his answer. Charon chuckled, opening the cooler and snatching me a new one. I accepted it, smiling at the frosty cold can as I cracked it open and mirrored his pose with a thoughtful sigh.

I knew he was keeping things back, and that he was doing it out of necessity. I was also sick and tired of asking questions only to receive bull-shit, half-hearted answers. Or purposefully vague ones. The gods were all in a club where they gave only cryptic responses. And even my allies were playing their own games. All answers were subjective.

"Sitting here too long will end my story," I finally said.

He nodded. "Makes sense to me. Or it could be an interlude if you had the right kind of song."

I nodded absently. Was he referring to the Elders? I knew their power had something to do with songs, and I'd seen Carl do some alarmingly frightening magic with a song.

I also knew he wouldn't simply give me a straight answer. Not because he was a dick—which he was—but because straight answers carried drastic consequences. Namely, that they could alter outcomes or outright nullify them. He was giving me what he thought I needed. A weapon he thought I could use, as long as I was wise enough to comprehend it. Glancing around at my surroundings, I suddenly recalled an item on my to do list. A promise I had made.

"I need you to do me a favor."

He turned to look at me, waiting.

"I'm going to take two people to the River Styx for a swim," I said, choosing my words very carefully.

Charon studied me for a few long moments. "I do believe that would have consequences. It is not a place to beef up your warriors—"

"They're kids," I interrupted softly, thinking of Calvin and Makayla. I'd promised their parents, Gunnar and Ashley, that I would take them to the River Styx to hopefully make them as impervious to harm as Achilles.

Charon stiffened. "Oh."

I nodded. "They're in danger—through no fault of their own—and it's the only way I can think to keep them safe until they're old enough to take care of themselves."

I didn't mention that—although young and inexperienced—Calvin and Makayla were incredibly dangerous. Freya had bonded them from the womb, lending them some of her powers to keep them safe. Unfortunately, this meant that harming one of them also harmed Freya, and vice versa. And her protection had the strange consequence of them being born as pups rather than children—less than a year ago, I might add—and gave them the curious ability to turn into giant mist wolves. They'd been innately powerful enough to break through some of Fenrir's chains—which had been strong enough to keep the giant imprisoned.

Despite these mysterious powers, they were just babies. Puppies. I wasn't confident that they had matured enough to be able to take care of themselves. And Freya had her own enemies, which could result in them sharing her fate.

The fact that they were naturally powerful actually put them in *more* danger—because they were young enough to be abducted by my enemies and then molded from a young age into something wickedly deadly. And when they did finally manage to transform into human skins, they would be nothing more than scrawny children. Possibly seven years old, or so.

You know, because dog years were seven-to-one. My crazy life made perfect sense at times.

But I didn't want Charon knowing any of that. I didn't want anyone knowing the particulars of their powers, parentage, or anything. Especially not that they'd helped me break Fenrir out of prison. I was their godfather, and I'd turned them into rabid little felons.

Charon was watching me thoughtfully, almost as if he could read my mind. Now that I was a godkiller, I knew that wasn't the case. Still, the intensity of his gaze was...concerning.

"What you request is beyond difficult," he finally rasped. "First, you'd have to get them down here. Without being seen. Cerberus takes personal offense to that. Then there's the Management," he said, looking as if the word tasted foul. "There are a lot of us, you know. Different pantheons war for power over their little pockets of Underworlds. Right now, it is split pretty equally among Hades and Anubis, but there have been a lot of private, closed door meetings lately. Odin and Freya still hold a large chunk of power, even though Odin hasn't been here in a while." He trailed off, as if noticing that he'd been rambling. "Anyway, chalk it up as politics. There are a lot of politicians looking for angles they can use to acquire more power. I'm kind of the mascot for this place. If I disappear for a personal...errand, it won't go unnoticed."

I nodded. "I wasn't asking you to do it for me. I'm letting you know that it *will* happen, and that I'd like someone to throw up some cover fire of some kind. Anything that will give me a few minutes to get it done and then get them back out unnoticed. This isn't a power play. This is a keep kids safe play."

He squirmed uneasily. "I will do what I can. Will this be happening soon?"

I laughed harshly, thinking of my current situation in Zeus' prison cell.

"I have no idea. Pretend that it will, just to be safe. Keep an ear open for my imminent arrival."

He smiled. "I already do that. I always know when you come here."

I flinched. "Can others do that?" I asked, fearing that Hades was about to appear and tattle on me to his brother, Zeus.

He shook his head. "No. Don't worry. Even Anubis can't track you, Catalyst. He bitches about it constantly since you're technically on the payroll. Good times."

I relaxed marginally. "Then how can you?"

He chuckled, cracking open another beer. "Family secret."

I frowned at him, my shoulders suddenly itching. "You're not a Temple, are you? Because that might just melt my brain," I admitted, hanging my head in my hands.

He chuckled. "No. I'm not a Temple. I merely stand in the shadow of their illustrious dynasty." I slowly lifted my head, frowning at him. "Well, *stood*, past tense. But that's all I'm going to say about that."

I let out a nervous breath, liking his elaboration even less than the fact that we might be related. Maybe I'd actually fallen asleep, and I wasn't really astral projecting right now. Maybe none of this was real—

"It's real, idiot," Charon said, tiredly. "Wait. Where are you going?" he demanded, reaching for his oar spear.

I felt my soul leave Hell faster than a nun could clutch her rosary after mistaking a sex dungeon for a soup kitchen.

4

I was suddenly standing in a jail of some kind—much different than the one I shared with Carl. I momentarily panicked, wondering if I had been caught—that Zeus had discovered my astral travels and had jerked me back into an imagined prison for my mind.

I let out a breath of relief to see that I wasn't actually behind bars. I was in the hallway leading to a collection of cells. And there were some serious health-code violations going on here. In fact, it didn't look like it had been updated since pre-colonial times.

Despite being here on the astral plane, the heavy stench of brine, iron, rotten leather, and decomposing fish clogged my nostrils, making me gag. The stone walls were wet with constant condensation, seeming to sweat despite the frigid chill to the air.

I flinched as a fishy female fiend flopped past me, her wet webbed feet slapping the ground like a bipedal frog fresh out of water. Her slick, scaly skin glowed in the dank darkness. She was covered in orange scales with wild arcs of white crisscrossing her skin, looking like a mutated Koi fish. She stared right through me, not registering my presence, and I let out a breath of relief as she walked away.

"Nemo Christ," I murmured under my breath. Where had Charon gone? How had I gotten here—wherever here was? I gagged as an aromatic perfume of sea rot rolled over me, making my eyes water. What the hell? It smelled so bad here that I could smell it on the astral plane?

I leaned towards the bars of a prison cell as I sensed movement within. A figure rose up from the darkness, their hair matted and filthy and even frozen into dingy dreadlocks in places. Their shirt was crisp with frost, and it cracked and snapped as they moved, indicating that the body wearing the clothes should have suffered frostbite long ago.

But they—no, she—hadn't. It was a woman. I thought.

As she leaned closer, pressing her face against the thick bars of her cell to squint at me, I took a step forward, surprised as all hell that she could see me.

"What the hell are ye doin' here?" she demanded in a heavy accent that was some sort of amalgamation of Irish and Bostonian.

"Oh, hey," I said to the stranger, scratching at my jaw in confusion. Maybe Poseidon had stepped in to give me a seaweed beating to help out his brother Zeus. But I didn't want this woman getting her hopes up that I was some kind of savior. "Well, damn. This isn't where I parked my car," I muttered, feigning aloofness as I stepped closer to the cell to get a better look at the woman.

She reached out to grab me with a feral claw of numb, frozen fingers, catching me completely off guard. Her hand came within an inch of my jacket and struck an unseen force. She jerked her hand back with a startled look on her face, flexing her fingers with a grimace of discomfort as if she had been zapped.

I was more surprised that she had even seen me.

I eyed the woman suspiciously as she let out a string of imaginative curses under her breath, not even seeming to realize she'd done it. She cursed like nuns prayed—often and reflexively. Something about that tickled my memory, but I definitely didn't recognize the bedraggled, beaten, frozen creature before me. Her cell was too dark to make out her features.

I found myself smirking at her mild pain of trying to molest me without my consent. Served her right. Trying to touch me without my permission. Who did things like that? You never invaded someone's personal space without their consent.

"Seriously," she asked in that harsh accent, "what are ye doin' here?"

I frowned as I surveyed the adjacent cells and the dingy hall behind me, verifying that we were alone. Others might not be able to see me, but this woman wasn't trying to hide the fact that she had made a new, imaginary friend—which would lead to questions if any of her guards overheard her.

I finally turned back to her, getting a better look as she shifted a tangle of hair from her face. Red, red hair. And that damning accent and filthy mouth...

"Hey, wait...I know you," I murmured suspiciously, cocking my head as I struggled for the answer. I snapped my fingers as it came to me. "You're that Irish woman. Othello's friend. The thief."

"What the hell d'ye just call me?" Quinn MacKenna hissed like a doused cat.

It had been a very long time since I'd seen the magical relic thief from Boston. I'd let myself into her apartment to discuss a business proposal. She had irrationally called it breaking and entering. I'd fought some demon ex-lover of hers, which she hadn't appreciated either.

All in all, Quinn was very unappreciative, in my opinion.

"Sorry, that wasn't supposed to be an insult," I said, waving my hand at her cell. "But then, and I do hate to be the one to point this out, you are behind bars..." I added, dryly.

She glared back at me, not having any footing for an argument. She looked like a refugee. She'd been here for a long time. Either that, or she'd been caught after a very bad day.

In my current clothes, I looked like I was about to hit a nightclub.

"I didn't steal anythin' to get locked up, ye idget," she finally snapped. "And ye still haven't answered me question. How d'ye get in here?" She looked hungry for the answer. Desperate.

"Not sure," I replied. "I was trying to find someone, but it looks like I failed. Again."

"Find who?"

"Someone useful." I flashed her a tired smile, hoping to temper my phrasing with a dash of empathy. "Anyway, I better go. Looks like I've got miles to go before I sleep." I was on borrowed time. I couldn't do anything to help her in my current state.

I prepared to leave this hellish place, focusing more intently on my original destination since my errant thoughts had accidentally brought me to Hell and then here.

Quinn, like a manic fucking psychopath, lashed out with one hand, looking as if she intended to punch my heart out of this solar system. Rather than recoil at the pulse of power she'd felt the first time, she gritted her teeth, obviously intending to weather the storm of power that had prevented her from touching me earlier—which had surprised the hell out of me, even though I'd hidden my astonishment. Her hand should have swiped right through me like smoke.

This time was even more of a surprise.

She latched onto...something within my chest, and her jaw locked up while the gaunt flesh of her cheeks rippled as if she was being zapped by pure electricity. Luckily for me, I felt the same blast of electricity rock through me—like she had stabbed me with a taser. Like a maniac, she held on, refusing to let go of whatever force was between us. After a few seconds, she let go with a yelp, wincing in pain.

"What the hell was that?" I barked, clutching at my chest and panting raggedly. I looked down to see that I no longer wore my imagined dress clothes, but instead resembled my physical body's current state after Ares and Apollo's dutiful care. My bare skin was sunburnt and peeling, almost purple at the shoulders, and I was back in my tattered clothes. My wrists were covered in scabs—some of which were freely bleeding. Quinn grimaced in surprise, as if imagining the pains for herself. She looked... strangely empathetic for being such a hard case. I had expected her to look victorious.

"What on earth happened to ye?" she asked softly, holding her own injured hand to her chest, looking as if she was trying to ride out her own pain.

I cursed at her revealing my injuries and immediately closed my eyes to bring back my disguise. In seconds, my nicer clothes reappeared and my wounds disappeared. Quinn stared at the sudden change in stark disbelief.

"It took me a while to figure out how to alter my appearance," I admitted. "Astral projection isn't all it's cracked up to be, but it works a lot better if you don't pop in on strangers looking like a leper."

"Astral projection?" she asked.

"It's how I'm here. Well, sort of here. It's complicated. Let's just say I'm making the best of a bad situation."

"What situation would that be?"

"I got myself in a bit of a bind, that's all."

"Imagine that," she drawled, seeming to bite back an amused grin. "Go on."

I appraised her pensively, wondering how much I could trust her. She straightened her shoulders defiantly, looking oddly determined to hear my answer. It wasn't sympathy. It looked...almost like she was *demanding* an honest answer. That I owed it to her for some reason. I knew the feeling well. "I pissed off a god," I finally admitted.

She snorted. "Which one?" she asked sardonically.

I blinked at her in surprise, wondering why she hadn't batted an eye.

"We can swap stories later," she continued, reading into my body language. "Which god d'ye upset? Wait, wait, let me guess...d'ye break into Hestia's house?" she asked dryly, her eyes twinkling beneath the filth, looking like gems in the mud.

I rolled my eyes at the reference to me breaking into her apartment—she'd remembered, and been just as unappreciative of my heroics as I'd assumed. "The goddess of the hearth. Clever." I said in a dry tone. "That was a long time ago. And I didn't break into your place. I just wanted to ask you to get something for me, and you overreacted."

She took a deep breath, looking determined to bite back her knee-jerk response. I was still wary of how she had freaking touched me—not that it seemed beneficial in any way. She'd tased me. That was the opposite of helpful.

"What was it ye wanted?" she asked curiously, obviously referring to my initial break-in.

"Doesn't matter, now. A jewel, I think." I lied easily, not wanting to mention the Devourer I had been looking for at the time. "A lot has happened since then. More than I care to think about."

She frowned, looking suddenly uneasy. Like she might have had a jewel she didn't want anyone knowing about. Curious. But I let it go. Pressing her to reveal her secrets would only open me up for return interrogation.

"Anyway," I said, "it wasn't Hestia I upset, though you're on the right track. See, I sort of set Prometheus free. And, in the process, ticked off the god who put him there. Since then I've been, you know...hanging around."

She winced knowingly. "How long have ye been Zeus' prisoner?" she asked, obviously knowing enough about Prometheus to guess correctly. And she'd known about Hestia as well. Interesting.

"I'm not sure, anymore. This is how I escape, how I stay sane. When I'm like this, it doesn't hurt." I was fudging the truth a little. No reason to tell her that I had only just figured it out.

"And your friends?" she asked. "Aren't they comin' to save ye?"

My smile grew brittle and weary, and I didn't bother to hide it. "Shouldn't you be worried about yourself?" I asked instead, gesturing to the bars of her cell. "That doesn't look cozy. What did you do to get put in there?"

"It's a long story," she said, after a moment's hesitation. It was almost comical how cagey we were both being about our current predicaments. Her next words froze my blood. "This is the Titan realm you've wandered into. At least, I t'ink it still is. I was chasin' someone with a grudge against ye, tryin' to stop him before he hurts anyone, and that's when—"

"A grudge against *me*?" I interrupted, fearing Prometheus had gathered allies to hunt down his enemy, Tainted Nipple—since he hadn't gotten my name correct. Then again, if Quinn knew a Titan with a grudge against me, Prometheus must have figured out my real name. "Wait, is that what you said?" Maybe I was lucky enough to have pissed off two Titans.

"Aye, and don't ye sound so surprised, like you've never done anythin' to harm anyone in your life," she chastised. "Ye and your friends killed his father, who was a member of the Wild Hunt tryin' to track ye down for the Queens of Fae. And let's not forget your parents stole an hourglass from under his watch, which got him exiled. Frankly, he has good reason to hate ye, all t'ings considered. But when he signed on to work for the Winter Queen to see ye killed, he started crossin' lines, lines he shouldn't have crossed."

I stared at her, my jaw hanging open. It was a relief to hear that my own personal Inigo Montoya was of the Fae, rather than a Titan, but where the hell had she learned all that about me? Had she been fucking spying on me? That had been a *long* time ago. I pinched my nose, debating how I wanted to respond. It wasn't like I could actually do anything about it in my current state. "This is ridiculous. I mean, we did fight the Wild Hunt once. But that was ages ago. And my parents...the hourglass..." I drifted off. "It wasn't stolen. Or, if it was, I'm sure they had a good reason."

Which was the biggest lie yet. No one had known that the Hourglass was not the property of the Fae. In fact, it was undeniably the property of my family—since the sand inside was actually the pulverized bones of my ancestors. It was what I had used to open up the Elder Realm in the Mausoleum.

"That's what I'm told," she replied bitterly. "Always a good excuse, Calvin and Makayla Temple."

I was suddenly pressed against the bars, my eyes a little wild. I instinctively wanted to kill her. Who the fuck did she think she was? She didn't know my parents. I realized that my skin was smoldering with vaporous light, and that I was somehow gripping the iron bars.

The very *real* iron bars. But none of that mattered right now.

"What," I said through gritted teeth, "do you know about my parents?"

"More than you'd t'ink," she replied, seemingly unfazed. She gripped the two bars farthest from my hands and leaned in, careful not to get too close, but stubbornly refusing to back down from my hostility. She was defiant, despite her current living conditions. "If it weren't for your parents," she continued, "I might never have been born."

I blinked, my anger flickering like a candle in the wind. "Wait, what does that even mean?" The mysterious, unbidden power roaring from my flesh dimmed and I let go of the iron bars.

A sudden cry erupted from above our heads, but it didn't sound natural. Nothing from Quinn's current environment, then. She hadn't seemed to hear anything. Was...it Carl? Trying to wake me? It hadn't sounded like a voice. But...it had sounded raucously familiar.

I cursed, turning back to Quinn. "I have to go," I said. I considered her thoughtfully, wanting to finish this conversation more than almost anything. "If you ever get out of here, you little delinquent, come find me."

None of Quinn's answers would matter if I didn't get out of my own prison on Olympus. I hoped she found a way out of hers.

And, with that, I left her, pursuing the sound I had heard. Because the more I thought about it, the more I realized it had sounded like an epic asshole of a raven.

Hugin or Munin.

Then the cawing sound abruptly cut off and I felt a sharp pain on my arm.

5

I opened my eyes to find Carl gripping me by the arm, shaking me violently. The prison cell door crashed open and I scrambled to my feet with a grunt, my heart racing. Zeus stormed into the cell as Carl calmly rose like some kind of Zen monk.

Panic raced through me as I tried to embrace the sudden shift in realities and the fact that I now felt trapped inside a straightjacket—my physical body. It hurt, and I felt like I'd just woken up from a coma, my body slow to respond to my brain's commands.

Zeus waved a hand at our chains, and they unhitched from our manacles, falling into piles with a loud metallic clanking sound. "Follow me," he growled. Then he simply walked out of our prison suite, leaving the door open behind him.

I shot Carl a questioning look, wondering if I'd missed something pertinent while astral projecting, but he shrugged his shoulders, looking concerned. With nothing better to do, I followed the God of Lightning out of the cell. I motioned for Carl to keep an eye on our rear.

Despite somehow being able to access a power of sorts—without intending to—on the astral plane, I currently couldn't do more than swing my fists or kick my feet. So, making a run for it was off the table. Even if I could escape, I wouldn't have the use of my powers with these cursed manacles clamped onto my wrists. And I'd be abandoning Carl and my satchel.

And if I tried to attack Zeus with my bare hands—a monumentally stupid plan—I had no way to defend myself once Ares or Apollo showed up. I needed to find out why the hell we were being held hostage, and this was the first potential opportunity outside of seemingly meaningless torture. He obviously had something to say, and I obviously needed leverage.

The hallway outside our door actually hugged the face of the mountain, leaving the opposite wall a vast sweep of open sky, high above the clouds. The architect had thankfully built a two-foot tall safety wall—the perfect height to almost miss and trip over it in a potential mad dash for freedom. I felt a violent rush of vertigo and had a sudden desire to grab the wall beside us, as far from the open sky as possible.

Thankfully, there was a ceiling of marble arches spanning overhead and supported by thick marble columns on the inside of the trip-wall, making it feel more like an incomplete tunnel, which added a sense of solidity to the hallway. Still, the yawning sky pulled at me like a vacuum, reminding me of how small and insignificant I really was in the face of nature. The ocean of clouds looked almost inviting—a siren song lulling me closer to a final, epic swan dive that would end Charon's *Legend of the Catalyst* on the exact opposite of a cliffhanger.

Zeus walked ahead of us on silent footsteps, utterly unconcerned about his unprotected back.

He had dressed more formally than his earlier white toga-jammies. He now wore an armored white kilt of sorts, consisting of leather straps affixed to a wide leather waistband that was decorated with Greek symbols cast in silver. He wore a matching white leather shoulder guard over his left shoulder, but I couldn't make out the details. It looked like a screaming eagle.

He exited the hallway and the mountain opened up onto a vast expanse of flat rock. We were obviously at the peak, and a quick full-circle sweep made me feel like we were on a stranded island in a sea of clouds. I saw no elegant marble structures or shining streets full of Olympians, and I saw no other nearby mountains. A thirty-feet-wide set of stairs stretched up towards a raised pavilion ringed with more Greek columns and topped with decorative marble entablatures to form a perfect circle overhead. I eyed the elevated platform warily, realizing that it was different from the one where I had first encountered Zeus before our imprisonment. I also didn't see the area where Prometheus had hung for millennia. We were on a different mountain.

Accidentally freeing Prometheus hadn't earned me any points. In any other scenario, I would have instantly understood the reason for my endless torture, chalking it up as punishment for freeing Olympus' Most Wanted Titan.

Except Zeus had kidnapped me *before* I'd freed Prometheus.

And by *freeing*, I meant I had knocked Prometheus off the mountain, sending him plummeting to Earth with a giant, hungry eagle pursuing him, so it wasn't like the Titan had a soft spot in his heart for me, either. He hadn't even gotten my name right. "Tainted Nipple," I muttered under my breath.

Carl frowned over at me, absently reaching for his chest to check his own nipples. I sighed, shaking my head.

The pavilion up ahead was also not the one where I had killed Athena.

Zeus had a lot of random pavilions, apparently. Like McDonald's buying up every highly trafficked corner lot in every major city across America. Location, location, location.

Zeus strode up to the stairs, so we followed suit. Even from our new vantage point, I saw no gleaming city in the distance—only a better view of the endless clouds—and I saw no guards or monsters hiding in wait to keep their boss safe. We were alone. Which probably meant we weren't alone at all. Or Zeus was mocking me, rubbing my face in my situation.

Yeah. Probably that.

It was now an irrefutable fact that Zeus didn't want witnesses to my imprisonment—or our impending conversation—which tracked with his vague initial request before he'd locked us up in our prison cell. He needed my help with something, and it had sounded suspiciously like he'd wanted a godkiller on retainer. It would be counterintuitive to hire a secret assassin and then let his potential targets know of my presence.

But...where the hell was Mount Olympus? Were we at least close to the fabled city?

Zeus came to a halt in the center of the pavilion, turning to face me as I made my final approach. I stifled my surprise when I noticed the Temple Crest carved into the center of the polished marble floor, directly beneath Zeus' sandaled feet. It had to be eight feet in diameter and was ringed with twin bands of solid gold and silver. He smiled arrogantly.

His white beard was thick and long, and his eyes crackled with inner lightning. Although obviously old, he had enough carved muscles to shame the most devout bodybuilder. The only other indications of his age —other than his storm cloud gray hair and white beard—were faint wrinkles at the corners of his eyes.

I stopped just shy of the Temple Crest in the event it was some kind of trap. There was every possibility that merely standing on it would cause some reaction. I was the last of my bloodline, and to find my family symbol here among such an old pantheon was unnerving. It implied that our families had once been pals—a long, long time ago.

Which was highly suspicious and unlikely, leading me to assume it was all theatrical. My family couldn't be *that* old, could it?

I tried to dismiss the obvious implication, but it was too loud of a thought. Was I...an Olympian? A demigod? Was that the reason for all the insanity in my family? The reason for Hermes' past help? The reason so many damned Greeks had made Missouri their home?

If so, had I become a kin-killer when I'd killed Athena? Was that why Zeus was so uneasy around me? Or was it more like my family's relationship with Odin, where my parents had roped him into serving our cause?

Or maybe Zeus was just a fucking liar. Anyone could draw my family crest. He'd said so himself when I'd first mentioned the similarities on his belt.

I'd already known he needed me, and there was only one reason he would keep me imprisoned and spend the last week torturing me. He wanted me—needed me—to do something for him that no one else could. And it was something he was entirely certain that I wouldn't want to do. He'd skipped threatening my friends and gone straight to breaking my spirit and body.

Which meant that he *really* needed me. Badly.

"Who do you need killed, old man? I've had about enough of this shit-hole and your syphilitic groin spawn, Ares and Apollo."

Zeus regarded me with pursed lips, not reacting to my slight about his sons. "Your torture was punishment for freeing Prometheus," he began, clasping his hands behind his back. "I have a reputation to protect, after all. If I didn't punish you for that offense, I would appear weak."

He paused, but I didn't offer a comment on his bullshit speech.

"It seems you have ascended, godkiller, and you are also the Catalyst. I cannot permit the other gods to see me letting you off with a mere slap on the wrist. It's just business," he said with a cold smile, flashing his perfectly white teeth. "I hope you understand. Our families are old friends, after all." He pointedly glanced down at the crest below his feet.

I'd heard the word ascension a few times, now. But I was still a little hazy on the details. "Thank you for your apology," I said in a pompous tone, knowing full well that he had not apologized. His shoulders stiffened slightly, but he didn't correct me. "Explain this ascension business, and I'll consider forgiving you. Right after you upgrade our rooms, free of charge."

He did not find my tone or words funny because he was obviously a man devoid of joy and happiness. Because I knew I was hilarious. I even laughed at my jokes, which was the best barometer for humor.

"Your ascension onto a new level of power. It has caused quite the stir among the gods of all pantheons. You are, in many respects, equivalent in power to the gods." His gaze shifted to a more threatening undertone. "Of course, there are many levels of power among gods. We were not all created equal."

I sniffed at the air. "You smell that?" I asked. "Smells like someone's cooking up some fresh patriarchy with a side of elitism and misogyny." He stared back at me, unimpressed. "You should probably hire a good PR firm. That kind of stance doesn't fly these days."

Zeus stared at me blankly, not seeming to follow along.

"Pantheon restructuring is one of the many services I can provide. For a sizable fee, of course." I leaned forward, speaking in a stage whisper. "It usually starts at the top, with the immediate replacement of the executive team."

6

His glare grew brittle and I sensed his shoulders tensing. It wasn't like he could expect me to be meek and submissive—not in general, and definitely not after how he'd treated us. It would have seemed strange had I *not* mouthed off to him. I had a reputation to protect, too.

Instead of reacting, he exercised godly restraint and resumed his earlier topic. "Here, we call ascension by a different name—Apotheosis. It means to make something or someone divine. In simpler terms, when a mortal transcends into godhood." He eyed me as if I had a pungent aroma. "Of course, becoming a godkiller was not the original intention of this rite of passage. It was a loophole we seem to have overlooked."

"That's me. Always sneaking through the back door." I swept my gaze across the columns and clouds. "Is there a committee or something? An inter-pantheon union? Or was this just a participation trophy for offing Athena? You're welcome, by the way. I'll give you that one for free." I had to force myself to appear disinterested and unimpressed while choosing inflammatory words to describe his daughter's death.

After a few moments of tense silence, I turned to look at him. Pressing him in such a disrespectful manner also validated my theory that he needed me. Otherwise, he would have killed me for the slight. A calculated gamble, but there was no return without risk.

"You do have an admirable track record for...restructuring pantheons, as you put it. Like what you recently did with the Norse Aesir gods. In a way, that is why you are here. That, and our two families share a long, illustrious relationship, of course," he added, again bringing attention to the crest by tapping his foot against it.

He watched me, looking about as pleased as a cat with a mouse under its paw—which was oddly poetic since he had his feet firmly planted on my family crest. I suddenly had a very bad feeling. Worse than I'd had before, and that was saying something. "Yeah, well, I don't offer friends of the family discounts, I'm afraid. If what you're claiming is even true," I muttered.

"Why do you think there are so many Greeks in your city?" he pressed. "Asterion. King Midas. Achilles. Leonidas. Athena focusing her war on your own home." He leaned closer as if to impart a secret. "Hermes giving you a lucky coin to use against the dragons years ago," he added, smirking conspiratorially. I felt the hair on the back of my neck stand on end, and I hoped that I successfully masked my facial twitch. "Your family has worked with me for centuries. The Fates decreed it."

Charon had claimed something eerily similar—how he'd stood in the shadow of the Temple dynasty. I scoffed, not bothering to hide my opinion on the matter. "Times change. And if this is all above board, why are you holding me prisoner at an Olympian black ops site? Your story doesn't hold up—not if we're friends, and not if you want the world to see you making an example of me for releasing Prometheus."

"Let's just say that I trust a handshake over bloodlines."

I arched an eyebrow at him. Then again, judging by the myths...he had a solid point.

"Well? What do you want me to do?"

He chuckled. "That's just it! I—" He cut off abruptly, glancing over my shoulder. "Ah. Perfect timing. They need to hear this as well," he said, chuckling again. And he strode past me, making his way closer to the stairs. He gave Carl a wide berth, which was difficult, because Carl was suddenly hurrying over to my side, glaring towards the base of the steps as if to protect me.

I spun to find three people striding up the stairs. I spread my feet shoulder-width apart and clenched my jaw as I eyed the crew of thugs.

Ares led the way. He wore a crimson toga with gold embroidery at the hem and a wide leather belt. His fiery red hair was tied back in a man-bun, and his scarred cheeks peeked over the top of a thick, wiry beard. His head resembled a misshapen hunk of granite, and his eyes glittered with hatred. He was fucking huge, but not in an aesthetically pleasing way. He made Gunnar look anorexic in comparison. He must have taken a nap, because he didn't look quite so murderous as when I'd last seen him stomping out of my cell in a hissy fit.

Apollo came next, tall and lithe, like a...well, like an Olympic swimmer. He had broad shoulders but looked as if he'd missed every single leg day in his athletic career. He wore a white and gold toga, and his long blonde hair looked professionally straightened. He had a gaunt, imperious look on his face as if he was always looking down upon anyone who might attempt to talk to him. He was that guy who showed up at the pool party in a company polo and khakis, hemming and hawing about his Ivy League degree while he daintily sipped a bottle of microbrew—that he had brought himself, of course—with his pinky raised. The man who wanted everyone to know how special and unique he was—while everyone else was busy congratulating each other on a new keg-stand personal record.

The guy who demanded that the peasants worship and adore him, even though he secretly scorned them for their inferior upbringing. So, still smart and dangerous, but arrogant and elitist to such a degree that he made me look like Mother Theresa.

I grabbed a firm hold of my junk, tugged it with a salacious hip thrust, and blew him a kiss. "I missed that magical way you rub oil into my shoulders. Next time call before you cancel our appointment, you heartbreaker." I winked suggestively.

The vein on his temple bulged and his cheeks reddened with outrage at my inelegant greeting. He even looked embarrassed that I had singled him out—as if not wanting his fellow Olympians to assume we had any kind of social relationship whatsoever, let alone a romantic one like I'd implied.

Ares curled his lip and took a noticeable step to the side so as not to catch the apparently contagious homosexuality molecules in the air around his brother. Homophobia for the win.

Last, but certainly not least, a stunningly beautiful woman brought up the rear. She had long, lustrous, thick brown hair, perfectly plump cheeks, and a narrow chin. Her almond-shaped eyes were big and wide, and her vibrant green eyes drew me in with an almost physical pull that made my tongue and jaw tingle for some bizarre reason.

She wore a sheer toga that flowed loosely around her rather than hugging her flesh. I had a perfect view of absolutely every asset in her investment portfolio, since the fabric of her garment was more transparent than a wedding veil.

And, like the wedding veil, what lay beneath that single sheet of fabric was a groom's greatest desire. An experience that menfolk waited their entire lives to attain. A course of learning that every male student in existence would pay any price to attend, even if they were destined to fail the exam. Because even failures could impart unforgettable lessons.

Starting with the first letter of the alphabet and giving her top scores for looks and an *I will eat your heart while you thank me for it* vibe, I assumed this was the infamous Aphrodite.

She took a firm position on the use of undergarments—she didn't wear them. Period. She walked with a seductive sway, but not like a porn star or cabaret dancer. Her grace had class and distinction despite inciting obvious lust. She wasn't just about sex—she was about forcing men to become the best possible form of themselves so that they might earn the right to at least witness her in passing.

It was...unsettling. Like her very presence made me want to become a better person. That wasn't to say that she exuded a divine sense of goodwill or anything. I had the perception that Aphrodite's call to bring out the best in people didn't grade on a curve.

Whether your calling was to be the best professor at your college or the most feared among hostile dictators—as long as the man was giving it their all, Aphrodite was satisfied.

The three of them watched me with varying degrees of uncertainty and hostility. They gave Carl a wide berth, refusing to look at him as if they could pretend he didn't exist. But their body language gave them away—tense and uneasy.

Carl smiled, flicking his tongue at them in greeting. "Hi, syphilitic groin spawn," he said very meticulously. Then he glanced at me. "Was that what he called them?" he asked me, not so discreetly jerking his chin towards Zeus.

I smirked at the familial hand grenade he'd come up with—especially how he'd implied that their own father had said it rather than me. It almost brought a proud tear to my eye. "Yes, Carl. That is what he called his own children."

Zeus was studying his children with a glare that demanded their attention over Carl's jab. "Where is Hermes?"

I heard a metallic flutter behind me and I spun, rearing back with my fist to sucker punch any biological entity in my personal bubble.

Hermes luckily leapt back a step before I had time to deliver him a four-knuckled message. Well, he leaned back, technically speaking—and glimmering, metallic tattoos covering each of his calves suddenly peeled off of his skin to reveal metal wings as thin as paper. They whisked him away as swiftly as a dandelion seed at the faintest gust of wind, propelling him to safety.

He met my eyes. "Apologies. The crest is where my coin's Gateways open up," he said, brandishing a golden coin between his thumb and first knuckle. Huh. Kind of like my Tiny Balls, except reusable. "Security measure my Father put into place. He's somewhat paranoid, you see."

"Get over here, Hermes," Zeus growled. "You're not only incompetent, but you're late."

Hermes waited until Zeus looked away to smirk and flash me a mischievous wink before fluttering over to his siblings, landing beside them in utter silence. The ankle wings wrapped back over his lower legs, making me think of the wings on the golden snitch in those Harry Potter flicks.

Hermes was a wild card. He was very tall with wavy golden hair, and his golden irises seemed made of the molten precious metal. He was also in excellent physical shape, but he looked like an awkwardly growing teenager when standing beside Apollo and Ares—like he was waiting on one more growth spurt before his voice stopped cracking and the bulbs in his man garden sprouted their first pubiflora.

I turned to Zeus with a resigned sigh. "You were about to tell me what you need me to do for you since our families are such good friends."

Zeus nodded with a faint grin. "I will be taking a short trip. While I'm gone, I don't need you to do *something* for me...I need you to do absolutely *nothing* for me." His smile stretched wider.

His children frowned thoughtfully, sharing furtive glances out of his view. Carl continued to watch them with a suspicious glare. "While you're gone," I repeated, trying to wrap my head around the comment. He didn't want me to kill someone. He wanted me out of the way. "Wait. Your evil plan is to leave me up here?"

He nodded. "It's better for everyone that way. Once I return, we can discuss the logistics of you handing over the Armory to me. It is mine, after all. The majority of its contents are Greek."

I stared at him in disbelief. "What Armory?" I asked, lamely.

7

Aphrodite smirked in amusement before catching herself, but Ares had noticed her look. The rapid scowl on his face let me know that he'd decided I was now competition for a prize that I hadn't known I was playing for—his sister's affections.

Hermes watched the exchange pensively, his face blank but his eyes calculating. He was the dangerous one—the watcher. *Always watch the watcher*, my dad had often warned me.

Apollo had a thinly disguised sneer on his face, as if mentally tallying the dozen other, more important, matters he should be attending to rather than suffering my presence. Like polishing his participation trophies while reading Tony Robbins mantras out loud in the first person.

I am amazing. I deserve to be loved. I am special. And god damn it, people like me!

Zeus was utterly confident and unflustered, now seeming to flaunt his position of power over me. "The Armory. The stolen collection of Greek antiquities your family has guarded for me all these years. The Armory we will use for the upcoming war when you join my forces. You will be my general. Once you prove your loyalty, of course."

My blood ran cold at mention of the upcoming war, but even more at the fact that he wanted me to be his general. Anger soon took over and made my blood boil. I was stunned by his audacity, that he thought there was a world where I would work with him...*for* him.

Ares' face purpled, and Apollo shot a wary look at Hermes. Aphrodite looked abruptly nervous, and Hermes looked as calm as a cucumber. Carl watched the siblings as studiously as a psychologist, taking notes with his eyes. There were games within games afoot, that much was obvious. "That's just a rumor."

"Reputations and rumors," Zeus mused, nodding. "Like the one that you hold my niece, Pandora, hostage." I kept my face blank. "I will have her back," Zeus said in a firm tone. "Then there is the rumor that you are a Horseman, for example. I truly didn't believe that at first. I knew you had the blessing of the dreaded Four, but I didn't know a second band of Horsemen could roam the world. That you could be a Horseman in your own right. Hope," he growled, not sounding pleased. "As offensive as that is, I would be willing to forgive you that disrespect in exchange for you marshaling them under my banner against a common foe."

So, not only the Armory, but my Horsemen as well. My mind raced, wondering how best to play this turn of events. Go along and find a way to double-cross him—which seemed like the avenue some of his children had taken—or to outright laugh in his face. The problem with the latter, more truthful, option was that I was currently his prisoner, and it would get me nowhere. Well, it would get me right back in my cell. I couldn't do anything from my cell. Which he was well aware of.

Bastard.

And why had he waited a week to tell me this? Why lead me to believe that he wanted someone dead? What games was Zeus really playing here? What games were his children playing? What had Zeus been doing while I'd been locked away, and what had changed for him to suddenly decide to share his travel plans if those plans had literally no impact on my current living conditions?

"But the Armory isn't as important as your little trip..." I said to Zeus.

He shook his head. "I require a weapon to kill a certain god. Believe it or not, I seek a weapon you once wielded," he chuckled. "Once I conclude my personal vendetta, we will map out the logistics of your new career as my general. I wanted you to have time to think about it. To come up with ideas. To prevent any untoward delays that would result in friends and allies coming to harm."

The threat was obvious. My allies were leverage that he had no issue using. And with me locked up, there was jack and shit I could do about it. Still, if I caved easily, he would suspect me of playing games. I had to live up to my reputation. And, to be fair, it was my honest answer.

"And you expect me to just sit here doing nothing. Then to hand over the Armory when you get back," I said dryly, wondering what I was missing. "Hard pass. I'm not giving you anything. Especially when I get nothing out of it."

Zeus sighed with resigned annoyance. "Then my children will break you. They will continue to torture you until you see reason."

Ares punched his fist into his palm. "Gladly," he growled murderously. Apollo had a twisted grin on his face as well. Hermes, once again, observed in silence.

Aphrodite cleared her throat and glided forward a few steps. "Perhaps honey is better. Pain obviously does not work on Master Temple. Neither do threats. Has anyone tried to show him how none of us find this desirable, but that we do, in fact, share a common enemy and must unite to survive. Has anyone tried appealing to his needs?"

"That's a long list, lady," I said, dryly.

"Oh, I'm counting on it," she murmured huskily, sauntering closer in a deliciously slow swaying movement. "Perhaps a woman's touch is what he truly needs while you are traveling, Father. Pain has gotten you nowhere. Perhaps it is time for a little pleasure…" she said, eyeing me hungrily.

"I'm not really into the whole dominatrix thing," I said, hoarsely.

"Perhaps you are into the whole endless orgasm thing," she replied, biting her lip dramatically. She whisper-fucked me with her tone, her words seeming to hit the erogenous zones of my mind like magic. "We will find out what kind of fetishes you are truly into. I promise to introduce you to a few of my favorites."

Ares instantly began arguing against Aphrodite's suggestion and I found myself smirking faintly. I'd almost forgotten that Aphrodite and Ares shared more than a sibling relationship. Although she was married to Hephaestus—the Olympian Armor God—she didn't try to hide her sexual promiscuity. One of the most notorious horses in her sexual stable was her brother, Ares.

Which, unless you were a pharaoh in Egypt, was just gross.

Also...even *if* you were pharaoh, that's gross.

And he didn't want Nate Temple diddling his sister. It was so ridiculous that I burst out laughing—which shut everyone up. Ares' face darkened and Aphrodite pursed her lips, looking hurt. As much as I didn't want to have any kind of romance with Aphrodite—on a rational, personal level— part of me was definitely drawn to her allure.

But that was just her godly power. It wasn't me actually wanting it. It was her slipping me a mental roofie.

Zeus stepped forward. "I am willing to give you this opportunity, daughter."

I raised my hand, but I didn't wait for anyone to call on me. "I'm not interested in acquiring venereal diseases from before Christ, thank you very much. I think I've been pretty clear."

She smiled sweetly. "I cannot get a sexually transmitted disease. I am actually the cure to any and all sexually transmitted diseases. Fuck me once, immunity on you. Fuck me twice, oblivion on you. Fuck me thrice..." she grinned expectantly, "well, you'll see."

Well. As campaign slogans and suicide options went, that was a top contender.

Ares folded his arms stubbornly, muttering darkly under his breath. I ignored him and arched an eyebrow at her. "You literally have a magical hoo-ha? Wow."

She was suddenly directly before me, and I couldn't move a muscle. Carl tensed anxiously, knowing that if he moved, I might just be murdered. I was more focused on the fact that she had grabbed a firm hold of my happy place and there was a dark grin on her face.

"Honey," she whispered, "you have no idea how much of an under-statement that is."

Before I could reply, she was a safe distance away, and I could move again.

"Aphrodite can be quite convincing," Zeus mused. "Perhaps her suggestion has merit."

Ares folded his arms, furious. Apollo rolled his eyes and shrugged.

"He is a rather broken soul," Aphrodite said, eyeing me up and down. "I wager he won't last five minutes before giving in. It has been years since he's had sex, the poor dear. He's dying for attention, looking for love in all the wrong places. My kind of places," she added with a smoldering grin.

I gave her an unimpressed look—which took effort, let me tell you. "It would be incredibly difficult to get it up for such a broken wreck as your daughter. I've never been into pity sex."

Her face paled and she clenched her fists. Carl slowly swiveled his head to stare at me with wide eyes, shaking his head as if even he thought I'd crossed a line. Aphrodite's voice was pure venom. "It seems I will have to resort to more drastic measures, Father. I will fuck him so completely that he will do whatever you wish to get back into my bed faster."

I'll admit, she made a compelling case.

"It is decided," Zeus said matter of factly. "Aphrodite will have first stab at Nate tonight. Moving forward, the three of you will each get two sessions per day with our guests. May the favorite child win," he said with a cruel grin, assessing each Olympian.

Ares and Apollo looked annoyed—and competitive. Hermes was busy watching his father, as if waiting for something. Aphrodite opened her mouth. "I ask only that—"

"That will be all," Zeus interrupted in a commanding tone. "Your job is to open your legs, not your mouth."

Aphrodite stiffened as if slapped. "Yes, Father."

I raised my hand, but spoke before anyone could deny me. "Does Hephaestus know you're banging his wife?" I asked Ares.

He smirked darkly. "No one cares about the tinkerer. Right, Aphrodite, my love?"

She nodded her agreement, but I saw the mask she wore over her true feelings—whatever those actually were. "I did not ask to be shackled to Hephaestus, so I don't know why everyone seems to be waiting for me to trip over my own heart. He was a punishment, if I recall correctly." And those pretty little eyes grew glacially cold, frosty, and barren as they locked onto her father.

Zeus grunted, looking unhappy that his efforts to punish Aphrodite with a lame husband hadn't led to the desired effect. Hell, maybe it was because he was offended that a woman—even if it was his daughter—had overstepped an imaginary line.

One thing was becoming increasingly obvious. They were all psychopaths, and Zeus had turned his children into broken, wretched voids of emptiness, clamoring for a heartless father's love.

And I'd thought my parents were assholes. Sheesh.

8

Zeus brushed his hands together as if cleaning them of the matter. "Well, I must be off. The world isn't going to save itself."

My mind searched for anything to keep him here. "What about Prometheus? If he sees you down there, he will kill you."

Zeus smirked, turning to Hermes without a word. Hermes obediently waved a hand, drawing my attention. I flinched as whatever his spirit fingers did caused Zeus' form to shimmer and…

I was suddenly facing my doppelgänger. I leapt back a step, staring at him in horror. Hermes had made him look exactly like me. Well, the prettier version of me. Not the current prisoner version.

Hermes was damned good at illusions, just like his counterpart in mischief, Loki. Perhaps he wasn't as disfavored as Zeus had made it seem. His siblings definitely looked about as shocked as me—and equally suspicious that their brother had a side project with their father. It was painful watching them vie for their father's attention. All the worse for the fact that he seemed to relish in the competition rather than handing out the reward.

"Prometheus wants to kill me even more than you," I said quietly, not understanding the benefits to his choice of illusions. I subconsciously felt my mind creating and discarding a dozen monikers for my doppelgänger. Nate-ning Bolt? Natericity? Electro-Nate. I settled on the last one.

Electro-Nate grinned. "I know."

And I suddenly understood why Zeus wanted me locked away. Because his little trip was going to involve some act of carnage that would piss off a lot of people. And he was going to do it while wearing my skin. He'd already said he sought a weapon I had once wielded.

This was a frame job.

Shit.

My doppelgänger studied me, eyeing me up and down with an arrogant smirk. That prick-ish grin really got under my skin, and it was a surreal moment for me when I realized that this was how many others likely saw me.

That even I wanted to sucker punch me in the mouth.

Electro-Nate studied me with that shit-eating grin. Then he studied himself, grimacing distastefully. He slowly lifted his head to stare at me until he matched my posture and we faced each other evenly—like I was staring into a mirror.

Other than the fact that the real me was all beaten up and bloody, of course.

"You are a *monster*," he said with an indifferent shrug. "There's no use crying about it. Own it. Like your ancestors did."

And I knew my therapist was going to earn her retainer this year when I tried to explain what was stressing me out—that my double had psychoanalyzed me.

Accurately.

"And you are a coward," I fired back on reflex, feeling an odd sense of honesty to be telling my reflection that—as if this was some corporate retreat where we were told to shout out our weaknesses at our reflections in the mirror.

Had my reflex comment been directed at Zeus or...myself?

I cocked my head at a sudden thought, and had to bite back a laugh. "You know that merely looking like me won't let you get into my satchel, right? Is that what this is really about?"

Electro-Nate waved a hand dismissively. "I merely wanted to check if it was full of my Armory's weapons. Realizing it wouldn't be that easy, I considered other avenues to get what I wanted. I'll admit, my first intent was to kill you. Hermes convinced me to think on it, and find a way to use you instead. Rather than kill the other player's army and weapons, find a way to acquire them for myself."

Hermes smirked proudly, relishing in the rare praise. His siblings practically snarled.

"Then, I began to see the benefits in a collaboration." Zeus said. He studied me appraisingly. "I see much of myself in you, Nate Temple. I have done my homework, and you are to be commended."

"Oh, and how did I earn your approval? I think your children are dying for that answer."

He didn't even bat an eye. "You are a monster," he said simply, repeating the earlier accusation. "And monsters, like blades, must be used to retain their edges. And I know a thing or two about using monsters."

"I'm not a monster," I growled. If being a monster was the key to earning his love, Apollo and Ares should have been tied for favorite son.

He laughed. "Even your own people don't want you. Everyone is scared to death of the toddler with the figurative hand grenade. I'm choosing to give that child candy, because I see the man he will one day become."

I let it go, realizing that I had no interest in understanding the inner workings of a madman. As simply as that, I no longer cared about his rash judgment of me. I wasn't a monster. Sure, some thought so. But they were worse monsters. Sore losers, some might say.

"Unfortunately," he continued, "monsters must be kept on leashes until they learn who their master is," he said, smirking at my manacles. "The only way out of the Titan Thorns—other than me—is to be well and truly in love with someone. Unconditionally." He smiled wickedly. "And that is an impossibility for one such as you, isn't it, Temple? You can't do anything unconditionally."

Rather than rise to the bait, I immediately focused my thoughts on Callie Penrose, hoping to seize on his slip of the tongue. Love was the key to my Titan Thorns, and I loved Callie Penrose. How could Zeus be stupid enough to tell me how to break free—

Nothing happened.

My forehead burst out into a cold sweat at the sudden, startling implication. Callie Penrose, my on-again/off-again, someday-maybe lover was a wizard from Kansas City. The sexual tension between us was possibly strong enough to give even Aphrodite a proximity orgasm, because we had never actually acted upon our obvious shared feelings. We'd openly talked about it, but it always got pushed back in favor of taking out some dire threat on her end or mine. But we loved each other...

Didn't we? Memories of a conversation with Kára—a bartending Valkyrie—beneath Yggdrasil suddenly came to mind. How she'd thought I was single and ready to mingle, because I had never once spoken about my relationship with Callie in anything other than a formal manner. How I'd spent many evenings in her company rather than visiting Callie.

It hadn't been intentional, of course. Callie had been busy, and so had I.

But I'd sure sent Kára mixed signals about my love of Callie Penrose. Of course, Callie hadn't made any effort to reach out to me, either. We'd both sat around, waiting for the other to make the first move, and it had begun to chafe on me, subconsciously—which had led Kára to believe that we were no longer an item.

If love was the key to the Titan Thorns...well, Kára's analysis suddenly carried more weight.

I realized that the pavilion was silent and that everyone was staring at me. Aphrodite had a sad, understanding look on her face. Apollo had a victorious sneer, and Hermes looked gaunt and pale. Ares, the ginger bastard, burst out laughing, doubling over to slap his knees.

I ignored them and turned to Zeus, careful to keep my face blank. He nodded with a cool smile. "Did you think me stupid enough to give you the key to your imprisonment if I thought you could actually use it? Your heart is broken, Temple. Permanently. Irrevocably. You chose to become a monster rather than a lover. That choice will haunt you forever, much as it has me." A haunted look drifted across his eyes, like a passing cloud over sunlight. "Like I said, there is no use crying about it. Reap the benefits of your decision, and fuck whom you will. I did. I wouldn't be offering a partnership if I didn't see a little of me in you. Potential."

I stared at him, not knowing how to react. I was literally speechless—both at his admission and the unbidden revelation about myself. Was he right?

Or maybe love had nothing to do with the manacles, and he was using my self-doubt to make me buy his claim that I was a heartless monster. Because how could he have known about my true feelings for Callie? I'd seen how he treated and managed his offspring—the equivalent of tossing a rusty knife on the breakfast table and murmuring that the last kid standing was the most loved. I had to admit, he was incredibly talented at reading and manipulating people.

Had he done so with me? Was that one of the things he'd learned from torturing me for a week? Had I said something to Ares and Apollo? Or something to Carl when they'd left? Had our cell been bugged and he'd merely bided his time to exploit a weakness?

He picked up on my obvious frustration, and gave me an empathetic shrug. "No one can escape the Titan Thorns, especially not a man without a heart." I narrowed my eyes, sensing that he was incredibly devious, or that it wasn't an empty brag. "The more power you have, the less likely you are to break free of them. The Titan Thorns are like the Sensate the Norse Aesir gods use. No one will find you. Even if they were standing just outside your cell."

No wonder none of my friends had attempted a rescue. The fact that the Titan Thorns also blocked my own magic only lent credence to his claim. I frowned suspiciously, wondering if he was truly that manipulative about the love angle. To use an internal flaw or fear of mine to justify something totally unrelated, knowing that I would conflate the two together as fact. I'd already watched him mentally abuse his children today, so it was safe to say he was attempting the same with me.

"I am the only one who can unlock your manacles. They were made by Hephaestus."

I thought about Hephaestus, the legendary weapon smith of the Olympians...Aphrodite's husband. Was he in on this shit show, too?

But if all the Olympians were working together, why was my prison so far removed from Mount Olympus?

"I will not be removing your manacles until you give me a reason to trust you. On that note, I will walk around looking like you, precisely because it bothers you so much. Until you give me a reason to trust you. Until you show me that you are more than just potential, and that my expectations are not misplaced." He straightened his toga, smiling arrogantly.

"What can I do to earn your trust?" I asked, gritting my teeth. "I won't pretend I like the situation, but I'm hyper-rational when it comes down to it. I'm willing to work with people I dislike to defeat a group I dislike even more." I let my words hang in the air. "So, who is our mutual enemy in this upcoming war? I've never heard a solid answer."

Zeus considered my questions in silence for a time, and I could see his own children leaning closer in anticipation and dread. "Your list of crimes is extensive." He began ticking them off, one-by-one. "You freed Prometheus, you killed Athena, you killed Hercules, you even had the audacity to plan on using the River Styx as a dog bath..." He watched me closely, and it took everything in my power to keep my face blank. How had he known about me wanting to dip Calvin and Makayla into the River Styx?

I noticed Hermes in my peripheral vision, but I didn't focus on him for fear of accidentally confirming Zeus' claim. Hermes had visited me outside the Temple Mausoleum, hinting that he knew of my plans. The only others who knew were Gunnar and Othello.

"We face war, no thanks to you. Of course, you cannot take all the blame. This war was set in place long, long ago. You are merely the Catalyst—important, but not the initial cause. You were set up just as much as the rest of us. You are merely the first domino to be flicked."

I frowned thoughtfully, recalling Raego's father, Alaric Slate once saying something similar, years before. How he wanted to be the one to flick the first domino and cause chaos. Was he behind all this? He was dead now—twice, technically—but that didn't mean he hadn't set up a failsafe. Had he been working with Zeus? "The Omega War," I said, choosing one of the terms I'd used to refer to the apparent prophecy.

He nodded grimly. "I mean to win this war. To do so, I must make alliances I would not usually make. You are faced with the same decision." He turned to stare out at the sky. "I have seen what becomes of those who work with you," he said. "They do not usually survive. At best, they find themselves in your pocket. This is not acceptable."

I waited in silence. He wasn't wrong. The Aesir pantheon was a mess, although I wasn't sure how long that would last. Odin had been masquerading as my butler, and I'd just helped Loki break his son, Fenrir, out of prison. Fenrir, as in the wolf foretold to help kick off Ragnarok—the Norse Apocalypse.

Shiva and Ganesh were essentially my pals. I worked for Anubis—as his Guide to Hell—yet he seemed downright terrified of me. I was friends with the Boatman, Charon, who also seemed to terrify Anubis, despite being his employee. I was close friends with the Biblical Four Horsemen. The Fae Queens owed me a favor. I had helped put Alex—a new King Arthur—on the throne.

Yeah. Zeus wasn't wrong.

Still. Extortion usually only served to make things worse.

"You have amassed quite the following. The Elders have long been servants of the Temple Clan. Now that you have finally opened the portal to their realm, you will soon transfer that alliance to me. You will marshal your forces under the banners of Olympus. My pantheon will survive this war, one way or another."

Carl—already silent—had grown utterly still. He didn't even appear to breathe.

I licked my lips nervously. I had assumed as much from the Elders, but I had not verified any of this servant business as fact. Maybe they had once served my family, and Carl seemed content to continue in this relationship, but he hardly spoke for his entire people.

I cleared my throat. "I have never met with their leaders, and I doubt they would believe anything I said if I showed up in manacles. They would know I am acting on another's behalf. And, in case you've forgotten, they don't seem to be fans of gods."

Zeus nodded stiffly, still staring out at the skies. Thunder and lightning crackled and boomed on the horizon—a reflection of his thoughts. "The Elders are a necessity. As are your Horsemen. And you will give me back the keys to my Armory. For this, you will be compensated."

I chose my words carefully, preferring honesty to his current attitude. "To speak plainly, those artifacts and weapons were obtained honestly. And it is a thin stretch to define compensation as allowing my friends to live. Extortion is not payment."

"Desperate times," he said with a shrug. "You are not qualified to lead this war by yourself. You wear too many hats as it is, and you have no experience running a war of this magnitude."

I grunted. "I'm not arguing with that, although prophecy seems to disagree with us."

Zeus was silent for a time. "Destiny is what I say it is."

My eyebrows almost climbed off my forehead. I was pretty sure that wasn't how fate worked, and I'd heard conflicting information on Zeus' control over the Sisters of Fate. In fact, some stories said even Zeus was not immune to their spinning. However, this wasn't really the place for that. "Have you spoken to them? The Sisters of Fate?"

"Yes."

I waited for more, but he was obviously not willing to elaborate. The real question was whether or not I believed him. Regardless, my current predicament was set in stone. Whatever I had to do to keep my friends safe was all that mattered—and I couldn't do anything if I was stuck on this mountain. Zeus had me. We both knew it.

He turned to glance at me. "We are too close to war to risk more gods dying. We will need every single one of them to face what comes next."

I stared at him, feeling a shudder of very real fear. "What the hell are we supposed to be fighting that is stronger than all the gods?" I whispered.

"That information will be granted to an ally I know I can trust," he said, firmly.

9

I stared at him, wondering if maybe he was right. Zeus, apparently wasn't finished with his sales pitch. He began lifting his fingers as he ticked off perks of my new job. "If you wish to dip your friend's children into the River Styx to protect them, only I can grant such a wish. If you wish to remove the Titan Thorns, only I can grant such a wish. You embarrassed my counterpart, Odin, by letting the world believe Thor had freed Fenrir. I can help appease his displeasure. Even now, he hunts for your head. Well, he's using a Valkyrie to do so, at least. He is occupied with the capture of his son, Loki. And Fenrir, of course."

I stared at him in disbelief. Odin wanted me dead? That...sounded like a lie. He was probably still scouring the world for Gungnir, which was safely tucked away inside my satchel in my prison cell. Why would Zeus lie?

Fear.

Was...Zeus afraid? I appraised him pensively, thinking back on how he had treated his offspring. How sometimes, men overcompensated. At least I'd heard the allegation a time or two—never directed at me, of course.

And I realized that it felt right. Despite how tough he was acting, he was terrified and trying to bully me into agreeing with him. So...what else was he lying about? Everything?

He continued on, not able to read my mind now that I was a godkiller. Thankfully. "Telling you my plans now will give you time to consider a strategy for when I return."

I studied my doppelgänger. "I'm not agreeing to shit until you tell me why you need to look like me. What are you after? Who are you after?"

Electro-Nate studied his new look with an amused smile, looking proud. Hermes folded his arms smugly, satisfied at the makeover he'd whipped up for his father. "I intend to kill a very powerful person—practically a god. To do so, I need to obtain an item that I should not be able to obtain." He settled his heavy gaze on me. "When the other pantheons see the godkiller—you—steal it, they won't think anything of it. You are a godkiller, this is a god killing weapon." He laughed abruptly. "And one you've already toyed with."

That could mean dozens of things. Which was his point, obviously, hence the evil laugh.

"And it will give you leverage over me since I bet the theft and the murder are going to piss off a lot of people," I growled, clenching my jaw.

He nodded unashamedly. "Yes."

"Who are you going to kill?"

His eyes glittered with desire. "Someone very important. Everyone will know soon enough. I will share the details once the deed is done."

His children looked anticipatory—and not in the way that implied they already knew the target. They were just as in the dark as me, and it rankled them.

"My friends will be able to see through the illusion—through the character of the man using my face. They know me well enough to understand what I will and won't do. They will know that your actions don't match up with your appearance—"

Electro-Nate burst out laughing and I cringed at the sound of my own voice mocking me. "Everyone is absolutely terrified of you, Master Temple —*especially* your friends. You said it yourself. No one knows what you will or won't do when your back is against the wall. What lines you will or will not cross. Maybe they knew once, but you are no longer the man they befriended." He smiled devilishly. "You have gone through ascension. Apotheosis. You are more god than mortal—and I'm talking about your moral code, not your body's ability to withstand harm. You are the monster to the monsters. There is *nothing* you wouldn't do. Why do you think I *like* you?"

His words hit his children like a punch to the gut. Each of them grew still.

I stared back at him in silence, feeling sickened. I knew that I always had the best intentions, but I sure spent a lot of time trying to convince my old friends that my purposes were for the good of all. I had even taken to hiding my actions from them so as not to have to deal with their judgmental looks. Which...

Was exactly what Zeus meant. Damn it.

Even worse, the more loyal the friend, the more sympathetic they might be to whatever Electro-Nate was cooking up. They would argue that I had to have a good reason for doing what I was doing, which would convince everyone else. Gunnar would assume the best of me, and the rest would fall in line.

Still...

"The moment you open your mouth, my true friends will see through the ruse. We have too many past experiences for you to be able to pull this off as genuine. The moment one of my friends makes a comment that you don't respond to in the right way, they will all close in on you."

Electro-Nate nodded absently, not looking even remotely concerned. "Your friends will receive Hermes for an official meeting. He will inform them that the Olympians are helping to search for you ever since you went missing after rescuing Fenrir. Then I—as you—will likely make a few casual appearances to flesh out the story, if necessary. Then, if they see the real me wandering around, they will assume I am working with you and they will aid me. Once they learn that you not only escaped your abduction but that you are actively hunting another target, they will clamor to your call, praising Zeus and his mighty Olympians for helping you. Greeks flood to your city already, and the Olympians rally behind you. It is almost poetic, when you look at the big picture." I stared at him incredulously, finding hardly any flaws in his plan. "It is no secret that Hermes has helped you in the past, so they will believe him. As I intended so long ago when I first ordered him to give you that coin. To establish trust."

I felt a cold shiver run down my neck again. The first meeting with Hermes and his help with the coin had been...a set up? All the way back when the Minotaur had given me Hermes' coin to fight the dragons? Zeus had been playing the long con this whole time? That was...

Wait for it...

Inconceivable.

Then again, if he had the Sisters of Fate wrapped around his finger, it was entirely plausible that he had been watching me this whole time, moving me around as he saw best for this future Omega War.

The fact that he had not punished me for killing Athena told me he wasn't an unconditional love kind of god. No one made plans this perfectly without great amounts of help.

Like the Sisters of Fate. But I'd already sensed a lie or two, and knew that he was afraid.

I simply couldn't decide which part of his claim was the lie—whether he truly had set all this up long ago or whether he was merely capitalizing on the current situation. He either had the Sisters of Fate under his thumb, or he absolutely did not, and he was scrambling to work around them in some way I couldn't comprehend. Was that even possible—to defy fate?

He chuckled at the look on my face. "I have thought of every angle, Master Temple. I am not one to sit idly by. I study my enemies and allies in equal measure. I have considered every weak link in the chain and set up contingency plans for every possibility. For example, one contingency should matter above all others. If I sense your Horsemen plotting against me, I will kill them all. I will not grant them the chance to explain themselves. I will simply end them. Hermes has already set up enough firepower to destroy every single person you have ever loved within one moment of my signal. I will have them under surveillance at all times. I wouldn't be surprised if one of your own friends turns the others in—thinking they are being loyal to you." He pressed a thumb against his chest, enunciating the last word to remind me that he meant my doppelgänger—himself. "You will sit here, locked away, and watch them all die, knowing that their loyalty demanded they make the call, thinking they are actually helping you, not that they are doing anything wrong."

I stared at him, shaking my head. "An alliance would have worked so much better," I whispered—not out of fear, but speaking entirely honestly. I also realized that I had subconsciously spoken in the past tense, as if I'd already made my decision.

Zeus shrugged. "Alliances are for negotiations. This is an ultimatum." He brushed his hands together. "I suggest you get some rest. It will be sunset in several hours, and if Aphrodite has any say in the matter, you have a long night ahead of you." He chuckled raucously. "You should be thanking me. The audacity to believe you are a prisoner when you get to fuck the Goddess of Sex as much as you could possibly handle."

He didn't even have the dignity to look at his daughter, so he didn't catch the brief glimmer of fury in her eyes. It was gone so fast, I almost hadn't caught it myself.

He was talking about his own daughter as if she was a salaried family whore. Even if she was okay with her job, the fact that her dad was so callous about it...well, it told me a lot about their family dysfunction. And that maybe Aphrodite was more independent than she seemed.

I wisely kept my mouth shut. Sex was not happening, no matter what she thought. "I'm pretty sure my time with Apollo and Ares will balance the scales of pleasure and pain."

Zeus shrugged. "You brought down their ire upon yourself. A godkiller must endure and carry the consequences of his actions for his entire immortal life. What doesn't kill you makes you stronger," he added with a dark chuckle. "I imagine you will be quite formidable when you are ready to work with me. When you see what is at stake. In two nights, to be precise, I will require your answer. There is supposed to be a truly epic storm that night—if I have anything to say about it," he chuckled absently at his funny little joke. His eyes grew distant. "I do not seek your friendship or good favor, Temple. Gods and godkillers cannot afford such whimsy. I hold you to a higher standard—that you will do whatever is necessary, despite your personal feelings—for the betterment of existence." He stared out at the clouds, a euphoric look on his face. "Zeus will save the world, and everyone will worship me again," he breathed, looking as if he could already hear the billions of humans—or however many survived this upcoming Omega War—chanting his name. He was drunk on his own power.

I stared at him for a few moments, knowing how dangerous unchecked arrogance could be.

"I have a friend who named his dog Zeus. Little terrier or something. One of those yapping, obnoxious, shoe-sized little rodents." Zeus' knuckles crackled dangerously, but he didn't rise to my bait. "There was an epic storm one night, and he got run over by a car much bigger than him. Mine." Zeus clenched his fists but didn't turn to look at me. "Funny how the world turns," I added. "Come on, Carl."

Carl nodded and followed me as I turned back to head to our cell.

What the hell was I supposed to do now?

Zeus muttered something, and his children were quickly falling into place to escort us back. Ares and Apollo took the lead while Hermes and Aphrodite picked up the rear.

My neck itched to have Hermes at my back, but I managed not to twitch. My mind raced with plans, most of them epic failures. Hermes— although mostly silent—was the scariest one of the bunch. He made my skin crawl. And he was the one who had supposedly tried to help me up until my abduction. He'd warned me not to trust any Olympian. Even himself.

Except Hermes had been playing me from the very beginning. Him and his fucking coins—

Wait a minute...

10

As we made our way back down the tunnel, I let my crazy plan percolate, wondering how to incorporate it. Our Olympian escorts kept themselves at a safe distance, obviously troubled by some of Zeus' comments. I could use that.

I leaned close to Carl. "Give me a distraction. Now."

Carl suddenly got right up in Apollo's face. He had his hands clasped behind his back to signify he meant the Olympian no harm. I knew that if Carl tried to hit Apollo, the manacles would prevent him from actually making contact—an annoying little limitation of the cuffs. I'd almost forgotten about that, and was now doubly thankful that I hadn't tried taking a swing at Zeus or his ilk.

Apollo tried to step back and Carl followed him, maintaining his invasion of Apollo's personal space.

"Make him stop, or I swear I will kill him," Apollo whined in a nasally tone. He stepped back and Carl pursued him, not lessening his proximity for even a heartbeat. "Ares! He's trying to attack!"

Ares grinned, suddenly amused. Aphrodite seemed similarly curious. Hermes flicked his mercurial eyes from face-to-face, watching everyone.

Everyone but *me*. Perfect.

I'd given the watcher something to watch.

"I am not touching you, sunshine man," Carl said, calmly. "But I am thinking about thrusting my claws into your chest cavity—as slowly as a lover's first mating session—while I drink down your fear and wrap myself in your dying screams. How my claws will carefully detach your heart and slowly pull it back out. How your blood will moisturize my scales for decades to come. Ichor makes the best lotion, you know."

Apollo blanched, breathing rapidly through his nose—both transfixed by and furious with Carl's melodic, almost hypnotic threat. "I will roast you alive—"

"And I will let you try," Carl interrupted calmly, matter-of-factly. "I will purr at your futile attempts to harm me, embracing them like a lover's arms around my shoulders."

"That's it. I am going—"

"To *die*, godling," Carl interrupted again, in a voice like a loving father's lullaby. "You are going to *die*. In my arms. Tonight."

I grinned. "It must have been something you said," I chuckled. No one paid me any attention. Everyone was staring at Elder Carl in very real fear. He'd been so fucking quiet this whole time that they believed ignoring him had worked to dial back the creepiness.

But Carl had no chill.

His creepy dial didn't go any lower than eleven. That was his *starting* point.

Carl flicked his tongue out, almost hitting Apollo in the nose. "After I finish feasting on your still-beating heart, I will lovingly carry your cold corpse to the Boatman," he said in a dreamy tone. "Yet I shall not pay him. No. Because killing you would be a charity to the world." Carl leaned closer. "I will do this thing, sunshine. I swear it."

Ares coughed and Aphrodite stared at the Elder in absolute horror.

Apollo stared at Carl with a nauseated look on his face, unable to pull his gaze away.

Poor Hermes didn't see me coming. I tripped into him, accidentally knocking loose the pouch of coins hanging from his belt. Olympian gold spilled everywhere, jarring everyone out of their staring contest with Carl.

"Shit," I cursed, wobbling on my feet dazedly and clutching at my head. "Sorry. I'm feeling a little dizzy."

Hermes glared at me and Ares laughed.

"Maybe if you imbeciles actually gave them enough food and water, he would be able to stand on his own feet for more than an hour," Aphrodite growled. "Now he's wasting my time."

"I said I was sorry," I mumbled, bending over to begin scooping them up. I made a show of collapsing to my knees with a groan, fumbling about with the coins.

Hermes wasted no time, slapping my hand away as he bent down to do it himself. I realized the moment he saw the four coins I had palmed between my fingers.

Mainly because he suddenly hoisted me to my feet and slammed me against the door to my prison cell, snarling at me from so close that our noses almost touched and my feet dangled a few inches off the ground.

"I bet you four coins that I can beat Zeus," I breathed before he could say anything.

In his eyes, I saw a split-second of hesitation, but his face remained furious. "You dare touch me again and I'll take my turn at torturing you, boy," he snarled. Then he very openly plucked the coins from my hand. "But try to rob me again, and I'll cut off your fingers. I'm the god of thieves, you fucking moron."

Then he reared back and clocked me in the jaw hard enough to send me to my knees. He bent down, scooped up his coins, and stormed away.

Ares and Apollo opened my cell door and ushered Carl through, first. He was chained back up and I was being dragged by my boots into the cell before I managed to clear the stars from my eyes. I heard the snap of chains as they connected to my Titan Thorns, and I climbed up onto all fours, shaking my head in both pain and true dizziness this time.

The door slammed shut and I spat out some blood, tonguing a loose tooth.

"It almost worked, Master Temple," Carl said, softly.

I glanced over at him and then slowly reached into the pocket of my jeans. I pulled out four golden coins and grinned at him. "I don't play almost, but I do like to place bets," I croaked.

Carl's eyes widened and his nostrils flared with hope.

"Not much help, since they only take us to the pavilion, but better than nothing." And I told him about the impromptu bet I'd placed with the world's most dangerous bookie after I'd failed to rob him. Talk about a stroke of luck.

The real question was why Hermes had slipped them into my pocket when he'd pinned me up against the wall. What fucking game was he playing now?

Regardless, my plan had worked. He was the god of thievery and trickery and gambling. He also favored mortals, historically. So, he had chosen to place a bet, putting his purse where his mouth was. This in no way helped me, but it could result in him dragging his feet when Zeus made a request of him. I'd found a fissure in their ranks.

A crack in their foundation.

Well, they hadn't exactly hidden it. I'd just exploited an obvious weakness. To be fair, Hermes wasn't risking all that much, and his potential for gain was very high. I analyzed the situation, murmuring to Carl that it was very likely our cell was bugged, so we should definitely be discreet in our conversations.

He nodded without hesitation and promptly went to his cot to rest.

I sat in the center of our cell, analyzing the situation. Now, how did I crack the foundation of the Olympian household even further?

Zeus ruled his crew with fear and infighting. Distracting them by pitting them against each other. He also used leverage to keep them in line —at least in a few cases, like Hephaestus over Aphrodite, then using Ares' jealousy over Aphrodite. I wasn't sure about Apollo and Hermes. They were wild cards. At least where it concerned how Zeus was controlling them. What motivated them? Apollo had a self-image weakness. He wanted everyone to know how important, pretty, valuable, blah, blah, blah he was. But he obviously had a fragile ego.

While I ruminated on the various pathologies of the goon squad, Carl decided to take a nap, but there was no rest for the wicked.

Zeus was drunk on his own name. True to Zeus' claims, I sensed alarming parallels between the pair of us. He was obviously at the furthest end of the narcissism spectrum, but I was close enough to bake him cookies and show up unannounced on his front porch—like a good neighbor. So, the real question was...

How would I beat myself? With Zeus now looking like my doppelgänger, it wasn't too hard to imagine. I had to put myself in his shoes, much like he'd put himself in my skin. If I went all-powerful Nate, what would be my greatest weakness?

The people I loved. Especially the kids. I felt my skin flush at mental images of Calvin and Makayla or Alice.

My allies, obviously. Then, the people I considered beneficial as leverage over my foes—those I knew who had value in the short-term but not the long-term.

Loyalty was the most important factor when considering an ally, and thinking of betrayal—justifiably so, thanks to my parents—kept me up most nights. The fear of deceit.

Fear. I needed fear.

And a few very frightening ideas began to simmer in my mind as I started considering beneficial allies who would likely terrify Zeus. Or those who were at least strong enough to put a chink in his armor that I could slip a blade through.

If a man thought so highly of himself that he thought he could remake the world into a better place—in his own image—well, that never ended well. Zeus was beyond irrational and already imagining the merchandise sales of his rebounded worship.

He thought he could win that worship by using me to win the Omega War for him.

None of this mattered if I couldn't get out of these damned Titan Thorns and get out of here. I'd have to play along with his plan to get a chance to take him out. I had to find a way to earn his trust. Even after that, I couldn't go to my allies or Zeus would kill them. I also seriously doubted that I was strong enough to go head-to-head with Zeus on my best of days.

Even if I was, I still didn't know who he wanted to kill, or which weapon he was trying to find. I had no leads. Just because I'd used this weapon once before didn't actually help me. I'd used dozens, hundreds, of weapons—and the ones I valued the most were within my grasp. Either my satchel or the Armory, and Zeus was willing to wait for the Armory. The weapon he sought was elsewhere.

I was certain he couldn't get inside the Armory without me—even if he looked like me. A Beast, Falco, ran my mansion. Two actually protected it, now that Ruin lived in the treehouse outside. Zeus couldn't get close without me. Pandora was safe, for the time being.

What kind of fall-out would there be once Zeus assassinated his target while looking like me? Because if I got out of here, it was going to become a big problem for me since everyone would believe I had done the crime in the first place.

Unless I teamed up with Zeus, hoping his ultimate intentions were good—that the end justified the means. Whether they were or not, he might be my only ticket to freedom. I leaned back, sighing in frustration. I stared out the small window high above, watching the clouds pass by. We were so high up that I couldn't even hear birds.

I took a calming breath, shifting my focus away from Zeus' current trip. There were too many potential options to discern his target. I needed to break him from within.

I needed to destroy his already crumbling family. As much as he scorned them, he needed them. For now. And as much as they wanted his affection, I'd seen enough dark looks to know they could be turned—if I played my cards right. I pulled out one of the golden coins and kissed it for good luck.

My bloody lip print stained the surface, and I smiled.

11

I woke up to Carl shaking me determinedly. Noticing I was awake, Carl turned to face the door, sniffing at the air warily. "Aphrodite is coming."

I narrowed my eyes, checking the window of our cell. It was dark outside, so I must have slept for hours. "Not if I have anything to say about it," I growled. Then I frowned, running my choice of phrasing back through my head. Damn it. At least Carl hadn't picked up on it—

Carl nodded his agreement. "Do not let her climax. This is a good strategy, Master Temple."

I sighed. "Technically, both are true," I admitted. I knew beyond a shadow of a doubt that I wasn't going to have a little slap and tickle under Aphrodite's sheets, no matter what she believed. I firmed my resolve. One thing I knew for certain—we were going to talk about our comings and goings.

She was attempting to direct me towards our comings, but the only thing I cared about was my goings—which, in all honesty, pretty much summed up my love life in recent years.

I glanced down at my Titan Thorns. The only way to break free of them was by Zeus' permission, or if I was well and truly in love with someone. Unconditionally.

He'd implied that I was broken and heartless. Irrevocably so. That I had chosen to become a monster instead of finding true love. That Zeus saw me as a kindred spirit, encouraging me to embrace promiscuity, love be damned.

And thoughts of my relationship with Callie Penrose had done nothing to change my current situation, leaving a gaping, hollow hole in my soul. I had consciously known that something had come between us—mutually, not just for me—but I hadn't relegated it to a certainty. I had considered it something that we needed to address and get past.

But according to Zeus' claim, that must have been considered a *condition*.

And unconditional love didn't work like that.

It was, perhaps, the worst sort of irony that my lack of romance and sexual activity had led me to a prison cell where the Goddess of Sex was now determined to seduce me into being her lackey. Many, if not all, men would have committed the worst crime they could think of if the punishment was suffering Aphrodite's amorous advances.

But I just saw it as a curse. Karma, even.

The Minotaur would be rolling over with laughter if he could see me now. He'd once warned me that Karma would be gunning for me.

Apparently, Karma would be stripping for me, too.

I smelled Aphrodite before I saw or heard her: fresh cut flowers, hot savory sweat, warm scented oil, a primal, mouth-watering bouquet of desire—

"The sea beast is here," Carl said, covering his nostrils with a sickly demeanor.

Well. To each his own, I guess. It was no secret that the connection between Carl's nose and his brain was a dark, twisted tangle, causing him to find pleasure from the creepiest scents and nausea from the floral perfume of a sex goddess. Carl's nose was figuratively broken.

His assessment was neither polite nor accurate. A man comparing any woman's bodily scent to aquatic life was on the fast track to getting killed so hard that it rewrote history—removing his original birth from ever happening. Even the poor man's mother would unquestionably accept the consequence of losing a son's entire lifetime as fair justice for the slight.

Because women were all in cahoots. I was certain of it. Magical cahoots, I tell you.

These existential pre-murders obviously created time paradoxes, but it seemed that only menfolk had issues processing the ramifications.

That was why men had such difficult times remembering their carefully-crafted bullet points during arguments with their lovers—because our brains still registered the fact that the other man had once existed—as had all the things that the poor man had ever accomplished in his now-erased life.

Women, on the other hand, were hyperaware of the new status quo, that the man had never existed, and accepted it without question. They wielded that rewritten history like a guillotine to decapitate our arguments, leaving us to scratch our heads in confusion, wondering how we had lost an argument that we knew for certain we should have won. We'd had spreadsheets and flow charts.

The women were assassinating our memories—and then denying that the victims had ever existed. They were waging war while we were shooting slingshots at empty soda cans.

"Master Temple, are you all right?" Carl asked in a soft tone.

I realized that my conspiracy theory made entirely too much sense for comfort. I shook my head to focus on the fight at hand. I gave Carl a reassuring nod and climbed to my feet.

The door opened and...

Aphrodite came like a gentle, unstoppable wave on a moonlit beach at midnight...and all suddenly seemed right with the world. Her heroin of pheromones made me salivate despite my brain defiantly screaming at me to deny it.

Aphrodite was the goddess of all things that go hump in the night: not just sex, but lust, desire, love, and pretty much anything else related to silk sheets, hot flesh, whipped cream, melted chocolate, hot candle wax, throbbing...hearts, and salacious whispers and moans.

She had definitely turned up her charm from when I'd seen her outside on the pavilion hours ago, because my pants were suddenly three sizes too small.

For fuck's sake!

So much blood instantly flooded to my meat gavel that my freaking vision began to tunnel on me. I closed my eyes, breathing deeply, reminding my body that the biggest, tallest, hardest mast in the world was worthless without a ship to ground it and a competent captain to steer it.

My instinctive arousal verged on voluntary suicide—a mutiny against the captain of my ship.

I forced myself to focus on Carl's comment about the denizens of the sea and their aromatic perfume—preferring the risk of time paradoxes to the siren song of Aphrodite's love box—and it helped bring me back to a somewhat rational state.

I let out a breath and opened my eyes. Aphrodite was hungrily eyeing my nether-Nate region, and I was pretty sure I heard her purring like an actual cat. She even licked her lips, making my face grow hot as I struggled to focus my thoughts back on slimy, stinking, sea creatures to kill my desire. "Moby Dick practices abstinence," I declared with all the pride of an actor in a tenth-grade sex education clip.

She studied me up and down. "Nate—can I call you Nate?" she asked.

I shrugged. "My stage name is Ishmael."

"Nate," she cooed in a voice that made the hair on the back of my neck stand up on end, "it has been so long since you've had an orgasm that I quite literally do not know how you haven't destroyed the world yet." She frowned with genuine compassion.

She wasn't wrong. "Oh, I'm getting there," I rasped, gritting my teeth. "Although difficult, my abstinence keeps me grounded. Situations like this do not help get my mind off it."

"Your mind isn't supposed to get off on it," she said with an amused smile. "Your dick is."

Well. I'd assumed we would dance around the topic a bit longer, but Aphrodite was a real go-getter, and she didn't seem to have a parental guidance sticker on her toga. Carl was a terrible chaperone, for what it was worth. He just watched.

"Perhaps you wouldn't feel so grounded if you released a little...a lot of pent up frustration," she said, struggling not to laugh at our ridiculous argument.

I folded my arms stubbornly. Because I'm a man, and that's what we do when we're right.

She studied me up and down. "Sex is not a sin. It is nothing to be ashamed of. Neither is it something to be so picky about."

I pursed my lips stubbornly so they matched my arms. I needed to change the topic. Now. Because this was not the same Aphrodite I had encountered outside at the pavilion. She was just as dangerous now as she was then, but her motives seemed oddly more...genuine and determined. "Let's talk about—"

"Sex is instinctual," she cut in. "Mandatory for a well-balanced life. Imagine treating any other area of your life with such scrutiny." She clapped her hand over her mouth in a theatric gesture. "Oh, no! I had a steak for dinner! Does that mean I love my steak more than my potatoes? What if I want potatoes some day? It will hurt my steak's feelings! Then there's the grapes! They'll never come to my plate again if they learn about my steak. I must keep this a secret. It was an accident. A moment of weakness. That steak took advantage of me! I will never be weak again. I will find my perfect meal someday. Until then, to prove my dedication, I vow to starve myself." Her words seemed to echo in the small confines of the prison cell.

My face was beet red—both in embarrassment and anger. Carl, the asshole, was nodding matter-of-factly, not even aware he was doing so. I was on my own. "Love is not as simple as steak or grapes or potatoes, Aphrodite—"

"You are quite right. And you are quite wrong. Sex is a *simpler* decision," she argued in a gentle yet insistent tone, as if truly trying to convince me that she wanted the best for me. "I spend more time considering my meals than my mates."

I blinked at her, wondering how I could bring the topic back to what truly mattered. Getting out of my manacles or finding out why she was really here. Why she seemed so different.

"Do you know what happens to a person who denies themself for too long?" she asked in a soothing, calming tone. "They grow manic, angry, and violent. Irrational. Like a rope supporting too much weight, the braid starts to fray and snap. The safest thing to do is lighten the load and try again later."

I held up a triumphant finger. "Or get a stronger rope."

She rolled her eyes. "*You* are the rope in the analogy," she said, dryly.

My triumphant finger went flaccid. She studied me for a few moments, and the look of frustration and compassion in her eyes let me know that she really was concerned about my stance on this issue. It was pretty much her sole purpose as a goddess, and she was not going to let it go. She looked like a negotiator on a roof trying to convince me not to jump. She wasn't trying to justify her own actions for her sake—she was trying to prescribe me what she believed was the proper medication to heal my self-inflicted wounds. In her opinion, she was trying to save my life.

That didn't mean she was right, it just made the already difficult situation even more difficult to argue. "Aphrodite—"

She lifted a finger, cutting me off. "Continuing down this path will destroy the world. You will make a terrible mistake. You need release more than any man I have ever met. Even Prometheus wasn't in as much danger as your aura suggests you are. He was too focused on his unending punishment to give it any thought. You, on the other hand, have come close to the edge of release on repeated occasions, only to have it taken from you moments too soon. That is far, *far* worse." And I could tell by the sympathetic look in her eyes that she was no longer only talking about sex. She was talking about love.

Indie had been my last physical release, and that had been years ago, before she had gone crazy with power. Ironically, Indie had unintentionally set me up to square off against Athena—

I blinked as Aphrodite's warnings suddenly took on a whole new meaning. "Athena..." I whispered aloud. I'd killed Athena by introducing her to lust. Being a virgin goddess, she hadn't known how to handle the alien emotion, and it had utterly destroyed her. Wasn't that a conflicting argument, though?

Aphrodite's lips thinned and she nodded. "Yes. See what abstinence gets you? A person begins seeking out other means of self-fulfillment. In her case, anger and power." She studied me sadly. "Everyone seeks the sensation of a lasting embrace, anything to fill the empty vacuum of existence—either via a grave of black soil hugging their body close for eternity or the silky-smooth embrace of flesh on flesh. Those who disregard sex find themselves with a manic desire to fill that void of depthless anger with overwhelming ambition. Violence. War. Death."

I considered her grim analogy. She made a fair point. We all wanted a hug, but I had never likened a coffin to a hug before. "War...like your lover, Ares?"

She nodded without hesitation or shame, even though I had seen how he treated her—the blatant disrespect and possessiveness. "Why do you think we are so attracted to each other? He fills me—rather snugly—with his fire, and I send it back out, safely dispersing it back into the universe." She met my eyes. "A proper climax is your charitable donation to the world of man. A climax a day keeps the carnage away."

I stared at her, dumbfounded. Then I burst out laughing at the mental image. "You have got to be kidding me," I gasped, bending at the waist to support my weight on my knees.

Aphrodite was not laughing. Oddly, she didn't look offended either. In fact, she looked deeply concerned. Scared, even. My reaction terrified her. "Sometimes, a soul is so broken that it no longer sees clearly. Sometimes, it is up to the maid to clean the filthy window to prove her claim that the glass beneath is cracked—even when her master mocks her for it." And then she began sauntering towards me, swaying her hips determinedly.

I squeaked, backing up a step. "No, Aphrodite." Was she intending to freaking force me into this? "What about love?" I demanded, taking another panicked step back. Carl watched the two of us thoughtfully, seeming to consider her arguments rather than protect me.

Aphrodite gave me a sad smile, not slowing her advance. "Love is more complicated, true. But it should never be used as a weapon, and it should always be reciprocated. Oftentimes, love is misunderstood, causing more harm than good—thinking that you are supposed to love a specific someone when, in fact, you do not. Love is not destined. Love is a choice, and it is intended to make both parties stronger. All else invites the carnage."

Her enunciation was clear and concise, and it was the second time she'd used the obscure word. "The carnage?" I asked, grasping for anything that might halt her advance.

She flicked her fingers and my arms suddenly shot above my head like she'd hoisted me up by the manacles. I danced up on my tiptoes, no longer able to move backwards. Aphrodite eyed me like a butcher eyeing a slab of beef. "Don't you fret about that, Catalyst. I will suck the carnage right out of you to save you from yourself. I will protect this world."

Carl finally remembered his job of keeping me safe and lunged forward to protect me. Aphrodite did the same flicking motion with a thin, smooth, manicured finger, and he was suddenly dancing up on his clawed toes as his arms were hoisted upwards. She hadn't even looked at him.

The goddess sauntered closer, licking her lips. She dropped her silk gown to the ground, revealing a tanned expanse of mouth-watering curves. Goosebumps pebbled her flesh, and her nipples stood erect. She lowered her hand with the speed of dripping honey, and my surroundings slowly dimmed to darkness—as did all sensation of Carl's struggles against his chains.

Instead, I heard the crackling of fire, the aromatic whiff of enticing incense and fresh flowers, and the atmosphere changed to warm and humid with a pleasantly sweet taste to the air.

As the lighting slowly returned, I realized that I was no longer in my prison cell.

Carl was on his own. I'd been abducted by the seductress.

12

I quickly noticed that I was in a rather swanky bedroom. I was no longer standing either. I was sprawled out on an extremely plushy collection of furs, pillows, silk sheets, and thick blankets that filled a wide concave bowl cut into the very floor—much like the seating areas inside my Sanctorum at Chateau Falco. The lip of my recessed bowl was even with the room's floor, and was large enough to fill with water to transform into an in-ground hot tub of sin.

The chains of my manacles were affixed to a thick metal ring hammered into the floor above my head since our little love nest sat at a lower elevation. I had enough slack so that I could move them to my sides but not block my goods.

Aphrodite stood within the bowl near my feet, towering over me. Her dark hair hung down over her shoulders, and she had oiled her skin so that her body glistened, reflecting the firelight of the room's several braziers. I couldn't help but stare in profound awe.

"Um. Your toga fell off," I mumbled. "Yet you fund underwear." She now wore only purple silk panties and matching garters. I absently realized that purple went really well with all that tanned sexiness. My lips were tingling for some strange reason and my cheeks felt flushed. I was beginning to sweat in the relaxing humidity.

"Oh, no," she said with mock concern. "Whatever shall I do?"

I averted my gaze, hoping to find something—anything—to get me out of this situation. The room was still dim compared to my prison cell, illuminated only by crackling braziers near the red stone walls. The ceilings were too high up for me to actually see—disappearing in a cloud of shadow—yet royal purple silk curtains draped down from somewhere high above, swaying at the faintest motion or gust of air, effectively partitioning the room into a dizzying array of private nooks and crannies.

This was not exactly what I had envisioned when she'd offered up her persuasive skills to her father. This felt...like she was running her own angle, and that it just might be the most important thing she'd ever done. I saw it in her eyes. The desperation and determination.

Not necessarily in a sinister way, either. Whatever this was, she was committed, and she was more afraid of me not learning her lessons than she was of her father's wrath.

A tenacious, nubile nymphomaniac was a nefarious nemesis to contend with.

How best to battle such a foe? How could I fight and win? Stubborn argument would just be a form of denial. I needed her to know that I acknowledged her arguments—especially her good ones—and that I could withstand whatever tactics she tried to employ. I couldn't participate, but I couldn't childishly not participate. She needed to see me kiss her fire, sample her sweetness, and then pull away, standing firm on my position. Otherwise, she would just keep dialing up the lust.

Aphrodite slowly, deliciously, lowered herself down onto all fours and began crawling towards me, licking her lips. Her irises glowed golden—reminding me of her brother Hermes, unfortunately—and her plump lips were engorged with blood. She settled into a kneeling position at my boots. Then she calmly reached towards her garter and withdrew a purple dagger that I had mistaken for some sort of decoration or buckle. Rather than stabbing me, she sliced through the laces of my boots and yanked them off before I could say anything. She flung them out of our love nest.

"You won't be needing those anymore, my love," she whispered. "I'll be making your toes curl hard enough that you would have destroyed them anyway," she added with a dark chuckle.

"You can't do this," I pressed, unsuccessfully trying to scoot away. "I don't consent. I do not want this," I growled.

She paused with a sad smile, settling back on her haunches in an effort to calm my agitation. "Nate..." she said, looking at me.

I stared at her beautiful face, not even needing to study her mesmerizing nudity. Her face was captivating enough to stop all rational thought. Had she looked this pretty outside earlier? It was a feral, primal yet elegant, combination.

"I would never do this without consent."

I let out a breath of relief, ignoring the sweat dripping down my temples. "Good. I do not consent—"

"But before I reach your lips, you will beg me for this," she promised me in a calm, utterly confident, and hungry tone. "Without any magic or power used against you, I promise that you will beg me for this lesson. And you should. It has nothing to do with me being the goddess of sex and desire. You deserve to be seduced and savored," she purred, and I felt myself nodding in agreement. "It is not my problem that you have been misled by unconfident women who do not know that they are playing with fire." Her eyes twinkled in the light from the braziers, casting reflections of what momentarily resembled Kama Sutra highlight reels. "Your first love, Indiana Rippley, was a weakness. You were not in love with the woman herself. You were in love with the concept of being in love." She very specifically enunciated the difference, making sure I caught her meaning. "She knew how to feed your beast—your primary love language."

"My primary love language?" I asked, snapping out of the hypnotic lull of her voice upon use of the word beast.

Aphrodite nodded. "I believe it is physical touch, but I intend to test my hypothesis."

I shifted awkwardly and Aphrodite smiled in faint amusement. "Indie is old news. We all see how that turned out for me. In fact, it scarred me, if I'm being honest."

Aphrodite nodded delightedly, as if suddenly encouraged by my answer. "It did." I momentarily froze to stare at her in surprise. She smiled compassionately. "Indie birthed the carnage within you. Unchecked, it will destroy everything you have ever cared about."

I shook my head stiffly. "No. That isn't true. I have...Callie," I argued.

With my hormones on full blast, it had taken me a moment to remember her name.

Aphrodite studied me in silence. "Oh? Your fellow Horseman? Dismissing the well-known dangers of romance with a subordinate, how has your sex life been with the White Rose? Have you unfurled those silky, pious petals? Have you buzzed about and tasted that nectar, little bee?"

I blushed at her analogies. "Well, not very sexy," I admitted. Then I blushed. "I mean no sex. Callie is exceedingly sexy."

Aphrodite licked her lips. "She is indeed," she agreed with an amused smile. "There has been no sex because even you know, deep down, that you two are not compatible. You could be, but both of you have made choices to prevent it, even if you did so subconsciously. That is often the most honest of decisions."

I stared at her, struck silent. Did...she have a point? Callie and I had never made time for each other. The best word to describe our romance was—

"Later," Aphrodite whispered, pouting out her lower lip. "The surefire blade to love's heart. Love is like an errant spark from a bonfire. It cannot be saved for *later* or it burns up. It must be fed *immediately*. Nurtured, cared for, protected from the storms of wind and rain that threaten to douse it. Embers and sparks hold the power of creation—of life itself."

"I thought you gods could no longer read my mind?" I demanded uneasily, knowing that their particular parlor trick was no longer a tool they could weaponize against me. Not since I'd embraced my ability to kill a god.

Aphrodite nodded. "I am reading the mind of an uncertain, love-weary man by looking at his face and his eyes. Nothing godly about it, godkiller. This is my purpose."

I let out a frustrated breath, refusing to let hormones and healthy relationship concerns sway such a serious concept as my feelings for Callie Penrose. "It's complicated. Callie has a lot on her plate, and so do I. It's not easy to make time for love when you're constantly fighting wars."

"It is not easy. But it should be natural," Aphrodite countered. "Love and war are two sides of the same coin. Anything worth keeping is worth fighting for. If the embers of love were so easy to grasp, they wouldn't be nearly so powerful. There would be no need for war without love."

I sighed, accepting her answer and silently chastising myself for not having foreseen it.

"And for the record, Ares has never let war neuter his desire. Quite the contrary. Your other friends have found love, despite their duties. If even gods can find love, surely a wizard can. You have had ample opportunity to bridge the gap with Callie Penrose, but neither of you have done so. You think you are a monster, and Callie Penrose teeters between anger, vengeance, doubt, guilt, and a dozen other emotions." She pursed her lips clinically. "Know that this failing is not your fault alone. Callie is complicit in stirring this cauldron of carnage. She is next on my list to cure."

My cheeks heated at the brief mental image of Aphrodite teaching Callie about sex. I licked my lips anxiously, trying to think of anything to stall her. I could withstand some teasing without succumbing. She'd promised she wouldn't take advantage of me.

Aphrodite sighed in pitiful amusement, reading my body language. "You square your shoulders, and face every manner of physical danger with your chin raised, but you run and hide from your own thoughts and fears. I will help you confront them, whether you want me to or not. Running is no longer an option, my pet," she murmured, her eyes smoky and dripping with desire.

"Unchain me!" I snapped. "If you think you can seduce me, you shouldn't need chains!"

She smiled at me. "Oh, my precious lamb. You are not wearing chains. You haven't been wearing chains for some time, now."

I flinched, glancing up at my wrists. I still wore my manacles, but no chains. I stared in disbelief. I leapt out of our love nest.

Or...I tried to. I hit a soft, invisible wall and bounced off, falling down onto my back on the pillows, right where I had just been held captive. I glared at Aphrodite. "No chains, you say?"

"You are not allowed to run away from your problems any longer, Catalyst. I'm about to blow your mind and suck out every drop of carnage in your body and soul. I have told you this several times. Now, lie back and take your medicine."

My face flushed deep purple as she speared me with her eyes. I didn't bother chastising her for her phrasing because there was nothing chaste about the goddess of sex. Instead, I focused on the situation. She wouldn't force herself upon me, which was a relief. But she wasn't going to let me flee. Which meant that I needed to prove to her that I was addressing her concerns—I needed to withstand her torturous foreplay without succumbing prematurely. My earlier plan was my best chance at a victory —taste the meal she was offering and then turn my nose up, respectfully, at the plate. She was obviously too good with words, and I was betting she was even better at the brass tacks of physical persuasion.

I needed to prove to her that this carnage she spoke of was not a threat to me. Or that I was strong enough to handle it. "Carnage. Explain it."

"I am trying to do so, but it is not a thing of words." She pursed her lips, leaning her shoulders back to consider her response. "The words do not mean anything until actions are undertaken. You will see after I ride you into oblivion, and then through it, before steering you back out unscathed." Her eyes smoldered, and I realized that her long fingernails were trailing up and down the arch of my foot in a calming, sensual manner—and that I hadn't even noticed it until my eyes saw it. It felt...euphoric.

I took a calming breath. "Fine," I growled, resolving myself to my plan of last resort. "Bring it on. You will not tempt me, woman," I said defiantly, even though at least several respectable inches of my reputation disagreed with the words—that part of me was unsurprisingly curious to learn and experience what bedroom games Aphrodite had mastered.

Because she had likely forgotten more about sex than all of mankind collectively knew. And here I was, trying to withstand her wiles. If wizards were chasers of wisdom, shouldn't learning the martial arts of love have been a mandatory prerequisite to life? Especially when everyone sought it at one point or another over their years. How had no one heard of this carnage?

Part of me accepted many of Aphrodite's arguments as facts, even though the dominant part of me committed to doubling-down on my position—turning my abstinence into the Alamo for a hopeless last stand rather than allowing myself to relish in this orgasmic arcane field of study with the master of all professors, Aphrodite. But my principles were at stake.

I loved Callie—

"You do not love the White Rose," Aphrodite murmured, forcefully but gently.

"She loves me—"

"Again, she does not. You *both* dangerously misuse the word love based on an incorrect definition. You *both* expect unconditional love while—at the same time—giving each other unspoken conditions. It truly is quite baffling to watch," she said, sounding vexed.

"What is wrong with me loving Callie?" I asked, fearing she had a personal stake at risk. Maybe that was her angle—why she was so different from when I'd seen her hours before. She wanted me for herself.

She flung her hands up aggressively, startling me. "NOTHING!" she snapped. "If you two truly wanted each other, I would be your greatest supporter! I am the goddess of love, not home wrecking. I literally cannot get in the way of love without figuratively stabbing myself in the heart, much like a wizard cannot cast a fireball at his own chest. Similarly, I cannot abide a perversion of the definition of love because you lack the proper lexicon and define love subjectively."

She was panting, seemingly on the verge of a mental breakdown. In that moment, I knew she believed this with her entire heart. She couldn't get in our way without weakening her godly essence. This wasn't some game. Even if she saw me as an enemy, she could not let this stand.

She took a calming breath. "Enabling your idiocies will cause the world great harm. You two are both entirely too powerful to walk into the Omega War thinking you are wearing armor when you are actually wearing neon, flashing bullseyes painted on your backs and chests."

I arched an incredulous eyebrow. Aphrodite was visibly huffing air— which had a delightful effect on her currently non-existent toga. I shook my head, raising my focus to her face.

Aphrodite noticed and laughed, my testosterone-fueled reaction serving to calm her down. She locked eyes with me and tried again. "You think you want each other because you think you are *supposed* to want each other. You've heard the term a bird in the hand is worth two in the bush?" I nodded. "You are both choosing a bird in the hand...not realizing that you each have a noble eagle already perched on your shoulders. Eagles that you placed there of your own volition, even if you both seem to have forgotten." She shook her head angrily. "If I wasn't looking at you right now, I would have assumed you had both been spelled to not notice the eagles." She pursed her lips, questing for a different, better metaphor. "I'm watching you crying about how you wished you had ten dollars when you're holding a twenty in your other hand."

I blinked at her. "Are you trying to say that we are settling for each other?" I blurted. "That's insane. Callie is one of the most amazing women I've ever met."

Aphrodite shook her head, looking frustrated—as if I'd momentarily come close but then missed it in an entirely new manner. "She is. And you are. One man's ten is another man's twenty," she said, moving her lips as if tasting the phrase. She pinched the bridge of her nose and then closed her eyes, still not satisfied with her analogy.

I was simply glad that I had so far delayed her advances with my apparently asinine beliefs.

She snapped her fingers eagerly. "How about this? I am also an amazing woman. Tory Marlin is an amazing woman. Every single woman standing behind you, beside you, and against you is an amazing woman—for many different reasons. That does not mean any of them are the most amazing woman for *you*, specifically. Nor does it mean that they are *equally* amazing. Everyone has different tastes. Although you know Tory is amazing, something in your own mind admits that she is not the right woman for you. You have numerous reasons, whether consciously known or not. Understand?"

I stared at her. My arms stretched out to either side in an inviting manner—to show her that I was not curling up into a ball to hide from her advances—or my own emotions. She needed to know that I was confident in my claims, not that I was arguing to delay the inevitable—which I totally was.

Unfortunately, Aphrodite was a master debater. She knew her way around the circular arguments of love and personal pleasure. I wasn't certain that I perfectly understood her points, but I was getting close enough to see the writing on the wall. Damn her. Who was I to debate love with the fucking goddess of it?

"You're saying that no matter how amazing we could be together, we could be even greater with someone else. These eagles you mentioned," I said, wondering who she thought these eagles were. Did Callie have another suitor waiting in the wings? Did I?

She nodded. "Yes, and based on your own feelings, not mine," she clarified.

I nodded thoughtfully, wondering why she was so confident that she knew how I felt about Callie or vice versa. "How can you be so certain?"

Aphrodite smiled sadly, and something about the look in her eyes told me that I had used up my last delaying tactic. She gripped one of my ankles in each hand and gently spread my legs apart to establish a landing strip for her express flight to my groin. I tried to keep my face composed but I probably wasn't doing very well. My magic staff was still betraying me, for one thing. "Settling for something other than your heart's desire does not cause immediate harm, but it does create a vacuum of unfulfilled desire. And, in that vacuum, the carnage will eventually find you and eat you alive. The both of you." She licked her lips. "All this will be readily understood once I've finished with you, Master Temple."

And then Aphrodite leaned forward, crawling towards me again. I swallowed audibly, forcing myself not to whimper. "Luring me into sleeping with you will only serve to prove your point that I don't love Callie," I pressed. "So, all I have to do is withstand your advance to prove that I do love her."

Professor Aphrodite was apparently finished talking. She was old school. This was no longer a lecture on love.

This was an apprenticeship in pleasure.

13

T he flaming braziers around the room dimmed further, and I heard the faint sounds of a marching drumbeat—but it was more primal and savage, dark and chilling, like an old Viking war song. And then a man's rasping but musical voice began chanting to the drumbeat. The melody was faint and raw, as if we were listening to a dream—or nightmare—given life.

If I hadn't been so focused on my surroundings, I might not have even noticed it at first. Despite the grim background music, I felt every hair on my head rise up, and my skin suddenly felt inflamed by the musical call to arms.

Aphrodite was establishing the mood. And it wasn't sexual.

It was war, just like she'd said earlier. Love and war, two sides of the same coin.

Two armies of inflamed, passionate flesh, sweat and blood, slamming into each other across a silken battlefield that was soon to be soaked with the bodily fluids of first contact.

And—goddamn it—her tactics were working. The strong scent of incense had now filled the room with lazy tendrils of shifting smoke, giving life to the haunting melody, and the silk curtains seemed to ripple and sway in time to the beat, bringing all my senses into sync. My hands were balled into fists, gripping the silk sheets like a lifeline.

Aphrodite came to a halt about two millimeters before my crotch. She leaned forward, her hair spilling forward like privacy curtains. She eyed my dirty tee and smirked at the caption. *Let me see your O-face*, with a happy donut. "What an appropriate shirt," she murmured, winking at me. She set one finger at the hem of the tee and slowly drew it up towards my throat, neatly slicing the fabric in half like she was using the world's sharpest scalpel.

The wild monkey-sex queen peeled me like a banana.

I panted as the warm air struck my naked chest and abdomen, twitching when her knuckles brushed my skin in a feather stroke of murder. She reached the collar and the shirt fell to either side. She calmly gripped both ends and flung her arms wide.

The goddess of sex knelt between my upper thighs, her sweat-kissed breasts bared, and she bit her lower lip with a devilish grin. Distantly, I wondered why she was trying to seduce me if she wanted to reaffirm my love for another woman. Wouldn't that hurt her power source, like she'd earlier claimed?

I watched her prepare her meal, and I was having a very difficult time recalling what we had been talking about moments ago. At some point in my distraction, she had entirely removed my pants, leaving me only in my boxer briefs. I hadn't felt a thing. I was so transfixed by the raw power of her presence, that I wasn't even embarrassed about a certain part of my body openly giving her efforts a glowing five-star-rating.

Our bodies glistened with sweat, and we were both panting desperately. My skin felt alive and electric to the touch.

And...I hadn't tried to stop her even once. I hadn't shifted from beneath her entrapment. I hadn't spoken. I hadn't denied her actions in the slightest. In summation, I might as well have been handcuffed for all the struggle I physically put up.

My only solace was my mind, and even that was crumbling—not from lust, but from self-doubt. Because her arguments had filleted me much as her fingernails had shredded my shirt. Did I really love Callie Penrose? If Zeus hadn't been lying about the Titan Thorns—which he very likely could have been—why hadn't they opened when I thought of Callie?

Was I denying Aphrodite due to my assumed love for Callie or because Nate Temple denied anything that was forced onto him?

I'd already questioned my feelings for Callie—internally—but that had been more related to a consequence of our new roles as Horsemen. Freya had warned me that being the direct superior of a lover was beyond difficult and not recommended. And I knew she was right.

But that wasn't the only issue.

Something had changed between Callie and me. Perhaps that was simply because we hadn't given each other a true shot. We had avoided privacy at almost every turn.

"Later is reserved for death, not love, Catalyst," Aphrodite whispered, and I realized that the ninja nymphomaniac was now straddling me. The thin strip of silk covering her sex was as hot as fire, and I knew I was about to have the biggest fight of my life.

Not against the sweet nirvana beneath Aphrodite's purple panties.

Against my own mind, body, and soul.

Because I could no longer discern whether Aphrodite was friend or foe.

This situation was its own kind of torture—not wholly unlike what Apollo and Ares had heaped upon me. And the only way to truly win was to make myself actually participate in this battle. Standing stiff on the sidelines—lying beneath her like a blind, deaf, and dumb fish—would not constitute a win. That would just prove my stubborn denial—my refusal to honestly stand up to, and address, her arguments. Much as I'd stood tall against physical torture, I needed to stand against this mental, seemingly self-imposed, torture.

Especially if Callie Penrose was the love of my life. I needed to prove, or disprove, it to myself. This was a crucible. I needed to toe the line—to get as close to the fire as I could manage without getting burned. I needed to tempt fate like Icarus and his wings had tempted the sun—not flying too high and burning my wings, and not flying too low and dampening them.

I lifted my hands, ignoring their violent tremors, and gripped Aphrodite's hips. She trembled and whimpered, and I looked into the seductress' eyes. "Bring it on," I growled.

She licked her lips and leaned towards my throat. "I swear on my power that this is not trickery," she whispered, her breath tickling my sweat-slicked skin. I nodded in relief, feeling reassured that I could at least disregard that worry—that this was all some sort of trap to trick me into thinking I didn't love Callie Penrose. Aphrodite had sworn so on her power.

I knew there were ways around that particular oath, but something about her tone and intense eye contact told me it was the most honest thing she'd ever said out loud.

Ever.

And it backed up our earlier debate. I nodded. "Thank you."

"Think of the woman you love," she whispered.

I nodded, defiantly focusing on Callie Penrose.

Aphrodite's tongue touched the hollow of my throat and my heart almost exploded as she licked my sweat. She stayed there for an eternal moment, tasting me, and my toes curled hard enough to crack. I gasped, alarmingly dizzy as she whispered, her hot breath caressing my skin like a feather.

"If you truly believed Callie Penrose was destined for you, your sweat would have scalded my tongue. My own power would have turned against me. If, deep down in your heart, you knew she was the one, my tongue would practically be incinerated right now."

She lifted her face to hover over mine as she stared into my eyes with a sad, but satisfied smile. She showed me her perfect tongue.

My mental fortress fractured and cracked as if hit by a cannonball. If not Callie, then who did I love? "Maybe I don't love anyone," I whispered, more to myself than anything.

Aphrodite shook her head. "No. There is someone in there," she whispered, tapping a finger against my chest. "I can feel the eagle waiting, watching, hoping—ready to swoop in for the kill," Aphrodite breathed, so softly that I thought I had imagined it. "If this was not the case, we would have already started to make love."

I shuddered, my entire body tensing at the brief visual. I didn't tense far, since every inch of her own steaming flesh pressed against me, pinning me to the pillows. "No," I croaked, trying to get my head into the game. "I need to understand this. Understand myself. Teach me," I begged, committing myself to withstanding her advances, but only if she gave it her all.

Aphrodite moaned savagely, her eyes shutting as my words almost set her off. Her entire body clenched atop me. "This woman better be worth it, Nate, or I will never forgive this cruel foreplay," she snarled.

I laughed harshly. "I'm betting my night will be far worse."

She chuckled her agreement. "You poor thing," she said with a resigned smile. "Since we are both gluttons for punishment, I agree to teach you. There are more names to test. More eagles to hunt."

Callie Penrose was not my true love. I felt numb even thinking it. But... numb in multiple ways. Numb with guilt, but also...with a surprising sense of relief. As if my shoulders suddenly felt lighter.

Even knowing that Aphrodite had the ability to lie, I knew beyond a shadow of a doubt that she was speaking the unadulterated truth. The look in her eyes had convinced me, because I saw that she wasn't pleased to prove this point to me. She was not pleased that the revelation hurt me.

But she *was* pleased that she had helped teach me a vital truth—much in the same way that seeing your child stick a penny in an electrical socket taught them the dangers of electricity.

I had been lying to myself about Callie Penrose. I'd stuck my shiny penny into Aphrodite's socket—figuratively, of course—and gotten zapped.

Frustration soon reared its ugly head. I didn't have time for this kind of crap right now. I was Zeus' hostage and I couldn't trust any of these Olympians. Unless it got me out of these damned manacles. But to earn my freedom from the Titan Thorns, I needed to conquer my own mind— to conquer my own heart. Only then could I stand up to Zeus as an equal.

As his *better*.

Aphrodite surprised the hell out of me by slowly sliding her sweat-slicked skin across my chest and collapsing beside me with a frustrated shudder—her own bodily desire fighting against her mind. She maintained physical contact by keeping one of her long legs wrapped over mine and resting her hand atop my chest as she cuddled against me. I stared up at the lazily shifting curtains of silk above, wanting nothing more than to get out of my own head.

I could feel her studying me empathetically. She trailed the backs of her fingers from my neck down to my lower ribs in a soothing, affectionate gesture. "I know it hurts, Temple, and I know you must hate me for pulling back the curtain to show you this side of yourself," she admitted, her voice cracking faintly.

I grunted, not meeting her eyes. "What do I have to complain about? I'm cuddling with the world's most beautiful woman," I muttered, full of scorn. "An amazing woman," I added, using her own words from earlier.

She sensed my sarcasm, but she didn't point it out or take offense. "True. Yet you are unhappy. This revelation alone should tell you much."

I frowned, glancing over at her. "Such as?"

She leaned down to rest her cheek in the crook of my shoulder. "That there truly is someone else closer to your heart, even if you do not openly acknowledge them. Otherwise, we would be doing a lot more than cuddling right now. I can assure you that my pheromones quite literally scramble the minds of men—unless another has already claimed his heart. I cannot recall ever being let down in my own bed. It is...somewhat refreshing."

"Um. You're welcome?"

She laughed lightly. I realized I was brushing my fingers through her hair in a fond gesture. As frustrated as I was—physically and mentally—I was definitely not mentally overtaken by Aphrodite's charm. I was now utterly certain that the Aphrodite I'd seen at the pavilion had been playing games in order to get closer to me. All so she could have this private moment with the Catalyst. She wasn't working for her family, she was working to find a way out.

The question was...why?

I let out a sigh. "Well, what's the next gauntlet of fire I have to survive?" I asked tiredly.

She laughed lightly. "Garter, not gauntlet," she teased. "You aren't ready for the tantric gauntlets."

Even hearing that she had a name for such a thing made me shiver with fearful curiosity. "Right. We should probably get on with the next lesson. Someone will notice I'm no longer in my cell, especially since we're being watched."

"Your jailers will think I am doing as I was commanded," she said, sounding amused. "And I am, in my own way. You do feel broken, yes?"

I nodded. "Way worse than the physical torture," I admitted.

"Then this has been a success."

14

She sighed, and lifted her head, sitting up in the process. She rested a possessive palm on my chest, studying my face. "You need rest before we continue. Otherwise your mind will be barren and infertile. You are too upset about the first revelation, so will numbly accept or deny my next lesson. You need to replenish your stamina before our upcoming twilight escapade. To process what you have learned about yourself."

I narrowed my eyes. "This is not a couples retreat, Aphrodite. Zeus wants me to lick his boots and become his thug on a leash. Whatever he intends to steal and whomever he intends to kill is only going to make matters worse. As pissed off as I am right now, I want to understand what the hell this is all about between you and me. Callie and me. Mystery woman and me. So that I can choose whether to believe it or not. Just because I apparently have very strong internal doubts about Callie does not concretely prove that Callie and I have no future together. It just means we need to freaking talk rather than avoiding each other."

Aphrodite looked crestfallen by my argument, as if I'd taken two steps back for our one step forward. "I knew you were stubborn, but I didn't anticipate the depth of your denial. I presumed that it would not be nearly so bad when you learned your opponent was your own heart."

I squinted at her. "Whenever someone tells me I can't do something, I always get combative. And I usually wind up destroying the person when I learn that they had an ulterior motive." The double meaning was clear—did Aphrodite have an ulterior motive?

She studied me, calm and unafraid. "You do know that you could kill me with your bare hands right now, yes? That I knew this before and that I decided to take the risk anyway? To bare my breast to you, knowing that you held a naked dagger to my heart and that your carnage had possibly made you unstable enough to stab first and ask questions later."

I frowned. "My powers are blocked." The fact that she kept telling me I was angry and irrational when I wasn't only served to make me feel more irrational and angrier.

She scoffed, leaning back on the pillows beside me and raising her arms above her head. "I have calmed the carnage for now, my lamb." I blinked at her choice of pillow-name for me. An erotic dubstep version of *Mary had a little lamb* played in my mind as Aphrodite continued. "Your power is in your blood. There is no blocking a godkiller. All Zeus could do was trap the numerous other powers at your disposal, and hope to trap the flesh containing the blood. He could hide it in plain sight with a bit of illusion. Or Hermes, perhaps."

I stared down at her, stunned by her words, but also to find that I was now kneeling at her side, looming over her. "What?" I rasped. Her big, serene eyes stared up at me, submitting to my physical dominance in such a way that I somehow knew that she was actually the dominant between us. That her submission was so complete that it unquestionably established her dominance.

Showing me that Aphrodite, more than anyone I had ever met, knew exactly what the fuck she wanted, and that she was more than willing to risk her life to get it. I leaned closer, gently gripping her delicate chin between my thumb and knuckled forefinger. "I can still use my godkiller powers?" I asked her, not knowing exactly what my godkiller powers even were.

An illusion, she had said, which made perfect sense. Since my imprisonment, I hadn't once seen my veins glow beneath my skin—a typical warning sign whenever I was around gods. Aphrodite lifted a hand and calmly brushed her soft fingertips down my taut forearm from elbow to wrist. In the wake of her caress, veins of golden light bloomed beneath my ravaged skin, serving to illuminate her in a warm, golden glow.

She stared into my eyes and bit her lip in what looked like awe, letting me know that they must be glowing brightly.

She'd revealed—or unmasked—my godkiller powers. I felt no different, but now the telltale signs were back. This was huge. I could break free! Right? But my elation rapidly faded as I realized that I couldn't feel anything powerful enough to break my manacles. Just the light had turned on. I empathized with an un-stocked vending machine—the light might be on, but I was empty inside.

"Zeus had it covered up so that you wouldn't get any...*bright ideas*. With all of us around, you would have been permanently glowing. Unless you already know how to dim it?" I nodded, focusing on my veins so that they no longer glowed, casting us back into our dim, romantic light. Her eyes widened marginally, impressed. I was too busy realizing how big her pupils really were. How I could lose myself in them if I wasn't careful. "It will do nothing to break your manacles, unfortunately. As long as he stays out of your immediate physical reach, he is safe and you are still his prisoner."

I continued to stare down at her, my silence speaking volumes. Because Aphrodite was wholly within my immediate physical reach. Not safe, according to her words. Trapped beneath me. Yet she'd intentionally placed herself there—all of her own volition.

She wasn't just the dominant between us. Her mind was dominant of her every emotion and physical choice she had ever made. Quite literally, this goddess of emotion and lust seemed to be the most rational and calculating person I had ever encountered. And she wasn't ignoring her emotions to do so. She was embracing them to such an extent that her entire purpose seemed to be to show me the truth of my own emotions, no matter the consequences.

She locked eyes with me, unblinking, as she gently but firmly gripped my right wrist. Then she slowly guided my hand towards the left side of her chest. She pressed my palm over her feverish flesh so that I cupped her upper breast, and I knew that there was nothing erotic in the gesture. Instead, it was us disrobing our souls so that she could show me something vital. Whatever she was doing was of the utmost importance, far more meaningful than letting me cop a feel of the world's top-rated breasts. She slid her hand down to my thumb and carefully spread my fingers so that my thumb and pointer finger formed a crescent shape over her flesh.

She waited, staring into my mind through my glowing eyes—which had winked back on so that I could get a better look at...the ritual, of course. Her entire body was bathed in the brilliant golden light of my eyes and veins, now, despite the dim room.

She then took hold of my other wrist so that my palm hovered over her face between us. She released her grip and made a pinching gesture with her finger and thumb, and touched them to my palm. Then she began to draw something out of it, and I gasped, my other hand gripping tighter on her breast by pure reflex, as pain bit into my palm.

Not lethal pain, but melted candle wax pain. I stared, transfixed, as she pulled a golden dagger out from my palm. Within seconds, a nine-inch dagger of molten gold—my ichor—extended from my flesh.

Still, she did not break eye contact with me. She wrapped my fingers around the blade and then guided the dagger towards her left breast. She calmly, bravely, set the tip of the ichor blade against her flesh, right in the center of the crescent shape formed by my other hand's fingers.

And I realized what she was doing.

Her heart lay directly between the points of the crescent.

Her heart lay directly beneath the tip of the ichor dagger.

She slowly trailed her fingers down my ribs, leaving a wake of goosebumps, until she gripped my oblique muscles. With surprising strength, she pulled me atop her, forcing me to straddle or stab her. I settled my weight over her, feeling a tear roll down my cheek from the strain of not blinking.

"You must be in control of everything, Temple," she moaned, taking a deep breath so that my blade actually pierced her skin enough to draw a bead of blood. My forearm tensed as I suddenly felt a thrill of adrenaline —a godkiller responding to a god's blood. My muscles grew rock hard and my glowing veins bulged with anticipation. Aphrodite licked her lips, and then arched her head back enough to bare her throat and press her chest against the blade, taunting the killer inside me. "In control of everything," she repeated in a breathy whisper. "Especially yourself. At all times. If you lose that—giving into those base urges—you will lose yourself. I will not permit this, so you will have to kill me if you wish to continue an existence of ignorance. I will swallow your carnage," she repeated firmly, letting out a gasp that made my heart race wildly.

She continued gripping my waist, waiting for me to make my decision.

She had let a godkiller into the silken sheets of her bedchambers, and she was letting him see just how dangerous of a decision that had been— for her. All to prove that she believed her lesson more important than the personal danger.

Or she was seriously into some kinky fetishes involving danger in the bedroom.

What the fuck did she really want that made her take such a risk? It couldn't be just to save my heart. No one was that altruistic—that giving.

I finally let out a gasp and withdrew my hands. The ichor dagger evaporated like smoke. I stared down in fear and Aphrodite spoke in a calm, reassuring murmur. "It drains quickly, and costs much. Do not use it unless absolutely necessary," she whispered with an edge of fear.

I nodded, and suddenly felt a violent surge of vertigo tilting the room at a sharp angle. She reached up and caught me, cupping my cheeks in her palms and pulling me down to her mouth.

I collapsed into her arms, my muscles feeling like jelly. Our lips touched and I cried out, my body spasming as my veins erupted with a jolt of energy. Her hands reflexively clutched my face tighter and she let out her own involuntary whimper so that for the space of a single heartbeat, we tasted each other's breath. We both clamped our lips shut at the same time, and then clutched each other tightly, trembling in unison, both blindsided by the physical response. If I had accidentally tasted anything beyond her lips, I might have lost all control. Judging by her response, she trusted herself just as little.

And that was the danger of our little game. That our hormones would take the wheel if we weren't careful. If we weren't in control. But whatever that had been, it hadn't been natural.

That being said, the feel of her maddeningly warm lips against mine was more satisfying than any tongue-on-tongue action I'd ever experienced. More exciting and impactful. Even more bizarre was the fact that I knew there had been nothing even remotely sexual in her action. And yet...there had been more love in that kiss than anything I had ever felt. It was almost as if I'd accidentally licked her soul and suffered an euphoriagasm.

A heartbeat of experiencing raw, unadulterated, true love—what was truly possible between the right pairing of individuals. It wasn't that Aphrodite loved me in such a way—I could tell that by her shared surprise —it was that I had unintentionally glimpsed the source of her godly power. Her silent, shaky reaction also told me that it was not something that should ever be discussed. That I was never to voice what I'd just glimpsed within her—which was ironic, given how open she was about flaunting her nudity.

Her naked soul, apparently, was an entirely different matter. As was proper.

Coupled with the dizziness of my ichor dagger evaporating, I was a physical and emotional wreck. I fell to her side, still pressed up against her. I wrapped my arm across her body at the diagonal, gripping her opposite hip and pulling her close. She reached out to rest a palm on my cheek, humming a private song that had probably remained secret for thousands of years, and...

I began to cry, softly, out of sheer exhaustion and frustration, feeling the weight of the world bearing down upon my shoulders. All the days of torture that I had buried deep within. All the fear I had smothered to appear strong against Ares and Apollo. To look strong for Carl.

She let me, comforting me with her loving hum and gentle strokes. "It's okay, Wylde," she cooed, using my Fae name in a familiar way. "I know it hurts. But you have survived the deepest stab. Now, you may begin to heal. I will kiss your pains away until you are restored. You will be stronger for this. I swear it, my lamb."

"I don't understand, Mary," I rasped.

"Who is Mary?" she asked softly, sounding alarmed. "I haven't heard you mention her before, but there is something about Mary—"

My sudden laughter cut her off, and served to instantly dry up my tears. I tried not to think about the movie, biting down my unbidden giggle. "Slip of the tongue," I reassured her. "You called me lamb, so my mind went to the nursery rhyme."

She was silent for a moment. "You...are lying next to the goddess of sex, and you're thinking of nursery rhymes?" she asked in a dangerous tone.

"Perhaps I have been too careful with you. Perhaps I will grab the tantric gauntlets after all—"

I laughed heartily, shaking my head. "Oh, you did fine. I apologize. No need for the sex toys." She relaxed under my embrace and I let out a sigh of relief. "How can something so...irrelevant as my love life matter right now? When I'm Zeus' hostage and the fucking world rests on my shoulders —allegedly. Why cry over a woman I thought I loved? A woman who does not love me? It's all...so fucking stupid," I muttered, exasperated.

Aphrodite growled unhappily, her body quivering beneath my arms like a warning grumble from a cat after three tummy rubs. "Do not forget with whom you talk. Love is not *irrelevant*," she hissed. "It is the most important thing. The fact that you do not know this is the very *reason* for my existence as the goddess of love. It is proof that we Olympians have not done our jobs in many years." She sounded furious at this admitted failure. "Men used to know the value of love. As did women. It is why all great stories revolved around a kernel of love: the Trojan War, Romeo and Juliet, and thousands more. The absence of love leads to such atrocities as Hitler."

I stiffened, turning to look at her in hopes she was joking. She wasn't. "You...um, you can't say things like that. Hitler had at least one or two other major character flaws," I said, deadpan.

She clenched her jaw, stubbornly. "The carnage devoured him heart and soul. Hate consumed all love in his soul. That is the war I fight every day. I battle the carnage."

I pulled her close so that her back was pressed up against my entire length, and I buried my face into her neck, wanting to douse her quivering fury. "Carnage is hate?" I whispered.

She let out a frustrated sigh, slowly melting into my embrace. "Carnage is what happens when life loses love. It can take many forms—it is not one simple thing like hatred. That is merely one of many possible symptoms. Such as becoming a monster, a tyrant, a murderer, or dozens of others. Carnage manifests in different ways depending on the power of the life suffering it."

I shuddered. I...had a *lot* of power at my disposal. What would carnage do to me?

15

Was that why she was so adamant about breaking my heart with the Callie revelation? Because she knew the potential danger it would lead to if she didn't? "I'm sorry. It's just not something that was on my mind. Mary," I added with a grin.

She gave my bicep an angry slap and I burst out laughing. She growled, tugging my arm closer to her body and draping her own arms over it as if to keep me there. "Because your mind had already discovered the true answer to your heart's desire—you just refused to listen or acknowledge it. Why you refused to listen to your inner self is what I will help you learn. Those lessons can be as pleasurable or painful as you prefer," she said, kneading her fingers into my forearms in a sensual, massaging manner. Like a cat's paws.

Silence stretched between us, the only sound the crackling fires from the braziers. Her breathing began to slow, and I felt my eyelids growing heavy. I blinked rapidly, realizing that we were falling asleep. And just like that, I was suddenly hyperaware of the fact that her breasts were pressed up against my upper arm.

Boobs. I'd been bewitched by godly boobies.

She chuckled in amusement, sensing me tensing. "Ah, men. So

predictable," she said, nudging me with her hip to indicate she'd sensed something else entirely.

I stammered awkwardly as I pulled my arm away and sat up. I cleared my throat, staring down at the Titan Thorns on my wrists. I was one step—and a pair of blue balls—closer to removing them. It didn't feel like a victory. It felt like battered kidneys and sorrow.

Despite my sudden discomfort over embracing Aphrodite so forwardly, I found that I didn't hold a shred of concern that I was almost entirely naked. It just didn't seem important. "Why do you care so much about this?" I asked her. "It can't be all about me. If you hate Zeus that much, just leave. You don't need anything from me."

Aphrodite sat up and studied me cautiously, made uneasy by my question—scared that her answer would put her in great danger. That this beautiful, confident, caring woman...had serious trust issues, should have been obvious to me. Her father was a real peach.

"My reasoning will become apparent in time. Perhaps I wanted to teach the most important man in the world about his most important muscle." I smirked and she rolled her eyes. "His heart, you fool," she said with a resigned sigh. "That would be an achievement the goddess of love would be interested in." I waited, my look letting her know that I hadn't been taken by her lack of answer. She took a deep breath—and a big risk. "Who I am in the bedroom is not always the same woman I am in public," she said, meaningfully.

I smiled. "You're a freak in the sheets but a lady in the streets."

She gave me a hollow smile, and I knew she was beyond concerned. "I must wear the toga I've been dealt. Reputations can be the safest armor. The best disguise is often to cloak yourself in your own legend. To let people fill in the gaps between your actions with well-known, historically consistent, motivations."

The look in her eyes told me that she was trying to warn me about what I might see during our next encounter—that she would maintain her enemy guise if we were in public. That her very life might depend on it. Zeus would not approve of our real bedtime shenanigans. Got it.

Aphrodite, the goddess of sex, had figuratively rolled over the next morning and told me that she'd had fun but that this never happened. Which...was an entirely new experience for me.

I stared down at my current state of undress. "This will raise questions. There are areas of my body where I would rather not get a sunburn the next time I hang out with Apollo."

She smiled uneasily. "Your clothing has already been sewn up." She pointed at a nearby pile of clothes, neatly folded if not clean. I saw no rips or tears from her deft fingers.

"What if you are Zeus' target?" I asked, softly. "Or what if he means to use me against you?"

She sighed. "You will do as you always do—make up your own mind, befuddle everyone in the process. Whether you kill me or not is a moot point. As long as my lessons are successful, I could die a happy goddess. I would not hold it against you." She paused, tapping her lips thoughtfully. "The particulars of our bedroom lessons should remain a secret." I felt uneasy with her sudden change of tone. "If the truth becomes known, I guarantee that I will be dead before I have a chance to utter a word." My blood chilled. Zeus would kill her. Period. Wow. "You will die with your lessons incomplete. The world would suffer for it. My death would be a relief compared to what price everyone else would pay."

I frowned uneasily. She didn't seem to care one way or another about herself. She seemed more concerned about the impact on me and the world than her own life. Love truly was selfless.

She glanced at my Titan Thorns, and took a deep, seemingly nervous breath. "I can get you out of here," she whispered in a rush.

I stared at her for about two solid seconds. "What?" I hissed.

She nodded. "I can break you free of the chains and get you out of here, but I cannot remove the Titan Thorns."

"Why didn't you say something sooner?" I demanded.

"I needed to know you were worth the price I will pay for betraying Zeus. If you clung stubbornly to denial over Callie, my sacrifice would have been for nothing. I hadn't been certain how long it would take to bring you to that precipice. I anticipated three visits, but I am now certain that you are ready."

I looked over at her, sensing the fear in her voice. So, her ulterior motive had been...her own safety. "You're a prisoner as well."

She nodded. "We are all prisoners here," she said in a haunted tone. She straightened her shoulders, seeming to gather her resolve. "But he was correct regarding the Titan Thorns. Only his permission—or true, unconditional love—will unlock them. Which is why, even if you escape, our lessons must continue. Or it will all have been for nothing. My death will have been in vain."

I studied the goddess warily, my mind racing with sudden plans. "How would these lessons help me? Exactly? How will more of this torture serve to bring me closer to an answer? Because, to be very honest, I'm not sure I've ever felt this frustrated—mentally and physically—with a naked woman sitting beside me."

She smirked, beaming with pride. "Or this *good*, right?"

I considered that, and finally nodded with a resigned sigh. "Yeah. I guess so."

"My lessons will harden you against temptation and seduction. I will bring your subconscious out from within by making you fight your own bodily desire—the part of you that wants nothing more than to fuck me like an animal." I realized I was clenching the sheets in my fist and shakily let them go. "This will help you learn the name of the woman you love. It will let you unearth what you have hidden from yourself. It will let you find your eagle."

I was breathing heavily. "Couldn't you just tell me?"

She shook her head vehemently. "No. This must come from your own heart or it will be stained with suspicion—that you only love this person because you were led by the nose."

I closed my eyes, taking a deep breath. I knew she was right, but this was ridiculous. "If I can't take off the Titan Thorns, I can't use my powers."

She nodded. "Correct."

"But I still have to stop Zeus from doing whatever he's trying to do."

"That is imperative," she said, wincing.

"And on top of Zeus' power play, I have a Cinderella story on my plate. To find my Princess Charming so I'm not consumed by the Wicked Queen Carnage."

She nodded, looking amused. "You have already met your Princess Charming. Now you are hoping she finds your glass slipper, or that you find hers, I guess," she said with an amused grin. "Zeus and my siblings could fill in the roles for the evil stepmother and stepsisters," she added, chuckling. I didn't point out that she was part of that crew. Her humor faded at the seriousness of the situation. "I can help you with your heart—your fairy tale—but the rest is on you."

I nodded wearily. "How can I be certain that this—you—isn't all part of Zeus' plan?"

She shot me a cool look. "You are too clever," she said, dryly. "Zeus' ultimate plan is to hold you hostage by setting me up to suicidally free you." I winced at her frosty tone. "The moment you leave, I must also leave—and hope that you find a way to beat him—or he will kill me." I'd killed the romance like a snuffed candle. "Don't make me regret it."

I bowed my chin. "I had to ask."

She nodded regrettably. "I know."

"Thank you, Aphrodite. And I'm sorry. I'll do my best."

My mind raced with plans and schemes, taking into account the dangers Aphrodite was about to face. First Hermes taking my bet, and now Aphrodite offering to break me out. And neither seemed aware of the other. I didn't have high hopes that Ares and Apollo would be equally friendly, but I could still sow some seeds of chaos.

"What about Hephaestus?" I asked, thoughtfully. "Aren't you sentencing him to death by doing this? Do you truly love Ares that much? Or despise Hephaestus that much?"

She growled, shaking her head. "I lied earlier, when I spoke of my husband," she said, a faint smile curling the corners of her lips. "I am doing this *for* Hephaestus. I sleep with Ares to protect mankind from war—and to make everyone think I don't care about my husband. Otherwise, they would use him as leverage against me. Hephaestus is enslaved much as you are."

I blinked, somewhat surprised to hear he was a prisoner as well. "So, why help me if it gives away your position? Hephaestus will be punished. Zeus will know it was your fault, right?"

Aphrodite nodded grimly. "I will have to flee, of course. And hope that I can help teach you to hear the beatings of your heart faster than Zeus' beatings strike Hephaestus. Only then will you be free to stand up to Zeus and possibly save my husband and me." Her eyes glistened with unshed tears. "You also look after someone who is very important to my husband. Someone the world—and Zeus—fears. You do this even though you do not need to do so."

I frowned. Then it hit me. "Pandora?" I whispered incredulously, remembering that Hephaestus had supposedly made her. The task had been forced upon him by Zeus as punishment to mankind for...

Prometheus giving mankind the gift of fire. Damn. It kept coming back to the Titan. Was that a good thing or a bad thing? I was fairly certain he wanted to skin me alive.

She nodded. "Hephaestus suffers a similar fate as Prometheus. Punishment for sneaking hope inside of Pandora's Box."

I winced. "Hope. Like me." She nodded. Was hope really a power? Like, an actual magic that I could somehow wield? I sure...*hoped* so.

Badump, bump.

"You inspired me to be a better step-mother to Pandora. I learned that love isn't about blood. I refuse to let Zeus break the child worse than he already has. She was conceived in a placenta of guilt and shame and horror, born in a womb of embers and sparks from Hephaestus' forge. Hephaestus did not put hope inside the box for mankind—he put hope inside the box for *her*. To protect Pandora from herself. Hope was to be her knight in shining armor." I stared back at her, stunned. "And look who is now the Horseman of Hope. You, and only you, can save her."

My mind reeled with all the interwoven pieces, trying to connect them into a clear picture.

She sighed, lifting her hands in a helpless gesture. "It is time to collect Carl and get you home. Unless you prefer to stay here?" she asked.

I didn't. Not at all. But I understood her point. Where would I be most effective? Going back home without powers wasn't ideal, especially when I needed to beat Zeus on his mysterious treasure hunt. And...I couldn't approach my friends directly. If I said or did anything contrary to Electro-Nate, they would know something was up, and could very likely assume that I was the doppelgänger.

Or Zeus would just have them all killed.

But I had a few ideas. "I must go home." I took a breath, gathering my courage. "But not yet." She cocked her head curiously. "Let's get me back in my cell. I need a few minutes to think this through."

She nodded, climbing to her feet. Between one moment and the next, I was suddenly back in my cell. I had no idea how long I had been gone, but Carl was sleeping on his cot and I could see a crescent moon in the sky through the barred window. It might have been my imagination, but a drifting cloud resembled the shape of a heart, situated directly between the points of the moon.

Just like the symbol Aphrodite had made with my fingers when she'd shown me how to use the godkiller ichor dagger.

Carl must have sensed something, because he abruptly sat up, turning to stare at us with a wary frown. He narrowed his eyes to see Aphrodite escorting me. After a pointed silence, Carl glanced over at me with a grimace and flicked his tongue out, tasting the air. "You smell like a million dying souls. You had unhappy sex."

I gritted my teeth at Aphrodite's sudden laugh. "Yeah. That sounds about right."

Carl shot an angry glare at Aphrodite. "This is not acceptable."

She laughed even harder. "Not my fault. Ask him."

I sighed. "Later, Carl." I turned to Aphrodite and prepared for her to argue my sudden idea. "We cannot leave yet. I need one more visit from each of your brothers. It will buy me time. Otherwise they'll be after me the moment you let me go."

She winced uncertainly. "That is risky..."

"Just be ready with another bottle of your Ambrosia when you see they're done."

She nodded. Then she lifted her hand and my chains snapped back onto my manacles. She appraised me thoughtfully. "You are not who I thought you were."

"I aim to disappoint," I said with a smirk.

She smiled. "Be ready for my return." And with that, she disappeared.

Carl watched me. "Did I just watch you turn away our escape?"

"You did," I admitted.

He was silent.

"It will make her think. Confuse her."

"Ah. This is punishment for your blue balls."

I coughed, shaking my head. "No. But thanks for reminding me," I winced, gasping at a sudden flash of pain.

"I hope this plan isn't so clever that it kills us. Then again, it will show them you can't be controlled," he mused, the plan growing on him. He nodded proudly. "This is an honorable death. Not even blue balls can keep you from making a rational decision."

I sighed, not wanting to explain it. That only made things worse with Carl. My groin suffered a tsunami of pain with each step, and I found myself practically panting, taking short, sharp breaths, and even shorter, stiffer steps.

Carl growled his displeasure. "Unacceptable. Orgasms are simple. I will talk to her for you."

I gritted my teeth, shaking my head. "No, Carl. For so many reasons."

He shook his head unhappily and then rolled over on his cot to resume his sleep. We'd need it for our next torture session, so I made my way over to my own cot. Strangely enough, I was looking forward to the brothers. Not the pain, but poisoning the Olympians and turning them on each other.

Maybe it would bring them one step closer to the carnage.

16

I shifted back and forth in a realm of misty apparitions, meditating for clarity. Carl still slept, but I'd been unable to go back to sleep after waking from a truly baffling series of dreams involving Quinn MacKenna.

Mainly because they'd seemed so real, yet I knew they were not. Because they had all been strange distortions of our memories, taking strange turns at climactic moments. Quinn got to see some of my distorted memories, and I had been able to see hers. Yet it had been closer to astral projecting, because we had been on the outside looking in...mostly.

One thing I'd decided upon waking was that Quinn and I really needed to hang out more. Maybe I'd visit her in Boston for St. Patrick's Day and then invite her down to St. Louis for Mardi Gras—see which city we could tally the most crimes in.

It had been startling to learn how many mutual friends we shared and how often our individual choices had impacted the other—yet we had never spent any significant time together ourselves. Other than that one time when I broke into her place and picked a fight with her ex—who had been a demon, in my defense.

But the most troubling aspect of the shared dream was the one where I'd been forced to relive that moment where Pan and I had fought...and he had died. That was pretty much the most painful memory I held in my heart, and it kept me awake many, many nights, although I never told anyone about it.

Except...in this dream, Quinn had somehow changed history and saved the horned god. I'd woken up in a cold sweat, panting, wondering if it had somehow been real. If Quinn had somehow managed to save Pan, my number one father figure from my time in Fae—

I was violently snapped out of my meditation by a boot hammering into my ribs, hard enough to elicit a cracking sound. My eyes shot wide open to see Ares looming over me, already rearing back for wake-up call number two. I gasped and grunted with each blow, protecting my vitals as best as I could— the pain of his kicks made all the worse when coupled with my aches from my night with Aphrodite. Throughout it all, I remembered my crazy plan.

I was actually glad that Ares had visited us, first. He would be the easiest to manipulate.

Ares finally grew annoyed with me, turning to Carl—

Who stood inches away from him, staring him right in the eyes. The sounds of me getting my ass kicked must have woken him. Ares let out a startled sound, but not before Carl flicked his tongue out in a sucker-slither, hitting Ares directly in his right eyeball. The god of war punched Carl on reflex, stumbling back from the Elder. I heard ribs crunch as Carl also stumbled back a few steps, but Carl did not whimper or cry out. Ares wiped furiously at his eye, cursing under his breath.

I wheezed out a pathetic laugh, but struggled to my feet before he could resume stomping me. I wouldn't be able to trash-talk if he kicked my teeth down my throat or killed me prematurely.

The two of us stood facing the god of war, waiting for his chosen form of entertainment.

He saw the absent smile on my face and frowned, lowering his hand. His eye was red where Carl had tongued him, and I hoped it got an infection, if such a thing were possible. Elder pinkeye, or something. My smile stretched wider.

"What the fuck are you smiling about? You think it's funny that he licked me?"

And with that, I initiated phase one of my plan to mentally break the god of war. I cleared my throat. "That was merely the icing on the cake that was me fucking your sister last night."

Carl's eyes shot about as wide open as I'd ever seen, and Ares' face instantly went slack and purpled before the hilt of his sword struck me in the gut, knocking the breath from my lungs. I doubled over, wheezing with agony, but I forced myself to press on. It was only going to get worse from here, but I had to set the hooks deeply if I wanted to guarantee a clean escape from this hellhole.

"Sorry," I croaked, and Ares held back his follow-up strike. "But I was still more out of breath after your sister did that thing with her—"

The second blow struck me on the nose like a hammer, sending me crashing to the ground. I felt blood in my mouth, likely draining from my shattered nose. At least I hadn't accidentally bitten off my own tongue. That would have made trash talking impossible. I could have trash-lisped him, I guess.

I lifted my head to stare at Ares. "Let's play charades."

He cocked his head in confusion, likely wondering if he'd knocked me senseless.

I held up a finger. "One word. Here's a hint." Then I dramatically gathered the blood in my mouth and took my time spitting to the side, making sure that he couldn't miss my impression. He frowned at me. "I think we can both agree that I'm not impersonating your sister." And then I let a slow, wolfish grin split my cheeks as I flashed him a bloody smile and pointed at my spit. "That's just not her style."

Carl burst out laughing and Ares reflexively flung his sword, stabbing the Elder in the chest—alarmingly close to the heart—and turning Carl's laughter into a rasping, choking sound. I watched Carl's eyes fluttering weakly as he began to die.

Ares' eyes shot wide and he reached for a flask of Ambrosia hanging from his hip, moving in stiff, frantic motions as he unstoppered the life-saving elixir.

"You better not let him die or your father will utterly destroy you," I said, forcing myself to chuckle despite my very real fear that he'd gone too far with Carl. "The Elders will never team up if he dies. Period. Although, I'm sure we'd have a grand old time as cell mates."

Ares cursed, pouring the Ambrosia down Carl's throat in liberal doses, panting wildly.

Which gave me plenty of time to finish him off. Ares shifted to pouring the Ambrosia directly onto Carl's gaping wound, muttering under his breath as if praying for a miracle.

"You know, out of all the gods of war I've encountered, you're the most disappointing," I drawled, capitalizing on his inability to shut me up. "Which is funny, because you're one of the most well-known. I mean, I pretty much made all of the gods of war my bitch. Thor was a hot mess with hardcore daddy issues. He wasn't even worth my time, but I got his hammer out of the deal, so it wasn't a total waste, I guess," I admitted. "And Odin was my butler. He was pretty damned good at it, too. Maybe you would make a good replacement butler when I'm finished with you," I mused. "I could make you general of my kitchen cavalry. I'd even give you your own spoon if you showed some initiative. You could serve Aphrodite and me dinner before we retire for...well, you know."

I grinned madly at his furious curses and labored panting. He wanted nothing more than to get his hands on me, but he was too busy triaging Carl.

"Athena was a joke, too, but you knew that. I showed her only a little bit of the pleasure I showed Aphrodite a few hours ago and her brain literally melted. Aphrodite was barely able to handle my foreplay herself, now that I think of it."

Ares snarled, dumping the liquid on Carl and reaching for another flask. With two flasks of the healing liquid, I knew Carl was going to survive. Time for me to put a bow on it.

"The strangest thing was what she screamed when she climaxed. Well, the first three times, anyway. Number four was all *NATE!*" I crowed, cupping my hands around my mouth. "I really put my back into that round." I saw Ares reaching for his sword and Carl sucking in a rasping breath. Time to hurry. "I hate to tell you this, champ, but it wasn't your name she screamed the first three times. It was her husband's name—and loud enough to make my ears pop—"

His fiery sword stabbed me through the chest like a white-hot iron, cutting me off. He leaned over me, his face livid, his right eye red and irritated from Carl's tongue, and he was drooling like a rabid dog. "YOU LIE! ADMIT IT!"

I raggedly sucked in the deepest breath I could manage. I had one more thing to say, and it was a one-word answer. "HEPHAESTUS!" I screamed in my best falsetto impersonation of an Aphrodite-level climax.

Ares twisted the blade with a furious snarl, shouting at the top of his lungs and coating me with his drool. My vision tunneled, and the last thing I saw before unconsciousness took me was a medical certainty. Ares' rage had made him pop a blood vessel in one eye, and the other was most definitely going to be a nasty pinkeye.

And that is why you just say no to incest.

I woke up with a gasp, clutching at my chest. It ached like I'd been in a car accident, and my nose felt swollen and broken like I'd been knocked out by an airbag, completing the analogy.

Carl stared down at me with a look of awe. "This is an insane plan," he whispered, shaking his head. "You amaze me."

I coughed. "Wait until we see his brother, Apollo."

Carl grunted. "I feared Ares more than Apollo. What can his sun do to me? It's like a day at the spa."

I considered his words thoughtfully, and a dark smile soon crept over my face as I theorized how best to get under Apollo's skin. Not just his fragile vanity...but his incompetence. "Thank you, Carl. You just found the last piece of the puzzle." I spat to the side. "We have any more of that drink? I think he short-changed us."

Carl shook his head. "He gave us enough so that we would live but not heal much from our injuries."

I grunted. "What an asshole. Nothing like his sister."

Carl burst out laughing. "HEPHAESTUS!" he crowed, parroting my taunt to Ares.

I grinned. "How long have I been out?"

"Ten minutes. Once you were breathing again, he left. Well, he worked me over with his fists because I kept moaning Hephaestus' name as he healed you up."

I grinned from ear-to-ear. "Way to go, Carl!"

His smile faded, replaced by concern. "It took you ten minutes to come back to consciousness."

I nodded uneasily, hoping there were no lasting effects to this abuse. "Wake me up when sunshine gets here. I'm just going to rest my eyes for a minute—"

The door burst open and Apollo stormed in, his eyes shining with fury.

I sighed, slowly sitting up. Part of me was glad that I was closer to escaping.

But the crazy look in Apollo's eyes wasn't very indicative of a good time. I cocked my head, studying Apollo pensively. Then I turned back to Carl. "Ares was right. Sometimes the creator writes the jokes for us. Life is a field sobriety test for some people." Then I turned to Apollo with a faux innocent smile. "Good morning, sunshine."

17

Apollo's glare was dripping with disdain. He even turned his nose up at me and sniffed. "I don't know what you said to my brother, but it seems you need to be put in your place."

I blinked, wondering if he was narcissistic enough to have totally missed the fact that my taunt had been directed at him. Was it possible to be so arrogant that snark was a foreign language? I'd have to be a little more on the nose with him.

Between one moment and the next, we were outside on the edge of a cliff. Well, the sheared-off edge of a white marble floor, like one of the pavilions had broken off the mountain.

The sudden light was blinding, and there wasn't a cloud in the sky. Because Apollo was the god of the sun, it wasn't a relaxing, tolerable heat; it was like standing too close to a bonfire when it flared up. My skin tightened and I hissed instinctively. Carl murmured appreciatively.

Apollo tore my shirt off and then kicked the back of my knees until I crashed to the ground hard enough to possibly fracture my kneecaps. I hissed at the heat of the sun striking my unprotected back, flinching involuntarily.

I glanced up to see Carl also on his knees and Apollo glaring at us with a satisfied smile.

I frowned at Carl. "Well, I had a great time with Ares. Maybe he just overacted his part?"

Carl shrugged. "You did tell him and Aphrodite to be convincing."

"What do you mean, convincing?" Apollo demanded, his bravado slipping. "And what does my sister have to do with it?"

"Well, he didn't torture me," I said, as if it were obvious. "Ares asked if I was willing to work under him. Aphrodite was there as the honey to his stick, like she'd told Zeus. I told them I would agree if I was able to keep the Elders under my command." Carl nodded, going along with my lie. I frowned at Apollo. "Why are you acting like you don't know? They said they had already talked to you about it after they overheard Zeus' concerns about your inability to subdue the Elders with your sunlight."

He glared at me. "You lie. Ares was furious. And he is the worst liar I've ever met. I would have seen through it."

I nodded. "Yeah. He is a pretty bad liar, but he said he would try his best. We agreed that it was safest until he had a chance to talk to Hermes about it. Something about sending a message to Zeus to tell him the good news."

Apollo looked deeply troubled, and I wondered what the hell kind of chaos I'd just stumbled upon. "Do you think it was when I told Ares about Zeus' plan for the Elders?" I asked Carl.

He shook his head. "You did not mention that. Zeus told you to keep it to yourself."

Apollo sneered. "You think you can get in my head, don't you? I already know what my Father intends with you filthy reptiles." He got right up in Carl's face, gripping him by the throat. "You and your people will soon be licking my feet if I so much as look down. And the god of the sun is *always* looking down."

"Always a let-down," I mumbled.

Apollo flinched, shoving Carl away and rounding on me. "What did you just say?"

I winced. "I did that thing again, didn't I, Carl?"

He nodded, looking annoyed. "Yes, Master Temple."

"What are you two fools babbling about?" Apollo snarled.

I met his eyes. "Repeated something told to me in confidence. Zeus will kill me if I repeat it. He wanted it kept a secret."

Apollo clenched his fists and I felt a wave of heat settling on me with his glare. "Not from me. My Father has no secrets from me, or else he wouldn't let me in here with you."

I shrugged. "He said *especially* from you."

I felt my skin begin to burn. "Talk or burn. I'll bring you back and do it as many times as needed before you give me what I want. What was this conspiracy they concocted?"

"Fine!" I snapped, shielding my eyes. "I can't tell you shit if you give me third degree burns. Turn it down for a minute."

He did. Barely. Enough to be increasingly uncomfortable but not lethal. "Talk. Now."

"When Zeus spoke to me in private, he said the Elders would be mine to command. That he didn't trust you with them. You could only be trusted when Zeus set up a controlled environment for you to work in. He said it was like tee-ball."

Apollo punched me in the mouth and I fell to the ground, seeing stars. "What is tee-ball?" The god demanded from behind me, kicking me in my already aching kidneys.

I fell onto my back, staring up at him, panting. His eyes glowed with fire. "Tee-ball is a children's version of baseball," I said, holding up my palms. "Your dad sets the ball on a stick so the incompetent, gangly, awkward child can manage to hit the ball. It helps them develop their tiny, worthless minds to grasp the concept of hand-eye coordination. Teaches them how to, one day, do it all on their own." Apollo's face reddened. "Some peak early, though, never progressing to the real game of baseball."

Carl burst out laughing. Apollo rounded on him, his chest heaving. "Watch it, Elder. You have no idea what I'm capable of."

Carl grinned back. "Aphrodite told Master Temple that Zeus often laughs about how easily controlled you are. That you're in tighter chains than even Hephaestus, who is literally in chains. And you expect your father to give you command of my people? To prop the ball up on the stick for his incompetent child?" He burst out laughing even harder. "You can't even make a real sunbeam, godling."

Apollo suddenly held a bow in his arms. Faster than the speed of light, he let loose five arrows that struck Carl. My eyes shot open to find Carl pinned to a nearby column with a single arrow through each arm and leg, and another in his chest.

He was no longer laughing, but he managed to lift his head and meet Apollo's glare. "What's the matter, godling? All out of sunbeams?"

I flinched at the sudden sensation of eyes staring down upon us. I glanced up at the ceiling and saw a hazy ripple, but I couldn't make anything out. It felt familiar, though. Like Quinn. Was I imagining things? Something like that bizarre sequence of dreams? The sensation disappeared abruptly.

I shook my head free of the thought as Apollo strolled over to Carl, dumping Ambrosia on his wounds from a flask—but not taking the arrows out. I grimaced. He was letting the wounds heal with the arrows still inside the Elder.

So he could rip them out again.

The sick bastard.

Carl smirked. "Maybe you could cauterize them for me with your little flashlight."

Apollo yanked out the arrow in Carl's chest and then stabbed him with it again and again and again. His hair flew wildly as blood spattered his face.

Carl never stopped smiling, even as his eyelids fluttered weakly. And then he began to sing in a soft, loving tone. "You are my sunshine, my only sunshine, you make me happy, when skies are gray..." he sang in a rapidly weakening whisper.

Apollo screamed, slamming the arrow into Carl's chest hard enough that the shaft snapped as the tip struck marble on the other side.

He was panting laboriously as Carl's head dropped to his chest. Then, like Ares had done, he was pouring more of the elixir down Carl's throat. He waited until Carl began to breathe again before ripping out the arrows and dousing the wounds with a second—and then a third—flask.

Carl collapsed to the ground in an unconscious heap. But he was breathing.

"In his defense, Zeus did say you look ghastly enough that the Elders might take you for one of their own. Which was actually a compliment since they have no reason to fear your sunlight. Their sun is much stronger, you see. Your sun is like a cold moon to them. A passing beauty to occasionally glance up at and then forget." I grinned through bloody teeth, chuckling. "Puts a whole new take on something else Zeus said about you, now that I think of it."

Apollo stormed my way, his toga and face covered in blood. He dropped his bow and lifted his bloody hands as if aching to clench my throat. He was shaking. "What did he say?"

I shrugged, spitting blood out the side of my mouth. "They were laughing when he said it."

"They?" he whispered in a murderous tone.

I nodded. "Ares, Aphrodite, and Hermes. They all laughed along with their father when he said that even though you were terrified of the dark, you would always be daddy's little star—"

A solar flare struck me in the chest and everything went white.

Too hot for me to even feel pain.

18

I woke back up in my cell with a rasping gasp, feeling the drink coating my lips. Carl was just sitting up as Apollo's voice cut through the dim interior of our cell. "No light, and only enough Ambrosia to keep you alive. The injuries will stay until tomorrow when I open them back up to see how well you're healing," he snarled. The door slammed shut behind him.

I glanced over at Carl to make sure he was all right. He nodded stiffly, smiling weakly.

I tenderly touched my eye and winced. I was going to be sporting a wicked black eye, soon, and I couldn't breathe through my nose. Maybe the broken nose would help blacken the other eye for me so that I was at least symmetrical. I had once read that beauty was symmetrical. I waited a few more minutes, wondering if I'd gone too far with the conspiracy theory and ruined everything. What if Apollo demanded answers of his siblings, and then they stormed in together to beat the hell out of us and clear up the story for their fragile brother?

Or maybe he wouldn't trust them, and would simply keep a close eye on them.

I didn't dare speak in case we were being watched. Then again, if we were, Zeus would have already seen what I'd said to Ares and likely shown up himself to give me a little fatherly talk.

Hell, maybe he would be impressed with me. We slowly recovered over a long two hours with no interruptions. Then two more hours went by, and we began pacing our cells anxiously, wondering why we hadn't heard anything. My eye had gradually swollen to a slit and my head throbbed with every step, making my broken nose ache, so I'd lost interest in pacing. Soon, night fell, and I twitched at every change of wind whistling through our window.

I needed answers, and since I was just sitting around anyway, I decided to try astral projection again, wondering if I would be able to meet up with Quinn and ask her about our shared dream. She'd babble and curse at me in her usual Flogging Molly impersonation, making me smile in amusement, and then she'd call me an idget a few times for good measure before telling me I must have been drunker than I'd thought to have such a crazy ass dream.

Which was infinitely better than sitting here, worrying. I couldn't even drum up enough energy to consider Aphrodite's lessons, fearing that the door would kick in at any moment, catching me in a depressed mood about my poor love life, or lack thereof.

Running away from my problems sounded like a grand old time. I closed my eyes, and sent my soul off into the cosmos, looking for adventure. And answers.

I somehow skipped past the oppressive darkness with the crimson lightning, and found myself smack dab in the middle of some drama. My favorite kind, too—someone else's.

I hadn't expected the cast of characters before me, or the backdrop.

Yggdrasil towered over me, filling the air with the sound of a million chiming echoes. I sat down on a nearby log, sweeping my gaze across the scene and wondering why I was here. Colors were more vibrant, almost seeming to be highlighted with a neon pen at the edges.

Freya stood near the base of the World Tree, waiting as a Valkyrie in gleaming golden armor approached her. The warrior came to a halt, thumped the butt of her gleaming trident into the earth, and then knelt down on one knee before her boss. I picked up a pebble and threw it at them, wondering what kind of experience this was going to be for me. Interactive or observatory.

The pebble struck the Valkyrie in the helmet with a sharp clang, and my sphincter clenched as I jumped to my feet in sudden alarm. The Valkyrie cocked her head slightly and removed her helmet, frowning down at it curiously. When she lifted her head, I gasped sharply. I knew her.

Kára's long blonde braid hung over her shoulder, highlighting the shaved sides of her head. What the hell was she doing here? The two of them wore perplexed frowns as they quickly scanned their surroundings. Kára's dual-colored eyes—one green and one blue—passed right over me, and I let out a sigh of relief to learn that I was invisible. I saw another log closer to them, and I approached it warily, wondering how good my invisibility truly was. How the hell had my pebble hit her? How had I managed to even pick it up?

Whatever the answers, I knew that I didn't want to miss this conversation.

Kára turned back to Freya, dipping her chin respectfully. Her smile was forced, judging by her clenched jaw. Now that I was closer, I realized that Kára looked like she'd been through hell. Her armor was not as polished as I'd initially thought, and it even had scrapes and gouges across it. I frowned to see an intentional etching over her left breast, what appeared to be a crude lighthouse of sorts.

I frowned. Valkyrie armor was elegant and grand, decorated in ornate swirls, symbols and meticulous design. Why would Kára vandalize it? If she'd wanted a lighthouse on it, there were any number of dwarven armorers who would have done a much better job.

Also, it was fucking hard to scratch Valkyrie armor. She must have tried using her freaking trident to do it, explaining the low quality of the design. Perhaps there was a lighthouse god in the Norse pantheon. They were big on ships, so I could believe it.

Freya also seemed to notice it and pursed her lips in disapproval. But... she didn't openly acknowledge it. Strange...

Kára cleared all thoughts of her armor from my mind when she suddenly hefted her trident atop her palms and held it out to Freya in what seemed a formal gesture. Freya arched her brow, startled by the display. "What is the meaning of this, Kára?" she asked, sounding overly calm.

Kára cleared her throat, keeping her eyes lowered. "My loyalties are divided," she whispered.

I blinked, shaking my head. That couldn't be true.

"Your loyalties?" Freya asked, sounding doubtful. "Are you a traitor, then?"

Kára snorted dismissively. "No," she growled. "My heart is divided."

I froze, recalling our brief conversation about her feelings for me. She couldn't really be handing over her powers as a bet on us getting together. That was insane. We hardly knew each other. And as far as she knew, I was still committed to Callie—as I'd told her during our last conversation.

"Explain," Freya demanded, refusing to accept or even acknowledge the offered trident.

"I have used your gifts for my own benefit," Kára said, refusing to come off as meek and apologetic. "I watched those who should not be watched. I spied."

"Why?" Freya asked, and I realized that she did not look angry. She looked...curious.

"Personal reasons," Kára said, obviously not willing to talk about it.

"And what is this personal reason's name?" Freya asked, sounding as if she was struggling not to laugh out loud.

Kára missed it, still averting her eyes. She remained silent, refusing to answer, and I found myself appraising her for my own...*personal reasons*. Because my time with Aphrodite had scoured parts of me raw, permitting me to see certain things in a new light.

Kára was amazing. She'd been a comforting shoulder for me to figuratively cry on at her bar. But...I hadn't actually spent any time crying on her shoulder. I hadn't complained about Callie. I hadn't even talked about Callie. Little had I known that my lack of conversation about Callie had led Kára to assume that I was no longer in a relationship with Callie.

In her eyes, my weeks visiting with her at the bar had been...well, one long first date. In my mind, I'd found a friend I'd desperately needed. In some ways, I felt I knew the mysterious Valkyrie better than I knew some of my oldest friends. Even though we hadn't shared much about our pasts, we had learned about each other's character and values.

Which was way more important, in my opinion.

We'd bonded. And then she'd come onto me not too long ago, catching me entirely off guard. Only a hundred feet or so from where I now sat. That had been one of the first times that I consciously realized there was a major rift between Callie and me. Before Kára had made her intentions clear, I'd always assumed Callie and I just needed to take a vacation away together.

And now I had Aphrodite stripping in my peripheral vision, and she wasn't wearing Team Callie colors either. I shook off the thought, focusing back on the exchange before me.

Freya stared down at Kára and then let out a warm laugh, pushing down the offered trident with two fingers. "Oh, Kára. If I wanted your heart, I would have taken it. War and passion are two sides of the same coin." I flinched to hear Freya echoing Aphrodite's quote from earlier. "Only the greatest warriors know how to truly love. Taking that away from the Valkyries would render them impotent. Keep your heart. I want only your blade and righteous fury."

Kára frowned in confusion. "What if my loyalties pit me against my heart, or vice versa?"

"Then you will have an interesting dilemma," Freya said, smiling compassionately. "I recommend you choose your heart, child. Some of us do not have that privilege."

Kára stared down at her spear thoughtfully. "I do not think my feelings are reciprocated. In fact, I am certain of it."

Freya laughed again. "Men are fickle beasts. Which einherjar do you have your eyes set upon? I could apply some pressure."

Kára's cheeks colored. "He is not an einherjar..." she said slowly.

Freya cocked her head thoughtfully. "I see," she said, just as slowly. The curiosity was clear, but she didn't force Kára to answer. She also didn't seem to assume it was me. Maybe I was getting ahead of myself and Kára had already found a new lover. "Is he a good man?"

Kára was silent for a very long time. "I...do not know," she admitted, and I felt my heart thump wildly. That sounded like a Nate Temple answer, for sure. "But I do not care. I do not want a good man. Good men die swiftly. I believe he could become a great man—for better or worse. I wish to help him on his path, whichever path that turns out to be."

Freya waited, arching an eyebrow. "Oh?"

"If he strays down darker roads, I shall bring him back or kill him. And I believe he would want me to do so." I shuddered. Well, true love had just been tossed out the window. Or...had it? Wasn't that exactly what a man wanted? Someone to stand beside, not stand before.

Freya nodded. "Memento Mori," she murmured. "You would be his confidante—his conscience and his trusted executioner."

She nodded. "If he would have me." She straightened her shoulders. "I would tell him all of this up front—my full intentions. If he's the man I believe him to be, he would want me to."

And...she was right—if I was the topic of conversation, anyway. How did Kára seem to know me so well? She was the most insightful bartender ever.

"How long have you known this man to become so besotted?" Freya asked. I winced, already envisioning Freya laughing in her face when she learned that it had only been months.

"Over a decade, but he does not know this," Kára whispered.

I sucked in a breath. *What?*

Freya grew still, mirroring my thoughts. Even the wind stopped. She cocked her head, studying Kára apprehensively. She looked suddenly troubled. "I know you didn't truly die in a car crash. A Valkyrie is required to leave her old life behind."

Kára remained silent. I realized I was leaning forward, holding my breath. Kára straightened her shoulders and met Freya's eyes. "I owe you an apology. I have been working for Odin this whole time—at his request and vowed to secrecy. He wanted me to be his second eye," she admitted with a faint smile, "to safeguard you, Asgard, and..." she hesitated, "one other."

I stiffened. Me. She had to be talking about me.

"I see," Freya said coolly, not pleased to hear that her husband had stolen one of her Valkyries. "And now you've fallen for this...one other."

Kára shook her head. "That happened long before I died, but I was too much of a coward to admit it to him. It is only in death that I found my truth. And it is now because of that truth that I must forsake my vows to you. I can no longer serve two masters." She clenched her teeth, visibly trembling. "It. Is. Tearing. Me. Apart."

Freya seemed just as upset, riled up by mention of her husband—especially since she'd told me Kára was her favorite Valkyrie, even if she was the newest. I racked my brain in an effort to guess who she had been in her previous life. Which woman I had met who had never admitted how she truly felt for me. If true, it was no wonder why part of me felt like I had known Kára for much longer than a few months.

"This is not a job you can resign from," Freya said in a stern, yet concerned tone. "I mean that literally. If not a Valkyrie, you are just a soul."

Kára nodded stiffly. "I am aware of this. Before the first horn of war, a warrior accepts that she might die this day. That does not stop her from clasping on her armor and kissing her axe."

Freya sucked in a breath, looking as if it had been a blow to her heart. "I know that the exact details of your death were concealed from me, but that the main premise I was given was true. You saved a life when you died. Before you, I have never accepted a Valkyrie without their complete story unfurled before me. Yet I agreed not to press you on the matter."

Kára nodded woodenly, looking about as guilty and heartbroken as ever. She hadn't wanted to hurt Freya, which was why she'd tried to shrug off her duty by pointing out her failures in the very beginning—to make Freya's decision simpler. "I—"

Death suddenly appeared out of thin air, slamming his scythe into the ground between Kára and Freya. Both women leapt back, wielding wicked spears on reflex. I don't know where the hell Freya had pulled hers from, but it looked deadly enough to castrate an interrupting Horseman.

Death remained motionless, assuring them that he was no direct threat. Then he turned to Kára. "You. Will. Be. Silent."

"You have no authority here, Horseman," Freya said in a cool tone.

"The dead are my responsibility. I give you information on souls with potential and certain qualities you desire. You accepted Kára at face-value, and those consequences are yours to bear." He dipped his chin to show her he meant no disrespect. "That, and your conversation is not as private as you may think," he said, his hood hanging low to conceal his face from the two women.

And I felt his eyes lock onto me, unbeknownst to them. In that brief look, I sensed pain and conflicting emotions—a man forced to choose between two terrible decisions.

His next words struck me like a knife. "Some people do not realize how dangerous it is to spy on a god without their body to protect them. They do not understand that there are things worse than death, reserved specifically for nosy, wandering souls."

Both women spun towards me and, for the briefest of moments, I thought Kára might have seen me, because her eyes widened in disbelief. But I had already fled, not desiring to bet on the age-old question.

Does a spear fly faster than an apology?

19

I slipped back into my body and collapsed as pain suddenly overwhelmed me. I'd forgotten all about how beaten up I was. It was easy to forget when astral projecting. I groaned, climbing to my feet, trying to make sense of what I'd just seen.

Who had Kára once been, and why had the details of her death been hidden from Freya?

Why had Death interrupted her answer, only to turn around and save me?

And what would now happen to Kára?

When Aphrodite opened our door and slipped into our cell, I had moved to my cot, attempting to get some genuine sleep before my next big adventure.

I smelled her familiar perfume and groaned as I looked over at her.

The door softly clicked closed and she shuffled towards my cot on slippered feet, not making a sound. She knelt by my bed, wincing at my current state. My eye had swollen even more while I slept, and my nose felt like it was the size of my entire face. My head pounded something fierce.

"Oh, good. I bet family dinner was a real hoot," I mumbled.

Rather than answering me, she forced a drink from her flask to my lips, waiting until I downed it all. I gasped in relief as the Ambrosia instantly went to work healing me. As my muscles and bones knitted and clicked back into their proper place, she worked on Carl.

Aphrodite knelt back down by my cot, resting a hand on my chest. "What were you *thinking*? They are furious. I don't know if I've ever seen them so...rattled. Especially Ares," she added with an unhappy tone.

I chuckled unashamedly. "I tried getting him angry in other ways, but you were the hot button he responded to the most."

She smirked faintly. "I do know how to inflame the...hearts of men," she admitted with a proud grin. "But why did you do this? Why not just let them torture you and be done with it?"

I shook my head. "I needed them to go hard. Hard enough that they realized they'd gone way too far and decide to skip a session or two to harden their mental defenses against my superior ability to infuriate them."

She watched me thoughtfully. "Why? We need only moments to leave."

I reached out to settle my hand atop hers and smiled warmly. "You're risking your life for me. I need at least one Olympian to see that I'm willing to risk my life for theirs. Give you enough time to make a clean break." She shuddered, nodding stiffly...in gratitude? It hadn't been that big of a risk, not with their Ambrosia and Zeus needing us alive. I didn't point that out, of course. "If I hadn't, they might have decided to take turns every hour on the hour. I needed to guarantee that they did such a complete job that I also had the chance to buy myself the most time for my plans once I'm out of here."

Aphrodite nodded again, seeming to have regained her own composure, but I could tell that my actions had earned me a significant level of respect from her. "Well, it took me some time to calm Ares down and convince him to take the night to come up with a better plan. Apollo banged on my bedroom door for an hour before giving up," she admitted with a shameless smile. "Apollo left the mountain, apparently. Ares and Hermes went to look for him and find out what the hell you said to him, leaving me in charge. I complained about the responsibility dumped onto my lap, of course," she admitted with a smile, but I'd seen the curiosity in her eyes when she'd mentioned Apollo leaving.

"I told him you three were scheming to rope me into your—Zeus' plans —giving him the hint that he was being left out. Maybe something about his father mocking his incompetence and his siblings laughing about it. I imagine Ares and Hermes will not receive a...sunny reception."

She grimaced. "Well, it looks like I'll definitely be leaving soon as well. The moment you disappear with me as the only prison guard, I'll either be punished for my involvement or my failure. I'd considered staging the cell so that it seemed you had found your own way out, but that sounds contrived after you single-handedly mind-fucked my brothers." She didn't sound reluctant. Just resigned.

I nodded, resting my forehead against hers. "Thank you, Aphrodite."

All I could do now was hope the seeds of chaos I had planted took root. At least I was no longer crippled with pain. I could even see clearly and breathe through my nose. It was going to be a good day. "Well, we should probably get the hell out of here, eh?"

She nodded, pulling me to my feet. She closed her eyes and touched the chains connected to my manacles. Her fingers began to glow with a vibrant pink light, and I felt a steady hum in the air. The chains hissed, recoiling from her touch even as the crimson runes and symbols flared brighter. Then they abruptly winked out of existence. I grunted, cocking my head.

"Um. That didn't happen last time," I said, fearing she might have triggered a silent alarm.

She nodded. "Temporarily unhooking them from your Titan Thorns is simple. Untethering them from both the Titan Thorns and the cell is entirely different. They returned back to a safe lock-up in Hephaestus' workshop, out of dangerous hands." She looked surprisingly drained, her face pale and gaunt from her effort.

I nodded idly. It made sense. "How did you do it?" I asked, wondering if any of her brothers could be pinned for my escape.

She approached Carl and placed her hands on the chains, answering me without looking. Carl watched her, and he looked surprisingly nervous. "Love," she whispered back as I spotted a similar pink glow, the runes flaring with crimson light and a keening hiss. "The chains repel...love," she mumbled drunkenly. They winked out of existence and she instantly stumbled, her legs giving out.

I shouted, but Carl swept her up in his arms, catching her and holding her horizontally, with a panicked look on his face. Her head rolled dazedly, leaning against his shoulder for a moment before she snapped back into focus, blinking up at him in confusion.

"You fell," he said, gently. "And you did not adequately satisfy Master Temple last night, so I did not want you damaged until you resolved the matter."

She was silent for a moment, but I was too busy fighting down my embarrassed blush. "Fucking Carl," I muttered. "You don't *say* things like that. I told you I had it under control."

Aphrodite burst out laughing. "I...see. I think I can stand on my own now, Elder Carl. Thank you for catching me, and for...looking out for Nate's best interests," she said, not bothering to hide her grin.

Carl set her down with a satisfied nod, but remained close to support her if she fell again.

I scowled at the pair of them for good measure, and then I turned to my satchel. I still had no magic, but at least I wasn't chained to a wall. I walked over and scooped up my satchel as nonchalantly as possible. I might not have magic, but I finally had my bag of tricks.

I didn't want her to see how frantic I was to get my hands on it. As much as I trusted her...I didn't fully trust her. She was now on Zeus' shit list, and she might be angling for an insurance policy to put herself back in his good graces if things went south.

Right now, the contents of my satchel were my only means of self-defense. If I cackled like a mad lunatic, she might just change her mind about helping me. I deftly slipped Hermes' coins into the satchel, pretending to check one of the straps. I'd been relieved to find the golden Gateways still in my pockets after Aphrodite had shredded my clothes. The real question was, had she seen them? She hadn't said anything about them, but she'd sewn the clothes up with magic. Paranoia was the spice of life. I didn't know what I was going to do with them yet. Maybe I would toss one into a fucking volcano and turn this shithole into a tower of ash.

I grabbed Carl's shredded jacket and tossed it to him. "Do you love anyone unconditionally?"

He tensed and grew unnaturally still, his face blank. "No." Then he slipped into his coat, zipped it up forcefully, and caressed the filthy pink material with his claws, smiling delightedly.

Aphrodite frowned at his strange reaction—especially his adoration of the tattered pink coat.

"Where will you go?" I asked her, leaving Carl to his secrets.

A ghost of a frown crossed her face. "Hide until our next meeting and hope you can come up with a way to stop my Father."

I nodded. "I hope I can."

"That's all anyone can do." She flashed me a smile. "Especially you, Horseman of Hope."

I mirrored her smile. "Can you make a Gateway to Grimm Tech? I need to go shopping." Other than my satchel, I also had a company with a hefty research and development department. It was time to play Batman, and I even had a pale, scaly Robin. Despite everything, my heart began to lift with hope.

Aphrodite frowned. Some of the color had returned to her cheeks, but she still looked exhausted. "Not the Armory? You need protection, not paperwork."

I shrugged, keeping my face neutral. "I left a key to a safe house there. It's stocked up for emergencies," I lied.

She watched me for a few moments and then finally nodded. "As you wish." She waved a hand, creating a hazy Gateway. I couldn't see through to the other side; it just looked like a vaseline-coated window hanging in mid-air. I could make out the other side of the cell through it. "Jump through. I will come for you as swiftly as I can."

"Good," Carl said, nodding in satisfaction. "As long as you reciprocate."

I groaned, wanting to throat-punch him. Especially when Aphrodite smiled at him. "I think I like you, Elder Carl. You're...lively."

He cocked his head. "Well, I'm also deadly," he said with a frown.

She grinned even wider, patting him on the shoulder. "I have no doubt, Elder Carl," she reassured him. Then she turned back to me, winking. She assessed the Gateway, nodded, and then pointed at my Titan Thorns. "You should be immune to tracking, but I wouldn't depend on it. Be vigilant."

I frowned, not having even thought of Zeus tracking me via my manacles. I'd have to find a way to resolve that. Luckily, I'd had plenty of time to think about it and already had an idea. "Then we need to set up a time and place for our...lessons, right?"

Carl watched the two of us curiously. "Do all humans schedule sex in their calendars?"

Aphrodite smirked. "Only malicious wives aiming to break their husbands into a shallow grave or a hollow affair." I narrowed my eyes, realizing that her example made me the malicious wife in our relationship. She smiled playfully. "Do not worry. I gave you a talisman so I may find you. Check your pockets, my lamb," she said mysteriously. I did, and found a short pink and purple bow tied from a silk ribbon. I slipped it back into my pocket with a faint smile. "A happy bedroom is all about the unknowns and the potential for surprise. No schedules, no inhibitions. I will find you when you least expect it." She eyed me up and down, enjoying the shy look on my face. "Be sure to stay hydrated, Temple. You are going to need it... either way. Resisting is harder than releasing," she said, clearly enunciating the last word in another euphemism.

"I will make sure he is ready for you," Carl promised in a solemn tone. "It is my duty."

She beamed brightly, curtsied at Carl, and then she simply disappeared.

Carl flinched, staring down at the empty space where she had been standing, looking more surprised that her Gateway still remained. "I like her, Master Temple."

"Let's go before one of her brothers returns." I leapt through the Gateway, hoping this wasn't all some trap Aphrodite was setting up for us—her own form of torture. Without the ability to see through, it was a gamble. Better than a second longer in my prison cell, though. I hoped.

I glanced back and frowned, unable to see Mount Olympatraz. I couldn't see the Gateway either, just the same barely noticeable haze to the air, like a mirage. Carl appeared out of the center, and the haze evaporated behind him like a popped bubble.

I scanned our surroundings, wondering where, exactly, she'd sent us. I quickly found that we were concealed in a stand of trees just outside Grimm Tech. Thankfully, it was also night here. I let out a sigh of relief, glad that she hadn't somehow been able to send us directly inside. That would have meant the building was compromised—and similarly, all the experimental magitech items within.

She had expected to send me to the Armory. Could she have done so? I shivered. I needed to warn Pandora about the unfolding situation, but not until I knew I wasn't being tailed. As much as I appreciated Aphrodite, I was cognizant of the fact that she could teach me all about love and still stab me in the back for her father. Or her husband. Or anyone else. She could be playing me much like she'd claimed to be playing her father. Much like I was playing all of them.

Carl leaned in uncomfortably close. "The red heels you bought me," he whispered, flicking my ear with his tongue so that I jumped. "I love *them* unconditionally."

I arched an eyebrow and stared down at his cuffs. Nothing happened. "Shoes are not the same as a person."

He nodded sadly. "They are better," he whispered reverently. "People hurt you. People do not make you feel pretty. They make you feel self-conscious."

He was staring off into the distance as he said it. I was surprised at the depth of his statement. I frowned sadly. "You didn't need to be self-conscious about that, Carl. You could have said that when I first asked." He looked down at his feet, not meeting my eyes. "If we make it out of this, you're getting a new pair of shoes," I promised him.

He looked up, grinning happily. "Yes!"

"First, we have to rob the local billionaire of his extremely volatile, experimental gadgets. Shoes are for winners."

Carl's eyes narrowed competitively. "Then we must fucking win. For shoes and glory."

I sighed. "Yep. That."

20

I reached into my satchel and pulled out a velvet *Crown Royal* pouch. I opened it and knelt in the grass, carefully spilling a collection of glass marbles out before me. I began sifting through them, inspecting the markings on each one. "Okay, Carl. We're going to break in and I'm going to grab a few things. I need you to be on look-out because we have to be stealthy. Security cameras are everywhere, and I'm not sure if Ashley or Othello has any permanent guards on duty." I frowned, unable to recall where Ashley now fit into the hierarchy of Grimm Tech. Othello had taken a more active role recently, where Ashley kind of coasted on the day-to-day operations, much like me.

Some CEO I was. I shook my head, realizing I didn't give a shit. The revenues were good and I trusted them. Whatever system they had was working better without me nosing into it. Also, when that same CEO was currently planning on robbing said company, it wasn't very rational to criticize the management structure.

"There might be werewolves and wizards on duty. Maybe some Shift students as well. We can't hurt them. They're just doing their jobs. And we can't knock on the front door or else everyone will hear that I'm back and Zeus will thunderbliviate the complex, and maybe all of St. Louis."

Carl nodded, unfazed. "Can I make them bleed? It might be necessary."

I winced. "I'd rather they not even *see* us, to be honest. We don't want them recognizing us. An Elder is obviously an Elder. Well, you might pass as a shifter dragon in the right lighting," I mused, eyeing his silhouette in the moonlight. "But we do have to get out of here cleanly, so if we have to hurt a few in the process, we will. But no serious harm. If we hurt any of them and they recognize us, we're fucked long-term. They will think I turned against my own people."

Carl nodded uneasily. "This sounds like a bad idea. Why not just go to the Armory?"

I shook my head adamantly. "This is a step up from a terrible idea, which would be heading straight for the Armory. What if this whole 'release from prison' thing is a ruse? What if they're somehow playing me much like I was toying with Ares and Apollo? What if they're watching us right now and we lead them straight to fucking Pandora?"

Carl grimaced, glancing over his shoulders suspiciously. "I sense no one," he said, not sounding convinced.

"They are *gods*, Carl. Let's not pretend that we know their limits and capabilities. Neither should we give them too much credit," I admitted with a growl, still shifting through the Tiny Balls. "It's all a balancing act. Until I'm certain we don't have a tail, we're staying low."

Carl glanced at his tail with a frown, shaking it for good measure. I rolled my eyes.

"Also, the moment I step foot on Chateau Falco's grounds, the mansion will likely respond to my presence and everyone will know I'm back. I need to figure out a way to get into the Armory without alerting everyone. If Zeus is watching, he won't be able to miss all of my friends being suddenly excited about my return because my Beast, Falco, couldn't keep a secret."

I sighed, realizing that I was getting agitated. I turned back to the Tiny Balls spread out before me. Most of these were designed to lead to specific places—marked with a rune or word on the inside of the clear glass marble. I held them up to the moonlight, quickly reading and discarding them: Falco, Sanctorum, Plato's Cave, Kansas City...

I closed my eyes for a moment, took a deep breath, and set that one to the side. Callie was in Kansas City. Another thing I had to deal with. I paused, realizing that I'd just referred to Callie as a *thing to deal with*, as if from a checklist, and I imagined Aphrodite's smile of confirmation that she'd been right. I didn't love her.

Kára's predatory grin hit me a millisecond later, victorious that she had been right about the fact that I treated Callie more like a business partner than a potential girlfriend.

Was I really that much of an asshole? Not wanting to answer the obvious, I focused back on my task, fondling my Tiny Balls. I saw two for Niflheim and hesitated. That...could be helpful, actually. Especially with Aphrodite's warning about needing to mask my presence in the event our Titan Thorns could be tracked. Last I'd checked, there were a ton of Sensates there.

I shoved that one into my pocket. We also needed somewhere to sleep away from prying eyes, and any god who chose to come to Niflheim had to suffer the effects of the mist that drained their powers. I wasn't sure what lasting effect it might have on an Elder or a godkiller, but it was better than getting a hotel room since we needed to stay off the radar. Hotels had cameras and paperwork.

And any of my known properties with a bed would be an obvious guess for my hunters.

Because if the Olympians weren't playing me, Ares and Apollo were going to turn over every rock to get me back into their torture chamber. They were personally invested in my misery, now, because their father was going to make them pay for their failure. Even if Aphrodite had freed me, that might not have happened if the brothers hadn't left her unsupervised.

Zeus would find a way to make each of them feel guilty for it, capitalizing on their need for his affection. He truly was a sick man.

I almost let out a shout of relief to finally find a Tiny Ball linked to Grimm Tech. I carefully put the rest back into the velvet pouch and tucked it away inside my satchel.

"Here we go, Carl. Just keep a lookout so I can grab a few quick items. Stay close because we won't be there long. We're going straight for the Vault," I said, holding up the marble.

The Vault was where I stored the most secret, dangerous, experimental projects involving magic and technology. I had a team of wizard scientists and engineers working around the clock to pretty much come up with the craziest shit they could think of. Or find a way to create any of the craziest shit I randomly emailed them. It was the research and development section of the company, and most of the company's other employees knew nothing about it.

They only heard about the items I approved to be sent to market—the nonlethal ones.

"How do we get out after?" Carl asked, studying the marble in the moonlight.

I stared at him for about five seconds. "Shit." The Vault had been warded to prevent Gateways in or out. I knew the Tiny Ball in my hand would work to get us in—because it had been designed to do exactly that —but any Tiny Ball thrown inside the Vault would do absolutely nothing. And that wasn't even considering any new wards my employees might have put up.

Who was even running the Vault, now?

Regardless, escaping directly from the Vault was probably a hard no. If I had access to my own magic, I knew I could find a way out no problem. But the Titan Thorns prevented that. A new fear came to mind. Would our manacles set off the alarms? They were incredibly powerful, after all, and might be construed as weapons depending on what new wards had been implemented. What if Elders had been included in the wards? They might even have their own alarm tone.

My arms suddenly pebbled with the realization that it was a terrible, terrible plan.

I slowly turned to Carl. "Remember what I said about our plan being one step above a terrible idea?" He nodded. "Scratch that. We're...going to need to purposely set off the alarms."

He arched an eyebrow and pursed his lips. "Why?"

"Because without magic, the only way out of the Vault is through the only door in the room. I've got a code, but who knows if it's still good." His tail began to twitch nervously. "We need to alert security so they'll open the doors for us. We'll sneak out the door in the confusion. Once we're out of the Vault, we should be able to use a Tiny Ball."

"While the security guards shoot at us or try to kill us with fang and claw," Carl said softly.

"And magic," I added. "But there are plenty of things in the Vault that I can grab to help in that regard. Maybe I can find a shield of some kind."

"This is no longer a stealth operation," Carl said, staring towards the imposing warehouse. "And even though we will set off alarms, alert security, and then attempt to sneak past them...we cannot let them see who we are." I nodded. "I hope I pass for a shifter dragon, then."

I cringed, wondering if I should leave him out here. But I needed his eyes to keep watch. And he was much better at physical confrontation than me, of course. I needed the muscle. "Me, too."

I ran through the mental list of items I knew we had inside the Vault, assessing what I could use to help our escape. As long as those items were still present and accounted for. There would likely be some kind of illusion spell.

"How many guards are we talking about?" Carl mused. "I can't use my powers with these manacles, which leaves my only weapons right here," he said, holding up his lethal claws.

I gritted my teeth. "Okay. You're on look-out and distraction detail. I'll be theft and deterrent." I didn't have anything in my satchel that would help in that regard—because I carried death on my hip. Nothing so juvenile as non-lethal weapons; my enemies played for keeps. I hoped the Vault personnel had been productive, making something that I could use for our escape.

I reached into my satchel, hoping to find a hat or bandana to help conceal our faces. I came up with nothing. Thankfully, it had rained recently and the air was warm. I quickly scanned the ground and found a muddy patch. "Perfect!" I began scooping globs of the dark mud onto my face and hair. Remembering that my shirt was familiar to my friends, I liberally coated that in mud as well. Carl sighed and began doing the same. Carl was a germaphobe and meticulous about keeping clean, so this was worse than our upcoming robbery to him.

He looked particularly depressed about further dirtying his pink coat. "We'll find a warm place to wash up after," I promised him. He suffered in silence.

Once finished, we stood facing each other, unable to bite back faint grins at how ridiculous we looked. The CEO and one of the most dangerous creatures in the known worlds now looked like a mud lizard and a homeless vagrant. At least security wouldn't instantly assume me a wizard since the Titan Thorns blocked my powers. We might just be able to pull this off.

I took a deep breath and held the Tiny Ball up to the moonlight. I kissed it for luck, leaving a muddy smear on the clear surface.

Then I threw it on the ground, waited for the Gateway to scream open with a flare of sparks—an ominous start to our stealth operation—and leapt through.

21

Carl landed beside me and we quickly scanned our surroundings in a full circle, back-to-back like we'd done it a million times. Then his tail almost ankle-swept me onto my ass. I stumbled, but managed to keep my balance and step out of his range. It was the middle of the night, but that was when security was most alert.

The dark inner warehouse of the Vault was utterly silent and empty, and I let out a breath of relief as the Gateway winked shut behind us. We were standing in the center of a wide aisle, and about ten rows of massive shelves climbed twenty feet high on either side of us. The single entrance to the Vault stood behind us—complete with a glass-walled breakroom that hadn't existed during my last visit.

At the opposite end of the warehouse was an open-concept laboratory, complete with tables of laboratory equipment, work desks, and filing cabinets. I spotted a few shelves bulging with dusty magical books. The computers were apparently hooked up to the massive monitors hanging from the ceiling, but I didn't want to risk booting one of them up and trying to log on. That would defeat the purpose of hiding my identity, even though it would make my shopping easier. Because one thing was obvious.

Grimm Tech had developed far beyond what I had imagined.

For example, rather than chairs, I saw only workout balls. I rolled my eyes.

"Fucking millennials. Ruin everything. In my day, we wore chains to work and didn't get to eat until we got home. We didn't even *have* chairs! Whoever is running this place is too soft."

Carl eyed me dubiously. I ignored him. He wasn't a CEO. He didn't know my troubles.

Several forklifts had been abandoned between the rows of shelves, and I saw a row of hazmat suits hanging near the lab area. That made me cringe with concern. But if the room itself had been poisonous, the hazmat suits would have been outside the Vault, not in here. The quarantine suits must have been set out for the handling of specific items on the shelves. Still...

What the hell had they been working on to need them?

Some of the storage rows had more shelves than others, depending on the size of the magitech stowed. The ambient security lighting bathed the room in a pale blue glow—just enough for us to make our way while remaining masked by shadows.

I straightened, relieved that an alarm hadn't immediately announced our arrival.

"Okay, Carl. Take a quick look around for cameras or motion detectors. I don't know what kind of security upgrades they've made in here. The stupid chairs and breakroom are new, so who knows what else they changed. Let me know what you find, and don't accidentally set any alarms off," I warned him. I waited for him to nod. "I'll start gathering stuff."

He crouched low and stalked over to the first aisle, turning out of my sight.

I slipped into the closest row, which was a few down from Carl, and took a quick inventory. Each shelf featured placards behind plastic sleeves, indicating the items stored on that particular shelf. Large blocks of tiny text that I couldn't read in the dim lighting filled each card, and I suddenly felt overwhelmed at the dozens upon dozens of slips of paper...on this shelf alone.

I didn't have time to read all of them. Not even all of them on this row. We needed to get out of here as fast as possible.

I froze, squinting at one of the placards. I rubbed my eyes in disbelief.

The millennial invasion...

Had saved my life. I was forced to concede that they had made at least one worthwhile donation to humanity.

One of them had probably been annoyed that his older coworkers always needed their reading glasses, so he had decided to include little symbols that indicated pertinent information on each inventory item— using a single symbol. No doubt to save himself from being endlessly harassed by his geezer coworkers who couldn't read the damned microscopic print in this abysmal lighting—

I cut off, narrowing my eyes. "I'm an old geezer," I admitted in a stunned whisper, horrified.

Emojis—the name of their strange, hieroglyphic-based, alien tongue— filled each placard.

Shields. Icicles. Fireballs. Skull and Crossbones. Chemistry flasks showing skulls with crossed-out eyes on the front. And dozens more. Rather than reading the texts, I resorted to scanning the emojis, silently thanking the millennial movement. Maybe I'd let them keep their stupid workout ball chairs. One of them. Only for the guy or gal who'd done the emoji thing.

Even with the symbols speeding things up, many of them were vague enough to make me hesitate. What did a yellow exclamation mark mean versus a green or red one? Safe, or not? Good deadly, or bad deadly? Time was not on my side, because I had no idea what time of night it actually was. What if it was close to morning?

I was currently in some kind of clothing section. That much, at least, was obvious. So, rather than wasting time, I made the best of my bottomless satchel, and transformed myself into a coupon-clipping all-star on Black Friday.

I flipped open my satchel and began tossing in absolutely anything that looked even remotely beneficial. I quickly scanned the placards to make sure the items wouldn't explode or poison me on contact. Seconds later, I was scooping up the relevant placards along with the clothing.

The next shelves held massive machines, so I skipped over them, deciding that no matter what they did, they wouldn't be practical in any upcoming fights. I saw a row of tiny stone Guardians and almost screamed in alarm, fearing they were active. They stared back at me lifelessly, and I let out a sigh of relief. I shoved them into my satchel and flipped the lid closed. Then I carefully moved two rows down, spotting blades and guns on the row closest to the door.

I grabbed a few strangely shaped blades and their respective placards before spotting an item that definitely didn't make any sense. A stuffed teddy bear with shaggy brown hair—looking like those old Teddy Ruxpin toys—sat on a shelf all by himself. In the weapons section.

I stared into Teddy Ruxpin's big plastic eyes, with a wary frown. I slowly scanned it, stepping laterally to make sure the eyes didn't follow me or anything else similarly creepy. Nothing happened. I lunged at it aggressively, wondering if it would counterpunch me in the testicles or hit me with the People's Elbow.

Teddy Ruxpin remained inert, daring me with his cute blue eyes and happy smile. Why was he in the weapons section? I would have thought he had been misplaced, but he had a placard with a crescent moon on it. "Silly old bear," I muttered.

A forklift was parked between me and the next area of weapons, so I scooped up Teddy Ruxpin with a nervous laugh, and made my way around the obstacle, yawning...

I BLINKED BLEARILY, wondering why I suddenly felt so sleepy. I frowned to discover that I was sitting in the seat of the forklift I had meant to bypass. The Teddy Ruxpin bear was laying on the concrete floor, smiling savagely at me, his blue eyes looking demonic in the dim blue lighting.

I flinched instinctively, but I couldn't halt the massive yawn that threatened to dislocate my jaw. Teddy watched me like a predator watching prey. "Creepy ass bear," I mumbled, rubbing at my eyes. Why was I so tired, and when had I climbed onto the forklift?

My eyes settled on Teddy Ruxpin, and I noticed the placard had also fallen out of my hand. All I could make out was the crescent moon—

I stiffened, my eyes shooting wide as I immediately snapped out of my daze, panting.

"Motherfucker," I whispered, violently slapping my cheeks in an attempt to wake up as I glared down at the stuffed animal. "Talk about lazy parenting," I muttered, wondering who the hell had approved the idea to make a Teddy Ruxpin with the power to knock out his owner kid.

"Roofie Ruxpin, more like," I growled, stumbling out of the forklift.

Carl came rushing around the corner and jumped in fright to see me climbing out of the forklift. "There you are!" he hissed, changing course to sprint my way. He looked panicked. "We need to *go!*"

My sphincter tensed at the tone of his voice. "Why? What happened—"

The lights in the room suddenly clicked on, almost blinding me. I cursed, dropping to the ground and hiding behind the shelves as I squinted to protect my vision. Voices suddenly filled the room as the security door opened and...a *lot* of fucking people walked into the Vault.

"I couldn't find you," Carl hissed, crouching down beside me, using the only row between us and our visitors to hide. Luckily, it contained the large machine devices, so we were safely out of view. "Where were you?"

I blinked at him, peering through the shelves to see about thirty goddamned people walking in through the main door. Luckily, none of them were guards.

Unluckily, they were worse. "Employees," I hissed, staring at their white lab coats.

"*Wizard* employees," Carl corrected in a grim whisper.

I nodded. "Shit," I breathed. "This is bad. So fucking bad. Do you think we can sneak past them?" I asked. The wizard technicians were now filing into the breakroom, speaking in hushed but animated tones. Several couches and chairs, along with a few large tables and a small kitchenette, filled the glass-walled breakroom.

One woman was holding a plate with both hands, and the rest were all gathered around her. "What are they even doing here in the middle of the night?"

Carl frowned at me. "We've been here for *hours*. I thought they had caught you!"

I blinked at him, utterly baffled. Just over Carl's shoulders, I spotted Roofie Ruxpin. He was silently laughing at me, grinning with demonic glee. "You," I hissed to my arch nemesis. Roofie Ruxpin had knocked me the fuck out, putting me in a coma. I must have dreamily crawled up onto the forklift, searching for a nice place to nap. Carl was obviously shit at hide-and-seek, and had somehow overlooked me.

I remembered snapping out of my sleep to find the bear on the ground. Dropping him must have woken me up. Carl had followed my attention and was frowning down at the teddy bear beside him. He began reaching for it and I slapped his shoulder. "Don't. That thing is dangerous," I warned.

His frown turned to a scowl. "It looks cute. I want to touch it." He stubbornly reached back out for it, ignoring my warning. I slapped at his arm and he bumped into the forklift with a grunt. Then, surprising the hell out of me, he shoved me back, lunging for the deadly bear.

Roofie Ruxpin laughed and laughed and laughed, watching the world burn in his wake.

I grabbed Carl's ankle and knocked him on his ass. Within seconds, two grown ass men were in the middle of a slapping contest, wrestling over Roofie Ruxpin's friendship.

"Carl! Stop!" I demanded in an adamant hiss.

"No! I want it!" he snarled back.

"It will knock you out!" I argued, gripping him in a choke hold as he scrambled to grab the cursed bear. I knew I couldn't hold out for long before he overpowered me or we drew attention. "I touched him and passed out. That's why you couldn't find me."

Carl froze, jerking his hand away as if burned, which sent us both crashing into the shelf behind us. I shoved him off as I heard something rattle on the shelf above me.

Of course, it was something loud and metallic, seeming to echo in the cavernous warehouse. Carl's eyes widened as he looked up towards the sound. Then he lunged forward to catch it.

He missed, and the item crashed to the ground nearby.

The warehouse instantly went silent and the lights blinked out, plunging us back into darkness. I cursed, jumping to my feet and peering towards the breakroom, ready for the fight of my life.

The Man against the working man—his employees.

22

I continued staring towards the breakroom, wondering how they planned to attack. My shoulders slowly relaxed as I saw that no one was coming for us. The wizards still in the breakroom, huddled around the woman with the plate. Except it was now on fire and her followers...well, they followed her out as if in some dark, nefarious ritual. Maybe she held was some kind of divination device to find the source of the sound.

Or they were offering a sacrifice to Roofie Ruxpin.

To finally bring him back to life after thousands of years so he could lay waste to creation—

I checked over my shoulder to find that the bear remained inert, and that my imagination was getting the best of me.

Still, I kept him in my peripheral vision as I turned back to the gaggle of wizards. Maybe they were pooling their magic for one ultimate finishing move. Since I didn't have access to my magic, I couldn't sense if they were holding theirs or not. A slow smile crept across my face as I realized that they weren't looking at us. Had they not heard the commotion? They were still a problem, but at least we still had the element of surprise on our side.

Carl shifted beside me. "What do we do? The only way past that many wizards is to kill some of them." He glanced down at Roofie Ruxpin. "Are there more of those? We could throw them at the wizards."

I shook my head. His shelf had been empty—for good fucking reason, apparently. What the hell else had I inadvertently grabbed that might incapacitate me? "The Vault isn't for mass production," I whispered, "it's experimental. They usually only make one or two of each item."

The horde of wizards were slowly approaching the entrance, whispering conspiratorially. Maybe it was some kind of protective fire magic and they were simply evacuating before sending in security. Attacking them might just get us killed.

At least they weren't heading our way. My eyes settled on two strangely out of place items on the shelf above the machinery. Two eyepatches made of a rough metallic ore. I glanced down at the placard and saw an emoji of an eyeball with a red line bisecting it. I grabbed the pair and shoved the placard into my satchel. "Put this on," I whispered to Carl, hoping I was fluent in emoji and that it wouldn't stab out his eye or something.

He snapped it on so that the patch hung over the top of his forehead and he stared at me.

"No. Put the patch over your *eye*, Carl," I muttered, reaching out to shift it into place for him. I accidentally released it when he moved, and the stone patch thwacked him in the eye. He cursed and immediately vanished. I gasped. "Carl!" I hissed. "I'm so sorry!"

"What?" his voice whispered, sounding terrified. He suddenly reappeared in the same exact spot, having shifted the eyepatch to his forehead again.

I stared incredulously. "You vanished!" I hurriedly snapped the other eyepatch over my head.

Carl hissed, his tongue flicking out to taste the air for me or something. He cocked his head warily, obviously not sensing me. Was that because of the eyepatch or his Titan Thorns? I watched him put his back into place, and his form suddenly shifted to a hazy silhouette, like he was made of glass. He hissed again, probably seeing me as a glass silhouette as well. "I can see you now," he whispered.

I grinned excitedly, slapping him on the shoulder. "We're invisible! Maybe we can walk right out of here! Only we can see each other."

He nodded excitedly, flicking out his glass tongue. The center of his eyepatch seemed to shine like a polished mirror under my current vision, even though it had been rough stone before we'd put it on. I frowned, wondering why that sparked something in my mind. Moments later, it hit me. "It's a dragon scale, not an eyepatch!"

Carl grinned delightedly. Regardless, there was no reason to tempt fate and stay any longer. We needed to get out.

Thanks to Carl's claws, part of my shirt had been ripped during our wrestling session. I tore off a large strip and wrapped it around my hand. Then I cautiously reached for Roofie Ruxpin.

I didn't black out, so I let out a sigh of relief. I waved the bear at Carl. "Non-lethal defense if we run into guards. But we might be able to walk right past everyone."

He nodded excitedly and followed me as I slipped from our hiding spot and out into the center aisle. The gathering of wizards had silently congregated before the entrance, their backs facing us. Whatever hellish ritual they were up to, I wanted no part of it. Maybe it was a cabal of traitorous Academy wizards spying on my company, and I'd caught them in the act. I could actually do some good as a CEO later when I told Othello about it.

I took us back towards the wall with the door, keeping our distance from the group so we could flee if they saw through our eyepatch disguises. I held the bear out before me, glad to see that it was also similarly invisible, looking like glass.

I felt like I was dripping with sweat as we finally came into their peripheral vision. If they were going to spot us, this would be it. They remained unaware, and I let out a soft breath I hadn't known I'd been holding. What the hell were they doing all huddled up in the dark around the woman with the fiery plate like psychopaths? She was buried within the huddle, so I couldn't make out anything specific, and I didn't care to get close enough to figure it out.

We crept along the wall, making our way towards the door. Not one of them looked at us, even though it felt like we were in plain sight. Most of them were staring at the door expectantly.

We came to a nervous halt about five feet from the large door. Thankfully, I knew it opened inwards, so we would be able to slip out if any conspiratorial stragglers slipped in. I couldn't very well walk up to the door and open it—not with all of them staring at it.

So, we waited. They waited.

Roofie Ruxpin silently laughed his mad cackle.

The group shifted as if someone had thrown a pebble into their midst, and I finally got a clear look at the fire on the plate. I blinked rapidly, my brain short-circuiting for a moment.

The door opened and the Reds—shifter dragons—backed into the room, only a few feet away from us. I could have taken a step forward and touched them. They were giggling excitedly as they tugged a familiar, tall, blonde-haired man behind them. He had a blindfold around his head and he wore a paper crown. He also wore a gaudy sash crossing his body from shoulder to hip.

Shit. Shit. Shit. I suddenly realized why the dragon scale eyepatch had looked familiar. I only knew one dragon who could make himself invisible. And, out of all the people who could have walked through *this* door on *this* day—

"Happy Birthday to you," the crowd of wizards belted out in a startlingly loud, mismatched chorus. The Reds tore off the man's blindfold, joining in on the song. "Happy Birthday to you! Happy Birthday, dear Yahn. Happy Birthday to you!"

"The best boss ever!" Someone else crowed, and the crowd burst out laughing and clapping, blowing party horns and throwing confetti at him. Boss? When the hell had that happened. I tensed in alarm, fearing that some of the confetti may have hit us and revealed our ruse. Thankfully, I appeared devoid of party favors.

Yahn was a glass shifter dragon, and could camouflage himself to nigh invisibility. And we were apparently wearing his own scales as eyepatches. Any other time, I would have applauded his endeavor to weaponize his scales. But not today.

Because if he sensed us, I would have to crash this birthday party with fire.

Yahn beamed from ear-to-ear, shaking his head in good cheer. The Reds planted wet kisses on his cheeks as he faced the crowd, laughing. Luckily, one of the Reds had kicked the door stop on her way in, so we weren't trapped at the birthday party—which I'd always felt was a death sentence, even under normal circumstances.

I held my breath and carefully shuffled past him—only five feet away

—paranoid that I would make a single sound to draw his attention. Carl followed me, holding his tail in one hand so it didn't bump into anyone. Luckily, the cheers and celebration drowned out our movements.

I reached the doorframe, walking backwards to keep an eye on Carl and Yahn.

The crowd of wizards were shouting for Yahn to blow out his candles and make a wish, and the Reds were smiling happily, nodding along delightedly. All in all, a happy moment.

But Yahn was sniffing at the air with a slight frown. Because dragons had good sniffers. Especially when he smelled his own scales sneaking past him.

Carl stepped up beside me right as Yahn spoke in a suddenly suspicious tone. "What is that smell?" I prepared for a wall of flame and claws and birthday cheer to destroy us as we darted out the door, scrambling backwards. The moment we crossed the threshold, sirens and alarms crashed over Grimm Tech.

Shit. The experimental weapons I'd borrowed must have been tied to the ward, setting off an alarm. I shoved my free hand into my pocket and grabbed our Tiny Ball to Niflheim right as Yahn spun and leapt after us with horrifying agility. "You are mine!" he roared. The door slammed closed as a security measure, right as he slipped past it, his long glass claws aimed straight for my face.

I frantically tossed Roofie Ruxpin at him, and shouted, "Happy Birthday!" While simultaneously lobbing the Tiny Ball a few feet behind me. Unfortunately, Yahn had too much momentum to simply catch the dreadbear, pass out, and drop to the floor. He reflexively wrapped his glass claws around the demonic plushie in midair with a perplexed frown on his face to hear his attacker's parting birthday greetings. Then his eyes slammed shut.

One one-hundredth of a second later, he barreled into me hard enough to knock the breath from my lungs as I scrambled backwards for our escape. His unconscious bulk hammered me into Carl, and sent us all crashing though the Gateway to Niflheim.

I landed atop Carl and bounced off him onto the misty ground. Except I hit a rotten log, snapping it in half with my spine. The Gateway winked shut and silence surrounded us. I lay there for a few seconds, panting wildly, watching the mist dance around me like living tendrils. Then I scrambled to my feet to find Yahn curled up into a fetal position around Roofie Ruxpin.

Carl stared at me in horror, barely visible through the ridiculously thick fog. Much thicker than the last time I had been here. Carl seemed made of the vapor himself since we still wore our eyepatches.

"Fuck," I agreed.

He shook his head adamantly, holding a long claw to his lips. Then his gaze slowly rose above my head...

And kept right on going—higher, and higher, and higher. I felt the hair on the back of my neck stand on end as a growl as loud as a Diesel engine suddenly made my entire ribcage rattle.

"Looks like we're having dragon and eggs for breakfast, Father," a giant growled from behind me, his breath knocking me forward a half-step.

23

I spun towards the threat only to find a colossal wall of mist towering over me, concealing the giant. Crooked trees pierced the darkness here and there, hiding the full tree so that it made the mist look like it was growing gnarled, spooky branches.

Two glowing eyes glared from just within the mist—at least twenty feet overhead. I slowly side-stepped, keeping those eyes in view as I reached into my satchel. The eyes remained fixed on where Yahn lay sleeping, oblivious to the birthday gift I'd given him—certain death. The giant hadn't sensed us—only Yahn.

My hand wrapped around a wooden shaft. I whipped Gungnir out of the satchel and everything suddenly changed.

The giant snarled viciously, even as it leapt back in a hasty retreat. The glowing eyes stared directly at me, suddenly able to sense me now that I held Odin's spear. The one everyone—including Odin—thought missing. I released my hold on the weapon, not wanting him to attack my general location since he hadn't sensed me until I touched it. Carl scooped up the sleeping Yahn and I urged him to get the fuck away from our last known location.

Thankfully, the moment Yahn touched Carl, he also vanished. Just like Roofie Ruxpin had.

Moments later, the fog turned into an inferno of fire. I jumped back in alarm, only to realize that the fog wasn't actually aflame, but that something beyond or within the fog was on fire and the mist had emphasized its size, reflecting the light throughout the mist.

"Fuck off or die!" a new voice boomed through the mist.

I froze, cocking my head. "Loki?" I shouted. "Fenrir? It's me, Nate Temple! What the fuck are you two doing here?" I demanded, realizing why the eyes had been so high up in the mist. Fenrir was a giant.

Literally. A Jotunn. No wonder he'd sensed Gungnir. It was the weapon prophesied to kill him. Utter silence answered me, as if I'd asked them a difficult trivia question. I heard Loki muttering to Fenrir, demanding answers.

"What did you do when we first met?" Loki demanded, sounding uneasy. "Answer wrong, and one thousand axes will fly at your face!" True to his word, roughly a thousand glinting reflections abruptly formed a wall of death within the fog, aimed at the spot where Fenrir had last seen Yahn and the general area where he had sensed me holding Gungnir.

Carl had hefted Yahn into a fireman's carry and was sidestepping out of harm's way, now that we had long distance projectiles to contend with. I silently did the same, catching up to them. The axes remained aimed at the same spot, not sensing our movement.

Taking a risk, I stepped into the fog, hoping to flank the inhabitants of Niflheim in case it was not Loki and Fenrir after all. Or in case I got the answer to his question wrong. Because it was a damned vague verification question.

Despite how all-encompassing the mist had seemed, five steps into the fog, it was suddenly clear. Well, mist hung low to the ground, but nothing I couldn't see through with ease. I motioned Carl to keep back.

Loki stood before the fog, not seeming to notice me. This eyepatch was incredible. He wore a flannel robe and clutched a mug of steaming coffee that I could smell from across the clearing. The mug said *Real Unicorns Hate Rainbows* on the front with an image of a black unicorn obliterating a rainbow. I'd lost a bet to Grimm, and that had been the price to pay. That, and I'd promised to use it every day.

Odin must have stolen it from Chateau Falco, because that was my favorite mug and I thought I'd lost it. The thieving bastard. Loki looked ridiculous. His hair was tousled in wild disarray and he looked gaunt and exhausted. Almost sickly, as a matter of fact.

Fenrir looked leaner than I'd last seen him, but he was still fucking huge. And he still had that giant collar around his neck—the one we hadn't been able to remove when we'd broken him out of the manacles around his paws. Well, when Calvin and Makayla had broken him free, technically speaking. Did that mean they were here, too? With Gunnar and Ashley? Alucard? Was the Horseman of War hiding out here in Niflheim as well? Damn it. So much for a discreet hiding place. If they saw me here, Zeus might kill them all on reflex.

"Answer or die," Loki bellowed. "I have an army of Viking spirits poised to murder you," Loki shouted. His voice grew louder the moment it hit the fog—the mist acting as a megaphone—making his threat echo like thunder. He was using the fog like the goddamned Wizard of Oz used his curtain.

He didn't have pants on beneath his robe, and he was wearing dirty fluffy slippers. He barely looked like he could take a punch at the moment. I almost burst out laughing at the ridiculous lie. Then again, he had Fenrir for muscle. The wolf was an army, of sorts.

I hesitated to answer his question. When I'd first met him, we'd wrestled over Gungnir in the Armory—the room where Freya had been preparing to deliver Ashley's babies. But we'd immediately been teleported to Fae. Camelot to be precise.

I must have considered my answer too long.

"Nice try, deceiver! DIE!" Loki screamed. I heard the sudden eruption of projectiles hitting the ground, trees, and foliage back where we had been standing. Loki sagged at the expenditure of magic, but Fenrir lowered his muzzle in time to catch his father. Niflheim drained them of their power. Why the hell would they be here? It was killing them.

"I kicked you in the nuts, you fucking psychopath!" I shouted.

Fenrir whirled and Loki dropped his coffee as he spun to stare in my general direction—which was nowhere near the killing field he'd set up. My favorite mug shattered and Fenrir snarled a warning, hunkering his head low to protect his throat. Their eyes darted back and forth suspiciously, unable to see me.

I peeled off my eyepatch and held up my hands. "It's me, you lunatics. Nate."

Fenrir didn't look convinced. Loki stepped closer, shielding his eyes as if sunlight was an issue here. It wasn't. The realm of Niflheim was eternally gloomy and overcast. "Why are you so filthy?" he asked. "You don't look right."

I grunted. "I don't feel right either, to be fair. And you're not looking all that fancy, either."

He narrowed his eyes, muttering under his breath. Fenrir warily trotted over, sniffing the air.

"I've got Carl and a dragon with me, so don't eat them," I said, so as not to surprise them.

Fenrir came to a stop before me, sniffed a few more times, and then sneezed, blasting me with about a million gallons of wolf snot.

"Oh, for fuck's sake!" I snapped, wiping the goop from my face. "It's in my mouth," I gagged, spitting furiously.

Fenrir abruptly play bowed and his tongue lolled from his mouth. "It really *is* you," he whined, speaking out loud. He had also spoken to me in my mind before. His tail swished back and forth behind him, almost clotheslining his father, Loki. "But you look wrong."

I let out a sigh of relief and shook off more of his snot before giving it up as a lost cause. I folded my arms, hoping they didn't get stuck together. "Come on out, Carl. They won't kill us."

Carl and Yahn walked into view—mine, anyway—and the Elder set Yahn down on the ground. The moment his claws released Yahn, he seemed to appear out of thin air to Fenrir and Loki. Carl tugged off his eyepatch and waved, materializing out of thin air as well.

Fenrir and Loki did not look convinced. "Is this some kind of a joke?" Loki asked warily.

Fenrir cocked his head. "He's wearing that stupid pink coat, but that's not Carl."

I blinked, my shoulders tensing at their tone. "Of course it's Carl. How many other Elders have you met?"

Loki folded his arms. "That's a golden fucking dragon or an old man. Not a Carl."

I blinked, frowning at the bizarre statement. Then a sneaking suspicion hit me. They'd said I looked wrong as well. "What do I look like?"

Fenrir was looking from Carl to me, obviously certain it was me after he'd sensed me holding Gungnir, but he still looking perplexed by my apparent appearance. Now that I thought about it, Yahn hadn't immediately recognized us either, but that had been because we were invisible, right?

Fenrir looked at me. "You don't smell or look like Nate, but I sensed Gungnir once you touched it, and you have the satchel. Nate wouldn't let anyone have that satchel, and it would be worthless to them anyway, so I believe you. But you look like a frail, scared, homely man, not the godkiller who recently saved me."

Loki nodded. "I recognize your voice, but only barely. Like a trick of sound. He looks like a roguishly handsome older man, not an Elder. But he has golden dragon claws." He glanced at Fenrir and a tired smile split his cheeks. "Well, slap my frosty ass and call me Hilde! If Fenrir says it's you, I'll buy it."

I smiled crookedly at his strange phrase. "Right." But I was very troubled by their revelation. Why did we look wrong? "What's up with the new digs...Hilde?"

Loki pursed his lips, his smile slipping. "Needed somewhere to sleep where gods wouldn't bother us. I've grown attached to the place." He eyed me and then Carl thoughtfully. "You?"

"Same. Refugee status. Apparently, under an illusion that I'm just now hearing about."

I glanced at Carl, frowning. He shrugged. "You look like Nate to me." I nodded my agreement—Carl looked like Carl to me. Loki's words abruptly registered as I studied Carl's claws. Loki had said *golden* claws, and I'd only ever met one golden dragon.

Was he saying Carl looked like Alaric Slate? Then...who did I look like?

"I need a mirror," I said queasily.

Loki flung up a hand, and a sliver of reflective water appeared before us, almost as good as a mirror. "Make do," he rasped tiredly, his hand shaking at such a simple effort. "We don't have the luxury of mirrors here, my lord."

I stepped up to it and gasped, wiping away the mud and wolf snot covering my face.

"Peter?" I whispered, tugging at my cheeks in horror. I had indirectly killed Peter years ago when he'd partnered up with...

Carl stepped up beside me, but his reflection showed another blast from my past. Alaric Slate. The dragon father who had tried to kill Raego to become the Obsidian Son.

Peter and Alaric were back in town.

Two men who every one of my friends would kill on sight.

Shit.

24

Carl frowned, poking at his face and watching the older man's reflection repeat the gesture with golden dragon claws. "I killed this meat sack in Hell," he murmured uneasily.

I nodded, turning to Loki. He released the spell and studied us. "I can't sense any illusion, but I'm practically tapped after that axe thing." He narrowed his eyes at me. "Thanks for that, asshole. Now the mutt is our only protection, and he's losing energy fast. He wasn't quite up to strength to begin with after his imprisonment."

I shook my head, wondering what the hell we were going to do now. "Zeus kidnapped us. Imprisoned us. We broke free, but he locked these manacles on us. Titan Thorns, he called them, and they block our powers. Apparently, they must also disguise me. But why Peter and Alaric?" I asked, more to myself.

"Are you telling me that you might have led the Olympians here?" Loki rasped, sounding horrified.

I shook my head firmly. "No. They can't track us, apparently." I hesitated. "Or so I was told."

Fenrir chuffed uneasily, sniffing at the air beyond us and scanning the horizon above the mist. "We are alone."

"Zeus—the guy who kidnapped you—told you that he couldn't track you, and you believed him?" Loki asked, sounding as if he wanted to throttle me.

I shook my head. "No. Aphrodite did when she broke us out. Zeus is hunting her, too."

At least I hoped so. Unless this was all a ruse. But I didn't voice that fear. They looked panicked enough already. Little did they know, I hadn't even gotten started yet.

Loki let out a nervous sigh, only somewhat relieved. "If he had you imprisoned, why disguise your appearance?" he asked, scratching at his stubble.

"There is a lot more to the story. Do you have more coffee? When Yahn wakes up, he's going to be pretty fucking confused. Restraints would be awesome. If he sees that Peter and Alaric abducted him, he's going to lose his shit."

"Then why the hell did you bring him here?" Loki asked, motioning for us to follow him to the small hut in the distance. It was no longer concealed by Freya's vines and seiðr magic.

"I broke into my company's vault to steal some weapons since I can't touch my magic. He caught us before we could escape." I paused, wincing internally. "It's his birthday."

Loki burst out laughing. "You're shitting me."

I shook my head. "Nope. They had a cake and everything. They had just finished singing when we accidentally abducted him." I sighed, raking my fingers through my hair. "He didn't even get to blow out the candles and make a wish."

"And the teddy bear?" Loki asked, not bothering to hide his amusement.

"Don't fuck with the dreadbear. Roofie Ruxpin fucks back."

He glanced back at my somber tone and his smile faltered. He eyed Yahn, who was still utterly unconscious despite the loud growling, fire, swarm of axes, and being dragged around like a rag doll. He frowned thoughtfully, but didn't comment.

"We're going to need more coffee. And chains," he finally said.

I nodded. "Sounds like the perfect morning. Did you say you had eggs?"

"I lied," Fenrir growled. "I wouldn't trust any eggs you find around here. They also fuck back. Welcome to Niflheim."

Fenrir was too large to go inside the hut, so Loki led us towards a circle of stumps around a bonfire out front. Loki had slipped into the hut to emerge a few minutes later with three steaming mugs of instant coffee and a plastic bottle of vodka that was half empty. I shuddered when he offered it to me, taking a hard pass. He'd shrugged, filling up half of his mug with the blinding hangover juice. Then he took a healthy swig straight from the bottle, swishing it around like mouthwash. He even gargled it. Surprisingly, even Carl had looked eager to drink the caffeine, a testament to our exhaustion. That, or he feared plastic bottled vodka as much as me.

I decided to let Yahn sleep a little longer. I wasn't ready to confront him yet. How would I explain the situation? He looked so peaceful clutching Roofie Ruxpin, and I knew he would instinctively freak out to wake up and see that two dead men—Peter and Alaric—had abducted him. And that wasn't even taking Loki and Fenrir's presence into account. I had even considered using a Tiny Ball to send him back home, none-the-wiser, but I wasn't sure how wise that would be for me. If I released him, and he'd actually recognized Peter and Alaric at Grimm Tech, he would alert everyone and there would be a manhunt for us on top of everything else. The smartest option seemed to be keeping him prisoner—as ironic as that was.

So, Carl dozed sitting up, jerking awake every few minutes to check that Yahn hadn't woken. Fenrir kept a cautious eye on the blond shifter dragon as well. I'd caught them up to speed on my current situation with the Olympians—deciding not to bring up the conversation I'd seen between Freya and Kára. If Loki thought his mother or father were involved, he would find a way to meddle, and I had enough gods to deal with. Then they told me of their own adventures.

Apparently, Loki and Fenrir had broken off from my other friends, not wanting to risk their lives when all of Asgard came a' hunting for Fenrir's hide. Which was oddly considerate for Loki, generally speaking. I was betting Fenrir had suggested—and enforced—that plan, concerned about Gunnar's kids after they'd freed him from his chains. He still had his giant collar, but at least he was no longer locked up in the middle of nowhere.

They still didn't know who had locked him up, exactly, but Loki grew

passionate when he went off on a tangent about his prime suspects—
which was pretty much everyone, ever. Fenrir had rolled his eyes, shooting
me an amused glance. I didn't have the time to worry about the Norse
pantheon, but I was relieved to hear that Gunnar and Alucard weren't
about to walk around the corner with marshmallows.

I needed to keep my distance from them to keep them safe.

Loki and Fenrir had been on the run ever since their prison break,
much like us, now. They'd grown oddly guarded upon mentioning a cave
they'd recently occupied, quickly dropping the subject after saying that it
was now compromised, forcing them to come to the hut where we had
found them. Where Loki had been imprisoned for hundreds of years.

Obviously, he hadn't come here for the nostalgia.

"Whoever did your illusion has skill," Loki said, breaking the
thoughtful silence. "Any ideas which Olympian is behind it?"

I shook my head. "My money is on Hermes. He put a glamour on Zeus
to make him look like me. Whatever he's doing with my face won't be
good."

Loki pursed his lips. "Well, that's a splendid frame job. No wonder I
couldn't see through your glamour. Hermes is exceedingly good at them,"
he said begrudgingly. "And if *we* can't see through it, *no one* can."

Carl shot me a concerned look and I shrugged. I'd figured as much.
During my time in Zeus' slammer, no one had alluded to me not looking
like myself. Had it only happened once I stepped through Aphrodite's
Gateway? Had...she been the one to make us look like this?

And was that as protection so I didn't draw attention to my actions, or
was it a set up?

I could see it both ways.

Making me look different would prevent me from reaching out to my
allies—consequentially saving their lives from Zeus. But it also prevented
me from reaching out to my allies, leaving me alone to face my
problems.

I felt Fenrir's snot drying and hardening on my everywhere and
grimaced. "Is there some kind of shower around here?" I growled.

Loki scoffed, gesturing at himself. "Does this look like the Four
Seasons?" Fenrir growled disapprovingly and Loki let out an annoyed
breath. "Sorry. I've been on edge lately. There is a small pond to the West

of us." He frowned to himself, then looked over at me. "You don't have any heart conditions, right?"

"No..." I said, guardedly.

"Good. Because I think the water is zero degrees. Something about Niflheim prevents it from freezing, though. Isn't it grand?" he said, dryly. "Feels like instant castration without anesthesia, but the numbness hits about three seconds after the imagined surgery, so it's more like mild pain reliever. A Niflprofen."

I shuddered, debating how badly I wanted to wash off the accumulated mud and snot and blood. "Is it poisonous to mortals, like everything else here?" I asked, unable to wrap my head around the temperature.

"You ain't a mortal, godkiller," Loki said. "And it's no more poisonous than the rest of this place. I mean, if we're being honest here, the dragon would be dead already if Odin and Freya hadn't warded this area," he said, jerking his chin at Yahn.

I slowly lifted my head. "What?"

Loki frowned at me. "The mist kills mortals, idiot."

Fenrir wagged his tail excitedly, because he was a psycho.

I slowly turned to stare at Yahn, feeling sick to my stomach. I hadn't even thought of that. Niflheim was deadly to mortals. I'd almost killed the world's happiest dragon...on his birthday.

"Are the Sensates still here?" I asked, hoping to change the subject from my obvious oversight. I stared into the fire, rubbing my hands together for warmth. Niflheim was ridiculously cold, and a dip in the pond would only make it worse. Silence answered me, so I glanced up. Loki had a constipated look on his face, and his mouth was hanging open. "That's why you came here, right? To get some Sensates so you couldn't be tracked? That's one reason we came."

Loki's mouth clicked shut. "Damn. I hadn't even thought of that."

Fenrir glared at him. "You've got to be *shitting* me. We've been running for days, and now you're telling me that we're thirty feet away from a stash of Sensates that could have hidden us?" he growled.

Loki narrowed his eyes, frustrated. "I haven't been thinking clearly, son. I've never had to be ruthlessly calculating and paternally concerned at the same time. And those Sensates kept me prisoner for a good long while. My skin crawls even being here."

Fenrir's ears wilted guiltily. Loki glanced over in my direction, looking embarrassed. "Thanks for the hot tip," he murmured, averting his eyes. "I'll...uh, go get some."

I nodded. "Mind grabbing a dozen for me?"

He nodded stiffly, climbing to his feet. "Sure."

"Then I'll go take a bath." I glanced at Yahn, wondering how he would react upon waking. I couldn't risk letting him sleep too long in case there were side effects from Roofie Ruxpin that I wasn't aware of, but he should be safe for a short while longer. "A clean stranger is better than a filthy stranger."

Loki chuckled weakly. "That all depends on what you're into, and how you define *filthy*."

I rolled my eyes, not having the energy for...filthy jokes. I climbed to my feet, gathering my resolve for the arctic bath. "Let Yahn sleep until I get back." I didn't even ask for a towel as I made my way to the pond, following Loki's directions.

This place wasn't the Four Seasons, after all.

25

It had taken me a while to find the pond after my wandering thoughts —and the wandering mist—had briefly led me off the worn path. I'd hesitated upon finding a small body of water that looked more like a flooded puddle. I'd seen ripples under the water and had leapt back in alarm. The mist had also been much thicker there, so I'd continued on. Anyway, Loki had described a pond, not an ankle washer with Niflheim snakes.

A few minutes later, I found a large pond with hardly any mist and no suspicious ripples. Instead, the pond looked eerily calm. Probably because it was so fucking cold. It was definitely big enough for Fenrir, unlike the first one I'd discovered.

Knowing that wading into the frigid water would only permit me to wimp out, I'd taken a flying leap into the deepest looking area, keeping my feet down in case it was shallower than it looked. Midair, I changed my mind about wanting a bath, panicking, but it was too late.

I sunk entirely underwater and did not touch the bottom. The cold latched onto me like tentacles and I screamed out all the air in my lungs as my scalp exploded with pins and needles and unseen hammers pounded at my fingertips and toes. I was certain that my ears had simply snapped off and that my eyeballs had frozen. My Titan Thorns flared with brilliant, crimson light, seeming to fight back the oppressive darkness of the all-consuming cold. I frantically thrashed for the surface, experiencing a sudden existential crisis as every little fear that had ever entered my mind was reborn like a crackling explosion of icy phoenixes.

Why had Pan had to die?

How the hell was the pond so deep?

Who was Kára, really?

Where was the goddamned surface?

Why had Indie betrayed me?

How could water be colder than ice?

Why did Othello love Death?

Had I already frozen to death?

Why was Callie so cruel—

My head broke water and I almost forgot how to suck in air. Before my head plunged back under, my reflexes kicked in and I inhaled what felt like one thousand razor-sharp icicles. My heart thumped against my chest, as noticeable as if someone was thumping on the outside. And it was erratic and stumbling, slowing and speeding in panic.

My mind was literally panicking and short-circuiting. I broke the surface again, my arms and legs feeling like lead-weighted foreign objects beyond my control. I moved in stiff jerks and my bones ached as if they were being crushed, on the verge of shattering.

My eyeballs felt like brittle glass and the air somehow hurt more than the thick, slushy water. Icicles formed on my eyelashes and hair, and the water on my cheeks and nose froze in the arctic air. My toes finally touched bottom—an icy sludge of thick, sharp mud—and I cried out in pain, feeling like I'd stepped on burning shrapnel. My toenails and fingernails throbbed, hit with unseen ball-peen hammers in a drumbeat more consistent than my pulse.

I stiffly rubbed my skin and hair and face as fast as possible while scrambling towards the shore, terrified of literally freezing solid if I didn't keep every part of my body moving in some manner. My thoughts lashed onto my time with Ares and Apollo, how I'd suffered their torture by embracing the pain, and the dreaded agony abated enough for me to think rationally for a second or two. I grabbed my pile of clothes and ran back to the hut, tripping and falling awkwardly as my skin both erupted with flame and froze into more icicles.

Thanks to my ability to embrace the pain—and now that I was out of the panic-inducing water—I was at least able to aim my halting forward progression in the direction of my only salvation.

Fire. The hut had fire. My Titan Thorns blazed with red light, burning away the mist, and I heard unseen creatures and beasts screaming in outrage as distant branches and trees snapped and cracked in their hasty retreat. I hadn't even known I'd had an audience.

I tripped again, rolling over a ledge and crashing into the valley with the hut. I heard wild shouts and furious barks, but all I cared about were the slithering tendrils of immolation calling me home with arms out like a worried mother. Fire—someone who loved me.

I shambled to my feet, ignoring the nails seeming to stab through every inch of flesh on my body, shivering hard enough for my neck to crack and pop as I pressed on towards the fiery oblivion. Burning alive was nothing compared to freezing to death.

I somehow made my way to the fire, the heat washing over me like acid rain. Icicles dropped from my hair, but I couldn't even blink my eyes—they were frozen open.

I lifted my foot to actually step into the fire, but two sets of hands grabbed me—I saw them, but couldn't feel them—preventing it.

I must have fought back against them, judging by their growls and hisses, but soon I just felt weak, like my body was sinking into the ground. They held me up and my mind slowly began to thaw as I stared longingly into the fire. Finally, I was able to blink, even though it felt like my eyelids had been ripped off. At least my eyes no longer burned.

Loki grunted. "It's not that bad, pussy."

My heart thundered in my chest as I stammered a response. "C-colder t-than you s-said. D-deeper t-too."

Silence answered me. "It's barely waist deep," Loki began and then he abruptly cut off. "Wait, which pond did you jump in?" he asked nervously.

I couldn't answer him. The manacles on my wrist felt like lead weights and I feared they would stick to my skin and rip it off.

"He went into the Deeps," Fenrir murmured, sounding stunned.

"D-deeps?" I managed, almost biting my tongue off at the attempt.

Loki tore off his own robe and wrapped it around me, followed by another from one of my handlers. The god of mischief rubbed my arms, his eyes wild with alarm. "Not even Thor would jump into the Deeps," he breathed. "It's instant death."

Fenrir whined sharply. "I won't even jump in there."

I wanted to scream at Loki or shove him into the fire, but the three sets of hands held me still. How many fucking ponds were there within walking distance, and why hadn't they warned me about the *only* lethal pond?

"Can that dragon breathe fire?" Loki asked nervously. "We might need to light Nate on fire. As a precaution. Only a little bit. I think he's literally dying. I hear ice in his lungs."

"We are *not* lighting Master Temple on fire," Carl warned from directly behind me.

"It really is Nate," a new voice breathed—my second handler—sounding stunned.

I almost stumbled into the fire to hear Yahn at my side. "T-toe...t-tah...l-lee," I croaked.

He grunted, wrapping me up in a tight hug. Yahn began to growl and I felt his body heat suddenly wash over me. I heard Loki and Carl curse and then the sounds of a lot of things falling over. Fenrir yelped and began barking with concussive blasts of air like blustery gusts.

I melted into that heat, feeling suddenly loopy with exhaustion. I smelled something burning but I didn't care very much as that heat thawed me from the inside out. After an indeterminable time, the sensation faded and Yahn gently held me at arms' length. "You okay?"

I nodded sleepily, opening my eyes. The ground around us was charred and smoking, and everyone else was at least ten feet away.

"That crazy fucker lit Nate on fire, Carl!" Loki shouted. "Who does that?"

Carl gave Loki a grim glare for tattling on the glass dragon when he'd suggested it first.

The front of the hut was smoldering and covered in white foam. Loki held a rusty, battered fire extinguisher. He saw that I was alive and let out a breath of relief. "I saved him."

Yahn muttered a curse. "You ran screaming like a frightened girl."

Loki narrowed his eyes. "Who sleeps with a teddy bear? Honestly?"

Fenrir chuffed, amused. Loki shifted his attention to me. "Nate! You crazy fucking maniac! I'm a damned frost giant and I wouldn't dip my *toe* in the Deeps," he said, shaking his head in awe. "You're mental." He turned back to Yahn. "And you almost burned our only shelter down to the ground. You're about as helpful as twat-thunder," he growled, shaking his fist.

Carl arched an eyebrow at the curse combo. Yahn studied Loki with a flat look and then finally turned back to me, ignoring Loki's ridiculous taunt. He searched my face curiously, and I remembered that I didn't look like myself.

"Happy birthday, Yahn," I said, my throat feeling raw. "It really is me. Greta's favorite."

He shook his head, wincing. "The Reds are going to kill me. I ruined their surprise."

I grunted. "Well, technically I ruined it. But you ruined mine, so we're both complicit."

He smiled crookedly. "Yeah, but I think I'm going to have to blame you. Where the hell have you been? Everyone's been freaking out. Something about you disappearing on a mountain in Colorado, but they won't share any details."

I sighed, wrapping the robe tighter around me and sitting down on a smoldering stump. It was covered in foam, so it was better than standing on my aching feet. My toes still throbbed despite feeling only partly frost-bitten, but none of them were black, so I was probably fine.

Thanks to Yahn lighting me on fire. Christ. The crazy bastard had really done it.

"How good are you at keeping secrets?" I asked him warily, realizing that he had to hear the whole truth if he was going to be any kind of asset in my plan. Whether he'd dropped the bear himself or been purposely woken, it was too late to send him back.

He studied me. "I'm not thinking I have much of a choice, but I don't share secrets."

"What if a god threatens to kill everyone you love?" I asked in a soft tone. "Can you still keep a secret?" I slowly turned to look at him. "What if

they threaten to kill the Reds right in front of you? What if this god actually *starts* to kill them right in front of you?"

Silence answered me. Loki let out a long whistle. "He's not wrong."

Yahn stared at me, looking sick to his stomach. "I...don't know," he
whispered.

I nodded, waving a hand for him to sit down. "That's the right answer
to an unfair question. Which is why you're now on Team Temple. I'm
sorry."

He frowned. "I'm not going back, am I?"

I shook my head. "Not unless you're willing to watch Zeus kill the Reds
in front of you and still keep a secret. And if you could do that, I'd probably
kill you on principle—right here."

Yahn looked over at Carl. The Elder nodded soberly. "He speaks the
truth."

"Why don't you start from the beginning," Yahn said, sitting down on
one of the logs. And, for the second time in an hour, I shared my story,
urging Loki to do the same since he'd been involved with my allies—Yahn's
friends.

With only Yahn asking questions this time, it didn't take long, but I
only gave him the highlights, not the in-depth discussion I'd had with Loki
and Fenrir.

26

Loki finally cleared his throat after I'd finished catching Yahn up on current events. "You don't want our help on this. We're already fugitives, so inviting us would only bring on my brethren, directly involving them with the Greeks. That would be a colossal mistake in an already colossally fucked situation—potentially world-ending if either side thinks we're helping you. The Norse, although hunting me, will never allow the Olympians to come after me. Likewise, Olympus will unite against the Norse in full-blown war, even if Zeus has been acting on his own up until now. In fact, I would bet he's *hoping* you rope the Norse into this so he has an *excuse* to rally his pantheon. A justification for war, and a way for him to consolidate power. All neatly wrapped up with an enlightening dick-measuring contest between Odin and Zeus." He leaned forward. "And you're the judge."

I grimaced, shaking my head. "I never intended to involve you," I admitted. "If I had known you were here, I never would have come to Niflheim." I tugged my robe tighter around my body, hating the frigid chill of Niflheim. I'd refused to put my filthy prison garb back on. I'd risked hypothermia to get clean, after all.

Yahn sighed. "Everyone is searching for you. Hermes made an appearance at Chateau Falco, claiming they would help find you. Although suspicious, they largely seem to have bought it."

"Who?" I asked. "Who bought it?"

"Your Horsemen. Callie dialed in on one of their phones. She was in the middle of some craziness in KC and couldn't afford to leave town."

I pursed my lips to hear that Callie hadn't even come down in the flesh to get an update on me. No matter the reason. I imagined Aphrodite smiling at me sadly and shook my head.

Fucking Hermes was doing exactly what Zeus had warned—turning my friends against me. "But they haven't seen Zeus—either as himself or as my doppelgänger, right? What about Apollo and Ares? Aphrodite?"

Yahn shook his head at the onslaught interrogation. "Just Hermes. He said he owed you a favor." I grunted. That could have been a lie or it could have been referring to the bet he'd made with me over the four coins. I hadn't mentioned those to anyone except Carl.

I knew Zeus' modus operandi with his own children and pantheon—mental abuse. Which meant that as soon as he learned of Aphrodite aiding my escape, he would employ those same tactics on me and my people.

I didn't have the resources to beat him on his treasure hunt. I knew what he wanted after that, though. The Armory and my Horsemen. The only way to beat him was to outmaneuver him. To out-Zeus...Zeus.

"What is the plan?" Yahn asked calmly.

I continued staring into the fire, hating myself for what I was about to say next. Finally, I looked up at him. Whatever he saw in my eyes made him flinch.

"We're going to extort the other Horsemen."

Fenrir looked up sharply, licking his lips. Yahn scooted back from the dreadwolf's lunging distance, eyeing him warily. Carl nodded his approval. "For shoes. And glory."

Yahn frowned at him, looking even more confused.

Loki leaned forward. "Pardon? It sounded like you just said you're going to betray those most loyal to you."

I nodded. "It's for their own good. You probably shouldn't hear the rest of the plan. It gets crazier, and you shouldn't be involved. I can't afford to drag the Aesir into this on top of everything else."

He leaned back on his stump, shaking his head. "Well, fuck me. This almost sounds worth it."

"No thanks," I said dryly. "What I will need is for everyone to give me some space for a few hours. I need privacy and complete focus, so don't bother me unless the world is ending. Deal?"

They stared at me, brimming with questions from my bombshell of a plan.

"Great. I'll be inside the hut." Loki had his mouth open, clutching a bag of Sensates in his lap. I pointed at them. "Oh, and give those to Yahn. He's going to make my team three sets of necklaces and bracelets in case these Titan Thorns actually are trackable. On that note, one of you should scout our perimeter until our new jewelry is finished. That'd be you, Clifford," I said, indicating Fenrir. "We don't want any surprises, now, do we?" Carl beamed smugly.

Fenrir watched me silently.

"I am?" Yahn asked about his given job, sounding shaken.

I nodded. "You apparently run the Vault. Show me you're worthy of the job or I'll hire someone else later." I nudged my satchel, flipping it open. The contents of my robbery spilled out on the ground. And a roll of duct tape. None of my personal items fell out, because it was a magical satchel, and only revealed the treasures I wanted revealed. "You might need that for the jewelry. When you're finished, I need you to go through the stuff I stole and let me know what's useful—especially if I managed to snag a godly hand grenade. That would be super."

Loki made a strangled sound, sputtering incoherently in a failed attempt to speak.

"Don't tell him if you find a godly hand grenade," I told Yahn. Then I turned to Loki. "Sorry to intrude. We'll be out of your hair once I'm finished. Niflheim is all yours."

Fenrir burst out laughing. "Now *that* is how you fucking strut!" he growled proudly. His eyes smoldered and he dipped his head at me respectfully. "You do exceedingly well, godkiller."

"I do as someone must," I muttered, waving a dismissive hand. I just didn't have the time or patience to make everyone feel better. The situation sucked. I was going to unsuck it.

"But I have a mutual interest in your cause," he growled, eyeing my satchel meaningfully.

I nodded. I'd been waiting for him to bring it up, hoping that he wouldn't. "Gungnir stays with me. Period. I have enough handicaps at the moment," I said, brandishing my Titan Thorns, "to risk giving up such a powerful weapon. However, I swear on my beating heart that I will not hand it over to anyone without consulting you, first. My word on it as a godkiller," I said, squaring my shoulders to face him directly. "Non-negotiable."

Fenrir grew utterly still, not even appearing to breathe. "Why not destroy it?"

"It is leverage—and not just against you, brother. One does not simply destroy leverage."

He narrowed his eyes, refusing to blink. I did the same. He finally reared his head back, regarding me pensively. "So be it. Your word or your heart. Break it, and I will collect."

I bowed my head. "Thank you for your trust, brother."

Surprisingly, he bowed his head as well. I kept the surprise from my face. "It's not just you whom I trust. It's those who choose to stand by your side. I am particularly fond of the pups."

I grinned sadly. Calvin And Makayla. Gunnar's pups had helped break him free. "Me, too."

"Keep them safe, and I see no reason for conflict between us."

And just like that, I wasn't sure if I'd been threatened or complimented. Probably both, but I agreed with his sentiments, so I didn't press my luck. I glanced at his collar. "I'll make sure that thing comes off soon, Fenrir. I'm currently in similar straits, so I can't offer much help," I admitted, tapping one of my Titan Thorns. I studied the runes on my manacles and then frowned at his. I approached him thoughtfully, leaving the others by the fire. The symbols weren't identical, but they weren't all that different either. He had lowered his head for me to get a better look at the massive stone collar around his throat, leaving me a few feet away from teeth as long as my spine. "Have you ever heard of the carnage?" I asked him. No one else was close enough to hear my question.

Fenrir stiffened. "Now where in the *hell* did you hear about that?" he replied in a whisper.

I shook my head absently. "A friend warned me about it. Said it might be going around, twisting up some of the godly thought processes," I said, choosing my words carefully. Loki was studying us with a thoughtful frown, curious as all hell what we were whispering about.

Fenrir stared at me. "That...could explain some things. But it's highly unlikely."

I cocked my head. "Why?"

Fenrir considered the question. "Well, carnage could mean multiple things. Some even say a gathering of Beasts is known as a carnage." He chuckled darkly, but I found nothing humorous about it. "A flock of seagulls, a carnage of Beasts. The point is, they're just...well, fairy tales for fairies, or myths for the mythical, and legends to the legendary." I nodded, pondering his explanation with deep thought. "The carnage is one of the boogeymen of our world. One of the monsters of our storybooks."

I met his eyes, not blinking. "And what the Regulars—the humans—take as fairy tales and myth, we know to be true..."

He hesitated. "True."

"So perhaps this carnage is very, very real. We're the Regulars in this echelon."

He nodded very slowly, looking troubled. "I will think on it. Catalyst," he added the last word, as if it were an afterthought—and a verification.

"I would appreciate it."

"I'll take sentry duty," Fenrir growled, loud enough for everyone to hear as he straightened to his full height. He turned, departing the hut in pensive silence, his paws crushing stones beneath his bulk much like my boot might snap a dried twig. Yahn and Carl had knelt down before my satchel, poring over the contents, not seeming aware of my conversation with Fenrir.

But Loki was burning holes in my back with his eyes.

I called out to Fenrir. "Someone told me that knowing and accepting my heart's greatest desire was the key to removing these," I said, tapping my Titan Thorns. "Unconditional love."

He paused but didn't look back. "Good luck with that," he grumbled.

Then he was walking away again. I wasn't sure if he was pulling an Eeyore and admitting that such a solution would never work for him, or if he was mocking the obvious fact that I was a lifelong bachelor. Either way, he was an asshole.

"Great talk," I muttered. I turned and made my way towards the hut, ignoring Loki's eyes.

It was time to tinker with a little astral projection and spy on my Horsemen. The longer I waited, the better chance Zeus would find leverage against them first, or use my face to deceive them into following his plans, banking on their trust.

"May the better man blackmail first," I growled, shouldering the door to the hut open.

27

I found a clear space on the floor of the hut—not trusting myself to use the bed and possibly fall asleep—and sat down with a tired sigh.

I wanted current information on my Horsemen—Gunnar, Callie, and Alucard—direct from the source. Interrogating Yahn on their current activities was all well and good, but he wasn't high enough on the food chain to know what they might *really* be doing. You wouldn't ask a soldier what his general's secret battle plan was, because whatever the grunt had been told probably wasn't entirely accurate. It might even be intentional misinformation.

With astral projection, I could look right over their shoulders. Big Brother was watching. Death's warning at Yggdrasil didn't deter me, because I was made of sterner stuff—blinding idiocy, a splash of arrogance, and a double dollop of testicular fortitude.

I couldn't confront them in person; I would be signing their death sentences if Zeus found out. Accidentally abducting Yahn was risky enough. My only hope was that he truly was low enough on the food chain that Zeus did not notice his disappearance—or saw no danger in it.

I took a deep breath and split my mind from my body with a mental scalpel.

My soul tore away from my body like an old scab, and I suddenly felt free for the first time in days. I stared down at my—Peter's—body for a moment, feeling the same uncomfortable twinge as when I had caught my reflection or when Zeus had turned into my doppelgänger.

I zipped out of the hut—straight through the walls—and let out a mad cackle. I spotted Fenrir and Loki sitting on a rock, scanning the horizon in companionable silence. I smiled. It was cute to see them out of the public eye. I sensed a stronger bond between them. They were healing from their centuries-long separation. I'd done a good thing freeing Fenrir.

Unless he and Odin succeeded in killing each other, of course. That would suck.

I wasn't entirely sure how I did it, but I was suddenly hovering over the pavilion where I had met Zeus and his broken offspring yesterday. I wanted to see the aftermath of my mad escape. A rickety card table had been set atop the Temple Crest with two folding chairs on either side. A board game sat between two men.

Zeus and Hermes.

They were playing a familiar game that resembled *Go*. I'd last played it against Asterion when I had dueled him for the book on the Obsidian Son, *Sons of the Dying Sun*, to defeat the dragon invasion of St. Louis by Alaric Slate. I narrowed my eyes at that suspiciously. And we now looked like Alaric Slate and Peter. Coincidence? Not in my world.

One stark difference from yesterday were the puddles of golden ichor coating the marble floor, splashing over, and seeping into the outlines of, the Temple Crest. I shuddered. Gods had been brutally tortured atop my crest. Probably some combination of Ares, Apollo, and Aphrodite—if she'd been caught. It wasn't enough ichor to be a murder—I didn't think—but it was enough to make Hermes noticeably uncomfortable. His movements were stiff and uncertain, and his forehead was knuckled with concern.

Zeus appeared amused. He also wasn't wearing my face, which was a relief.

He'd left the puddles of ichor—still fresh—on purpose. Just like he'd chosen that specific spot to set up their little board game. Obviously, Zeus was also playing mentally abusive games with his son, like any stand-up father figure would. Because it built character, or something.

Had Zeus picked up on my bet with Hermes? The clouds below the mountain were a murky gray, but there was another ceiling of them above the two gods—unnaturally black and brimming with fingers of crimson lightning. I took a risk and drifted closer. Hiding up in the clouds would conceal me, but I wouldn't be able to hear their conversation. I got within ten feet of them, hovering just above the pavilion's floor like a spirit. I was in full view of Zeus but he didn't react in the slightest.

Shiva had been an expert at astral projection, and I'd feared that maybe all gods were.

I felt myself smiling. Zeus was so obsessed with himself that he likely had no understanding of what it meant to truly step out of his body and ride the astral plane. It required a slice of humility to accept that your existence wasn't the center of the universe. I must have skated by on a technicality, since I had no problems doing it.

His arrogance was actually a benefit to me right now. Even though he didn't currently look like me, I was very aware of our similar character traits. Zeus was what I could become if I didn't embrace humility and empathy. Food for thought. Unfortunately, the only way to beat him was to play his game—and become more like him in the short run.

Just in case he had a great poker face and was fully aware of my presence, I prepared to leave at a moment's notice. Hopefully, faster than he could hurl lightning—astral or real. I floated laterally so as to keep both faces in view.

Hermes rolled the dice, his face a mask of forced calm. He moved his pieces and then waited for Zeus. I noticed his hand trembling ever so slightly.

The god of lightning studied the board with a grimace. The bulk of the game was scheming, setting traps, and sabotage. A player could suffer great losses all the way through to the end, and it wouldn't mean he was losing. There was no winner or loser until that last toss of the dice.

I narrowed my eyes, sensing the correlation between their game and current events. The fun was in the set up, but the victory was in the last move.

Zeus grinned at Hermes, folding his beefy arms. "Did you do as I told you?"

Hermes nodded reassuringly. "Yes, Father. Temple's disguise is in place, and it's completely undetectable." Hermes studied his father with an approving look. "Now that he's escaped, that disguise will be even more valuable than you originally intended. Unless you knew he would escape..."

Zeus just smiled at him. I couldn't tell if he had known or was simply fucking with Hermes. I felt my hackles rising, though. Hermes had disguised us. So much for suspecting Aphrodite.

Hermes focused on the board, pursing his lips. "He tried to rob me, making it much simpler."

Zeus frowned. "Rob you? Why?"

Hermes tapped the coin pouch hanging from his belt. "Desperation, perhaps?"

Zeus chuckled. "I hope you let him succeed. He'll need a way to return, now that he's escaped," he added, his humor evaporating alarmingly fast.

I felt myself leaning forward, even though I could have plopped myself right down on the center of their board game, confident that they couldn't see me. This was the moment of truth. Hermes had betrayed me—but only at Zeus' express command. Now he had a free pass to come clean about our bet.

"No," Hermes said, wincing apologetically. I frowned in confusion. Why hadn't he come clean? He could have played both of us by admitting he'd handed me the four coins, possibly garnering favor from his dad. If nothing else, it would have covered his ass if I failed to win.

"But I used his attempt as an excuse to get close enough to lock his disguise to the Titan Thorns. He won't break it without your permission. He is no longer a concern, even if free."

Zeus grunted dismissively. "I was never concerned about Temple. But I am concerned about his Horsemen. You met with them, correct?" Zeus asked, leaning forward. Hermes nodded. "Did they believe your story?" he pressed, smirking in amusement.

I stiffened, holding my breath.

"They had a lot of questions, but they ultimately bought it. Especially now that I have released the wild card."

What the hell was the wild card? It didn't help that my mind instantly jumped to the famous quote, *Release the Kraken!*

Zeus grinned. "It's all falling into place, and even better than I'd planned. I still have a few things to take care of, but they will be concluded before tomorrow night."

Hermes nodded shakily. "What about Aphrodite?" he asked, his eyes darting to the pools of ichor near his sandals. "Was she working with Ares and Apollo?"

Zeus suddenly gripped him by the throat, hoisting him up into the air. "Know that you will beg for Prometheus' fate if you attempt to betray me." Hermes gagged, struggling to breathe but not using his winged feet to help relieve the pressure of Zeus' grip. I could tell he was nodding subserviently, but Zeus continued to choke him for a few more moments.

Zeus grunted, and tossed him aside, brushing his hands together disgustedly. Hermes struck the ground face first—right into a wet puddle of ichor. Hermes struggled back to his feet, his face smeared with his brothers' golden ichor, making it look like he was wearing tribal war paint. He wiped at his cheeks hurriedly, looking nauseated.

Zeus returned to his chair and calmly sat down as if nothing had happened. "Ares and Apollo are smart enough not to betray me, but they failed at the simple task I gave them—to punish and guard Nate Temple. Any imbecile could have done this. I had to punish their incompetence. We will all be worshipped again soon, as befitting our station. Our old personas—and failures—must be eradicated. I love you all too much to let you become anything less than your best."

Wow. That...I didn't even know what to make of this level of dysfunction.

Hermes sat back down. "I love you too, Father," he said in a croak. "What of Aphrodite?"

Zeus growled furiously. "Aphrodite has yet to be reprimanded for her part in his escape, but I guarantee she will beg for Ares and Apollo's punishment in comparison. For now, let her hide like the panicked rabbit she is. I hold her husband in chains, so I still have leverage—even if she denies her affections. I've heard them whispering to each other when they think no one is watching." He fixed Hermes with a stern, warning glare. "And I am *always* watching, my son."

Hermes nodded reassuringly. "Aphrodite can't remain long from Ares' bed either," he said. "She will be here tomorrow night, one way or another."

Zeus nodded. "Too much rides on this for her to do anything else. Same with the others." He waited, eyeing his son up and down. Hermes squirmed uncomfortably, nodding. "It is your turn," Zeus finally said in a cold tone. "And you know what will happen if you forfeit..." he added with a malevolent grin, chuckling.

Hermes nodded shakily. He scooped up the dice and tossed them on the table. Like a beaten child sitting at the dinner table with his abusive father, he said nothing—but I could imagine his thoughts. *The storm has passed. He really does love me. He just gets angry sometimes when I let him down. I'll do better next time.*

I clenched my fists furiously as they continued to play their game.

Hermes had betrayed me, but he'd also lied to Zeus—when it would have benefited him to tell the truth about the coins. Which horse was he ultimately backing, though—Zeus or me? Aphrodite was on Zeus' shit list, so whatever games she might be playing were her own. I wasn't sure if that made her completely trustworthy, but it made her more trustworthy. Enough to entertain her plan to break me out of these damned Titan Thorns. I had no other options, so she was the only game in town anyway.

My lack of trust wasn't even related to my own paranoia. After seeing how utterly broken this family was—the children, especially—I had to keep my eyes open. Kids this broken were unpredictable, but the statistics always pointed a similar direction.

Ultimately, they would fall back on their family when bullets started flying. Stockholm syndrome had started on Olympus.

I'd learned a few things. It sounded like Zeus still hadn't found his weapon or killed his god.

And he needed me back here tomorrow night.

I would oblige.

28

Rather than immediately zipping to my next destination, I decided I needed to take a moment to calm myself down. I was strangely empathetic to the Olympian children—not enough to forgive them their crimes, but enough to understand what drove them.

How I'd used that against Ares and Apollo. I didn't feel guilty, but I couldn't deny a small heap of responsibility for my actions. I had to accept that if I wanted to come out of this as my own man, rather than a mirror image of Zeus.

Not that I was even remotely as cruel. But...Zeus hadn't been this cruel at first, either. Each step had taken him closer to the god I'd just seen, and each step had likely seemed rational and obvious.

Also, Zeus had been born into a world where his father would rather eat him and his siblings than risk them rising above him. That...had to fuck with a kid's head. Then to castrate and kill him with a scythe, going to war with his siblings against his aunts and uncles.

Yeah. I decided that the world didn't need to worship a family like that.

So, I needed to get my head in the game and start rolling my dice. Tomorrow night was the big event. Zeus was setting up his pieces, so I needed to do the same.

I considered my intended moves, adapting them to the new knowledge

I'd acquired. Nothing major had changed. I need to take my Horsemen off the board, and that would require stealth here on the astral plane. Quinn had been able to see me and interact with me, even if Zeus and Hermes had not. To be sneaky, I had to be relaxed and unemotional. Thoughtful rather than reactive. Because my next decisions were going to look a lot like Zeus, and that was going to hurt me just as much as it hurt them—in the short run.

And in the long run, I could not be like Zeus. Could never be like Zeus.

I calmed my mind, taking slow, deep breaths. Breathing wasn't necessary, but it was something to focus on. I often used my crest to prepare for meditation, but right now, all I could see was my crest painted with godly ichor while Zeus mentally choked out his son.

After a few moments, I floated in a sea of darkness. Well, mostly. I ignored the familiar crimson cracks all around me. It almost felt like I was under a glass dome and that the red lines were attempting to shatter the protection. Or like a massive root system was fighting to break through an obstacle. Creeper vines, maybe.

Sharp, cracking echoes reverberated all around me, unseen, like calving glaciers, but I ignored them. Because through it all, I suddenly heard a raven cry.

I abandoned my plan to spy on the Horsemen, and sped towards the new sound without hesitation, reminded of hearing something similar when I'd been speaking with Quinn. The sound left a trail of energy in the darkness. Vaguely purple and as ephemeral as dissipating smoke.

I heard another raven reply—a slightly deeper caw than the first—followed by another jet of purple energy like a contrail behind a distant airplane. I knew I had been right.

The bird brains—Hugin and Munin—were here on the astral plane. Were they trying to get my attention or had I overheard them? Were they searching for Loki and Fenrir? If so, I needed to warn them. They wouldn't know that their location was compromised.

I latched onto the sound—the very tip of the ribbon of purple light—and I was abruptly yanked forward like in an unfair game of tug of war. I shattered through an unseen barrier and onto the ground. Unfortunately, my body could still experience high impact landings. I skidded on my cheek and then flipped head over heels.

I came to a stop, lying on my back, staring up at a morning sky, panting heavily. My head rang and stars twinkled in and out of my peripheral vision. My cheek felt raw and I sported several new bruises—to my soul.

Which were not as fun as bruises to my flesh. I could sense the point of origin for a physical bruise, but soul injuries apparently rippled outward like a pebble thrown into a pond, sharing that pain in concentric, echoing rings throughout my body.

So, my entire soul felt fucking fantastic.

My self-pity died as I heard faint laughter nearby. Familiar laughter. I sat up, wondering where the hell I was—where Hugin and Munin had taken me. I didn't see the bastards anywhere, and I could no longer see the contrail of power that had flushed my soul down this astral drain. But they had to be somewhere nearby or I wouldn't be here.

I froze to find Callie Penrose a dozen paces away. Her long white hair looked like spun silk, and her purple-flecked blue eyes seemed to suck in the sunlight around her. She wore canvas pants and a matching coat—both hugging her body tightly in a way that made me think it was more functional than fashionable. Like martial arts attire used for training. It was scuffed and dirty in places, verifying my analysis.

She was sitting on a stump beside a familiar, buff Asian man who wore black military BDU's. Straps and buckles and cargo pockets decorated his ensemble—most likely brimming with weapons.

His name was Ryuu, and I'd met him before. Recently. He'd done something stupid and I'd been forced to put him back in his lane. He'd held a sword to my back. He'd won the lottery by not getting himself killed.

Callie hadn't been pleased. I hadn't been pleased. Ryuu had been extremely pleased.

He'd also been somewhat approving of my response, respecting me for it and even humbly apologizing for his oversight—even though it had been Callie's oversight.

All that to say, he was a badass, and he led a group of ninjas who had chosen to guard Callie—the White Rose, as they called her. Callie had picked up quite a few strays in recent years. She even had a talking skeleton who seemed like a real riot. Xylo adored red balloons and he wore pirate boots. I had questions.

They were in some kind of wooded clearing, holding small cups the size of shot glasses. A bottle of sake—judging by the kanji on the label—sat on a quilted picnic blanket between them. A park in Kansas City, I presumed.

She...well, she definitely looked like she was too busy to come to Chateau Falco to meet with Hermes and make sure her old pal, Nate Temple, was safe. She hadn't even finished her bottle of sake yet. Gee golly, I was surprised she'd even had time to take the phone call from Gunnar and Alucard. I'd have to thank her for really going out of her way for me. Kansas City was practically on fire, judging by the tranquil scene spread out before me.

I mean, the park was obviously a hotbed of crime and intrigue, what with the chirping birds, the lush greenery, the lack of other park-goers, and the sunbeams shining down through the canopy. That picnic blanket looked downright nefarious, and the cheese and crackers were probably poisoned with greed—

I gritted my teeth and took a calming breath. After a few seconds, I begrudgingly admitted that I felt jealous. I also admitted that I was giving some serious thought to my visit with Aphrodite later.

I saw a pair of wooden staffs and training swords tossed into a pile not far from their picnic blanket. I frowned harder, eyeing the sake, the sunlight, and the weapons. Sake was not typically used in weapons training, as far as I knew. They had unfastened the top buttons of their jackets to cool off, and their hair was sweat-soaked from sparring.

They were laughing at some joke I'd missed. Carefree. I watched as she settled her hand on Ryuu's shoulder, actually wiping at her eyes as she tried to regain her composure.

I stared, refusing to blink.

All other sounds seemed to fade away, and I suddenly felt very hollow. A gentle breeze blew through the scene—not affecting me in the slightest—and I could almost taste Aphrodite's perfume in the air. I knew it was all in my head—a knee-jerk defense mechanism to seeing Callie enjoying herself with another man.

Ryuu laughed alongside her, and I saw the hidden embers of desire in his eyes. I knew that look well. I'd had it before with Callie. I didn't even breathe, wondering why I felt strangely hollow and empty inside even though I was full of anger, sadness, and jealousy. All irrational feelings, based on my lessons from Aphrodite. Because I was also confident of her claim that we weren't right for each other.

Despite the weatherman's forecast, the silent, all-encompassing hurricane of emotions raged.

Callie finally looked up. Ryuu had been watching her, so they ended up locking eyes from a hands-width away. Their laughter cut off as abruptly as if a plate had been dropped in a restaurant. I watched, the hair on the back of my neck rising up of its own accord, as Ryuu hesitantly leaned a fraction of an inch closer. Callie didn't pull back.

Instead, she bit her lip expectantly.

I stared at the two of them, ignoring the imagined, echoing sound of laughter in my ears. Aphrodite's laughter—not her laughing *at* me, but an echo of her laughter *with* me from when we'd hung out naked last night. I smelled a whiff of guilt in the air, but it quickly floated on by as I watched Callie hesitating to act on Ryuu's obvious advance.

Callie suddenly turned away, lowering her gaze to her boots, looking shaken and mildly angry. Her purple-flecked blue eyes sparkled, full of pent-up emotion.

I watched her, feeling like a dried husk of myself.

By the looks of it, Callie had similar conflicting emotions about us as I did, and that reaction hit me like a punch in the gut. Aphrodite...had been right. It wasn't just me. Otherwise, Callie would have punched Ryuu in the throat for even hinting at a kiss. It was obvious that part of her had desperately wanted to lean forward rather than away.

Surprisingly, it was...somewhat of a *relief*. Painful, but still a relief. My guilt about my night with Aphrodite slowly evolved to a mild—very mild; I'm not a saint—form of sympathy for her current emotions.

Irrational jealousy was apparently an inherited trait. It was science, so I didn't argue it.

Aphrodite had hinted that I did hold someone in my heart. Somewhere. Maybe Ryuu was Callie's soulmate. I wondered if she knew. If Aphrodite had paid her a visit, like she'd intended. Was that why Callie had hesitated, momentarily entertaining Ryuu's kiss?

"My apologies," Ryuu suddenly said. "I should take a quick walk and leave you to your thoughts," he said, abruptly standing, bowing, and spinning on a heel. Callie reached out a hand, her composure cracking with angst, but Ryuu was already striding away.

Her hand fell and her shoulders slumped.

I stared at her long white hair, refusing to blink. I gritted my teeth as she brushed a loose strand behind her ear. She was beautiful and talented and amazing. Sure, she had qualities I didn't like at times—much like any of my friends.

I loved her.

But I wasn't *in* love with her. There was a difference. I didn't currently know the identity of my mysterious soulmate, but that wasn't the point. Something deep inside me knew that she wasn't the one for me.

It was a strange dichotomy. I obviously cared deeply about her, and part of me clung to the idea of a relationship, even while another screamed for me to move on. Much like the convenience of the easiest, straightest path versus the longer, winding, more difficult road. They each led to the same place, but the rare vistas viewed from the more difficult route were not visible on the easier, straighter path.

29

I flinched as I suddenly sensed a new presence. I angled my neck to see a warrior in gleaming gold kneeling behind a bush. I stared, blinking incredulously. Her armor—pleasantly forged to show off the beauty of the feminine form—had not been repaired and still looked uncared for. She gripped a wicked trident in one gauntleted fist and glared at Callie from her hiding place.

Kára. What was *she* doing here? Was she looking for me?

I waved a hand at her to check, wondering if she could even see me. Although I was clearly in her peripheral vision, she didn't acknowledge me in the slightest. Damn it. Was she actually in Kansas City? In the real world? I crept closer, knowing that Ryuu would kill her if he found her. Thankfully, he was on the opposite side of the clearing.

Was she spying on Callie in hopes of finding me? Was that why Hugin and Munin had led me here? And where were the two miscreants—

A sudden flapping of wings drew my attention as two large ravens swept down from a nearby tree. Their raucous caws seemed to echo as if in a cavernous stone room, even though we were in a park. Which meant they were on the astral plane as well. I realized I was holding a large rock in my hand, ready to throw it at them if they attacked Kára. They landed on the bush directly before the Valkyrie with a rapid flap of their wings to slow their descent.

Kára's form dispersed like wind-blown smoke and she cursed up a storm. I froze. Wait. *Kára* was on the astral plane. Then why couldn't she see me?

Her form slowly rematerialized, and she glared at Odin's ravens with murderous intent.

"You should not be here," one of the ravens said. "Our agreement was to be your eyes. You being here jeopardizes everything."

"Fuck off."

I chuckled at her blatant disrespect of the ravens. None of the three heard me, so my humor swiftly faded. She obviously knew them well. But what was this about an agreement?

Judging by Kára's dented armor, her search for me had introduced her to many unsavory types—it was even more beat up than when I'd last seen her with Freya. As I focused on her trident, I noticed dried blood on the tips. Where the hell had she gone looking for me, and who had she poked?

I walked closer, seeing no need to hide my presence since they couldn't see me.

Kára rose up from behind the bush to a standing position. As she did, her form flickered again, as if she really was made up of mist. It happened every time she moved. My form didn't seem to do that.

Her upper body was adorned by a golden cuirass covered in eccentric sworls and curlicue designs, looking like an armored corset. Her lower half was somewhat covered by a short skirt of black leather strips—much like Zeus wore but a different color—with golden tridents on the lower tips. Beneath that skirt was a whole lot of bare leg. She wore furry leather boots, also decorated in golden runes and symbols. The fur was matted—with blood, presumably.

I was able to get a closer look at the hand-etched depiction of a lighthouse over the left breast of her cuirass, but I still didn't understand its significance. A closer look only showed me how bad a carving it actually was. Kára was definitely not an artist. I cocked my head, trying to get a better look. Maybe it was a tower, not a lighthouse. Or just a random stack of lego blocks.

Maybe she'd let Alice vandalize her armor for the hell of it. But Alice was actually incredible at drawing, so I doubted it had been her.

I gritted my teeth in impotent frustration as Kára's glare rolled right over me.

"You should not be here, Kára," Munin said, mimicking his partner in rhyme, Hugin. I studied the three of them, flapping my arms dramatically in hopes that the ravens were just ignoring me to be dickheads. They had led me here, after all. They didn't even blink, focused entirely on Kára.

"You should not be doing many things you are currently doing," Hugin added in a soft, almost compassionate tone.

"I must find him," Kára snarled, clenching her trident tightly. "I *will* find him." I stared at her incredulously, a kernel of hope blooming deep within my chest. She really had been talking about me with Freya!

"I think it's safe to say that he is not *here*," Munin drawled dryly.

Kára pointed her trident at Callie, nearly skewering both ravens in the process. Since they didn't react, I was betting they were immune to her blade. Or Kára's mist form couldn't touch them. "She might know something," Kára argued lamely, drawing her trident back and setting the haft into the ground at her feet. It wasn't entirely clear how Kára intended to get that something out of Callie, but the look in her green and blue eyes told me she was ready, willing, and able to spill blood.

Munin shifted from foot to foot. "She knows many things. How he tastes, for example—"

Kára's trident suddenly flared with light and she stabbed it directly over his head, missing him by millimeters. This time, he let out a panicked squawk, tumbling down into the bush. He winked back into existence a moment later, on a different, safer branch.

"You fucking crazy?" he screeched, flapping his wings angrily. Kára's form buffeted against the pressure, momentarily breaking up. "We work for your boss's boss!"

"Not for long," Kára growled under her breath, reforming even as she said it. Then she laughed harshly. "That was not a threat. I meant that I might be unemployed soon."

I frowned, having forgotten that little tidbit as a result of my own adventures—robbing corporate secrets, crashing birthday parties, and skinny dipping in a Frost Giant's version of a hot spring.

I did recall that if Kára got fired, she'd revert to soul-status—which wouldn't help her cause at all. And...mine either, I admitted, realizing I was smiling shyly—nervously. I started, shaking my head. I'd meant as a friend, Freud. I wasn't rebounding, but Aphrodite's lessons were on the forefront of my mind.

The ravens studied her and then each other. "Not it," Hugin finally said.

Munin narrowed his eyes and flapped his wings. "Ragnarok it all!" he cursed, hunching down as if preparing to take flight.

Kára grunted. "I already spoke to Freya about it. We didn't finish the conversation."

The ravens calmed, cursing under their beaks. "Why not?"

"We...had an observer," she said cryptically, turning away to conceal the faint smile tugging at the side of her lips.

But I sure fucking saw it. I grinned smugly, glancing over at Callie with an air of triumph. Ryuu was pacing worriedly behind her back. Callie was fidgeting with her small glass. It was obvious that both knew of the other's presence, and still needed a few moments to gather their thoughts. Or drink more sake.

"I'll see your ninja, and raise you a Valkyrie," I muttered with a pompous sniff.

Kára waved a hand at the ravens, gripping her trident tightly in her other fist. "Shoo. I need to hear what she says."

Why had the ravens brought me here? Or had they? Maybe I'd just hitched a ride somehow. They obviously hadn't seen me. The ravens left, and I realized that I was still staring at Kára.

I stepped up beside her. "Hey, stranger."

She didn't react and I let out an annoyed sigh. I glanced up at Callie and sighed again.

Kára—even though invisible to them—kept her distance, probably fearing that Callie might know some magic to detect her if she drew too close.

Which...wasn't necessarily wrong. Callie was alarmingly powerful— much more powerful than when I had first met her. I'd seen her carrying around a Beast of her own, as a matter of fact. An eyeless white fox with melted silver oozing from her vacant eye sockets. The fox wasn't in attendance, thankfully.

Ryuu walked up to Callie, and I was surprised to see the cool anger in his eyes.

"Too much to drink," Callie finally said, sounding embarrassed. "I'm a lightweight," she said off-handedly, still staring out at the scene as if she doubted her own words.

Ryuu remained silent. He made no move to resume their earlier moment, making me wonder if it truly had been an unplanned event. That he hadn't intended for it to happen but hadn't wanted to miss the opportunity. He just stood there, close enough for support if Callie needed it, far enough away to give her space if she needed that. And he was still angry. Actually, he looked a lot angrier after hearing her excuse and chewing on it in silence.

She fidgeted uncomfortably, not meeting his eyes. "What almost happened a few minutes ago," she began sheepishly, "never happened." She turned to Ryuu with a determined look in her eyes, and abruptly jerked back in surprise. "I..." she stammered, caught off guard...by her ninja's now furious glare. "I have feelings for Nate," she finally managed, lamely.

Kára growled savagely, clenching her trident tight enough that it seemed like she was trying to hold the weapon itself from attacking Callie.

I realized I was grinning boyishly. "I'm amazing."

He closed his eyes for a long moment, seeming to gather his resolve. "Then I guess I will echo your lie." She cocked her head, frowning. "I apologize for my actions," he said, dryly, obviously not meaning it at all.

Kára burst out laughing. "Damn. I actually like this guy," she breathed, smirking. I smiled along with Kára, nodding my agreement. Ryuu was clever. I'd give him that. Of course, clever people got killed all the time in this world. A tactic was only deemed clever *after* it worked.

Before that, it went by idiotic, reckless, or foolish. Three of my favorite words.

Callie's lips thinned as she finally comprehended his meaning. "I was not lying, Ryuu."

"This isn't the Riverboat Casino," he growled. "Doubling down on a lie will not save you."

Kára lifted her trident, hooting as she pumped it in the air. "Go, Ryuu!" I was more interested in Callie's dilemma—facing a man who wouldn't tolerate her bullshit, even though he worked for her. But I was smirking at Kára's vehement glee. Just hearing her smile and laugh as opposed to being broody and grim was enough to make me happy.

Callie brushed her hair behind her ear, patting the stump he'd occupied earlier. Ryuu sat down on the blanket instead, a respectful distance away. "We have more training to do, so we should make this brief," he said.

Callie glared at him. "I'm sorry for hurting you, Ryuu."

He studied her for a few moments. "Are you ready to continue training, then?"

She clenched her jaws. "Stop being an asshole. I'm trying to apologize."

He leaned forward. "Then stop being a fool. I don't care for your apology. I want your heart."

She stiffened, her eyes widening as she opened her mouth wordlessly.

Even Kára stared at him, cocking her head as if he'd appeared out of thin air.

Ryuu's anger faded somewhat, spotting a tear on Callie's cheek. He winced, reaching to brush it away and she slapped the shit out of him —THWACK!

Kára let out a whistle but I didn't turn to look. Wow. I was more impressed by the fact that Ryuu hadn't attempted to block it. He was a ninja, after all. In fact...

He was chuckling. He had a perfect red handprint on his cheek, and he was *laughing*. Callie blushed. She opened her mouth to apologize, but Ryuu held up a hand, cutting her off. "That was the most honest thing you've said in ten minutes. Your honesty echoed throughout the park." He smirked. "And my skull."

Callie's blush deepened, and a faint smile tugged at the corner of her mouth. She let out a frustrated sigh. "Fine. You win, fucking ninja Jedi," she snapped. "I'm not sure *what* Nate and I have! Happy now?"

Her words struck me like a gong, seeming to simultaneously echo throughout my body, the astral plane, and the wooded park. It wasn't sadness I felt, but hearing the words out loud...hurt.

Ryuu stared at her, waiting. Not giving her an inch. He did not nod. He did not smile. He did not gloat. He just waited, forcing her to do this on her own without his help. Just like she'd lied on her own and he'd called her on it.

Okay. This guy...was pretty damned badass. Even if his plan failed, he'd earned my respect.

I glanced over at Kára to find her grinning from ear-to-ear, leaning forward to watch the verbal sparring between the two. She licked her lips and I found myself smiling. To finally see someone fighting for me was a soothing balm to my hurt pride. Although Kára was sticking up for my side in this silent battle, the entire situation was a double-edged sword.

The chasm in my relationship with Callie didn't revolve around me and my feelings. It took two to tango. Callie shared my same concerns, even though she'd never told me.

I hadn't done so either, but I hadn't really even thought about it until Aphrodite stripped me down and trapped me in her bed. Which, if I was being fair, was much worse than Ryuu leaning in for a hopeful kiss in a romantic Russian roulette scenario.

"I think we are perfect for each other, but I also fear that we are not," Callie murmured, obviously struggling to put her feelings to words.

Kára sucked in a breath, leaning closer. I heard her knuckles crack as she gripped her trident tighter. Ryuu watched Callie, nodding encouragingly. "Thank you for admitting what I have known for some time now," he said gently. "That is all I ask for—honesty." He paused, a smile tugging at his lips. "Well, that is not *all* I ask for," he admitted, openly grinning.

Callie blushed, looking down at her boots, fighting back a matching smile. Ryuu did not press her further, because he was not an idiot.

"I can no longer sense Nate," Callie whispered. Ryuu's humor evaporated in an instant, apparently having had no idea. "Gunnar and Alucard are anxious, but I shrugged it off as their typical neurosis related to every half-cracked idea Nate decides to act upon," she said with a hollow smile. "He's apparently been missing for over a week."

"You spoke with the other Horsemen?" Ryuu asked.

She nodded. "And Hermes. He said the Olympians were helping search for Nate. To call on them if we needed anything." She swallowed grimly. "They found him, but he is doing something for them as a gesture of thanks. He hasn't visited Chateau Falco to talk with Gunnar and Alucard. Why not?"

I cocked my head. Hold up. I was back now?

Ryuu frowned. "That...is good, right?" he asked, obviously confused.

She shook her head. "They *say* he's back, but I do not *sense* him," she repeated.

Ryuu grimaced. "What about our own...problems? Kansas City is ready to blow."

She nodded tiredly. "I know. But something is wrong. I can feel it," she said, tapping her chest. "I think it's a Horseman thing."

"Where might he be?" Ryuu asked, no longer focused on romance now that danger was on the table—both with my disappearance and whatever he'd been referring to in Kansas City.

Callie was staring at the ground. "I do not know. He's just *gone*. Maybe he's in Fae..."

"No," Kára growled. I flinched, glancing at her.

"Or Asgard..."

"No," Kára repeated knowingly.

"Or Niflheim..."

Kára hesitated, seeming to consider Callie's suggestion.

Shit. That was not a good development. Not with Loki and Fenrir holed up there. "No. I'm not in Niflheim, Kára—"

She disappeared, obviously not having heard me.

Callie continued, and I let out a frustrated sigh, hoping to listen in for a few more seconds before leaving to warn Loki and Fenrir. "He hops realms all the time, but this feels different."

"What can I do?" Ryuu asked solemnly.

Callie shrugged. "Nate never tells me anything. Never lets me in. How am I supposed to help my friend if he keeps me in the dark?" she whispered angrily, punching her fist into her thigh.

Friend. She'd said friend.

I didn't need to hear anything else. That single word had been more honest than anything else she'd said. It was a painful word, but a necessary one. Just because I agreed with it did not mean I couldn't look back on old memories with a loving smile.

I would always love her. Just not in the same way.

"Goodbye, Callie Penrose," I whispered, blinking through misty eyes. A great weight shifted from my shoulders as I left.

30

I zipped back into my body and shuddered, feeling like I had just slipped into a shirt that was too tight. I controlled my breathing, thinking over the conflicting storm of relief and sorrow over Callie. I embraced it, accepted it, and then shoved it into a room in my Memory Palace for later reflection. I wasn't running from it, but I was on borrowed time. I needed to be cold, calm, and calculating. There was no room for emotion in the crimes I would soon commit.

I hadn't had time to check on Gunnar and Alucard, but I'd unintentionally confirmed my diabolical plan on the Callie front. How I would get one Horseman off the field and out of Zeus' thoughts for a short while.

But Kára taking off to search Niflheim for me had cut my astral adventure short.

I had to warn Loki and Fenrir...

I realized I was brushing my fingers through my hair, attempting to somewhat tame the chaotic mop, and wishing I had something nicer to wear instead of my stupid robe. Something more elegant and snazzier for—

I blinked. I was...stalling. Preening. Primping.

I...*wanted* to see Kára. I wanted her to see *me* in all my glory.

"Get it together, pansy," I muttered with a macho growl. "You're dashing, even in a robe."

Hell, I wanted to see anyone who actually wanted to see me back. And, preferably, someone I couldn't put in immediate danger from Zeus. Was a Valkyrie immune to Zeus' reach? He'd obviously been aware of her activities, but he hadn't seemed to consider her a friend of mine. Did he not know, or not care?

Either way, I needed to warn Loki and Fenrir, first. After they were safe, I could sit here and wait for Kára's imminent arrival without fear over roping the Norse pantheon into my mess. Freya had made it sound like Valkyries were somewhat autonomous—but that they suffered consequences as a result of that freedom.

Depending on how badly Odin wanted Gungnir, could he force Kára to turn on me? He might view me holding onto Gungnir as a risk worthy of imprisonment—personal feelings aside. His life was literally on the line now that I'd let Fenrir loose.

She might have to turn me in despite her feelings. I would trade one god problem for another.

I sighed, climbing to my feet. I made my way out the door and scanned Niflheim. Yahn hadn't heard me emerge, too focused on the arts and crafts project I'd given him. He looked frustrated. Carl was sleeping nearby, definitely not aware of any inbound threat. Not wanting to shout Loki's name in case Kára was already circling the skies or spying on our little hut, I reached out to Fenrir, hoping he would sense me through our shared godkiller bond.

I cursed, remembering the Titan Thorns on my wrists. I reached for the eyepatch hanging around my neck, and slipped it on, not wanting to alert Yahn. I didn't dare grab Gungnir, even if it would get Fenrir's attention.

I ran, aiming for the last place I'd seen Loki and Fenrir while astral projecting. I kept my eyes to the sky, wondering what Kára would look like with wings. I actually hadn't seen them before. The skies remained empty until I stumbled onto the rock and found Fenrir and Loki staring at a point on the horizon, looking alarmed. I heard a distant whining sound and froze.

I lifted the eyepatch to my forehead and Fenrir and Loki both jumped, shouting and growling at my sudden appearance. "Valkyrie inbound," I snapped.

"Another one?" Loki demanded angrily. "What color hair does she—"

"It's a different one. Blonde," Fenrir interrupted, eyeing the rapidly approaching Valkyrie.

Loki grimaced, rounding on me. "Give me my robe back."

I stared at him in disbelief, clutching the fabric tighter around my body. "No. You crazy bastard."

He narrowed his eyes in challenge, and I accepted the fact that I was about to wrestle the god of mischief for a ratted, utterly unimpressive robe. And that I was going to win. I wasn't going to let Kára find me naked in Niflheim. I had enough problems.

Loki took a threatening step forward and Fenrir growled, grabbed his father by the back of the neck—like a mother wolf—and then disappeared, abandoning me to the Valkyrie.

"Thanks for considering *my* safety," I muttered. "Also, you're welcome, assholes."

I let out a sigh of relief, straightening my robe as if it were a tuxedo at a ball. I faced the inbound blur of light, headed straight for me like a comet. I debated whether or not to slip the eyepatch back into place. Would Kára still sense me and attack the invisible threat on reflex? The alternative was to see how she would react to meeting a crazy man named Peter in Niflheim. I let out a frustrated sigh. "I'm down to my deadliest weapon. My charm." I glanced down. "And my robe."

I paced back and forth nervously, watching the approaching streamer of light. My heart both fluttered and raced, practically hopping up and down from my stomach to my throat. I rehearsed a dozen speeches in about a tenth of a second. Would she kill first and ask questions later? How could I convince her who I was, as quickly as possible? How would I explain my robe? Was my hair a mess?

I grunted. "Stop making excuses and just admit you want to see her," I muttered under my breath. "It's okay to care, idiot."

I took a deep breath, feeling a hundred pounds lighter after the pep talk.

The fog burned away in her wake as if repelled, and the keening wail grew loud enough for me to cringe, sounding like a kamikaze airplane. I stood my ground as the winged figure slammed into the ground before me. I stared in awe as her gleaming, ornate metal wings flared out to either side, beating at the ground to slow her descent, more closely resembling short swords than feathers. The tips were splashed with dried blood, and they glowed like cooling metal in a blacksmith's forge. They whispered shut like sheathed swords as she rose to her feet and assessed me.

Although showing its miles, the golden armor seemed to shine of its own accord, even though Niflheim was dim and overcast. Her left shoulder guard was about as large as her head, consisting of staggered layers of gleaming gold. I knew she could modify her armor at will, even making it disappear when necessary. She slammed her trident into the ground and stared at me in silence. I pretended not to notice the crude tower etching on her breastplate, even though it stood out like a sore thumb compared to the exquisite detail of the rest of her armor. I had a more difficult time ignoring the strip of toned abdominal muscles and the sharp curve of her obliques peeking over the waist of her war skirt. Her helm protected the sides of her jaw, but revealed her delicate chin and lips, and teased her glittering eyes. Death by Valkyrie wasn't the worst way to go down.

"Hi," I said. "I'm not who I look like, but I don't know how to fix it. And I am unarmed."

She stared at me from beneath her helm, her blue and green eyes glinting from within. She looked scary as hell, but I felt like a moth drawn to a flame. This was the woman who was scouring the world for me. The Valkyrie willing to risk her soul for me. The woman who hadn't let death destroy her heart, seeking me out even in her afterlife.

"Are you a pirate?" she asked in a tone that brooked no nonsense and was almost sharp enough to cut flesh. Reading the confused look on my face, she pointed at my forehead. "The eyepatch. You're wearing it wrong. Unless you are a cyclops." She eyed me up and down, smirking faintly at the robe I had valiantly fought for. "Or The Dude."

I pursed my lips, tugging the eyepatch down so that it hung from my neck. I straightened my robe self-consciously. This was not how my fantasy had played out. "I am not a pirate or a cyclops," I assured her. "And I wasn't in the *Big Lebowski*. There can only be one *The Dude*," I said reverently. She chuckled faintly from within her helm.

I had to be very careful here. She was looking for Nate, which meant she was very likely to run into Z-Nate, and he was a psychopath. I didn't just *want* to convince Kára. I *needed* to. Otherwise she might fall for Z-Nate's disguise and rally behind him—against me. The sick bastard would not hesitate to use Kára against me if he learned how she felt about me.

And I knew Kára had a burning desire to tell Nate how she felt about him.

I had a million ways to prove who I really was, but I couldn't be too direct, or she might kill me on reflex, thinking me a liar, or that this was some form of trap. "You were right."

She cocked her head and her helmet disappeared, letting her blonde braid fall down her back. "I usually am."

I smiled. "About a girl in Kansas City."

She stiffened, and I could tell that she was annoyed by her own reaction. "Who cares about Kansas City?"

I chuckled. "St. Louis is so much better, I agree."

She took a step closer, gripping her trident in a threatening manner. "Get out of my way, Pirate."

I held up my hands, reminding her that I wasn't a threat and that I was not trying to stand in her way. "Of course." She began to walk by me, obviously finished with our little talk. "I just wanted to thank you," I said after she passed. I knelt down to the ground and poked my finger into the wet earth.

I heard her pause and, presumably, glance back at me. "For?"

I finished writing in the mud and stood. "This," I said, pointing at the ground and backing up a step. *Nate Temple was here*, was hastily drawn in the mud.

She spun aggressively, obviously taking my cryptic answer as an implied threat. She saw me standing a safe distance away and pointing at the ground. She followed my gaze, read the words, and tensed. She whipped her trident up and I felt the center prong abruptly pressed against my Adam's apple—the weapon somehow stretching long enough to cover the seemingly safe distance between us. I'd apparently misjudged, thinking the distance was longer than it was.

A common malady for males, I'd heard.

"What is the meaning of this?" she demanded in a frosty, suspicious tone.

I very slowly held out my hands to again remind her they were empty. "I was just standing there, for the record." I carefully indicated my mud-drawn sketch with my chin.

She shot me a baffled look, probably thinking I was touched in the head. Then she grew still, glancing sharply back at the words. "You...were just standing there," she repeated haltingly.

I nodded carefully, her trident was still dangerously close to my throat. "Yes. And I don't normally look like this, but I can't fix it," I told her.

I saw that she understood my meaning, but suspicion prevented her from lowering the weapon. "What do you normally look like?" she asked. I pretended to ignore the trembling in her voice.

"A handsome son of a bitch who doesn't know a thing about women. And I'm not a robe guy. Well, sometimes, if the mood is right."

She dropped her trident to the ground—luckily it didn't sever my throat—and took a sharp step closer. "Who. Are. You?" she whispered, clenching her fists at her sides. The fact that she'd dropped her weapon was not an improvement. It simply meant that she was willing to get her knuckles bloody if I didn't answer correctly.

"I'm a local at a shitty bar in St. Louis, *Buddy Hatchet*. The bartender there is a fox, but I'm a wreck when it comes to women," I said. I didn't want to go too far and lead her to believe that we now had a chance to pursue a romantic entanglement. I wasn't going to resort to using her affection against her as a means to get out of my Titan Thorns—

She tackled me. My head struck the ground harder than I would have personally liked, but it didn't give me a concussion. It was simply hard enough to let me know she cared. On a hatchet scale of one to the movie *Misery*, it was a solid six whacks.

"Nate?" she rasped, her face only six inches away, and her body pinning me down to the cold, misty ground. Her green and blue eyes glistened with frustrated tears, confused by my looks.

"Yes, Kára," I said with a reassuring smile. "I ran into some trouble and now I look like a douchebag—"

"Shut *up*!" she cried out, gripping my cheeks with both hands. "If you lie, you die," she said, trembling dangerously.

"It's me," I whispered, staring into her eyes so that she might glimpse the man within.

Her thumbs tensed, squeezing my face harder, and then...

She kissed me. Fucking *hard*. But I didn't care.

I was momentarily, unequivocally, twitterpated. Bambi's laughter echoed in my mind. "*Sucker!*" Thumper thumped, cackling madly. I ignored them, flipping off Disney in general.

As I was still reeling, she detached from my lips, wrapped her arms around my neck, and collapsed bonelessly atop me, sobbing in unashamed exhaustion.

I suffered the beating like a man and wrapped my arms around her armored back, hugging her tightly. Even a Valkyrie needed a hug now and then, and no one was watching. She was safe. "Thank you, Kára," I whispered, relishing in her childlike embrace, oddly touched by her overwhelming reaction. It was one of those hugs that truly felt soul deep. "I really needed this hug," I whispered. "Even with all the sharp murdery bits. They just prove that you care."

She laughed, leaking all sorts of emotions on my neck. "Me, too," she admitted. "I thought you were dead."

"Not yet. But we have a lot to talk about."

She stayed where she was, squeezing me. "Not yet," she whispered. "Later."

I froze at the familiar word, suddenly understanding how much different that cursed word could sound—how much of a difference it could make in the right context. Callie and I had pushed our relationship to the side for *later*, choosing to prioritize the world's problems.

Kára was pushing the world's problems to the side for *later*, prioritizing this raw moment.

I grinned like a fool. It was all about priorities.

"You're not allowed to see a woman after she cries," Kára continued, taking my silence for hesitation. "Not until she gathers her composure. That goes double for us strong Valkyrie types. We have a carefully crafted reputation."

I smiled wider. "Liar."

"Just. Shut. Up. Nate," she whispered, and I felt her body relax even further, seeming to melt into mine. Not in any sexual manner, but in a way that let me know that her rope had been carrying entirely too much weight lately—that it, like mine, was frayed and shredded. That her body was shutting down for a reboot. That this was the first time she'd let down her guard in a long while.

I caressed her hair, protectively, pulling her closer and inhaling her scent. It smelled so familiar, but I couldn't place why...

I let the thought go for later, focusing on the moment.

Come to think of it, my rope was feeling a lot less frayed, now. I should explore that more.

But not right now.

31

We had finally detached after a good long while lying there together. She'd mentioned something about not wanting to dent her armor further, making my ears burn in embarrassment, before she'd rolled off and sat down beside me. She hadn't broken contact, though, keeping her thigh pressed up against my shoulder as if for reassurance.

I'd been careful to maintain that contact as I sat up beside her. We stared out at Niflheim together, the silence serenely deafening. We wanted it that way.

My thoughts wandered as we stared out at the shifting, deadly mist. Had Kára really been willing to end her career to save me? Even after I'd halted talks of a relationship between us? Although I hardly knew Kára the Valkyrie, on some level I felt I knew her better than anyone. Probably because she'd told Freya that she'd known me for over a decade. That she'd been too much of a coward to admit her true feelings to me, and that serving two masters had been tearing her apart. Technically, she'd been serving three masters—Odin, Freya, and her heart. *Who are you, Kára?* I thought to myself, studying her from the corner of my eye in hopes of a hint.

Without more information, it was impossible to guess. Ten years equated to a lot of acquaintances. She knew me too well to be some casual date or hookup from my youth.

But I doubted she was someone I'd actually dated long-term, either, or else she would have told me how she'd felt while we'd been together. Had she been a close friend, never crossing the rubicon of romance?

Another obstacle in my mental investigation was that a lot of people I had known over the years had died. A lot. And I didn't have the emotional strength to dredge up that list and revisit every friend I had lost, reopen every old wound and heartache in hopes that I might find a face that fit. My heart already felt heavy even considering the attempt. And, seeing the sad, haunted look in her dazzling green and blue eyes, my heart sank even lower.

Perhaps I should take on that review of my past—anything to get the weight off her shoulders. Because she had hinted that the answer was some kind of secret or a promise, so I doubted she was able to tell me herself. I needed to find it on my own.

In a way, I wanted to find it out on my own, rather than her giving me the truth. Because the moment she told me, I would have only a split-second to react—a split-second where she held her heart in her hands, awaiting my response.

But I might need time to consider what it meant to me. I wasn't gullible enough to blindly throw my heart at the first woman who secretly threw hers at my feet. That wasn't what Aphrodite had taught me. I needed to find my own definition of my heart's greatest desire.

Not love someone because they loved me.

But...it was impossible to deny that Kára was on the fast-track to winning my affection.

She was hauntingly beautiful, no question. She was obviously wickedly devoted to her values and to me—to her detriment, it seemed. And...that bit bothered me.

Here I was, searching for my heart's greatest desire, and *Valhallia's Secret—the Armored Collection*—model of the year was willing and eager to swoop down and stand by my side. It felt...too perfect. Like I was being played or being forced into making an emotional decision in a difficult situation. A setup.

Not that I suspected Kára of deceiving me. On the contrary, I feared she might be the victim even more than I was. Had Aphrodite set us both up? I'd already learned Hermes was playing both sides. Why not Aphrodite? Pun intended, naturally. She'd admitted to wanting to teach Callie a thing or two about her...heart.

I realized I was studying her but that she hadn't noticed—too lost in her own thoughts. I frowned as her fiery, dual-colored eyes momentarily shone in a familiar way. For a brief moment, I could have sworn she was Indie's twin sister, and I felt my heart skip a beat. No...

Indie? Could it be?

Kára didn't act like Indie, though. Sure, there were striking similarities, jokes, insightful conversations and debates, fiery passion, but...

Indie had gone *crazy*. I definitely hadn't loved Indie at the end—when I'd killed her. Power had destroyed the woman I had loved. Or, according to Aphrodite, the woman I had thought I had loved.

But...what if, upon death, people *changed*? Maybe they reverted back to their most perfect forms. What if the dark side of Indie had perished when I killed her, and the old Indie had returned as Kára, the Valkyrie?

Even more confusing was the fact that Indie had technically died *twice*. Death had helped bring her back as a Grimm. Had that fucked up the space-time continuum? Was Kára the pre-Grimm Indie? What would I do if that was the case?

I felt a massive headache forming at my temples, so I turned away, troubled.

I began talking, hoping to change the topic from our unspoken feelings to the more tangible issues at hand. She turned at the sound of my voice, her green and blue eyes arresting me for a moment, forcing me to look away. I caught her up on my recent adventures since I'd last seen her. I told her the main points of my current issue with the Olympians. How I'd been abducted, and that Zeus was playing some game—whether against his own people or me in particular, I wasn't entirely sure. I showed her the Titan Thorns, explaining how they blocked my powers and how they were the cause of me looking like Peter.

What I didn't tell her was obvious—how I was avidly working on removing the manacles, and who was helping me do so. Kára had a trident, after all.

Upon finishing my talk, we'd agreed to make our way back to the hut.

I'd told her about Carl and Yahn, watching her closely to see any flicker of recognition that might narrow down my suspect list for her true identity. She had been genuinely excited to meet these strangers. Then again, I'd probably mentioned them in passing before—over drinks at her bar.

She used her trident like a walking staff, her hips close to mine as her eyes quested our surroundings with hyperawareness. I smiled, recognizing it as protection. She was guarding me, even as she talked. Her scent was cool and faintly floral, reminding me of fresh growth beneath a heavy snowfall. Of melted snow at the tail-end of winter as the water tumbled down ancient streams.

As we walked, she told me what she'd been up to, which was a whole lot of nothing important, outside of hunting me down. She downplayed that, not mentioning anything about the talk between her and Freya that I'd witnessed. Had she realized I was the spy? If so, she had an excellent poker face. She also said nothing about her agreement with Odin—being his second eye to watch over me, Freya, and Asgard. Or her relationship with Hugin and Munin.

As the hut came into view, I saw Yahn and Carl sitting together, inspecting something between them. I cocked my head at a new thought. Luckily, I didn't blurt out the first words that came to mind, or I would've had accidentally admitted to spying on her.

"I hope Alice is alright. Is she still with Freya?" I asked carefully, not bothering to hide my genuine concern. I hadn't seen her at Yggdrasil with Freya—where she should have been.

Kára froze, her face instantly paling. "Oh, my god. I didn't even think of that."

My arms pebbled in sudden panic. "What do you mean, Kára?"

She swallowed, looking as if she was about to vomit. "Freya said you came to collect Alice," she whispered in a haunted tone, eyeing me up and down.

The implication was clear. I didn't look like Nate Temple. But someone else did.

"Zeus," I snarled, my vision throbbing red at the corners. "That motherfucker will pay."

Kára knelt apologetically. "Freya said you had returned, but no one else had seen you. Alice wouldn't have left with anyone other than you, though. Still, I had to verify for myself, because something about it all just seemed wrong. Not even your Horsemen have seen you. That didn't add up in my mind." She licked her lips. "When I finally found you, I forgot all about Alice. My relief overcame my concern. I am so, so sorry. Where would Zeus have taken her? Why would he have taken her?" she fired off in a furious, frantic, panicked tone. Because Kára cared about Alice almost as much as I did.

Her eyes were brimming with despair as she stared up at me, choking out a sob. "Where is Alice, Nate?" she whispered desperately.

"I...have no idea," I whispered back. "But you can bet your armored ass I'm going to find out and make him pay. I will make them *all* pay," I snarled, pulling her to her feet. "And you're going to help me. Don't fall apart on me now, Kára. I need you."

She nodded determinedly. "I swear it."

Carl and Yahn had noticed us and were staring warily. I grabbed Kára's hand and tugged her after me. "We're going to meet my friends, and then we're going to wreak some havoc."

32

As we neared them, I waved at Carl and Yahn so they wouldn't do anything stupid with whatever weapons they'd discovered from Grimm Tech. As they stood, I was relieved to see their hands empty.

"Yahn, Carl, meet Kára." I took a gamble, choosing my words carefully. "She's a Valkyrie and a trusted confidante," I told them. Kára stiffened ever so slightly at my introduction. I hadn't wanted to say friend—knowing how it had felt to be on the receiving end of that slur—and I'd wanted to subtly get her thinking about her conversation with Freya. Even after the alarming news about Alice, she hadn't voiced her suspicion that I had been the spy Death had warned them about. She hadn't even mentioned seeing Death, as a matter of fact.

Kára had regained her composure and dipped her chin politely—a warrior's greeting. Healthy respect to let them know she was honored to meet them and, for the time being, would rather not respect them so much that she had to kill them.

"What is a Valkyrie?" Carl asked curiously, and I remembered that he'd been gone from our world for quite some time. He probably knew, generally, what a Valkyrie was, but Carl loved hearing the gritty details.

"I scour the fields of the dead and lift up the most honorable to fight another day in Valhalla during Ragnarok. Our version of Armageddon," she said.

Carl's eyes glittered. "How *delightful*," he mused with utter sincerity.

She beamed brightly. "Beats sitting behind a screen all day, I guess. Travel package is nice."

Yahn watched her. "You own Buddy Hatchet. The axe throwing bar in East St. Louis."

She nodded. "Valkyries make great bartenders, by definition. Most of us spend our free time carousing in Valhalla's Mead Hall with all the dead heroes waiting for Ragnarok, but I find it depressing to hang out with a bunch of drunks who talk about their past and future glory days twenty-four-seven. Literally. Forever." I grunted. She made a fair point. She shot me an amused grin. "Heard you ran into another bartending Valkyrie in New Orleans. Same name, even. That's called a trend," she said with a smirk. "And a type."

"And that's called profiling," I said, narrowing my eyes. "We don't talk about New Orleans," I added with mock solemnity, "If I had ever been there, of course." She was talking about Gunnar's bachelor party and, now that I thought about it, I had met a Valkyrie bartender named Kára there, although she'd pronounced the first vowel in a harsher sound. Huh.

I wondered if she had intentionally or accidentally given me a hint about her identity. Or if she was just giving me shit. My tinfoil hat grew taller.

Yahn nodded thoughtfully, turning his attention to me. His eyes were full of questions he no doubt wanted to ask me in private.

Carl was openly fangirling, even flicking his tongue out in her direction. "You smell like death and cold light. Delightfully macabre. We will be good friends."

She arched an eyebrow and smiled, her lips tugging at her cheeks to reveal dimples. "Carl...you're a fucking riot. Has anyone ever told you that?"

He pumped out his chest proudly. "Now they have." He turned towards Yahn, frowning. "She took your place as my second favorite human."

Yahn rolled his eyes. "Oh, no," he said deadpan. "Whatever will I do?"

Carl narrowed his eyes suspiciously, but he wasn't well-versed in sarcasm. "Live a life of unfulfillment, naturally," he finally said. Yahn sighed, sinking his face into his hands, giving up.

Kára grinned her approval and turned towards Yahn. "I like your heart, dragon."

He stiffened, lifting his face. "I prefer to keep my heart where it is, Kára."

She smiled. "That was not a threat. I was reading your aura. It is what Valkyries do. I see that you are a brave and honorable man," she said, dipping her chin respectively.

He nodded slowly, warily. "What's your angle in all of this?" he asked.

She considered his question for a few moments, glancing at me for direction. I gave her nothing, wondering how she would respond. "I do not have an angle, as you put it. I do have interests, and they will more than likely put me at odds with my employer, Odin."

I kept my face blank. As long as we gave her no reason—

"Loki and Fenrir just left," Carl said, eager to be helpful to his newest friend.

"That's quite enough, Carl," I interrupted in a stern growl.

Kára studied us with a frown. "I have no interest in Loki or Fenrir. I am not a thoughtless spear to be thrown where I am cast. Valkyries have leeway in the pursuit of our tasks. Discretion is the better part of valor."

"Don't you have some kind of agreement with management?" I asked, wording my question very specifically in hopes she might let something slip. "Duties to be fulfilled in return for your new life?" I asked, indicating her armor.

"Perhaps," she said guardedly. "Some things are worth breaking rules for." Yahn cocked his head thoughtfully. "Those I care about and those I am sworn to protect *always* take precedence," she said in a bold, foreboding tone, meeting my eyes levelly. "Always."

Because we were having two different conversations. I was digging for secrets, but she thought I was alluding to Alice. Or maybe alluding to her thoughts on me, specifically. Yet...she hadn't chosen to air that laundry in front of my friends. For her own dignity or mine?

"Seems like a bad trait for a Valkyrie."

She shrugged. "I did not choose this," she said, sounding slightly haunted. "But it got me what I wanted. Some deals cost more than others. I exploit every loophole I can find. It's all the freedom I am permitted." She grunted. "Their oversight is my gain."

"You understand that I cannot allow the Aesir to get involved in my mess, right? I have enough gods to worry about at the moment, and I don't need Odin breathing down my neck because you went rogue. My life is not the only one at stake," I said, referring to Alice.

Kára nodded knowingly. "They will not. I have Freya's blessing." And that was all she was going to say about it, apparently.

I knew I could trust her, but I'd really hoped to jostle up a few new answers from her. Kára was well-versed in keeping secrets and holding back any breadcrumbs that might lead to her true identity. Damn her. Begrudgingly, I had to give it to her. She was good.

I turned to the hut, considering how to delegate duties among my expanding team, and I froze to find Aphrodite standing in the doorway, ten paces away, in full view of everyone. She was leaning against the door-frame, her hip cocked in playful laziness, and she was smiling. She had lit candles within the hut, and they illuminated her maddeningly perfect silhouette very, very well. Could anyone else see—

Yahn sputtered and gawked, jerking his attention towards her with a stunned look on his face. Carl grunted. "Easy, young buck," he drawled, smirking at Yahn. "She's not here for you." Yahn averted his eyes in embarrassment. Aphrodite had a way about her that lit a fuse to a man's lust, even if his heart was committed elsewhere.

Carl pointed a warning claw at Aphrodite. "Do better this time, woman. Or else."

Aphrodite laughed delightedly, and then crooked a finger at me, beckoning.

I realized that Kára was frighteningly silent, and I turned to find her idly fingering the blade of a dagger I hadn't seen her draw. She blinked languidly and then turned to me, arching an inquisitive eyebrow. The reflection of the fire's light twinkled in her dual-colored eyes, and I couldn't tell if she was jealous, protective, or...possibly amused?

"I...um. I have a meeting," I said lamely, figuring it would cover all my bases.

She regarded me thoughtfully. "Okay, Nate. Do you need protection at this meeting?"

My face reddened at the multiple ways *that* could be taken, primarily the one that included Kára helping me get seduced by Aphrodite. The goddess of sex would be totally fine with such an experiment. And as soon as Kára learned my dilemma was more torture than foreplay, she'd probably help a sister out to really make sure I took the lesson to heart.

The only thing that would have made it worse was if Carl piped in about Aphrodite being the cure for all STD's and that protection was not necessary. "No. I should be fine," I grumbled.

She continued watching me until I began to squirm. "I will be here when you are...finished. Shout out if you need anything," she said softly. Then she chuckled at her advice, assuming I'd be shouting out for entirely different reasons. And...

She really didn't seem too concerned about it.

In fact, she really did look amused.

Yahn and Carl busied themselves with mundane tasks, pretending not to notice. "It's not what it looks like," I argued to the group in general.

Kára grew still. Then she turned to look at me. "Oh? And what does it look like?" she asked in a maddeningly calm tone.

Even though I wasn't supposed to know how much she cared about me, there was one thing I was suddenly very consciously aware of. A jealous Valkyrie was not someone to poke a stick at.

Nor was it someone to admit you had spied upon.

I cleared my throat. "Tonight will come early—" Yahn fell into a coughing fit, interrupting me. Carl began smacking his back to help him. I ignored them, averting my attention so as to hide my now permanent blush. "We should all get some rest. We're going to be busy soon."

Yahn lost it. "One of us is getting busy!" he hooted. "And it ain't the birthday boy."

Kára swept her dual-colored eyes across the misty realm. "I'll stand watch. I'll let you know if I hear anything...strange." And then she was walking into the fog, hefting her trident.

I closed my eyes and took a deep breath. Then I made my way towards Aphrodite and her hellacious hut of hedonism.

33

I closed the hut's door behind me and warily scanned the room. I felt like I was walking into the cave of a great beast, wondering which shadow held the monster, but knowing I needed to keep going despite the danger. That something deep within this cave was worth the dangers.

"Aphrodite?"

"In here." Her voice came from the back bedroom. There really weren't all that many places to hide in the tiny hut. The door was only open a crack, emitting a narrow sliver of pale light. I fidgeted with my Titan Thorns absently as I approached, itching to getting them off.

At the door, I took a calming breath, focusing on my needs and wants for this meeting. Resolved, I opened the door and stepped inside. The door clicked shut behind me and I gasped to find myself in a twilight nirvana—not the hut's bedroom.

We were deep within thick, almost impenetrable foliage, and I knew that no man had ever ventured this deep into this magical forest. The same could not be said about my host.

Badump-bump.

Keeping the theme going, the forest seemed totally virginal—unexplored by mankind, her secrets unknown, and her magic unimagined.

Although untouched by man, there was a vibrancy of life to the place. Mystery and danger thrived in equal measure in this place.

It reminded me of the wildness of Fae.

Moonbeams of pale moonlight pierced the trees above, stabbing the dark forest floor with dozens of spears of white light. But my surroundings were not completely dark. I smiled at the pure, natural beauty of dozens of naked, glowing, will-o-the-wisps who were innocently bobbing through the air. They looked human, other than their gossamer wings and pointed ears, and were no taller than the length of my forearm. I smiled to myself, pleased to find magic untainted by sinful human nature. They were all dancing happily to the music of the forest, and some were using the moonbeams like...

I blinked.

Stripper poles. The goddamned innocent magical pixies were using moonbeams as stripper poles. What they lacked in size, they made up for in impossible acrobatics and enthusiasm. They...um, well, they were good. Very good.

I sighed. "Just when I begin to have hope that at least *some* magic can be pure and wholesome in this world, someone needs to hire a DJ to play *Pour Some Sugar on Me* and start flinging fun coupons," I muttered, my innocence shattered.

Their tiny throats emitted whispers of chiming laughter, relishing in my dashed dreams. Their fairy song filled the rolling slopes of thick green grass in a pleasant, tinkling sound, reminding me of wind chimes or the siren song of slot machines at a casino—enticing innocent fools with empty assurances of triumph.

One of them paused mid routine—upside down and gripping the moon pole with only two fingers in defiance of the laws of physics—and shot me an expectant smile. I grunted. "Money-grubbing pixie strippers," I muttered, storming past her. I was safe as long as she didn't have any bouncers waiting in the shadows. A troll, perhaps.

Other glowing blue fairies hopped from flower to flower, leaping tall bushes in single bounds and covering vast distances with expert somersaults and backflips, their wings whipping out at the last second to extend their acrobatic feats for a perfect landing.

The ground may have dipped and rose, but trees too thick for me to wrap my arms around filled the woods all around me, seeming to form a barrier to protect this haven. A steaming pond of crystal blue water occupied the area to my right, and I was surprised to see that a small waterfall fell from a rock face about twenty feet tall. I hadn't even noticed the bubbling, splashing sound, but I realized it was having a calming effect on me, causing my shoulders to droop. Not in lethargy, but as if an expert masseuse had finally removed the last knots from my shoulders.

The air was warm and moist, and tasted faintly sweet with each breath.

A handful of trees circled a raised, flat-topped hill that overlooked the pond, forming a canopy of thick, waxy leaves, and aromatic flowers over the hill's peak. From my position, it actually resembled a naturally grown garden tent. Dozens of candles—or perhaps glowing fairies restrained by their favorite bondage gear, given my luck—illuminated the space within.

Vibrant vines bursting with large, glowing flowers the size of my head, hung down from the canopy to the ground, serving as privacy curtains. Yet they did not block out the view of the steaming pond and waterfall. They served as an open porch to the magical oasis.

With a resigned sigh—not even bothering to question how the inside of the hut in dreary Niflheim had been transformed into a National Geographic Valentine's Day scene—I expertly parted the curtains with two fingers to enter the magical tent.

Of course, I found Aphrodite waiting for me.

The goddess of love lounged on a reclined, moss-covered stone slab. I was surprised to find her nudity both emphasized and concealed by the neon glow of bioluminescent body paint that covered her godly curves in mesmerizing swirls and maddening geometric shapes and symbols. I realized, with a start, that the place was not illuminated from within by BDSM fairies. The light was from her head-to-toe body paint. The moonbeams hitting the canopy above had somehow turned the space below into the equivalent of a teenager's blacklight bedroom.

Aphrodite's teeth gleamed a luminous white as she beckoned me to join her. Her flesh was a pale, bluish gray wherever the numerous splashes of neon paint didn't distract. Her hair was pulled back into a long, thick plait that curled over her shoulder and draped down between her breasts to rest on her belly, making me think of a sleeping serpent. She wore a woven crown of glowing, hot pink flowers.

She patted the mossy stone—wide enough for two, of course. I made my way over, not even surprised to learn that I had naked-ed myself upon entering her tent. I forced myself to play along with the scene that Aphrodite had so carefully crafted, even though my thoughts were on Alice's safety.

Because my chances of rescuing Alice would drastically improve once I removed the Titan Thorns. Which meant I needed to take one for the team. To save Alice. Right.

I briefly wondered if this was an illusion or if Aphrodite had actually taken me away from Niflheim. If Kára entered the hut, maybe she'd find me sitting on the floor naked, having a conversation with an imaginary goddess of sex, and write it off as me tripping balls on Niflheim shrooms.

I shrugged off the thought. It wouldn't be the most embarrassing thing my friends had seen me do. I'd downplay it as an arcane magical ritual. They *always* believed that one. Fools.

I sat down beside her. Surprisingly, the moss-covered stone was as comfortable as a broken-in couch, and my bare ass actually sunk into it a few inches. Without warning, Aphrodite pressed my shoulders down until I lay flat atop the angled, Tempur-Pedic mosstress. In utter silence, Aphrodite pulled over a wooden bowl of glowing yellow paste and set to work on my chest, painting wild, savage, geometric shapes down my abdomen and arms. I watched her work, marveling at the glowing symbols on her torso, finding myself unable to verify whether she was actually naked or not.

I knew she was, but the glowing paint broke her form into distorted segments of pleasant curves, darkness, and dizzying symbols. Each breast was different in both theme and color, but both were mandalas of infinite, impossibly tiny, unrepeated patterns that made my head spin so profoundly I forgot they were breasts after several seconds. So I tried again, naturally, to play pin the eyeball on the nipple. Temple's never quit.

As a whole, her body art reminded me of those Halloween costumes consisting of black clothes and a full-sized glowing skeleton on the front and back. The kid could stand on a dark street and wave at you and, just for a moment, your pulse would speed up and you would forget it was just a costume, not a *real* skeleton.

Except the amalgamation of Aphrodite's body art transformed her into a deadly magical spell come to life. Her unsettling and captivating canvas of vibrant symbols, letters, shapes, and designs turned her into something deadly and dangerous, tickling the distant corners of my mind. Something I wasn't supposed to talk about, but that I kept finding references to.

The Omegabet.

The longer I studied Aphrodite's glowing body paint, I began to grow more and more certain that some of those shapes and designs were not coincidental. Had she painted herself with the Omegabet—whatever that was, exactly?

I snapped out of my thoughts as I felt her hot breath kiss my damp cheeks. She leaned over me, focused on her work as she applied a glowing blue paste to my cheeks and forehead, decorating me with designs of her own choosing. It suddenly felt much warmer in our tent, as I became consciously aware of how close—and how naked—we both were. Even knowing how dangerous it was to let someone cover my body in spells, I had committed myself to trusting Aphrodite—anything to get me out of these manacles.

Finally, she smiled down at me, tucking a strand of my hair back from my forehead. She let out an approving sound and set a glowing finger over my lips. I stared back, silently glad that she hadn't decided to decorate anything below my waist. Judging by the intricate artwork on her lower half, I had feared she would focus entirely too much time on my more sensitive areas. To make sure we matched—and to be evil. Thankfully, she twisted around, reaching behind her. This gave me an alarmingly close look at her painted back and the glowing symbols trailing down her hips and over her —

She turned back to me, holding a flat wooden tray brimming with grapes. Smugly, I admitted that Aphrodite was way better at picnics than Ryuu. Chump ninja.

Aphrodite set the tray down between us and then plucked a grape out of the pile. She lifted it to my lips, forcing them apart to slip it in. Her finger—just the tip—wormed its way in for a quick second. She grinned before extracting it and scooping up another grape—this one for herself.

"This is how I first saw you," she finally whispered, the sound tickling my raw skin. This was the first she had spoken since my arrival, I realized. I nodded, recalling how I had been covered in war paint from Fae when she had seen me fight Athena. "I promised myself you would be my greatest conquest," she added in a serious tone.

I cleared my throat, convincing myself that the word conquest should not be used too many times, given the circumstances. "Is this all an illusion?" I whispered. "Because if not, you should know the fairies are pole dancers. Well, moonbeam dancers, technically. And I'm out of cash."

She pondered my question for a few moments, ignoring my quip entirely. Instead, she slipped another grape past my lips. I nipped at her fingertip and she let out a playful giggle. "This is an illusion, but not in the way you think. This is an *emotion*," she said, enunciating the word, "and emotions have the power to override current surroundings. Much as a memory of a loved one is particularly embellished and vibrant. How you remember a walk through the woods with a lover feeling romantic, yet the trail is painfully plain and uninspiring years later when walked in solitude. Without the lover's companionship, our trail through life is merely dust in the wind."

I nodded. "So, is this your emotion or mine?" I asked, studying our surroundings.

Aphrodite considered the question with a thoughtful frown. "I would assume it is a bit of both. I draw desire out of my lovers. Our surroundings reflect your desire as well as mine."

I nodded thoughtfully. "How did you find me? I didn't have your ribbon in my pocket, and I was in a realm outside of your...jurisdiction."

She pursed her lips. "I grew alarmed when I learned you no longer held my ribbon, but I found another way to locate you," she said, a coy smile replacing her displeasure. "You picked up a pearl on your journey. My lesson must be working."

I frowned suspiciously. Well, wasn't that convenient...

"A pearl?" I glanced down pointedly. "I'm not wearing pants, as you are well aware. And I would know if I was carrying around a pearl."

Aphrodite laughed, making the roof of my mouth tickle as I felt her breath roll over my tender skin. She set her palm on my chest, right over a symbol that looked eerily similar to the Omega symbol. "The pearl is yours, not mine. That is how you have chosen to symbolize your love. And I can always find a man looking for love. You must have progressed on your quest."

I shook my head. "I would never pick a pearl. That's lame as hell. Tell me the truth."

She rolled her eyes and then reached towards my solar plexus. She pinched her fingers and pulled back. I gasped to see her pinching a glowing white ball between her fingers. "Look. A pearl," she said deadpan. I reached for it, but she purposely dropped it.

I tried catching it but missed. The pearl hit my chest and slipped beneath my flesh like a pebble thrown into a pond. I gasped as I felt a faint flare of warmth in my chest, and then the sensation of it sinking impossibly deep.

I stared at her, angrily. "I want it back! Where did my pearl go?" I snapped indignantly.

34

She arched an eyebrow at my about-face on treasured stone preferences. "It went back inside your heart, of course. Where you chose to lock it up inside the tallest tower you could imagine. It should be out in the world, in the palm of another's hand, but you keep denying yourself this necessity." She paused, sighing. "At least you found it. That's progress."

I frowned. "Necessity?"

"Love locked away is a soul in disarray."

I drummed a finger on my chest, considering her words. "So, this pearl represents my love," I said, wondering where I had found said pearl. As obvious as the guess was, thinking of Kára didn't seem right. There were too many unknowns with her. "You said I subconsciously know who I love, so shouldn't it be with that person?" I thought, momentarily thinking of Indie being reborn as Kára.

She snorted. "If you weren't so thick-headed, yes. If that were the case, I could not find you so easily. I would not feel *compelled* to find you. You would not be in shackles."

I let out a sigh, leaning my head back on the mossy stone. Aphrodite slipped another grape into my mouth, smiling warmly. Her other hand absently trailed up and down my ribcage, both soothing and exciting me.

Any kind of physical touch was a great way to prematurely light a fuse to this bottle rocket, given my current frustrations and overall lack of romance.

"What have you been doing since we parted ways?" I asked gently. I didn't mention overhearing Zeus and Hermes' conversation.

Her face grew haunted and her finger stilled over my ribs. "Hiding. Watching. Spying."

"Learn anything helpful?"

She lowered her eyes and retracted her hand. "I have troubling news."

I tensed. "You learned something troubling, and you're only just now telling me? Only *after* spending twenty minutes painting my body with your glowing mud?" I demanded, swatting away the bowls of glowing paste beside us.

She nodded calmly, not reprimanding me for my outburst. "This paint —as fun as it is to play with—is actually a type of armor." She raked her eyes across my face with a slight frown of worry. "When I tracked your pearl to the cursed realm of mist, I was startled to find you wore a different face. Yet I *knew* it was really you. Because of your pearl."

I gritted my teeth, wondering why I hadn't even thought about that. "Hermes did this. He tied it to the Titan Thorns when I tried to rob him outside my prison cell. The spell must have been linked to the mountain or something, activating the moment I left."

She clenched her jaws angrily. "That snake," she hissed, livid. She took a calming breath. "Seeing that you were now under an impenetrable illusion shed new light on what I had learned. I hadn't considered it particularly relevant until I saw your new face."

I stared at her. "What the hell are you talking about? What did you learn?" I demanded.

She nodded, pursing her lips. "I had intended a different, more intimate, lesson, but I was forced to alter my plans in light of my findings." She indicated the mud painting our bodies. "Hopefully, it will keep us hidden while I enlighten you. My Father's plans were more meticulous and far reaching than even I had feared."

She climbed to her feet and held out her hand. I hesitated for only a moment. Then I accepted it and let her pull me to my feet with surprising ease. She was stronger than she looked.

"Come," she whispered.

I gritted my teeth, resigned to my unfair life. Lines like that from women like her should never give a man nightmares. I guess I was just lucky.

Between one moment and the next, our twilight oasis was gone and we were in an entirely different, heavily populated setting. Aphrodite stood behind me, her arms wrapped around my waist as she pressed her naked body up against my back. She rested her chin on my shoulder, whispering sweet nothings into my ears. Not the sexy kind. The *don't panic, we're safe* kind.

I stared out at a swarm of frantic activity. Dozens of men and women were shouting and arguing, running around like crazy people. One man stood tall and grim, violently calm, like a boulder in a raging river. I knew him.

Raego Slate, the Obsidian Son. The ruler of the dragon nation. We were on his lawn, facing a vast collection of inky, glossy, obsidian statues of humans and monsters. Except they weren't artistic depictions. They were his enemies—the ones he'd frozen in stone with his penchant for black fire. He found it amusing to show them off like lawn ornaments.

Dragons stalked the garden, hunting for something. Or celebrating Easter with an egg hunt. I watched as they checked behind bushes, inside sheds, all of them looking ready for immediate violence. Packs of two and three—some in human form, some in dragon form—stalked the perimeter of the property and, judging from the sounds and number of lights on within the home, they were tearing the house apart as well.

My heart began to race as I scanned the array of stone sentinels, wondering what they were so alarmed about. Aphrodite pointed out the area with the most activity and I saw Raego staring at an empty space I hadn't noticed. I sucked in a startled breath, knowing which statue should have been there.

Peter.

But it had been obliterated, leaving behind a pile of polished rubble. As I stared at the empty void in both fear and disbelief, I heard dragons repeating the news from one to the other. Raego abruptly turned, pointing at two familiar dragons—the Reds. The sisters I had taken Yahn from during the surprise birthday party at Grimm Tech.

Their faces were gaunt and pale, but their eyes glittered with unbridled fury.

"Fly to Chateau Falco. Tell them the security feeds from Grimm Tech were genuine. Peter really has escaped. I don't have an explanation for Alaric Slate," he snarled. "Yet." They nodded obediently and began to turn away. Raego grabbed Aria by the shoulder, drawing them up short. "Have either of you heard from Yahn?" he demanded.

I winced guiltily and Aphrodite hugged me tighter. The Reds shook their heads grimly. "No," they said in unison.

Raego cursed, releasing her. "Then Peter already has one hostage." The Reds clenched their jaws, looking as if they were on the verge of exploding with fury. "Alert everyone at Chateau Falco and find out if anyone has heard from Nate yet!" he snapped. "Peter will be coming for him next. Or me. We both had a hand in killing him." Then he dismissed them with a flick of his hand, muttering under his breath, "I should have listened to him and destroyed them all."

No fucking shit. I'd told Raego that his macabre collection was a pointless risk—leaving an army of his enemies on his lawn. Raego had arrogantly assured me that he had complete control over his statues, shrugging off my warning, even though he'd admitted to not knowing if they were truly alive or dead beneath the stone. That had been answered, now. At least one of the statues had harbored a living person, in spite of having his throat slit before Raego had hit him with his petrifying black fire.

Were the rest equally sentient—alive beneath a deceptively secure shell of stone? Because there were a lot of statues on his lawn. It was a veritable statuary garden. He could have charged admission, there were so many. An army of foes hanging around the throat of his stronghold.

I stared at the remnants of Peter's broken statue, seeing the section that had covered his face. It was a perfect mold of my old friend. The man who had betrayed me for power walked the earth again. I assumed he still had the bracelet that had made him so incredibly powerful.

And because that wasn't enough to cause irritable bowel syndrome, Zeus had disguised me to look just like him, knowing full well that Peter would soon walk the streets of St. Louis. This must have been the wild card he'd mentioned to Hermes. An insurance policy in case I escaped.

"Zeus," I cursed in a low, cold tone. Abducting Alice hadn't been enough. Taking my power hadn't been enough. Torturing me hadn't been enough. Lying to my friends hadn't been enough. He'd been involved as far back as my first confrontation with the dragons, using Hermes to give me the coin to defeat Alaric. I had to admit, his patience was unparalleled. "How can he still be alive? It's been *years*."

Aphrodite clutched me tighter. "Although alarming, I didn't appreciate the ramifications until I saw the disguise Zeus placed on you," she whispered into my ear. "I have spent some time here, gathering information, wondering if Zeus had woken this Peter to hunt one or both of us," she admitted. "I heard Raego saying that one of the cameras at Grimm Tech apparently caught sight of Peter abducting Yahn on their feeds. This concerned me, knowing I had sent you to the same place. But when I searched for you, I felt your pearl," she said, caressing my chest, "so I knew you were alive. Then I saw your disguise," she whispered, "and changed my plans, knowing the paint would get us close enough for you to see the scene for yourself."

I surveyed the scene, forcing my pulse to slow rather than thunder out of my chest. "How the hell did he survive a slit throat on top of no food and water for years?"

Aphrodite's arms suddenly tensed, tightening around my chest like a vise.

I looked up to see Raego pointing a finger directly at me with a furious snarl on his face. I froze, locking eyes with him. How could he see us? Aphrodite had said—

"THERE HE IS!" Raego snarled, partially shifting into his black dragon form. "TAKE HIM ALIVE!" His gaze latched onto my Titan Thorns and he hesitated. "He's armed!"

I shook my head frantically, holding up my hands, cursing his memory of Peter's bracelet. My fucking shackles looked nothing like it. "No! It's not—"

Aphrodite squeezed me hard enough to crack my ribs right as balls of flame slammed into the ground all around us, trapping us in a circle of fire. I felt something tug at my soul and the sounds of screaming and fire puffed out as if I'd only imagined it.

35

I panted wildly, jerking my head left and right for inbound threats.

But the only current threat was the naked goddess straddling my hips like a vise. Her bare flesh was pressed tightly against mine, her entire body hugging me close. I sucked in ragged lungfuls of air, noticing that we were on top of the Round Table in Chateau Falco's Sanctorum—not our secluded woodland strip club.

The sudden adrenaline rush caused by Raego's threat—even though our body paint should have protected us from detection—swiftly shifted course to give me an altogether different bodily response.

Never let energy go to waste, it said.

My skin hummed with electricity where it touched Aphrodite's skin. I bucked her off, and spun to pin Aphrodite beneath me. I stared down at her, panting in starvation, my rational thoughts a very distant whisper as blood pounded in my ears. My veins flared with golden light, triumphing in my dominance of a god now that I'd reversed our positions.

She was mine. As all gods should be—some in different ways than others, of course.

Torches along the walls suddenly puffed to life, casting the room in a purple glow as the Sanctorum responded to the Master's presence. This was my castle. Everything in my grasp was my plaything, to do with as I pleased.

Aphrodite whimpered, looking surprised—and then aroused that she'd been caught off guard and overpowered. Her pupils dilated and her breathing changed as she blinked lazily up at me. I hadn't realized I'd secured her arms above her head, holding them down as I loomed over her.

"Yes," she breathed, her lips barely even parting to let the word out. My grip clenched tighter and she whimpered in response, sucking in her lower lip. She was mine to command—whether to ravage or revile. "The carnage sings," she purred in a calming whisper. Part of me knew she was right. I could hear the encouraging whispers in my soul, tempting me. "I am the only vessel strong enough to contain it." She squirmed her hips beneath me, gaining a better position for negotiation—one that made my toes curl. "It will consume you," she warned. "Give. It. To. Me."

I shut my eyes, gasping for air as I struggled to think clearly. She would do anything to lull my carnage to sleep long enough to save us both. Nothing was forbidden and everything was permitted in the aim of that goal. This was to save the world.

Or the Catalyst would get a power boost he definitely should not have.

I...considered it. Anything to give me a fucking break. In my mind, I was on the edge of a mental cliff, staring out at an endless abyss and...

It was beginning to talk back to me in seductive, enticing promises.

And Aphrodite's seduction was the *protection* from that dark malevolence. Its antithesis.

She claimed I was not strong enough to contain it—that it would consume me. I felt a spark of defiance rise up in my soul, and the endless abyss of temptation hissed angrily, even at such a frail, pitiful ember challenging it. I fed that spark, rallying behind it in challenge to Aphrodite's doubts, feeling my head begin to clear. She thought I wasn't strong enough to withstand temptation. That ember crackled and flared, growing larger.

Aphrodite had obviously underestimated my tolerance for scrotal sorrow.

I was the king of unhappy sex. I could turn her and the carnage down. Easy.

The ember of my abstinence roared to a pillar of flame and I felt a faint pop as the carnage fled from my mind. I fell to the side, crashing to the table next to Aphrodite, panting as if I'd just raced a mile. Our bodies were slick with sweat, but the glowing symbols painting us had not smeared at all. On the other hand, my veins no longer glowed beneath my skin.

I craned my neck to see Aphrodite staring up at the ceiling high above, a stunned look on her face. "Impossible," she whispered.

I'd beaten back the carnage—and Aphrodite's ever so helpful solution of slapping skins like two wild animals atop King Arthur's Round Table in my secret, underground, inter-dimensional library. At my parents' house. Only now did I realize how sad and depressing my victory actually was.

"Chastity!" I cheered weakly, barely able to lift my shaking fist.

She slowly turned to look at me. "As impressive as that was, I have decided to make it my life goal to get you to have sex. You are a black hole of loneliness. You need this. The world needs you to need this," she said firmly.

I narrowed my eyes. "Hey. Let me enjoy this miracle without your nagging."

"I will murder your abstinence," she vowed, "as my duty to all of existence."

I grunted, lifting my gaze to stare up at the ceiling—a depiction of the night sky made from precious gems to indicate stars, constellations, and distant planets. I'd frequently come down here to stare up at them, liking to think that Kai, my old Beast, was up there somewhere looking down on me. It should say something that I felt more connected to a Beast than my ancestors.

But that was because my ancestors had all been assholes. Every one of them.

Aphrodite reached out and clutched my hand tightly. I squeezed back reassuringly. "To be completely honest, I'm open to negotiation on the whole find Nate a lover thing. Or else I'm going to need to invest in icepacks." I smirked. "All the icepacks."

She burst out laughing, squeezing my hand even tighter. "There aren't enough in the world."

My thoughts drifted to Peter.

The instant obsidian casting had probably served as a bandage to stop the bleeding of Raego's throat-slash, allowing Peter to actually heal beneath the stone over the past few years. He would be truly insane by now if he'd been conscious this whole time. He'd been halfway there before we'd sentenced him to death.

I needed to get these damned Titan Thorns off, and I needed to get my friends off the board before they accidentally hunted me down, thinking I was the real Peter. Raego had been convinced. I knew Peter would also want to hunt down his impersonator. And he likely had a bracelet overloaded with power that would get the job done. Unless Zeus had brought Peter up to speed already, maybe even pointing Peter at me as the price to pay for his release. Peter probably knew more about the current shitstorm than I did.

"How did they see through the paint?" I asked, frowning down at the runes and symbols covering my body.

She paused, looking uncertain. "I do not know. It should have been impossible." Her tone made me glance over, so I saw the raw fear in her eyes before she masked it from me. "Perhaps Zeus found a way to nullify my powers," she mused uneasily. "I obviously have no power to seduce you," she said, dryly.

I grunted. "Doubtful. I'm just infinitely defiant—even to my own detriment."

I swept my gaze across the Sanctorum, frowning uneasily at a new thought. Why hadn't Chateau Falco reacted to my presence? She either should have responded with a warm welcome if she saw through my disguise, or sounded an alarm if she hadn't. But the torches had flared.

"I'm not sure it's safe here," I said, sitting up.

Aphrodite sighed, sitting up as well. "You've proven you're worthless to me at the moment," she grumbled. "You are running out of time. I do not know what Zeus intends tomorrow, but it has a sense of finality to it. You must find a way to remove the Titan Thorns. It is your only chance."

I nodded my agreement. "I know." I took a deep breath and met her eyes. "I need you to do me a favor."

"What kind of favor?"

"I need you to return to Olympus. To turn yourself in."

She paled, licking her lips. "He will kill me."

I shook my head firmly. "No. He might torture you, but he has a sick dependency on his kids. He needs you to worship and revere him." She shuddered knowingly. "And he might not even torture you when you tell him that Hephaestus is the key to acquiring Pandora's Box."

She stiffened abruptly. "What?" she hissed. "That is impossible. My husband would have told me—would have told Zeus."

I met her gaze, unflinching. "Just trust me. Tell him that Hephaestus will no longer be used as leverage, or Zeus will castrate his own chances at acquiring Pandora's Box or the Armory." I smirked. "Use that word. Castrate."

She grimaced, knowing the reference. It was what Zeus' father, Cronus, had done to his own father, Uranus. Something to make Zeus ponder and fret over. "Is it true?"

I smiled at her, not answering. "I hope I can figure out these manacles without you," I said.

She smiled sadly. "You do not need me to confirm your answer. You need to give the question serious thought. When you say the right name out loud—with confidence—the Titan Thorns should fall free all on their own. I am merely here to help you wander the path—not to point out the path for you. And you found your pearl all by yourself."

"Any last-minute pointers?" I asked, hopefully.

She was silent for a few moments. "Think on what your goals are. Not now, but what they have always been. Who has embodied them to such a degree that you hold them in high esteem? Who could give you advice on such values and you would be least likely to question their source? Not just who would agree with you, but who would emulate your chosen ideals best. Also, don't disregard someone just because you might disagree at times. Iron sharpens iron, after all."

I grunted. "So, in summary, someone who might argue with me or someone who might not."

She sighed. "Yes, if you want to oversimplify it."

My thoughts immediately went to Kára's adamant declaration to Freya —how she wanted to be my confidante. Could she really be Indie? I kept toggling between yes and no, finding arguments for both sides. Either answer seemed wrong, unfortunately, despite genuinely liking Kára as a woman to *begin* a romance. She wasn't someone I *already loved* unconditionally.

"I'm definitely ready to return," I muttered.

"As you wish." She hesitated for a few more moments, lingering on my shoulder to the point that I wondered whether she was the figurative angel or devil attempting to influence me. "Be wary of the Valkyrie. Matters of the heart will not matter if you allow yourself to succumb to the pleasures of the flesh to hide from your heart."

I flinched, fearing she had read my mind somehow. "Christ, Aphrodite. Are you trying to depress me or help me?"

The room began to dim at the edges as my vision tunneled towards the center. "Yes," she whispered, her breath tickling my ears. "Love hurts."

36

I opened my eyes to find myself back in... "Niflhut," I murmured, nodding.

Thankfully, Aphrodite had left, allowing me to endure my walk of shame with dignity rather than having to escort the body paint version of the goddess of sex in front of my crew. Her scent still lingered on my skin.

I was seated on a dusty, rotted crate. I shifted my weight and it collapsed into splinters, sending me crashing to the floor with a curse. I jumped to my feet, brushing at my rear and groin, fearful of a poisonous Niflheim splinter skewering my ass or impaling my giggle berries like misty cocktail olives.

I froze to find that I wore a crisp dark suit with a loosely buttoned white dress shirt. I even had new shoes. "What the fuck?" I whispered out loud. It was a perfect fit. I frowned, spotting my robe in a wadded ball with a strip of paper resting atop it. I scooped up the note and read it.

The robe was hideous. Always wear protection.

I grunted, crumbling the paper in my fist. Protection? I got the joke, but was the suit armored in some way? I would find out soon enough. Regardless, Aphrodite had pimped me out—and she'd known my size more accurately than any tailor. I chuckled, shaking my head. At least she hadn't given me a toga. As I inspected my new threads, I winced at the illuminated symbols that still painted my skin.

I quickly checked for any kind of reflective surface to check my face. I found a sliver of broken mirror and immediately cursed to see the intricate designs Aphrodite had painted on my face and cheeks. I continued staring, touching at my cheeks thoughtfully. I looked...

Pretty damned cool, actually. An angled blue line stretched from my temple to my chin, curving to bisect my eyes and lips from either side. Another dashed line cut my face in half from my hairline to converge at my chin with the others. Random symbols and shapes filled out the rest of my face in a haunting mask that made me grin toothily.

It was a shame to have to wash it off, but it wouldn't do much for protection—as indicated by Raego instantly spotting me on his lawn, and it definitely wouldn't help with stealth. I sighed unhappily, searching the room for anything that might help me clean up. I found a bottle of water with the safety seal intact, verifying that it hadn't been tampered with. Must have been from Ashley's stay here. I popped off the top and wetted the sleeve of my robe, scrubbing at my face with the thin sliver of mirror as my only guide. I needed to hurry. As I worked, my thoughts drifted to the Omegabet, wondering exactly what Aphrodite had painted on me. I hadn't told her my plan, but it involved a lot more than finding the key to my heart.

Because if I was going down, I was taking a whole pantheon with me. Zeus' victory would be tarnished by blood and chaos, with ripples big enough to shake the world.

I would unleash a storm of consequences that even the god of lightning couldn't weather.

"Nate?" Kára called out from the other room.

I dropped the bottle of water with a curse of surprise and it splashed all over the floor. I dropped to my knees, careful not to get my suit wet as I soaked up as much as possible with my dingy robe. I didn't have any other water and I had wanted to wash the symbols off my chest as well. "In here!" I snapped, furiously wiping the damp towel at my face to remove as much evidence as possible. I didn't want to look like a glow stick when Kára came in. I could already imagine her ensuing interrogation.

"Nate?" she called out in a louder tone from just beyond the door, sounding concerned.

"Yeah. In here," I assured her, scrubbing my face hard enough to irritate my skin.

The door squeaked open on dry hinges and I felt the Valkyrie enter behind me. "I saw the glow under the door and it looked like it was moving," she said. "Where is the candle?"

"What?" I asked, keeping my back to her as I patted my face dry with the other sleeve.

"Whatever was illuminating the cabin," she said, as if I was particularly dim-witted.

"Oh, right," I said, gesturing at the puddle of water. "I dropped the candle in the water."

I finally turned to look at her, using her reaction as a mirror. She didn't jump back in surprise, so I must have done a passable job. She smiled crookedly, tucking her hands behind her back, which only served to emphasize her significant curves. She waited in silence.

I stood up, feeling markedly uncomfortable under her scrutiny—and her general presence. The goddess of sex's parting warning whispered in my ears. "So."

"Did you find your candle?"

I blinked, caught off guard. "Um. It...rolled away." Why was the goddamned candle so important to her?

She sighed, her smile fading. "I see." Her eyes darted about the cabin, obviously searching for Aphrodite.

"It wasn't what it looked like," I reminded her softly. "She's helping me with something."

"Okay," she said in a soft, almost hurt, tone.

I clenched my jaws, and attempted to walk around her, not knowing what I could do to make her feel better. My time with Aphrodite had hurt her feelings, but there was nothing I could do about it if she wouldn't believe me.

Kára, I learned, was not the kind of woman to let me run from confrontation. She grabbed hold of my shirt and jerked me close. I grunted in surprise as our chests bumped together, our eyes only inches apart. I realized, quite suddenly, that she was not wearing her armor. I'd somehow entirely missed that obvious fact. Instead, she wore primitive leather and fur pants and a linen shirt with an untied drawstring at the neck. She looked much smaller without all her armor yet she looked more imposing at the same time, commanding every inch of her height.

My anger dissipated as her scent enveloped me, replacing that of Aphrodite. I stared into her eyes, wondering what this was all about. She averted her eyes and stepped back, shattering the moment. I closed my eyes, realizing that my emotions were barely skin deep after my time with Aphrodite. Every problem seemed to have the same solution in my current state.

Fuck it.

For better or worse.

"Aphrodite is trying to help me make sense of some personal problems," I said stiffly.

She nodded. "It's okay, Nate." I could tell that it was not, in fact, okay. Kára was hurt, and she didn't know how to fight this foe.

Which sucked. I wanted to help her, but I was the source of the problem. She'd told me long before all this Titan Thorns nonsense, how she felt about me. I'd turned her down, using Callie as an excuse. Yet she now knew Callie was no longer an issue, and I'd yet to address the topic for round two. Even after our affectionate reunion when she'd hugged me.

But I could not afford distractions right now. And what right did she have being jealous? She'd seemed amused about Aphrodite earlier. She'd even teased me about it, so why the change? "I'm only going to say this one more time, Kára. I have no interest in Aphrodite. I lost something and she's trying to help me find it."

She nodded slowly, a faint smile curling her lips. "Like invisible candles?" she asked, pointing at my chest. I frowned, glancing down.

I sighed. My chest was glowing beneath my shirt, and she'd gotten an up close look when she'd grabbed me. Clever, clever, clever. "Right. You got me. I didn't have a candle, but the truth is a little more embarrassing. I wasn't lying to hide—"

"Nate," she said, interrupting me. "I don't give one flying fuck about the harlot." I blinked. She shrugged. "I cannot stop poachers from circling, but I can point out a vulture when I see one." She shrugged. "Competition is healthy."

"Then why are you angry?"

She watched me for a few moments. "I'm not sure if you are aware, but you should never ask a woman why she is angry." I smirked, nodding. "I was angry about your lie," she said, indicating the glow beneath my shirt. "Even one so simple as an invisible candle. White lies become habitual, and I'd rather be cut by honesty than stabbed by deceit."

I winced, lowering my eyes. "I understand. I'm sorry. This is—"

"I have no right to your secrets," she interrupted firmly. "Just do not lie to me. That's all."

We stood in silence for a few moments. Finally, I nodded. "That's fair, Kára."

She smiled to clear the air. "I like your friends. I got to know them very well while you..." she glanced about the room, "dropped candles," she said, teasingly. "Yahn said your collection of weapons is worthless. But he wanted me to give you this," she said, extending a black stone on a leather thong. The Sensate necklace. The cord was wrapped around the black stone, securing it in place. "Carl is already wearing his. Yahn said you'll need to tape the others to your manacles to guarantee they don't break contact—which is the whole point. A bracelet cannot guarantee that."

I nodded, accepting the necklace with a sigh of relief. I put it on. "Any difference?" I asked, hoping that my Peter illusion had dropped.

She studied me up and down curiously. "You still look like the douchebag."

I narrowed my eyes. "Ow. Thank you. I really needed that."

She grinned, slipping her arm around my waist and guiding me towards the door of the Niflhut. "You were looking a little arrogant. Humble pie is always beneficial—if not to you, to everyone else who hears it. Laughs cure all." She tugged at my jacket. "The suit is a nice touch. From the vulture?"

I chuckled. "She didn't like the robe."

"I did," she said with a smile. "The suit is durable. An armor of sorts, although I can't place exactly what it protects against."

I frowned. "Is it safe?"

She nodded. "Yes. I can sense that it is a genuine gift, not a trap."

I blinked. "You can do that?"

She nodded as she pushed the door open. It was still daytime. Unless there was no day or night here. I wasn't entirely sure.

Aphrodite's note had said to wear protection. And the suit was better than the robe. "I hope the Sensate works. Maybe they really can't track me through the Titan Thorns. Ares and Apollo would have paid me a visit by now if they could." Kára shrugged, not having an answer. I thought about Yahn's lack of success on the items from Grimm Tech. "I can't believe that none of the stuff is offensive," I muttered. "I really wanted to be offensive today."

She chuckled, catching my play on words. "He seemed remarkably concerned about a stuffed teddy bear. He said it was baring it's teeth at him."

I grunted, shaking my head. "Why? It just puts people to sleep."

She glanced at me. "He says it was designed for torture and that it breaks the mind from within. That the nightmares linger beyond waking if you hold the bear too long."

I frowned. "I didn't have any nightmares."

She shrugged. "It's what he said. Ask him your questions," she said, jerking her chin towards the fire. Yahn and Carl watched us, looking anxious.

37

I quickly caught them up to speed on what I'd learned from Aphrodite about Peter, leaving out the juicier personal bits. Because I was a gentleman, not because I was embarrassed to admit my abstinence had saved the world and given Aphrodite a new life purpose.

When I'd finished, Yahn let out a long breath. "Shit," he said, leaning back. "The Reds are going to kill me."

I rolled my eyes at his lack of professionalism. His love life was the least of our concerns. My love life, on the other hand, was extremely important. And I wasn't complaining about it. I was scheming. Like a responsible, professional adult.

Kára was watching me curiously, looking thoughtful to hear that my time with Aphrodite had indeed been informative. She had no idea.

"Peter and Alaric," I said, pointing at my chest and then Carl, "are actively being hunted by the scariest monsters in St. Louis—my Horsemen and the dragons. If they get their hands on us, we're dead. Period." Kára bristled, her armor suddenly whispering back into place. I sighed regretfully and she grinned. "And it's safe to say Peter is on the hunt as well—either working for Zeus and knowing full well who I really am, or because he's heard of an impersonator breaking into Grimm Tech."

Yahn grunted, shaking his head. "It seems like overkill."

I nodded. "You're not wrong. It's a complicated hit job, forcing me to come crawling back to Olympus tomorrow night if I want to survive. Staying here will just get me killed by Peter or my friends."

Carl grimaced. "Choosing Peter as a disguise was clever, but making me look like Alaric Slate was foolish. Everyone knows he is dead. Perhaps if I reached out to Alucard—"

I shook my head firmly. "No. This is my team." Kára murmured her approval, smiling. "We are going to use Zeus' own trap against him. I'm finished reacting. We're going on offense. I'm going to raze Olympus to the ground."

"How?" Kára asked, sitting down beside me.

I took a deep breath. "Kidnapping, theft, and extortion. We're not playing checkers," I mused recalling the board game I'd spied Hermes and Zeus playing. "The only move that really matters is the last one. Until then, we set up our pieces as best we can, taking hits when needed as long as it puts us in the best position for that last lucky roll. Then, we crush him."

Kára nodded thoughtfully, licking her lips. "Let us do this thing." She turned to Carl and Yahn. They murmured their steadfast agreement in a pair of growls.

Then Kára suddenly whipped two daggers out from who the fuck knows where and struck Yahn and Carl in the chest—simultaneously.

I hissed, my reflexes kicking in, but I abruptly noticed that Carl and Yahn were not gushing blood. They hadn't reacted. They hadn't even blinked. They stared back at Kára with grim resolve. I looked down to see her daggers had struck them hilt first, and that Kára's hands were dripping blood as she gripped the blades with her bare hands. She stared deeply into their eyes, silently demanding their commitment to the cause, not taking their earlier growls as sufficient.

"The fear of spilling your first drop of blood for a cause is a powerful thing. It will fester in your heart, slowing your reflexes and inviting hesitation." They nodded, mesmerized by her speech and actions. It seemed ritualistic. A Valkyrie tradition? "To that end, I chose to face that fear on my own terms. I have now spilled the first drops of my blood for this man," she said, the blood seeming to spill faster as her hands began to shake from squeezing the daggers tighter. "I now have nothing left to fear. I am already invested. My heart and mind are now impervious to self-doubt.

When the time comes to spill more blood for Nate Temple, I will laugh heartily, fondly recalling these two little pricks," she growled, lifting the daggers high so that the blood spilled down her wrists and forearms. The air seemed to pulse with energy, and I wasn't sure if it was magic or a mental boost of confidence from her words.

Kára lowered her daggers and flung them down at the ground, burying them to the hilt between Yahn and Carl's feet—one for each man.

Yahn calmly grabbed the blade between his boots, looking ten years older in my eyes. Actually, the look in his eyes was downright frightening. Had Kára done something to them, or was this the effect of a proper speech at the proper time? I wasn't sure I had ever inspired anyone quite so well as she just had. Hell, she'd even inspired me. Yahn locked eyes with Kára as he dragged the blade across his forearm, spilling fresh blood. "I spill first blood and vanquish all fear, Kára."

That vibration in the air was almost audible now. It was real. Some energy that was now bouncing back and forth between Kára, Yahn, and me. I had missed Carl drawing his own dagger, but it was impossible to miss him slicing into his arm, because he had to apply a lot more effort to penetrate his hardened scales. "I spill first blood and vanquish all fear, Kára."

The energy in the air practically crackled, and I felt a tingle of excitement race down my spine. The three turned to me, eerily calm. They looked more relaxed now that they'd bled all over themselves. "Thank you," I said, humbled. I held out my hand for a dagger.

Kára shook her head vehemently. "No. That is bad luck. We spill blood for you, not with you." I withdrew my hand, nodding my understanding. Yahn and Carl handed her back the daggers. Kára accepted them, smiling warmly at our group. "We are now family, and I bleed for my brothers and sisters." They echoed her oath.

"I don't think I have ever been so excited in my life," Carl whispered to Yahn, except he said it loud enough for everyone to hear.

Yahn chuckled, looking surprised at his own peace of mind. "Yeah. Me too, actually."

Kára smirked at their naivety. "You made an oath with a Valkyrie. It is a great honor. It is usually followed by days of feasting, fucking, and fighting. In whichever order suits your mood," she added with a grin.

Yahn and Carl shared a long look, smiling like thieves before a heist.

Kára flashed me a bright smile, wiping off the daggers and sheathing them. "When do we leave?" she asked, oddly jubilant.

"Soon. I am going to reintroduce Zeus to fear, but we're going to have to take a few hits on the chin to keep our true movements hidden. I'm going to Hell."

Yahn leaned forward. "What about us? I don't know if we could survive Hell. Literally," he admitted, not in fear, but speaking the simple truth.

Carl waved a claw dismissively. "It's lovely down there. I'll be fine." Kára eyed him thoughtfully, looking impressed.

I shook my head. "You two have other tasks ahead of you. Kára will join me in Hell." I glanced over at the Valkyrie. "If you would be so kind."

She grinned devilishly and scooped up her trident. "You didn't ask Aphrodite to go to Hell," she said smugly. "I win."

I grinned, shaking my head. "There's only one girl I would take to Hell."

She beamed appreciatively. "This is going to be fun. Since the gentleman made the arrangements, it's only proper that a lady follow his lead," she said, sounding amused.

I nodded, unable to deny the aura of confidence from my team—we were united. I was no longer alone. "I can open a Gateway..." I trailed off, staring into the middle distance.

Carl cleared his throat. "You cannot make a Gateway, Master Temple," he whispered.

I slowly turned to Kára, wincing. She was grinning. "I am a Valkyrie. We have our own entrance, but we might have to fly a ways unless you wish to walk through Niflheim." I grimaced, shaking my head. "Then it looks like the *lady* will make the arrangements, and the *gentleman* will have to follow *her* lead," taking entirely too much pleasure from the turn of events. Then she poured salt in the wound. "Wear something cute for me. It is a date, after all. I'll pick you up. Literally," she clarified, her metallic wings suddenly erupting from her shoulder blades.

Yahn was grinning. I sighed, admitting defeat, and Kára's wings tucked back in with a metallic whisper. "Well, it's only polite," I admitted, grinning. Then I turned to Yahn and Carl. "You guys are going to hate me..."

"What do you need?" Yahn asked, determined to prove me wrong. "It can't be worse than Hell."

I felt the eyepatch still hanging from my neck. I took it off and tossed it to him. "So no one sees you when you kidnap Ryuu, Callie's bodyguard. He's a ninja, by the way."

Yahn's smile slipped. *"What?"*

Kára burst out laughing, grinning like a cat with a saucer of milk.

Carl studied me thoughtfully. "What else?" he asked.

I met his eyes, refusing to flinch from them. "We need to kidnap someone close to Alucard as well." I turned to Yahn. "The Reds. Unless you think you could kidnap Tory."

Yahn shook his head numbly. "I'm as useful as a puppet against a Beast Master."

Carl considered it. "Not if you want her in one piece," he finally said. "But two pieces, on the other claw..." he suggested, trailing off to gauge my reaction.

I shook my head adamantly. "No. *One* piece, Carl." I waited until he nodded.

"What about Gunnar?" Yahn asked. "I really hope you're not planning on—"

"Let me worry about Gunnar," I said, interrupting him. That part of my plan had a few additional steps they didn't need to know about. "You're going to leave a note behind where the Horsemen can immediately find it. The timing is crucial. They need to instantly know they've been hit." Yahn gulped, his face paling. "Now, here's what your note needs to say. Not in my handwriting, and not in yours. They might recognize it."

Kára leaned closer. "I can write them."

"Good," I said. Yahn handed her a tiny Moleskine notepad and a pen from his pocket—a total manager move. I chose my words carefully. "*Tell a single soul and they die. Meet me at noon on Chateau Falco's front lawn if you want to see them alive again. —Peter.*"

Kára chuckled, scribbling on the pad. "A setup," she mused.

"How are we going to get them without hurting them?" Yahn asked. "They're all fighters."

I smiled, pointing at Roofie Ruxpin.

Yahn flinched. "I don't think you realize how dangerous he is. Touch him for too long and the nightmares might not ever leave," he said warningly. "We designed it for the toughest of foes, to override all sense of self-preservation or loyalty they have, and force them to spill their secrets."

"They only need to hold it long enough to get taken."

He sighed, nodding in resignation. "And where is that? Where are we going to house a group of hostages who want to kill us? Preferably, somewhere Horsemen-proof."

I smiled. "Buddy Hatchet."

Kára glanced at me sharply. "My bar?" she blurted.

I shrugged. "I've seen the security measures, but we won't need them. It's just a temporary spot. I need you guys to trust me on this." She sighed, finally nodding. Yahn and Carl looked equally doubtful, but they did nod. Good enough. "You have a phone?" I asked her. She nodded. "Give Yahn your number so we can stay in touch." She scribbled a number down on his notepad and handed it back to him. Along with his pen.

"Zeus will know you're behind this," Yahn said, reading the number and pocketing it.

I nodded, smiling. "And what could he do about it? The trap he set for me is so intricate that it will trip him up just as well as it does me. He can't very well tell the Horsemen the truth."

I watched them play it out in their heads, smiling as they realized my point. My plan was also the only way I could think to get Alice back safely. I swallowed my anxiety, briefly imagining her cold and alone, locked in my old prison cell or worse. I gritted my teeth. *I'm coming, Alice.*

I pointed at Yahn's eyepatch. "Use that to hide your identity." I turned to Carl. "Let them get a good look at Alaric Slate. I hereby promote you both to pirates."

"Aye aye, Cap'n!" Kára hooted. Yahn and Carl echoed her cheer.

But my heart had skipped a beat to hear Indie's familiar phrase come from Kára's lips. They were too excited to notice my momentary surprise. I managed a smile.

A very nervous one.

Yahn bent down to scoop up my satchel. He handed it to me, dipping his chin. "The Sensates and the duct tape are inside if you want to tape up your manacles like Carl," he said, glancing at my necklace.

"Thanks. I hope it works."

He nodded, gesturing at the pile of junk I'd stolen from Grimm Tech. "Kára told you it was all worthless, right? Nothing worth even keeping locked up, to be blunt. You must have the worst luck ever."

I narrowed my eyes. "Thank you."

He smiled. "I have a few Tiny Balls on me, but none of them go to Kansas City. Luckily, I know I have one that does at my apartment." He lifted a golden marble with a smirk. "And I always carry one to my apartment."

I nodded in relief. I was so used to being able to go anywhere I wanted at the snap of a finger that I rarely considered other means of locomotion. I reached into my satchel and fumbled around in my velvet sack of Tiny Balls, reading and discarding. I finally pulled out the one I had for Kansas City and handed it to him. "Here you go. Kansas City." He smiled in relief, studying it as if he didn't trust me—his boss. "Just curious, but where do your other Tiny Balls go?" I asked with a curious frown. He'd claimed to have a few on him.

He grinned. "Where my Tiny Balls belong. The Reds' house. AKA Alucard's house."

I laughed, shaking my head at his innuendo. "Luck." He shook my hand firmly, then turned to join Carl. I pointed at the Elder. "Do not reach out to Alucard."

He saluted at me. "Aye, aye, Cap'n!" I cringed.

Kára stepped up beside me. "Go to Hell?" she asked with a smirk.

"We have one other quick errand to run before we go to Hell. I meant to ask you sooner, but can you take more than one person with you?"

She frowned suspiciously. "Why?"

I told her.

38

I stood at the end of the long passageway, squinting at the purple flames on the walls, waiting for the alarms to go off in the event my theory was wrong. Kára stood patiently beside me. "Are the flames dangerous?" she finally asked.

I shook my head, not breaking my study of the passageway. "The whole place is dangerous."

She nodded, accepting my warning, even though nothing even remotely dangerous had happened. Thanks to Aphrodite taking me to the Sanctorum earlier for our nightcap, I'd learned that I could enter Chateau Falco without raising an instant alarm. I'd had an old, dusty Tiny Ball in my satchel that would take me here, but I hadn't wanted to risk setting off Falco's alarms, or having my friends learn of my sudden appearance.

"It's really me, Falco," I whispered. "I swear. I hope you and Ruin have been—"

The rafters groaned faintly. Not enough to alarm anyone else in the mansion, but enough to at least let me know she'd heard me.

"There you are, old girl," I said, patting the wall with a big goofy smile. Other than Carl, she was the only one to have recognized the real me, and it made my heart swell with love. I hugged the wall, leaning forward to rest my cheek against the cold stone. It instantly warmed.

Kára snorted incredulously. "Really? A hug?"

I pulled away from the wall and pointed at the spot I'd been touching with my cheek. She frowned suspiciously and then touched it. She gasped. "It's hot," she whispered, yanking her hand away. Then she touched the rest of the wall and frowned. "The rest is cold."

I smiled, nodding along. "That's my lady Beast, Falco. My one true love. She's never gonna give me up. Never gonna let me down."

Kára's smile faded and she nodded awkwardly. She had her trident strapped to her back, but I knew she had a handful of discreet blades camouflaged in her scuffed, but still elegant, armor. In fact, I was certain her armor had been designed to conceal the hilts. "Does that mean we can proceed? We still have to worry about the residents, and I don't think you have an escape plan, do you? No more safe destinations for your Tiny Balls?" I narrowed my eyes at her smirk and she chuckled, lifting a hand in defeat. "I had to. Who names such an incredible invention Tiny Balls? It's a blatant middle finger to everyone you know who will use it in the future, forcing them to say something ridiculous just to make you laugh."

I grunted. "Well, maybe someone more responsible should have gotten off their ass and imagined them. And Falco loves my Tiny Balls, because she's loyal. Right, old girl?"

I slapped the wall with my palm and the stone around us for ten feet suddenly glowed in the dark. My eyes shot wide open, momentarily panicking. That was a new reaction. At least I knew we were in a secluded, locked down area of the mansion—I was fairly certain we were on an extended plane of reality, in fact—and that no one would be patrolling here. I was one of the very, very few who had a Tiny Ball leading here. The only other way to the Sanctorum was walking in through the front door of the mansion—attracting the attention of everyone on the property—and approaching the magical door that only I could open. I glanced over my shoulder with a frown. Or through the waterfall behind us that led to Fae. Now that I thought about it, I really should have set up stronger wards for that back door. Always watch your six.

I made my way down the hall, speaking low to Falco. "Keep an eye out for me. We need to make it to the Armory without anyone seeing us."

The house rumbled and a sharp crack drew me up short as I held out my hands for Kára to stop. She gripped two daggers in her hands, staring over my shoulder warily. Then she gasped, drawing the blades and raising them towards the wall in a defensive stance.

I followed her attention to see what looked like a new door set into the stone. "Falco?" I whispered giddily. "Have you been holding out on me? A secret fucking passage?" I hissed. "You *know* how much I love secret fucking passages!" Kára smiled at my boyish reaction, lowering her blades.

I gripped Kára by the arm and tugged her after me, shouldering the stone block open. It grated loudly as it moved, but there was nothing for it but to press onward. The purple torches of the hallway puffed out behind us as I pushed the door closed behind me.

Our new tunnel was pitch black, and Kára was gripping my hand tightly, refusing to let go. I couldn't see her face, so I was happy that she couldn't see mine. I stood like that for a few seconds longer than absolutely necessary, taking in the sensation of her warm flesh against mine, and thinking back on Aphrodite's sybaritic syllabus of love.

It also felt nice that someone as tough as Kára reflexively trusted me to protect her.

With a sigh, I shouldered my satchel out of the way and rested my free hand on the wall of our secret passageway. The stone began to glow, stretching ahead of us with a cool blue light to help guide us. Kára's eyes reflected the gleam in two different ways, making them even more mesmerizing. She was staring at me with open interest, momentarily forgetting to mask her emotions. She abruptly lowered her eyes, turning to face the path ahead. "Sorry. It took a few seconds for my eyes to adjust."

I waited a moment. "You could have taken a few more," I said carefully, watching her reaction. Her shoulders tightened, but she didn't look my way.

"I did not know you were a cruel man, Nate Temple," she said softly.

I flinched as if she'd slapped me, my cheeks reddening. "Right. That wasn't appropriate. I'm sorry, Kára." I let out a frustrated breath.

She nodded stiffly. "I've made my feelings clear. I expect your response to be as equally...heartfelt and genuine. Not mocking."

I hung my head, seriously considering her words. Right now was not the time. Then another fact wormed its way into my thoughts. She saw Peter when she looked at me, not Nate. She'd been checking out *Peter*. My mood instantly soured. "This whole thing pisses me off. Knowing that people see someone else when they look at me is surprisingly disheartening, and it hits me about five seconds after the fact, catching me off guard. When they hear my voice, they're hearing a different voice. When they hold my hand, they're holding someone else's hand. When they hug me, they're hugging someone else." I met her eyes. "A man I *hate*."

She had flinched at each example, knowing full well they applied directly to her. She turned to look at me, meeting my eyes. "And do you think it's not equally infuriating for everyone *else*? For *me*?" she said in a low warning tone. "I'm forced to look at this douchebag," she spat, waving a hand at me from head-to-toe, "and I have to try to imagine the man I admire beneath. Perhaps when I hear your nauseating voice, I am twisting it in my mind so that your real voice parrots it. Perhaps when I smile at this disgrace of a creature, I am trying to encourage the real you to persist and not give up. Perhaps when I reach out to hold your hand, it is the act of a fellow warrior supporting you on the field of battle, ignoring the fact that you're now missing a goddamned leg! That I'm trying to be fucking *brave* for you, looking past all that you are suffering!" she shouted, her voice cracking through the passageway. Kára abruptly turned her back on me, visibly trembling with anger.

I tried to mentally sink into the stone floor, but Falco wouldn't let me. In fact, she seemed entirely too pleased about my comeuppance, shifting her glowing walls closer to Kára. So much for loyalty.

"There is a difference, Nate Temple," she said, still facing away from me, but speaking in a gentler tone. "I know a thing or two about suffering a new body. It takes a while to break in. At least yours is only temporary, and those who matter know who you truly are."

My heart split at the pain in her words, but I knew she didn't want me to call her out on them. Just like I didn't really want people reminding me that I looked like Peter every two minutes. But her admission also told me something I had only assumed. Kára was wearing a new body.

So...what had she looked like before? And why *this* body, specifically?

"I'm sorry for snapping at you, and I'm sorry for poking fun at you. If you like eyeballing douchebags in the dark, have at it," I said, holding my arms out wide to put myself on display.

She coughed out a laugh, glancing over her shoulder at me. "Okay," she said. She sighed, turning to face me. She assessed me up and down like a side of beef. "Consider yourself eyeballed, douchebag."

I rolled my eyes. "Okay—"

She stepped forward into my personal space, leaning forward to lock eyes with me from only inches away. "The reason I was staring was because sometimes I feel like I can see your eyes—not his—staring back at me," she whispered.

I held my breath, torn between which eye to focus on—the green or the blue—and wondering if I could take her advice, peering through her eyes to see the real woman beyond.

Finally, she pulled back with a resigned sigh. "Nope. Still the douchebag."

I let out a frustrated grunt. Kára's words cut deeper than anything I'd suffered from Ares or Apollo. Even Aphrodite wasn't as painful.

39

I frowned, scuffing the ground with my shoe. "Let's go before I make a bigger ass of myself." And then my mouth kept right on flapping of its own accord. "Just so you know, I'm terrified of the dark, so if I grab your hand, it's definitely not because you look ridiculously amazing in that armor and that you make it difficult for me to think straight. Even though my mind is going in a million directions right now, it all comes into sharper focus when I look at you. I know it's not fair, and I'm not trying to lead you on. When I'm with you, it feels so natural that I speak without thinking. Reflex flirting, I guess, and I'm out of practice."

My words echoed in the passageway, leaving behind their own kind of physical silence.

She slowly turned to look at me, and her eyes were dilated despite the glowing walls. "I feel your eyes on me often, Nate," she whispered. "If you had a mound of clay, I have no doubt that you could sculpt a perfect image of me in a dark room. I *know* this." She stepped closer, her armored chest coming within inches of contact. "Yet the next minute, you deny you have hands with which to sculpt. It is beyond frustrating."

I realized I was breathing heavily, clenching my fists. "I...see."

"Carl explained your little bracelets," she said, tapping them with a finger and making me jump, "in great detail. Your project with Aphrodite.

How you are stuck in a fairy tale, searching for true love to escape your prison."

I blushed. "That rat bastard."

She grunted. "Which was good, because when you told me I had been right about Callie..." she trailed off, licking her lips and suppressing a shudder, "I intended to restate my case to the Court of Appeals. Vehemently. Vivaciously. Scandalously. And shamelessly," she whispered.

Each word fell on my ears like she was removing an article of clothing, dropping it to the floor between us. I was panting, unable to break eye contact. "Oh?" I squeaked.

"But that is not what I want. If I merely wanted to seduce you, I would have already claimed my prize. If you wanted to be merely seduced, you would have let me. You claim you seek true love, but you are a blind, foolish, stubborn, idiotic man," she said, shoving my chest and forcing me to take a step back. She advanced after me, not relenting. "In our story, I am not the beggar shaking my tin cup for coins, and you are not the billionaire graciously helping the poor. I do not need—or accept—your *charity*. In our story, as you are now, you are the damsel in distress and I am the fucking knight in dented armor. Throw down your fucking hair already, Nate."

I stared at her, clenching my jaws and flexing my fists. "Did...you just call me a *girl*?" I whispered dangerously.

She scoffed. "If the shoe fits, Cinderella."

The glowing walls were still favoring Kára, for those at home keeping score.

Kára took a calming breath. "I did not ask for this armor, but when my time came, I accepted it. I'm a quick study, so I grew into it well. But that does not mean I don't want to someday be the princess. The difference between us is I now know when it's time to put on a dress and when it's time to put on my armor. The choice in clothing does not dictate or alter who I am beneath it. Our character roles are not static or permanent, because our fairy tales are darker and everlasting—requiring us to adapt or perish. You've worn the armor for far too long, and I see your shoulders sagging, your steed faltering, your sword and shield dragging," she whispered compassionately, lifting my chin with a gauntleted hand. "No matter what happens between us, take this to heart...your bartender is telling you to sit down, take off your armor for a spell, and have a drink before you get yourself killed. She has a shotgun under the counter, so she can keep you safe while you recover from your weary travels. Fucking let her, you idiot."

I was doing a lot more than breathing heavily at that point. Despite the lethality of her strong feelings, I was able to take them in the manner intended. She was a Valkyrie, after all—and maybe the key to a happy Valkyrie's bedroom was a lot of tender loving goreplay.

Right now, I might be the princess in my story, but I had been the knight for quite a while. And...it *was* wearing on me. "Who are you, really?" I asked, softly.

"Your bartender," she said softly.

I shook my head. "Who *were* you? How did you become a Valkyrie?"

She stared at me, her lips trembling. I knew she desperately wanted to tell me. "I...cannot," she whispered harshly.

And I knew my question hit her harder than any sword—and when she had no shield capable of blocking it. So, I let it go. For now. I let out a long sigh. "Okay, Kára."

She turned away, staring down the passageway, wiping at her eyes. "Which way are we going?" she croaked. "I feel like hacking something innocent."

I laughed, surprising myself. "Me, too," I admitted. Then I cocked my head. "Do you have a hatchet hidden somewhere in that armor?"

She turned to me with a frown, sniffling. "If this is one of your lame pickup lines, I might just have to kill you."

I grinned, shaking my head. "No. You said you wanted to hack something innocent to death, but I didn't see an axe."

She stared at me for a few seconds, and then her hand flashed to her belt, checking where her hatchet should have been. She frowned, looking mildly embarrassed. "Must have left it in the chest cavity of that troll. I can just as easily stab or poke something innocent to death." She eyed our surroundings. "This looks like a long hallway, and my patience is very strained at the moment."

"Well, then stop jabbering and let's get moving," I said, slipping past her before she could kick me. I kept my hand on the wall to make sure that the glow didn't wink out and leave her in the dark. As far as I knew, this tunnel shouldn't have existed. Hell, maybe Falco had made it specifically for me on the spot. Maybe Kára could get trapped down here if she didn't keep up—

"Nice ass, Nate. If I squint my eyes in this lighting, I can almost envision the real thing behind the illusion. Keep walking, just like that."

I blushed, glaring over my shoulder. "You're not allowed to say things like that. Only uncouth men can say things like that," I argued. "It's in the rules."

She snorted indelicately. "I'm the knight in this story, princess. And this knight has a filthy mouth. Deal with it. You're not the only one who gets free looks when you think others aren't watching. And I never said I played by the rules. I thought I made that clear."

I sighed, admitting defeat. Bantering back and forth with her was...fun. I hadn't really flirted a whole lot in recent years, other than the very occasional times spent with Callie. "Well, get an eyeful, woman. This ass is over thirty years in the making." I swatted my ass and continued walking. "I usually charge for long, dark walks through creepy underground tunnels. You're welcome."

She chuckled behind me and I heard her picking up her pace so as not to be left in the dark. As we made our way through the tunnels, I looked down, frowning to see finished tile beneath our feet.

"Not so secret, it seems," Kára said, noticing my attention.

I nodded, troubled to discover that Falco had shown us a real secret passageway rather than some magical tunnel formed on the fly to suit my needs. "Must have been over a hundred years since anyone walked here. Hell. Maybe longer." We pressed on, and soon we encountered alcoves set into the walls. They each held unlit lanterns that were definitely hundreds of years old. Our tunnel eventually opened into a vast cavern with arched ceilings. I stared, transfixed.

"It...looks like one of those roaring twenties subway stations," Kára breathed, spinning in a circle to take it all in.

"Light it up, Falco," I whispered. The cavern immediately bloomed with light, bright enough to make me squint. I stared at over a dozen arched doorways set into the walls. They all rippled like water, but I knew it wasn't water. I walked up to one, shaking my head in disbelief. *Niagara Falls* was carved into the stone above the rippling space. "It's a Gateway. A permanent fucking Gateway to New York." I slowly turned, taking in more arched doorways, all listing distant states or major cities East of Missouri. Even some in Canada. *Philadelphia. Boston. Charleston. Atlanta. Fort Malden, Ontario.* I gasped, recognizing the last one. It was also the biggest archway. I pointed at it. "Fort Malden...was one of the main points of entry into Canada for the Underground Railroad," I breathed. "This...isn't a subway, but it is a travel nexus," I whispered. Sure enough, I saw another carving in one of the more prominent arches. *Welcome to Temple Station.*

The depots used in the Underground Railroad had been referred to as *stations.* And...they'd called those who housed runaway slaves in their homes *station masters.* Masters. No fucking way. My ancestors had played a part in the war against slavery? Master Temple suddenly felt like a much heavier title. I needed to look into this more. This was incredible. A piece of my family history that wasn't dark and terrible.

Kára gawked, spinning in a slow circle.

I pointed at the doorways. "My family had permanent access to major cities in the thirteen colonies and more," I said.

Kára's eyes were misty, now that I could clearly see her in the light. "This is incredible."

I nodded, leaning closer to the Gateway with a nervous shudder. "And I'm pretty sure they still work."

Kára immediately grew tense. "What if someone finds the Gateways on the other sides?" she asked, slowly turning to count the number of arched doorways. There had to be fifty of them.

"That...could be very bad. I'll need to check all of these out later. Wall them up, maybe." I didn't say anything, but I was suddenly very concerned that some of my old living relatives like Matthias might know a thing or two about this. Hopefully not.

Because if he'd known, he definitely should have told me.

"Good job, old girl. Good job," I murmured under my breath. The walls seemed to purr at my praise. The station slowly began to dim, all except for a hallway extending out from the cavern that I hadn't noticed before. Those stones glowed brighter, beckoning us onwards.

I grabbed Kára's hand and pulled her after me. "Let's go."

40

Our tunneling adventure came to a halt at another solid wall, much like the one we'd first entered near the Sanctorum. I took a deep breath. "If it's clear on the other side, open her up, Falco," I said, hoping she understood my caveat.

The wall cracked open, this time swinging inwards without my assistance. Which was good, because there hadn't been a handle or anything. We stepped out into a familiar hallway, and I let out a sigh of relief. "We're close."

We were in the tunnels near the entrance to the Armory. The opposite direction would take us to a secret passage leading to my office.

Kára eyed the dim hallways warily. Despite the walls no longer glowing —so as not to give us away, I hoped—the space seemed to have an ambient light of sorts. Thankfully, I was familiar with it or I would have been concerned about—

"Come any closer and I'll burn you up," a reedy voice stammered from around the corner.

Kára whipped her trident out, and her helmet silently rolled down over her head like Iron Man, but infinitely sexier. A shoulder guard suddenly bulged into place as well, on her non-dominant arm. She shot me a hooded look from beneath her helm, but I shrugged. I didn't recognize the voice, but the oddly specific threat made me assume he was a wizard.

I didn't have any wizards living on the property, as far as I knew.

In fact, I'd kind of put a solid dent in my relationship with the wizard Academy recently. So, what was this assclown doing in my mansion, and more importantly, what the hell was he doing down here near the Armory?

I slowly rounded the corner to find a geeky stick of a boy—with about a dozen proudly displayed mustache follicles to his name—pointing a shaking finger at me. He pushed his aviator-sized prescription glasses up the bridge of his nose, and he might as well have wiped at his nose as an afterthought.

"Christ, he's young," Kára whispered from behind me. "You know him?"

I shook my head, holding my hands out so the boy could see I wasn't armed. "Easy, pal." I swiftly scanned the area, realizing that he actually seemed to be guarding the door to the Armory. All by himself. "Who left you down here all alone?" I asked in a soothing tone. Then I took a gamble. "Master Temple always says we work in pairs." I pointed a thumb over my shoulder, indicating Kára. "Like I am."

The boy looked uncertain all of a sudden. "No one knows I'm down here. I figured I would just wait until someone came because I don't know how to get out."

Jesus. Was he serious? He'd been *forgotten* down here? Who the hell was running things up top? It definitely wasn't Gunnar, or this kid would have been on the front lawn doing a thousand pushups a day to build character and make him slightly more threatening than a limp dish rag.

"Well, I'm glad we came across you, then. We were just making our rounds."

The boy's shoulders sagged in relief. "Oh, thank gods. It's been two days!" I made my way closer, shaking my head in both frustration at the lack of leadership and concern for the poor bastard. What if he'd fucking died down here? Would anyone have even told me?

"Who's your partner? We'll get this sorted out. Better yet, who sent you down here to patrol? This place is about as secure as possible and doesn't need a regular guard."

"Who sent me down here?" The boy repeated, and I realized that he suddenly looked older. Bigger. I paused, now only a few paces away. A grim smile split his cheeks and his eyes suddenly smoldered with inner fire. "Tainted Nipple sent me," the Titan growled. "Or should I say, Nate Temple—"

Kára's trident whistled past my ear and hammered into his torso, sending him crashing into the wall with a burst of sparks—which verified exactly who Kára had just impaled without provocation. I turned to look at her, my mouth hanging open.

"What?" She shrugged unashamedly. "He recognized you. And I *told* you I would stab something soon. Obviously, you didn't take me seriously. I win."

I continued to stare at her in disbelief. But she had a point. He *had* recognized me. He'd seen through my illusion. I ignored the pained cries behind me as the man struggled with the trident sticking out of his abdominal region. "That's Prometheus. The *Titan*, Prometheus."

She folded her arms stubbornly. "He was resisting. Or about to. I'm sure of it."

"Really?" Prometheus roared, sounding livid. "The liver? The damned LIVER? AGAIN?!" Prometheus shouted, sounding more upset about that specific vital organ than anything else.

Because that was the part of Prometheus' body the eagle had feasted on every day for at least a couple thousand years—Zeus' punishment for the Titan giving fire to mankind.

And Kára had just opened the old wound.

I raked a hand through my hair, wondering how I could calm everyone down as I turned to face the Titan. He jerked the trident out of his stomach, curled a lip at it in disdain, and then flung it to the ground in Kára's direction. "Nice fork, but you'll need a much better weapon to take down a Titan, girl," he sneered, clutching at his side. It looked like the coals of a fire rather than blood or ichor pouring out. And as I watched, the wound slowly closed. He had finished shifting into a closer resemblance of the ugly man I'd seen chained to the rock on Mount Olympus.

Thankfully, his wounds had healed up and he was no longer twice my size.

Kára scooped up the trident with her foot, flipped it into the air, and caught it. She smiled at the Titan. "Best two out of three?" She asked, hefting the trident playfully.

"Let's all calm down a second," I said, holding out my hands.

Prometheus held up a palm and I tensed, fully expecting a blast of flame. It was kind of his thing. But nothing happened, and I realized he was waiting for a high five. "Oh, don't tell me you're going to leave me hanging," he said, glancing up at his extended palm. "Again." He lowered his hand, but made no threatening move. What the hell was he doing down here? And why wasn't he attacking? He was obviously pissed at me.

I winced. "Yeah. That was not how I meant for that to go down." He pursed his lips at my phrasing since he had, in fact, been knocked off the mountain to fall to Earth. I sighed. "How can you see through this illusion? They're tied to my Titan Thorns," I said, lifting them up.

He grunted, eyeing the manacles in what I took for surprise. "Pissant Olympian illusions can't fool me," he said, folding his arms. He didn't comment on my shackles.

Kára watched him as she was if choosing her next target.

He eyed Kára curiously. "Where's that cross-dressing lizard? Not that I'm complaining that you traded up," he added with a dark, foreboding chuckle. "Even if she is...prickly."

"Hey!" I snapped angrily. Prometheus turned to me and I pretended not to notice Kára's approving smile. "Carl is not a cross-dresser." Kára's smile evaporated, realizing I had not intended to stand for her honor. She shot me a dark look. I just couldn't win. I focused on the Titan. "I...am so glad you survived. I would have preferred your escape over mine."

He stared at me. "Did he chain you to a rock?"

I grunted. "Zeus slapped these on my wrists and then let his psychopathic children play dissect the wizard. Daily. On that note, Ambrosia is not all it's hyped up to be in the stories."

Prometheus narrowed his eyes, taking in my Titan Thorns again. "I don't doubt it."

He studied us in silence and, finally, his shoulders seemed to relax. "Well, are you going to open the fucking door, or what, Tainted Nipple?" he asked, pointing at the Armory.

I grunted. "You know my name isn't actually Tainted Nipple, right?"

He smirked crookedly, a ghastly grin on his horrific face. "Better than the real thing. Nate Temple sounds like a sheep lover. And the Catalyst does not shag sheep."

I narrowed my eyes at him. "That...was not very nice."

"I never much concerned myself with niceties. I always got burned when I tried," he said, dryly, obviously referring to his affinity for fire, and what it had cost him. The multiple punishments Zeus had inflicted on both Prometheus and—

I blinked. "Pandora's Box." Zeus had unleashed Pandora's Box on the world as punishment for accepting Prometheus' fire. Even though they'd had nothing to do with the gift, Zeus had still saw fit to make them pay—to maintain his reputation and image. "Do you know Pandora?" I asked, wondering if he was friend or foe. He was standing right outside the door to her Armory. I watched his face closely.

"Nate?" A voice called out from beyond the stout wooden door. I flinched in surprise, as did Kára and Prometheus. "Is that you?" Pandora asked. "You sound strange."

"Yes, Pandora. It's me. Although I've been hit with a wicked illusion spell, so I look like a douchebag."

"I'd argue it's an improvement," Prometheus said.

"His ass is still nice to look at," Kára piped in helpfully. "If you squint." I shot her a dark glare. She smiled innocently, and I knew it was payback for defending Carl over her.

"Are you okay?" I asked Pandora.

"Yes, my Host. I've missed you."

Prometheus was glaring at the door, looking hurt. "You mean to tell me that you could hear me this whole damned time?" He snapped. "I've been hammering at this door for a week, hiding whenever guards came patrolling, and you pretended not to be home?"

Silence answered him. I waited a few seconds before facing the door. "Do you not want to see him?" I asked her.

"Trust isn't in my wheelhouse these days," she called out. "And I don't know what his intentions are. I do not have a chaperone."

I arched an eyebrow. "Really, Pandora? You didn't need a chaperone with Alex," I said, biting back a grin.

"Yes, well, I was acutely aware of what Alex wanted to do with me," she said, sounding amused. "And you vouched for him. I honestly can't keep track of who is your friend and who is your enemy these days, so my standing policy is no entry without your prior approval."

I nodded, feeling a great weight lift from my shoulders. "That is perfect, Pandora. Good job." Prometheus had folded his arms and was scowling at the world in general, settling his immediate displeasure at the door, me, and then Kára.

"What will it be, Pandora? Leave the ugly bastard outside or can he come in?"

The door disengaged and began to swing open on silent hinges. She wore her usual toga—sheer for his pleasure—and looked about as delicious as the first bite of a candy bar. She eyed me up and down, squinting. Then she beamed. "Nate!"

I smiled in relief, although confused. "You can see me?"

"I can see the rough edges. Enough to verify your story."

Prometheus lunged for Pandora with his arms outstretched—and promptly struck an invisible wall, bouncing back on his ass. I stepped over him, motioning for Kára to join me. "You are welcome to enter, Kára," I said under my breath. She crossed the threshold without issue, studying Pandora with obvious attention.

Pandora smiled back at her, eyeing her up and down with an interested hum. "Oh, my. My, my, *my*," she said, flashing her teeth at me in a mischievous grin. "Things are *happening* out there, eh?" she asked in a playful tone, winking at me not so discreetly.

Kára nodded satisfactorily.

"Not now, Pandora," I sighed, turning back to Prometheus. He was sitting up and glaring at us. "Do you promise you mean me no harm? That you will not betray my trust? The same for Kára and Pandora?" I asked.

He grunted, climbing to his feet. He repeated the promise, studying the door as he did so. I watched him for a few long seconds. I smiled and then nodded. "You may enter my Armory."

He did so, wincing as he crossed the threshold. Once past it, he let out a sigh of relief and grinned at Pandora. "Girl, are you a sight for sore eyes."

She smiled anxiously, her eyes brimming with hope. "Prometheus. You look well, considering."

He grunted. "Thank Tainted Nipple for that. He busted me out of my imprisonment. Happiest day of my life." She wrapped her arms around him in a tight squeeze and he let out a happy sigh.

Inwardly, I let out my own sigh—of relief. It was always a good day when you learned that a Titan didn't want to kill you to death.

"He's a special kind of asshole, but I won't hold that against him. The best of us are."

I strode past them, my mind already moving at full speed. My original plan had evolved upon running into Prometheus. Now that I knew Pandora was safe, I needed to find a way to convince them all that my plan wasn't as crazy as it sounded.

41

Prometheus sat in a loveseat, filling it all by himself, sipping a comically small cup of tea so that he looked like a father at his daughter's imaginary tea party. *Been there, done that,* I thought to myself. With Alice.

A flash of panic and fury raged through me at the thought. Was she okay? I didn't have the power or the army capable of storming Olympus, so my only hope was to play this smart. Emotionless. Just keep moving my pieces and setting up the board for that last roll of the dice.

And hope for the best.

I sat on the end of the couch closest to Prometheus. Kára sat beside me, and I was doing my best not to see her in my peripheral vision. She had shed her armor in favor of her leather and fur pants and the loose canvas top. I was acutely aware of her hip's proximity to mine and I tensed any time she shifted her weight. Our conversation in the tunnel had hit me deeply. Although she'd made solid points, I was finding it impossible to focus on anything but the Zeus and Alice problem. And Yahn and Carl were out there, risking their lives, too.

Pandora had rebraided Kára's hair for her—using it as a ploy to trap the Valkyrie in place as she whispered in dark, mysterious, estrogen-laden tones. Finished with their primping, the magical librarian now sat on

Kára's other side, occasionally leaning towards the Valkyrie to whisper something she thought I couldn't hear.

I could hear her—clearly—and it was making me blush and fidget.

I sipped my tea as I traded stories with Prometheus. As I spoke, Pandora's focus shifted to me, listening intently, looking troubled but trying to hide it behind false confidence. Apparently, Prometheus had hit the base of the St. Louis arch like a feathered meteorite a week ago. He'd dented it all to hell, inciting a panic about terrorist attacks in the Midwest, and then he'd immediately gone to ground.

Meaning he'd snuck into Chateau Falco to wait outside the door to the Armory.

"How did you manage to get in?" I asked, still impressed that he'd inadvertently vandalized a staple of the St. Louis skyline. To be blunt, I was jealous. "The house doesn't like strangers."

Prometheus grunted. "The Beast, you mean. Falco always was a sucker for the underdogs and strays," he said absently, slurping loudly at his tea.

I blinked, sloshing my drink. "You know Falco?" I demanded, stunned. Prometheus hadn't been walking the world of man since the Greek era. How the hell would he know Falco?

He shrugged. "Sure. Ignus is secretly in love with her." He snapped his fingers and a flaming specter the size of a matchstick appeared in his palm, staring back at us. He clapped a fist to his heart, emitting a burst of sparks. Prometheus cursed familiarly, swatting at his pants.

Despite his unassuming size, the power and heat radiating off that little matchstick man...

I leaned away, feeling like the skin over my face had been pulled tight. "A Beast," I breathed. "You have a Beast."

Prometheus nodded proudly, smirking at his tiny friend. "That's why I came here. We sensed that Falco was in town—shocked the hell out of me, especially when I learned she was yours. We sought her out and claimed sanctuary. Almost soiled myself a second time when I realized that, on top of that, you had Pandora, here, locked up in her own private pocket dungeon."

Pandora leaned forward, rolling her eyes. "So overprotective. It's not a pocket dungeon. It's a pocket *dimension*. And I like it here. I have hope," she said, pointing at me.

I shifted uncomfortably in my seat as everyone turned to stare.

Falco purred warmly and the flaming matchstick man waved up at the ceiling before blowing her a kiss of fiery lips that floated up into the air like an ember before puffing out. Prometheus grunted. "Enough of that, Ignus. Kai swooned her, first. The world isn't fair," he said softly, nudging Ignus with a finger. The little fire specter hung his head sadly and hugged Prometheus' finger in silent misery.

I felt a tiny hole burn its way through my heart, realizing what Prometheus had meant. Falco had found another man while Ignus had been chained up on the mountain with Prometheus.

The Titan looked over at me and shrugged. "Okay, maybe Ignus' feelings are not so secret," he admitted.

I stared at the Titan, shaking my head. I felt a migraine coming on. "You knew Kai, too?"

He shrugged. "Beasts are a close-knit group. Well, they used to be. The ones who landed on this rock, anyway. They're not so affectionate with those back home, from what I gather."

Ignus lifted his fists and began shadow boxing atop Prometheus' palm, sending out sparks and hair-thin tendrils of smoke with each blow. Falco let out an ominous growl that I felt in my boots. Ignus pumped his fist, backing up Falco's ire. I smiled at the little guy's attempts to win her over. Ignus was into big beautiful women. Big beautiful Beasts, technically.

"All right," Prometheus grumbled affectionately. "Get some rest, pal. I'll let you out once the dust settles." He glanced over at me. "If Tainted Nipple and Falco permit it, of course."

I rolled my eyes at his repeated use of my nickname, realizing now why it bothered everyone else when I did it to them. Ignus turned to me and did the fist clap to heart thing again—with another burst of sparks—and then snuffed out of view with a tendril of smoke. Prometheus' palm was covered in black soot, but it wasn't burned.

Kára studied me out of the corner of my eye, but I pretended not to notice. I did notice that her hip was touching mine now, and my heart skipped a beat. "Who else knows about all this Beast lore?" I asked the Titan, my voice cracking sharply at the end. *Smooth, Nate,* I chastised myself. *Puberty suave is really making a comeback this year...for middle-schoolers.*

Prometheus was frowning at me curiously. "You are an odd little man, Tainted Nipple. Why are your cheeks red? Did Ignus make it too hot in here for you?"

Pandora choked on her tea and I felt Kára's body shake in silent laughter.

I sipped at my tea and cleared my throat before repeating my question.

"Beasts are one of the original forms of magic, Nipple. Everyone knows about them. Where do you think us godly types got our powers in the first place? And why do you think most of us hate Tiny Gods so much? Why we make them think they're just dirt under our boots?" He laughed harshly. "We were all Tiny Gods, once. A fact that some gods—like Zeus—do everything possible to hide. Like, oh, I don't know, chaining a poor bastard to a mountain."

I grimaced. "Why didn't Ignus help you break free of your chains?" I asked, frowning.

Prometheus shuddered at the thought, shaking his head adamantly. "That's what Zeus wanted. He wanted to take Ignus for himself. Didn't think an irresponsible Titan like me deserved to keep him any longer. If I let him out on that cursed rock, Zeus would have taken him from me. The whole mountain was covered in runes to trap Beasts. Zeus is a bit of a collector. Not that he can do anything with them, no matter how much he tries. He has poor Hephaestus tortured every time one of his contraptions fails to solve Zeus' desire to harness the control of more Beasts. Zeus can't accept the fact that if the Beasts don't want to work with you, they won't work with you. So, Zeus thinks that if he can't have them *all*, no one else should have even *one*."

I stared at the Titan, feeling like my brain was a carton of smashed eggs. In ten minutes, I'd learned more about Beasts than I had over the last few years. And he acted so nonchalant about it. Most everyone else had been terrified to discuss Beasts.

Then again, they had been gods. Prometheus was a Titan.

As vitally important as this information was, I didn't have the time or the mental energy to add another issue to my plate. I needed to maintain focus on Zeus or the distraction might cost me—everyone—the game. If Zeus had his way, the world would be a much darker place in about twenty-four hours. Alice was in danger right *now*. I closed my eyes, biting back my sudden panic. Pandora was whispering to Kára again, and I heard her mention the healing hot tub. She'd only brought it up six times or so in the last twenty minutes—she was about as subtle as a frying pan to the nose.

"Oh, Kára," Pandora whispered, "you simply *must* go try it. Nate could show you where it is. A long soak is just what you two need, taking a few private moments from battle and stress to relax and heal, gathering your thoughts and rejuvenating your bodies. Think of how much more productive this conversation would be after a nice long soak—"

I cleared my throat, cutting her off. "We're on the clock, Pandora. This is serious."

"So is this hot tub," she fired back in a smugly sweet tone. "Truly," she added, placing a hand on the Valkyrie's thigh and pointedly shoving her against me. Kára did not resist as she turned to look at me—now all up in my personal bubble. She blinked slowly, arching an eyebrow, the question obvious. Pandora saved me. Kind of. "And you are not on any clock. Time is fluid here, remember? I could easily lock down the outside world for a day or two while you plan your war and...scrub each other's backs."

She smiled like a tiger, with the innocent eyes of a lamb.

I clenched my jaw defiantly, clutching tightly to my crown of abstinence since I didn't trust myself to be anywhere near Kára and hot water. Not without a chaperone. "Thank you, Pandora. Truly," I managed with genuine gratitude—because she wasn't wrong. The tension between me and Kára was heavy in the air. "But no. Zeus wants *you*. And he has taken Alice prisoner. I want to stop him. *That's* why we're here. Not for your hot tub."

I may as well have thrown a vase on the ground for how quickly my words silenced the Armory. Prometheus clenched his fist and shattered his cup. He winced apologetically. "Sorry, Pandora," he mumbled, bending down to scoop up the shards.

His fingers were not bleeding—or embering, I guessed—from the cup's shards, because he was a Titan. Pandora stared back at me, pursing her lips nervously, and I wondered if her earlier carefree attitude had been outright stubborn denial.

"He wants you more than anything," I continued, realizing that I finally had the upper hand on her. "He's already kidnapped Alice and freed Peter.

He wants to control you and me for the Omega War. To use us to *win* while he takes all the credit."

She slowly turned to scan the piles of weapons surrounding us, grimacing as if she were envisioning Zeus sauntering by with a squeaking shopping cart and a grocery list. Then she sighed dejectedly, knowing the store of weapons would be of little help against Zeus and his cronies. I wasn't even sure how many items in here had the power to make a god bleed. Judging by her reaction, not enough. Because it wasn't just Zeus. Ares and Apollo were out there. Maybe Hermes and, depending on Aphrodite's devotion to her husband, she could fall back on her family's side as well.

"He has Hephaestus locked up, too, Pandora." She flinched. "He made you, right?"

She nodded sadly. "The only father I ever had. The only man who genuinely cared about me as a person over what I could do for him. Well, other than you, my host." Prometheus grunted and she smiled reassuring. "And you, Prometheus, of course." He settled back into his chair.

With the pain on her face, I didn't mention what Zeus had said about Hope being locked up in the box to keep her safe. I feared it would be enough to make her break down. We both knew it. She'd already hinted at it when she'd told Prometheus she liked it here because she had hope.

Pandora settled her focus on my Titan Thorns and her frown deepened. "You can't do anything with those blocking your power, my host," she said sadly. "Even with all these toys."

"I'm working on that angle," I muttered angrily, feeling too frustrated to get in touch with my emotional storm at the moment. Right now, it was better to seek shelter and wait for it to pass.

She shook her head, studying my manacles. "No. That's what *I* was trying to do," she said, lifting her gaze to meet mine. "Two words. Hot tub."

I flung my hands up. "NO! Leave it alone already!"

Kára rose to her feet and calmly left the room. Pandora shot me an accusatory scowl and then left to go comfort her.

Prometheus was watching me, his eyes flicking towards Kára and Pandora's departure. "Well, that was poorly handled. Just go diddle her already."

I clenched my fists and my knuckles cracked. "Not like that. She is not a piece of meat and she's not an item on my to do list that I need to check off. That would degrade her. I'd only be doing it to get these off. She's more than that."

Prometheus studied me, nodding thoughtfully. "Well, then what is she?"

I studied him in silence for a few long seconds. "If I knew that, I'd be diddling her in the magic hot tub, idiot."

He grinned toothily, lifting up a hand in surrender. "I forget how touchy you mortals can be. Living with a Beast inside you leads you closer to a..." he frowned, questing for the proper word, "more primitive, simpler lifestyle. Latch onto what you want as soon as you can latch onto it, because a storm is always on the horizon."

I took a calming breath, nodding. "I used to have a Beast inside me. I know what you mean."

Prometheus blinked. "Bullshit."

I frowned, looking up at him. "Kai was mine. I freed him."

Prometheus lunged to his feet. "Now I know you're fucking with me. Kai was the greatest—"

Falco growled warningly and Prometheus clammed up. I narrowed my eyes. "What? Kai was the greatest what?"

Prometheus was shaking his head adamantly. "Nope. Missus made her feelings on the matter clear. I'm not saying shit else." With that, he quickly left the room. "I'm going for a walk."

I frowned, studying him as he slowed his pace to a more leisurely stroll once safely away from me. I stared up at the ceiling. "What was that all about, Falco?" I asked, softly.

She did not answer me. I sat alone on the couch, holding my empty cup for what seemed like days, lost in my own thoughts. If Prometheus hadn't believed that I freed Kai, what would he think when he learned that Kai had a son? What, exactly, was so special about Kai?

And what did that mean for Ruin?

It's a dark day when you learn that even your house kept secrets from you. Possibly bigger secrets than your lying parents ever kept. At some point, sleep soon took me.

It wasn't pleasant. Even my dreams were cruel. I blamed them on Roofie Ruxpin.

42

I woke to find Pandora laying a blanket over my lap. I smiled at the kind gesture, only to realize that Kára was fast asleep on the couch beside me, resting her head in my lap. My pulse abruptly skyrocketed and Kára let out a soft sound as my muscles tensed. I forced myself to relax and set my palm on her shoulder. She instantly calmed, burrowing her cheek tightly against me.

I looked up to find Pandora smiling sadly at me. "Relax. It's only been twenty minutes, but I didn't want to wake you." She shifted her sad smile to Kára, who tucked her chin beneath the blanket. I grinned. Lethal could still be cute and cuddly. "She won't wake for some time yet. I gave her something that she desperately needed."

My eyes widened. "You drugged her?" I hisspered—a sound between a hiss and a whisper that I had perfected over the course of thirty years of extreme stress.

Pandora smiled, shaking her head. "I gave her a shoulder to cry on, Nate." Pandora smiled sadly at the Valkyrie in my lap. "She's had a very rough time of it, I'm afraid. Whatever road she's traveled to get to this point..." she stared down at the sleeping Valkyrie, shaking her head. "She's given it all of her heart and soul. And then some. It won't be long now."

My thumb was making gentle circles on her bare shoulder, but it felt awkward the moment I noticed it. I turned back to Pandora and the gesture no longer felt as stiff. It became natural the moment I stopped thinking about it.

Aphrodite's warning about letting Kára become a distraction haunted me, tortured me, scoured my skin raw. "Why do you say that so sadly?" I asked, realizing that I wanted to hit something. Whatever it was that gave Pandora that sad look on her face. "Wait. You're not saying she's dying, are you?" I breathed.

Pandora stiffened and shook her head. "No. Christ, Nate." I let out a relieved breath.

"You don't say shit like *it won't be long now*, and expect a man not to freak out," I hissed.

Pandora rolled her eyes. "She's had a tough couple of days. Unlike men, women don't go from tough days to instant death. There is a long spectrum of emotions between those two points called 'holding your shit together.'" I narrowed my eyes at her but she wasn't looking. "Do you always jump to the worst possible conclusion?"

"I have abandonment issues and my mom never let me buy those green sneakers I wanted," I said dryly. "I know a thing or two about tough days and holding my shit together. Why is this different?"

Her shoulders shrunk. "Sometimes, when you chase something long enough, you realize it might not be what you imagined it was. That you focused so much on the destination that you forgot to appreciate the journey—and what set you on your quest in the first place." She studied Kára. "I fear she hit that wall hard, and it's rattled her." Pandora looked very small in that moment.

I grew very quiet myself, turning inwards. Was Pandora hinting at her own traumas? Or was she implying that I was the destination Kára had been chasing? She'd made it sound like she didn't know the path Kára had traveled, but that it had been rough. All I knew was that Kára had chosen to become a Valkyrie in order to get something she'd wanted. She'd said some deals cost more than others. I'd heard her with Freya, trying to give up her duties as a Valkyrie to find me—no matter the consequences—to make sure I was all right. And she'd promised Odin she would look out for me, in addition to Asgard and Freya.

So...what had her original destination been to make those other crappy deals? And what had changed? Or had she hit this brick wall some time ago, and Pandora was speaking generally?

I sighed, knowing well enough not to dig. Kára would tell me when she was ready. Or she wouldn't. That was her prerogative. But it was damned frustrating to ponder with her sleeping on my thigh, making my damned wrist cramp since I was forced to keep my hand on her shoulder to make sure she slept soundly—

I narrowed my eyes. I'd been suckered. Pandora had probably made up the whole sob story to make sure I didn't resign from my human pillow job. Magical cahoots. They were all in on it.

"What is the meaning of all this, Pandora? Can I, for once, just get some honest answers? Some clear-cut situations?" I unclenched my jaw, realizing I was actually straining to speak. "Can I get something that *I* want? Just once? Without all the mind games?"

Pandora frowned compassionately, her face breaking with emotion. "Oh, Nate. Perhaps that is your problem. *You* never let yourself get what you want. You're always worried about consequences."

"I'm a wizard," I argued. "I have to think about consequences."

She nodded. "Yet, when it comes to threats, you often disregard the consequences, trusting your instincts."

"And look how well that has turned out for me," I muttered.

Pandora shrugged. "I would say it's worked out incredibly well. Why else is everyone so scared of you? Your enemies fear to approach you head on. You have succeeded far more than you allow yourself to see."

"I don't see how that has anything to do with—" I cut off before I said Kára or Indie or Callie or Othello or Pandora or any other woman who'd once tickled my heart for one reason or another. "I can no longer afford to do what I want regardless of the consequences. That is reckless. To disregard the pain I would leave behind, means that other people shoulder twice the burden."

"Have your parents not left you twice the burden?"

I nodded vehemently. "Exactly—"

"And would you truly sit there and tell me you'd want it any other way? You would not have Gunnar in your life. You would not have me. You would not have any of your allies. You would be a lame wizard holed up in the Academy somewhere—an obedient little worker bee. You would trade that slow suicide for what you have right now?" she said, lifting up her arms. "It seems you have hit your destination, found it wanting, and disregarded the incredible adventure you took to get here—all the amazing and wonderful and insane things you experienced. Just. Like. Her." She pointed at the woman sleeping peacefully on my lap—her co-conspirator.

I frowned. But she wasn't finished.

"Burdens will always be carried, even when you overanalyze every situation. Carried by you or by others. All I'm trying to say is that burdens make people *stronger*. Do not disregard consequences, but definitely accept them. Allow others to take risks with their lives. Allow others to grow stronger." She paused, smiling gently. "Or you could ask Prometheus about his brother, Atlas. According to your arguments, Atlas is your role model— one man holding up the world all by himself."

I snorted softly. "That's unfair. And untrue."

"Is it?" She leaned forward, speaking so softly that it was barely a breath, but her words echoed in my ears. "How heavy is your heart right now, my host? Because from where I'm sitting, it looks like it's too much for you to bear. It brought you those manacles." She slowly leaned back, her eyes surprisingly intense. "Because you *let* it shackle you. Like a *coward*."

I flinched in surprise, causing Kára to stir in my lap. I stared at Pandora incredulously. Not an ounce of malice showed on her face. Instead...

I saw only pain.

"Sometimes, accepting too many burdens for yourself also has unintended consequences. Whether you like it or not, others already shoulder burdens for you without a whimper of protest. They silently carry burdens that you don't even know exist—burdens created by your own stubbornness." She stared at me flatly. "My shoulders are fucking tired, my host. I'd appreciate it if you stopped making me carry your baggage. Of course, I will carry it to my grave, no matter what you decide, but my own heart hurts twofold for every weight you tie to yours. And I am but one of the army of servants silently carrying our king's burdens."

She calmly stood, straightening her toga. "Rest, my host. I have slowed time so that you may recover properly. You two may not be physically wounded, but your hearts and minds are a train wreck of pain. All insinuations aside, you really could use a dip in the hot tub. By yourself."

And she left.

Somehow, the room dimmed, even though it was perpetually sunset here in the Armory. My mind wandered for a long, long time. Soon, I heard Morgan Freeman talking from the ether, and he seemed to be narrating the story of my life in his deep, syrupy drawl.

As a sleeping Valkyrie slipped into the world of dreams, a wizard's eyes caught the light, glimmering like precious emeralds. The wizard didn't seem to blink, and he definitely didn't move. He was watching over that Valkyrie, protecting her from unseen dangers. For far longer than absolutely necessary. Because they were in a safe place and had no enemies but themselves here. And the couch was more than big enough for two.

But he was a stubborn wizard, that Nate Temple. He only feared one thing in this world—

"Cahoots," I murmured sleepily, interrupting the voice of god at my peril, as my eyes slipped closed. "Magical...cahoots..."

43

Something was tickling my face, waking me from a deep, lethargic sleep—one of those semi-comas that felt almost like a dream in and of itself. I smiled. Maybe this was another dream. If so, I should be able to reach out and tickle my fingers down her shoulders and rib cage until I reached her lower back and she stirred with a sleepy yawn. She would roll over in my silk sheets—the ones we'd thoroughly disheveled several times the night before—and smile at me, her eyes hungry and ravenous as she beckoned me closer. I would grin back boyishly at the beautiful, mesmerizing face of—

I woke abruptly, feeling as if a bucket of cold water had just been dumped over my head.

Kára was nuzzling into my chest, one arm draped across me in a firm hug, and her hair tickling my face. We were lying down on the couch with Kára wedged between the backrest and my body, and she was baking like an oven.

I did not move a single muscle for fear of waking her.

Nevertheless, her breathing changed and she suddenly sat up straight, wiping at her mouth. Her dual-colored eyes locked onto me and then widened in a panic. "Oh! How long was I asleep?" she asked, sounding frantic.

"I have no idea. I fell asleep too," I said, sitting up so as not to look like a lazy bum. "You're really hot," I blurted, her panic infecting me.

She blinked in surprise and then stared at me. "Hot?" she repeated, biting back a grin.

"Warm," I corrected, trying to clarify my intended meaning. "You're very warm."

She cocked her head. "What's next? Tepid?"

I opened my mouth but couldn't think of an adequate defense under her cross-examination. She swiftly hopped off the couch and out of reach. "I'm going to go find a shower or something," she said abruptly. Then she left in a rush.

I stared at the spot where she'd been sitting moments ago. "Fuck."

"Smooth, Nipple. Real smooth."

I spun to see Prometheus lounging in an armchair facing our couch. "How long have you been sitting there, creep?"

He slurped at his tea and smiled. "A while, Nipple. A good long while."

"Fuck off, Zippo," I growled, spouting off the first fire-based nickname I could think of since his insistence on using Nipple was really starting to get under my skin. "I don't have the patience for your shit right now, weirdo."

"Later, Taint," he said, chuckling as he climbed to his feet. He whistled to himself as he left.

I closed my eyes and counted to ten. Then I got to my feet, shaking my head and stretching my neck from side-to-side. I made my way over to a familiar side table since I had nothing better to do and there wasn't any awake water here.

I was useless without coffee. Like Superman without a cape.

Plus, the side table had something I'd meant to grab before leaving the Armory—a wooden bowl of Tiny Balls that led directly here. Those would be a necessity for my hostages later. At least as a fallback if Kára's bar was compromised. And if Pandora agreed, of course.

I wasn't entirely certain where I stood on the female front right now. They could have sentenced me to death already, based on my recent inter-actions. I might already be walking around on borrowed time.

I scooped up a handful of the Tiny Balls and shoved them in my pocket, frowning at a basket brimming with rolled scrolls beside the bowl of Tiny Balls. Had that been here earlier? This table was usually empty other than my bowl—

"Ah," Pandora said from directly beside me. I squeaked involuntarily, my heart abruptly thundering in my chest. She arched an eyebrow, amused. Then she nudged me with her hip in a playful manner, shifting her attention back to the side table. "The Alexandria scrolls. Very boring."

I had regained my composure somewhat, and I found myself smiling down at her. "That's not what a librarian should say about her collection."

She grunted. "It's the truth."

I pointed at the Tiny Balls. "Do your new security measures nullify these?"

She pondered my question. "Yes. Why?"

"On a scale of 'holding hostages is acceptable' to 'I've always wanted to hold people prisoner,' where would you rate yourself?"

She folded her arms. "A solid no."

I sighed. "What if it's for a good cause?"

"Are these hostages victims?"

I nodded. "If I don't take them first, yes."

She sighed, looking annoyed. "Grant them permission and I'll let them in. For a short time."

I squeezed her in a one-armed hug. "Thanks. While we're at it, I want to revoke any Aesir access until I clarify a few things. I'm wary of Kára's bosses. And general chicanery," I added meaningfully, referring to Loki and any other ramifications from my recent Norse conquests.

She smirked, nodding. "That is wise. Consider it done."

I reached out and flicked through the scrolls, counting them as I told her who to expect. Before she could pepper me with questions on my new VIPs, I switched topics. "These are from the Library of Alexandria?" I asked her absently, frowning at the scrolls for some strange reason. I felt a mental itch in the back of my mind upon touching them, so I kept talking. "Why are they in the Armory?"

Pandora smiled. "A hint to a riddle, would be my guess."

Then she turned and left. I watched her stride over to the balcony, frowning thoughtfully. I mentally ran back through our conversation, confirming that I hadn't said anything to make her leave or somehow dig my hole deeper, and nodded to myself.

"That's a win, these days," I told myself.

Then I made my way over to the balcony to join her. I hadn't told her my plan yet, and I was suspicious about her tea, wondering if she really had drugged us to sleep. I reached her side and propped my elbows on the railing, leaning forward as I stared out at the windswept sands.

"How long did we sleep?" I asked.

Pandora smirked out of the corner of her mouth. "Twelve solid hours, believe it or not."

I sucked in a panicked breath.

Pandora gripped my forearm firmly. "It's only been fifteen minutes outside. Relax."

I forced myself to calm down, taking a deep breath. "Thank you."

She shrugged, removing her hand. "You needed it." She didn't say anything about our conversation from last night, or what she'd been up to with Prometheus during our slumber. She just stood beside me, smiling at the sands.

"I have an idea, but you're not going to like it."

She sighed tiredly. "It is what it is."

Prometheus drifted into the room, coming to a halt on the other side of Pandora. "Well? We finally talking about something worthwhile?"

I ignored him, turning back to Pandora. "I need you to lock yourself up tight in here until this all blows over."

"No." Her tone brooked zero argument. "I will fight this time." I remained silent, pursing my lips with a frustrated look. "You cannot make me stay here."

"I can," I said softly.

"You wouldn't," she clarified, turning to glare at me.

I was silent for a few moments, and then I let myself smile. "Okay."

She narrowed her eyes. "What is this? Are you trying to pick a fight?"

I let out a breath. "I get the general sense that anything I suggest these days incites an instant argument from my female superiors. Since they are wiser than me, I choose not to argue."

She narrowed her eyes and Prometheus began to laugh. "So, you gave me something to argue about to get it out of the way," she said in a cool tone.

I smiled, shrugging. "We both win."

She folded her arms. "You're exasperating, my host. What is your real plan?"

"I prefer incorrigible," I said, chuckling. "Do you still have your box? Or urn. I can't remember."

She stared at me for a long moment, likely wondering if this was another ploy. Which had also been my intent. "Yes."

I shied away from that look, wondering what it signified. "Good. We're going to need it."

And I told them my plan. Pandora looked uneasy, but Prometheus was soon grinning. "It's taking a page out of the old story," he growled eagerly.

"Do you think it's too obvious?" I asked.

They both shook their heads. "It's perfect," they said in unison.

But where Prometheus sounded exuberant, Pandora sounded resigned. The reason for that was perfectly clear, so I didn't comment on it.

"I'm going to go check on Kára," Pandora said. "Make sure she doesn't need anything." She curtsied to us both and glided away from the room.

I turned to watch her. "Are you okay, Pandora?" I asked, frowning. "It was just a little fun to ease the tension."

She paused, her back to me. "How ironic. I was experiencing significant shoulder strain, even before your little game," she said without looking at me. And then she continued on, disappearing from view.

I turned to Prometheus with a questioning look. "They do that a lot around you," he said.

I frowned. "Do what? Get upset?"

He shook his head. "Leave."

I turned to look out over the sands, biting back my knee-jerk response. "You're not wrong," I finally admitted. "You're not wrong at all." But my thoughts drifted to one woman who hadn't left me. I'd left her. Othello. In the end, that hadn't worked out all that well, either.

"She's just concerned for you, Nipple. It's a difficult thing when hope seems lost." I glanced at him from the corner of my eye, but he was speaking conversationally, not seeming to regard the weight of his words.

Which only made his words heavier on my heart.

I nodded absently, staring out at the windswept sands, thinking about tight shoulders. "I think it's time for me to hit something. Hard."

He grinned. "Atta' boy." He finished his drink and set down his cup.

Then he glanced down, tensing in surprise. A small ornate wooden box rested between us. I hadn't even noticed that Pandora had left it behind— or that she'd even had it on her *to* leave behind.

Prometheus eyed the infamous Pandora's Box anxiously. It was made of black wood and carved with symbols not unlike the runes on my Titan Thorns. In fact, they began to glow for the first time since leaving my prison. I shuddered at that. Had it been carved with the Omegabet?

And were they protections or curses?

I picked it up warily, waiting for the world to end. I let out a sigh of relief, echoed by Prometheus. It was surprisingly light. "Any idea how to use it?" I asked.

"I think you just open it. The world ends all by itself, I'd imagine," he said somberly.

"This is the way the world ends. Not with a bang but with a whimper..." I quoted.

Prometheus stared at me. "You have a little girl to save, right? Alice?"

I nodded, clenching my jaw. "I have more than one girl to save," I said, thinking about Kára. And Pandora. And Alice. And Aphrodite.

The funny thing was, they were trying to save me. And we were all tripping over each other in the process. Maybe it was time for them to save themselves.

"Then let's make Zeus whimper," Prometheus growled, snapping his fingers. Ignus crackled to life on his palm. The little pyromaniac grinned at me.

"Okay. Let's make Zeus whimper," I agreed.

44

I'd taken the time to sneak into the healing hot tub and clean off. Aphrodite's paint still decorated my chest, but it had stopped glowing upon leaving Niflheim. I washed it off anyway, just to be safe. The brief soak had felt marvelous, washing away the small aches and pains of my body and somewhat helping to clear my jumbled thoughts.

It did nothing for my heart, but two out of three was better than nothing.

I found Kára waiting for me on the couch. She had her armor on and held my satchel in her lap. I'd stowed Pandora's Box inside, already updating her on my modified plans.

She stood, holding out my satchel with a warm, hesitant smile. "How was the hot tub?"

"Tepid and unsatisfying," I grumbled, accepting the satchel. "She totally oversold it."

Kára laughed, resting a hand on my shoulder as we made our way out of the Armory. "Mine as well. Technically, we didn't follow her directions," she said.

I smiled, nodding silently. Kára had been giving me mixed signals since our walk to the Armory, so I wasn't about to tempt my fate.

As we left the Armory and headed back towards the secret passageways, I glared up at the walls of my mansion. "Don't think you're off the hook, Falco. I have a lot of questions," I said, thinking back on the Underground Railroad, Ignus, Kai, and all the Beastlore I'd learned.

I'm pretty sure the responding groan was an amused chuckle. Kára glanced down at her phone—which had its own little pocket in her armor, believe it or not—and pursed her lips. "We have three abductions before lunch. That's ambitious for six hours."

I nodded. "Maybe Carl and Yahn have already taken care of theirs. Have they called?"

Kára shook her head. "I still can't believe it's only been an hour since we left Niflheim."

I nodded absently, hoping Carl and Yahn were okay. "You get used to it." Before we reached the spot where the secret tunnel had dumped us out, I paused, turning to Kára. "How sneaky can you be?" I asked, placing my hand on the wall. The section of stone swung open silently—Falco reading my mind and responding to my need through physical contact alone.

Kára smiled. "I'd conservatively estimate that I'm the best in the world. Why?"

I nodded, hiding my frown at her strange answer. "We're here, and our hostages are likely here. It would be a good time for reconnaissance." Considering our time restraints, I made a decision. "Chateau Falco is huge. We should split up so we can cover more ground. Meet back here in one hour. See what you can learn. Hopefully Alucard and Gunnar are here, making our job easier."

She nodded, barely hiding her suspicion about us splitting up. "I do not know your home as well as you, so my movements will be limited."

I glanced upwards at the ceiling. "Mind helping us spy on my people? Help her stay hidden?"

Falco purred approvingly, and the walls of the secret passageway began to glow.

"Looks like she likes you," I said.

With a final, somewhat tense, look, we dipped our heads and Kára slipped into the tunnel, the stone closing shut behind her. I let out a sigh of relief as I continued on down the hall. I wanted to head to my office. See if I could learn anything on the Grimm Tech situation or how their manhunt for Peter was going.

Othello had pretty much taken over my office, and if anyone had answers about Grimm Tech, it would be her.

Falco knew more than one secret passageway. She knew magical corridors so recondite that the ones I had been so proud of for years might as well have sported illuminated exit signs.

I crept up to the wall of the new tunnel she had shown me and, I shit you not, peered through two shaded holes. One look, and I knew beyond a shadow of a doubt that this exact spot on the other side of the wall held a painting of my father.

I was totally staring through the eyes of a portrait.

Bucket list item, checked.

And it had a direct view of my desk. Well, Othello's desk. Where my father had stored his camel bone chests of Gurkha Black Dragon cigars, the world's most notorious hacker had upgraded to an array of curved monitors that dominated the wide antique desk.

I noticed the screens because they emitted light.

But I noticed Othello because she *was* the light. My breath caught and I stared, resting my palms against the wall. It warmed beneath my touch but I didn't really notice.

Othello was...stunning. Seeing her this close—even with a wall between us—brought back a montage of our past relationship, starting off with how we'd originally met in an advanced Russian class in college.

She'd been quicker to learn than me, and had agreed to be my tutor when it became obvious that I was falling behind. I invited her to Chateau Falco and she immediately decreed that we set a one-hour timer where neither of us had been allowed to use English. Those hours had been long and silent at first, full of playful teasing and stilted, abrupt phrases and comments. With her my superior—not by all that much—I'd been forced to watch and listen to her attempt to babble at me in complete gibberish.

We resorted to charades, pantomiming and laughing more than we actually spoke. We wore the silly fur hats and played their National Anthem, marching somberly before falling onto the couch in fits of laughter.

My parents had thought me insane or a possible Russian sleeper agent, although not a very good one.

We didn't care. Everything outside those hours of study simply ceased to exist for me, and I realized that I was slowly falling for her, one perfectly rolled R at a time.

Forced to stare at each other for hours each week, we found ways to encourage one another with non-verbal cues and a lot of heavy, supportive eye contact as we struggled to master the vocabulary and conjugations. We celebrated the simplest achievements together—every word a well-earned triumph in our war against the oppressive hour of near silence. We also learned not to be cruel with our teasing—pruning a tree helped it flourish but hacking the trunk with an axe was not conducive to growth.

Still, she'd often tease me by asking if I wanted to play *Russian Tourettes* since I had about a one-in-six chance of belting out a Russian curse word when I failed to wrangle a complete sentence together.

I'd quickly capitalized on the fact that Othello had no problem rolling her R's.

But I did.

With the criminal genius of a con artist...I'd milked it, feigning incompetence and annoyance to get her to teach me her impressive tongue work. It turned out that I was much better with my tongue than I'd portrayed and, because I had already performed one crime in my con scheme, I added another to my criminal resume.

I stole my first kiss.

And that's when our spark kindled to a flame.

Our Russian improved rather swiftly once we were both properly motivated to get through our hour of classwork.

Soon, she shared her love of computers—both the good and the bad—with me. She was a hacker by trade. Never having been a fan of authority, it fascinated me.

I watched her work from my vantage behind the wall. She typed furiously on her keyboard, biting her lower lip absently as my memories sped faster: cool silk sheets, long talks over bottles of wine under the starry night sky in the gardens of Chateau Falco, purposely getting lost together in the labyrinth—for hours, listening to the cicadas chirp outside the open window as we stared up at the ceiling, simply enjoying the feeling of bare flesh against bare flesh.

How she always fell asleep on movie night, and how I always woke her up by tickling her. How I knew she faked half of those moments, because she knew I would tickle her and we would then find something more fun to occupy our evenings.

Finding the seediest bars in town. Hopping in the car at a moment's notice to travel halfway across the country on an impromptu road trip— only to end up staying in a simple hotel nowhere near our intended destination, distracted by some billboard for some random local touristy destination in *wherever-the-hell*, America.

Waking up before her in the mornings but pretending to be asleep because I knew she'd use the most...creative ways to wake me up—and I'd taken a page out of her movie night scam.

I sighed, the montage slowly fading.

We'd gotten to know each other through silence, and that had birthed a spark that neither of us noticed at first. We would later discover that neither of us could extinguish it. One of us would try, but I was now realizing that I was a terrible fireman. This fire had only gone to ground, smoldering deep below the surface. For years.

I'd fucked up. We hadn't ended on a bad note—not at all. But I hadn't fought as hard as I should have to keep her close when an opportunity arose for her overseas. And then, much as silence had conceived us, time destroyed us. We'd grown apart, living two very different lives, staying in touch sporadically and warmly—but neither of us willing to give up our own personal adventures or careers.

I closed my eyes for a moment, knowing I would punch something if I didn't get a grip.

Alice's life was on the line, and I had a lot of work to do.

45

Othello sat behind the screens, typing furiously on a keyboard and chugging from a bright can of digestible jet fuel—an energy drink of some type. Knowing her, probably an illegal one.

Although beautiful, Othello looked tired and haggard—as if she hadn't slept in days. She wore a black tank top and had her hair tied back in a ponytail. Loose strands had escaped their confines and hung down her sharp jawline; I found myself staring longingly. I firmly closed my eyes and leaned away from the visual, silently chastising myself. I didn't dare speak in case the sound traveled through the pinprick holes in the painting's eyes. Thankfully, the holes seemed to be covered with a type of dark mesh so I didn't fear her seeing my shifting eyeballs from her side.

Marginally composed and hormones somewhat in check, I took another gander of my office.

And I almost jumped to see a second figure looming only a few feet away from me. Luckily, he had his back to me. Unluckily, it was Hemingway—the unwitting cock-blocker supreme.

Or, as he was more widely known, the Horseman of Death. The Pale Rider.

I controlled my breathing, chastising myself all over again. That wasn't fair of me. I had been involved with Indie—regrettably—when Othello wandered back into my life years later. After a tense few days with my old flame helping me fight the Academy Justices, I'd made the conscious decision to leave the past in the past and focus on my future with Indie. Death had swooped in like a specter, stealing her heart, body, and soul.

Literally, as it were.

Granted, his package had been impossible to turn down—his *benefits* package, to be clear—because he'd brought her back to life after my fight with the Justices had resulted in her dying. Well, Death had officialized *my* unsanctioned act of bringing her back to life, because I'd borrowed *his* Horseman's Mask to do it. Apparently, I'd forgotten some of the paperwork.

With my sudden recap of our old relationship on my mind, it was very easy for me to find someone to hate. Someone else to blame.

That, and my continuing torture with Aphrodite—and now Kára—wasn't helping my chill.

Upon stumbling back into my life during the Justices fiasco, Othello had made it abundantly clear that she hadn't forgotten about me. The only obstacle had been Indie, my lover at the time.

Had I known Indie would get corrupted by foreign magic and go batshit insane years later, my response to Othello's invitation would have been drastically different. Hindsight could suck a big one.

Regulars, I was beginning to realize, did not handle power all that well. Freaks didn't either, to be fair, but it almost seemed like Regulars were genetically disposed to epically worse outcomes when they got their grubby meat hooks on magic that hadn't been given to them upon birth. Like the universe was putting the smack down on the have-nots.

Although that seemed unfair, the results were undeniable.

Now that I thought about it, Death had been behind bringing Indie back, too. He'd had to make her into a Grimm to do it, and that had been the beginning of the end for Indie—setting her on a path that would ultimately end in me being forced to kill her to save my best friends, Gunnar and Ashley. The same night Aphrodite and Hermes—and who knew who else—had watched me kill their sister, Athena, on Mount Olympus.

I hesitated, my tinfoil hat's antenna vibrating ominously.

Here I was, confronted by the Olympians and Death—who had apparently been making more shady deals than Donald Trump and Rumpelstilt-skin combined.

I hesitated, dampening my suspicion somewhat. I couldn't blame Hemingway. It was his freaking *job* to meet the dead. He wasn't the one who killed the people. He was the one who took them to their next bus stop.

Still...I had questions. Pertinent ones. Because he was leaving messes behind that were causing me all kinds of grief. Then again...he'd warned me about that. A few times.

Point a finger at someone and at least three more point back at you, or whatever the saying was. Some flowery motivational poster garbage.

"No one has seen Peter since the break-in at Grimm Tech?" Death asked Othello in a clipped, frustrated tone, snapping me out of my reverie.

Othello shook her head angrily. "Nothing. And we know for a fact that Alaric Slate is dead."

"Twice dead, to be more precise," Death clarified. "I never met this Peter fellow." I rolled my eyes. *Because Peter never actually died*, I thought to myself. Death continued. "What do you know about him?"

Othello threw her hands up, glaring at her screens. "Nothing!"

Death shook his head. "Yes, you do. Check the memory shard," he said, pointing at her amulet. My eyes latched onto the prominent jewelry. I'd almost forgotten about that. Death had given it to her after she came back from the dead. I'd seen it block a magical attack, so I knew it was powerful, but Othello hadn't been able to answer my questions when I'd asked her about it.

I'd never heard it called a memory shard before. What was this all about?

Othello looked embarrassed for not thinking of it herself. She touched the amulet and her eyes closed, flicking beneath her lids as if she was dreaming.

A moment later, she opened her eyes and let out a breath. "Peter was his best friend, but he betrayed Nate for power to partner up with Alaric Slate," she said, as if reading a report on her computer screen. "It didn't end well for either of them."

Death nodded thoughtfully. What the hell was going on here? Did

Othello have amnesia or something? Had she forgotten about Peter? She had met him a few times. How could she have forgotten—

I winced at a sudden thought. Had Othello lost some of her memories when I brought her back to life? Was that what her amulet was for? To help her remember? It had multiple purposes, obviously—defensive and restorative. Was that why she'd been cagey about explaining the amulet to me? Out of embarrassment for her foggy memories?

"This *has* to be some kind of illusion—at least with Alaric—but the security feeds at Grimm Tech are above reproach," Death muttered nervously, pacing back and forth. I understood his anxiety. This was an epic job failure if Death was screwing up...well, death. He was also coming alarmingly close to the truth, and that was not good. If he thought I was in danger, he might take action and doom my friends. My plan to kidnap their loved ones was now a necessity. Anything to keep my Horsemen far away from a friend with good intentions.

Othello fingered her amulet, glaring at her computer screen. "I can't fucking find Nate either. Anywhere!" she snapped. "If he really is back like Hermes said, then he's gone analog."

Death sighed, calmly drifting closer to rest a hand on her shoulder. "It's okay, my love. You'll find him."

Othello snarled, scooped up a jar of pens, and then hurled it across the room. It shattered out of my view. "*She* would have found him by now," she muttered. "I'm only the second-best hacker in the world." She released her amulet with a bitter smile. "Although, pulling off this lie for so long with none the wiser technically makes me the best—"

Death's grip on her shoulder abruptly tightened and she cut off with a short whimper.

46

He instantly released her, taking a step back and looking sick to his stomach as he apologized profusely. But even as he spoke, his eyes darted about wildly, eyeing the rafters warily.

I frowned in confusion. What had she been talking about? What lie had she pulled off? Was there another hacker out there who had finally bested Othello?

"You mustn't speak of such things," he said urgently. "It mustn't be said out loud—at all—even in private. You *know* this. Even I cannot stop the consequences."

What the *hell* were they talking about?

Othello nodded guiltily. "I know." She leaned back in her chair, taking a deep breath and closing her eyes. "I'm sorry."

"And I am sorry for hurting you," he replied, sounding just as guilty. It was obvious the poor bastard cared for her more than he should. He'd lived a long, lonely life. Othello had been the best thing to happen to him in thousands of years. And, looking at her now, it was undeniable how she felt about him. He'd given her what I never had. A future. I had no right to feel bitter.

Othello sighed, sagging her shoulders. "It's fine, my love. It just gets overwhelming sometimes. I wish we could just—"

Death cleared his throat. "Never," he repeated firmly.

She grunted, kicking her feet up on the desk. She wore yoga pants and no shoes, and she'd painted her toenails a vivid green. "I don't understand why Peter took Yahn. Or what the hell he was doing at Grimm Tech—let alone how he got in," she added with a low growl. "Alucard and Tory are frantic, not to mention the Reds."

She tapped a few buttons on her keyboard and scrolled a few times with her mouse, reading several of the screens in rapid, practiced motions. "Raego and his dragons are still hunting for Peter and Alaric. No luck yet." She folded her arms, swiveling to face Death. "Alucard and Tory visited his estate to have a stern talk about the statue failure. Tory locked down every shifter on the property and Alucard almost killed Raego." She paused. "Luckily for Raego, a Good Samaritan jumped in and prevented bloodshed. Barely. Raego promptly destroyed the rest of the statues on his lawn —like he should have done a long time ago."

Death grunted, turning away. "Someone needed to stop the Horseman of Absolution from making his grand debut on a shifter ally. I had a talk with them both. A long, pointed talk."

Good fucking lord. Alucard and Tory had almost eradicated the shifter dragons? Over Yahn? And Death had prevented it?

Othello assessed her lover in silence. Whatever she saw chilled her, and she turned back to her screens. "It seems one of Callie's men was abducted in Kansas City, but that's all she's saying." I let out a sigh of relief. Carl and Yahn had gotten Ryuu. The fact that Callie hadn't mentioned specifics gave me hope that she'd gotten the note and was following instructions.

Death began to pace again, clenching his fists. "I do not like this. As far as I know, Callie never crossed paths with Alaric or Peter. They were before her time."

Othello nodded, still reading her screens.

"Which means they are trying to draw Nate out," Death finally said, sounding as if the words had been pulled out of him by force.

"Is Nate still working on his secret project with Zeus?"

Death didn't answer for a few moments. "So I hear. Nate has always been secretive, but I don't like the fact that no one can sense him. Hermes said he's covered in protective runes for a reason, but why hasn't he met with anyone directly? People have seen him here and there, but not for longer than a few minutes, and always at a distance."

"Hermes answered those questions. You were there."

Death punched a fucking hole in the wall, about two feet from my face. I almost fell on my ass to see his skeletal fist poking through my side of the stone wall. He pulled it out and I remained leaning against the wall, wondering if I had been made. With the now larger hole in the wall, I could hear them even clearer. Which meant they could hear me easier as well.

It had apparently been a reflexive action, because Death answered her in a calmer tone. Jesus. He'd almost pulverized me without even knowing I was there. Talk about irony. How had he sensed me on the astral plane but not here? Did he have more power there? That was a scary thought.

"Hermes is worse than Loki in many ways. He is the confidence man on Wall Street selling you shares in a lucrative, stock of the century, investment. Loki is the man selling timeshares to Branson."

I smirked to myself. That was a good way to put it.

Othello shifted his focus back to current events. "Everyone is coming to Chateau Falco later for a meeting. To discuss matters of Peter. Maybe Callie has an update that could help us track him."

Death grumbled something vaguely affirmative. "What else?"

"A Valkyrie has gone rogue," Othello said.

I eagerly stepped back up to my viewpoint. They were talking about Kára.

"I know," Death said. "She got involved with Quinn MacKenna, believe it or not. That girl is almost as infuriating as Nate."

Othello leaned forward interestedly, dropping her feet from the desk. "Really?" I was just as surprised as her. Kára hadn't mentioned that. Did that mean Quinn was really out of her jail? Had my follow-up dreams with her been as real as they had felt? That was troubling.

"It had nothing at all to do with Nate," Death explained. "Just an unhappy coincidence. I hope Callie Penrose isn't half as troublesome as those two. Especially if she's coming here for this meeting. If you tell me Quinn is also on her way, I'm leaving." I saw that he was smiling, and that Othello was smirking back at him.

"Have you spoken to Odin?" Othello asked after a few moments. "Does Freya know about...the rogue Valkyrie?"

Death regarded her with what I assumed was a cool warning, judging by how she seemed to shy away. Death had a hardcore resting bitch face, so maybe he'd unintentionally hit her with the full-frontal RBF. "I have a meeting with him tomorrow night. I'm sure the topic will come up."

I arched an eyebrow. Death was meeting with Odin? What was that all about? Was Kára in trouble? And why hadn't she mentioned running into Quinn? *Where* had she run into Quinn? On the astral plane like I had? It seemed like a stupid thing to hide from me. Maybe she just hadn't wanted to stress me out since I had enough going on.

"I know this might not be the right time," Othello began, staring at Death's chest rather than his face, "but maybe we could visit my—"

"NO!" Death shouted, cutting her off. His eyes flicked up to the rafters. Chateau Falco quivered in agitation at the booming sound of his voice. My eyes bugged out of my head with desperation, needing to know what she had been about to say more than almost anything in the world.

"I'm sorry," Othello whispered. "I didn't mean—"

Death enveloped her in a tight embrace, looking torn. "No. I'm sorry, Othello. I shouldn't have shouted. But these walls have ears." I flinched instinctively, fearing he was about to punch through the wall again and grab his Peter with a triumphant cry.

I frowned. Even my thoughts were a barren field of mistaken phrasing.

She nodded. "I know. I'm sorry. It was a slip of the tongue."

"I love you, Othello," Death said, clutching her tightly. "Even though it risks my own soul."

She sighed in defeat. "Take me to bed. I need the distraction."

Death eyed her hungrily. "Of course, my love. Perhaps a break is just what we need."

She eyed him with a smokey gaze. "You're about to break off a piece of that ass in my bed, Horseman," she said, chuckling huskily.

He actually blushed at the role reversal. Then he eyed the room thoughtfully. "Why waste time finding a bedroom?" he asked mischievously. "This desk looks sturdy..."

"Didn't you say the walls have ears?" she teased.

"If they're lucky, maybe they also have eyes. I want them to see and hear you scream," he said. "Our pleasure is nothing to keep secret."

I felt an icy dagger stab into my heart with each word, seeming to take my breath away.

In response, Othello ripped off her top and I blushed to find she wore no bra.

I managed to peel my eyes away from the torrent of naked flesh and hastily discarded clothing, but I could do nothing about the sounds as I walked away. The panting. The kissing.

I forced myself to focus on the meaningful aspects of their conversation. My Horsemen were coming here to Chateau Falco. That presented an opportunity. As I slipped away, making my way back through the tunnels to the Armory, I couldn't shrug off concerns about Othello's memory shard amulet.

And what the hell had Othello been trying to say before Death cut her off? My old friend was racking up secrets—and all of them seemed to involve me. I knew he viewed me as a brother and would do anything for me—he'd proven that numerous times.

But sometimes families had the most secrets...

47

I made my way back to the entrance to the Armory, feeling numb. I continued to ruminate on what I'd heard.

Othello had mentioned that Ryuu had already been taken. At least, I was pretty sure she'd been talking about Ryuu—as long as my pirates had taken the right ninja. I hoped Yahn had made use of his eyepatch so as not to be seen—or Callie and Alucard might very well go to war. Alucard was a hair away from going postal, according to Othello's news update. Almost killing Raego? And Callie would raise Hell—literally—to get Ryuu back after his heartfelt statements at their picnic. Callie worked with angels and demons. I hoped Carl hadn't painted a holy target on his back by following my plan.

I stood at our rendezvous point for about ten minutes before I even considered wondering why Kára wasn't back yet. It had to have been an hour by now. It had felt like a lifetime for me.

What if Kára had been caught? Falco wouldn't let her get into trouble, unless Kára grew cocky and wandered out in the open for some reason. She didn't know the mansion like I did, and I wasn't sure if her confidence about stealth was arrogance or magical. If she was caught, it might give up my whole plan. Othello already knew Kára was hunting for me. If they found her here, difficult questions would be asked—and no one seemed in the mood for peaceful interrogation tactics.

"Falco, take me to Kára. Now," I demanded, snapping out of my mental funk.

The wall beside me cracked with a dusty expulsion of mortar and stone, revealing a different door. I shook my head, biting down my concern about this new development with my mansion. How I could just tell it where I wanted to go and a pathway would be provided. Did it have something to do with my own powers or had she been able to do it all along?

"Thank you. And don't think I've forgotten about our talk. I'm not mad, I'm just disappointed," I added, taking a line from my parents.

The door promptly disappeared as if I'd only imagined it.

I stared at the stone wall. "You've got to be kidding me," I muttered, glaring up at the rafters. "You can't blame me for feeling deceived!" I called out, my voice echoing.

Falco remained steadfast. "Fine. You hurt my feelings. I know you had your reasons."

The mansion purred begrudgingly, but no door appeared.

I flung up my hands. "I'm sorry!"

As if I'd said *open sesame*, the door reappeared. I muttered inaudible curses—so Falco could not make sense of them—under my breath as I shoved the door open. She was likely to lock me in the tunnel if I didn't get a grip on my temper.

I quickly made my way down the tunnels at a nervous jog, trusting Falco to take me to the right place. Ten minutes went by before I heard voices from another peephole just ahead. The tunnel branched off to the right, but I halted abruptly when I heard Gunnar's familiar voice.

I leaned up to the peephole to see him talking with Ashley. He was shirtless, pacing back and forth in what looked like one of the upstairs bedrooms. Ashley watched him with a stern look on her face, and I knew he was in the doghouse, figuratively speaking.

He must have told her about our quest to free Fenrir, and how he'd allowed his minor children to join in on the crime, making it a family affair. The Court of Ashley would sentence him and the pups to a few years of doghouse arrest for that. As long as he didn't snitch on The Godfather—

me—I'd let him ride out his sentence worry-free. I began pulling away to pursue Kára's tunnel when his words drew me up short.

"It was so ridiculous that I thought it was a prank," Gunnar chuckled. "Peter walked around the shelves for a while, grabbed a ridiculous amount of worthless junk, and then he took a two-hour nap on a forklift with a teddy bear. Alaric Slate ran around like a maniac, searching for him. It was almost like they were playing hide-and-seek."

I gritted my teeth. It had been way more dangerous than that. I'd been stealthy as hell.

"But he had Nate's satchel, right?" Ashley asked nervously.

Gunnar nodded. "It sure looked like it, judging by how much he took. It's concerning, but Nate's been spotted numerous times, and he trusts Hermes. Even the Minotaur vouched for Hermes. And Nate picked up Alice to keep her safe. Freya didn't bat an eye over it, and Freya will do anything to protect children," he said reassuringly, implying how much she cared for their own kids. She'd literally bonded her godly powers to them to keep them safe. "Whatever Nate's up to, it's some crazy-ass plan that will only make sense when he's finished. Maybe he is dealing with Peter and we just don't know it—lulling him into a false sense of confidence by giving him that satchel. It's only useful to Nate, after all. No one else can get anything out of it."

Ashley sighed. "I hope you're right. What else did they do at Grimm Tech? Set traps?"

Gunnar scratched his head, frowning. "Well, they got into a slap fight over some item, but I don't know what it was. Peter was choking Alaric out at one point, and then they knocked something off the shelf. Minutes later, they both disappeared. And that was well before Yahn was taken. Maybe someone else was in the Vault, too," he said, shrugging. "Because the Peter and Alaric show looked like the Two Stooges."

I grimaced angrily, my pride wounded at their rendition of my robbery.

"Anyway," Gunnar continued, his humor evaporating in an instant. "Callie just arrived, and she's out for blood. One of her ninjas is missing, but she won't talk about it for some reason."

Ashley sat up straighter. "And Alucard?"

"He was at the gate with Tory and the Reds a few minutes ago. He's probably downstairs now. I told Callie we would meet in the office in ten minutes. I texted Alucard to meet us there, as well," he growled, raking his hands through his long blonde hair. On the nightstand, a marvelous hammer stood, hilt up, and his eye kept drifting towards it subconsciously.

"You planning to use that today?" Ashley asked, only faintly kidding.

He jerked his attention away with a mumbled curse. "Let's just say I'm not leaving it out of sight anytime soon. Where are the pups? With tempers this high, I don't want them wandering around by themselves."

Ashley stood, looking furious. "You can't mean that."

Gunnar faced her, squaring his shoulders. "Someone took Yahn, and I don't think it was Peter. Now someone has taken one of Callie's people," he growled, sounding troubled. He turned his back on her, clenching his fists as he faced his hammer again. Mjolnir...and he was considering bringing it to a meeting inside Chateau Falco—that was how concerned he was. *Damn it, Gunnar*, I thought. *Stop being such a good detective. Just for a little while longer.*

Ashley slowly approached her husband, setting her hand on his broad, muscular back. He was breathing heavily, looking as if he was preparing for a boxing match only moments away. He flinched under her touch, but she didn't let up. Finally, he let out a shuddering sigh.

"You are Wulfric." Her words had an immediate effect.

He spun, gripping her by the waist, and pulling her close. She gasped in surprise, melting into his advance. He kissed her deeply, growling as he did so. Finally, she pulled away, placing a dainty looking palm on his massive chest.

"You are the Horseman of Justice. It falls to you to broker a peace between your fellows in Nate's absence."

He nodded affirmatively. "I agree. The question is whether my fellows feel the same way. Hence, the hammer," he said, extending a hand to the side. Mjolnir zipped into his grasp and tendrils of electricity rippled up his arms, making his veins pop out.

Ashley regarded her hulking husband with an amused grin. "Perhaps you should put a shirt on *before* you grab your hammer. The pecs might distract Callie for a second or two, but they won't help you with Alucard," she teased.

Gunnar stared back at her, and then grinned wolfishly. He set the hammer down and tugged on a plain white tee that had been tossed onto the bed. Then he grabbed his hammer again.

Their conversation abruptly ended at the sound of barking from the halls. Panicked, nervous, frightened barking.

Gunnar snarled. Ashley snarled.

I squeed—maybe even peed, a little.

The tunnel leading to Kára led suspiciously close to the source of the barking. Damn it! I raced down the hallway even as I heard Gunnar blast through the bedroom door with his hammer, not even bothering to try the handle.

"Shit. Shit. Shit," I panted, sprinting down the hall. "Stall them, Falco. Please!"

I felt the mansion rumble, but it wasn't a relief.

Because it sounded suspiciously like wizard's fire, werewolf howls, and vampire screams rather than her offering sanctuary to Kára.

48

I reached a solid wall and took the gamble of all fucking gambles, pushing it open without concern for anyone on the other side. I didn't have magic. All I had was the element of surprise.

I fell out into a hallway and stumbled directly into Kára. She held a large black puppy with white paws under one arm—Makayla—and her trident in the other. The other pup—Calvin—was white with startlingly pale blue eyes, and he was currently dancing about like a madman, weaving back and forth between the Valkyrie's legs. The pups took one look at me and began wagging their tails.

Werewolf howls echoed down the corridor and I heard Callie's familiar voice cursing from a different adjacent hallway. "Why isn't my Gateway working?" she demanded, and I hoped to God that it was because Falco was covering our asses.

I stared from Kára to the happy pups with a bewildered look. She stared back at me, her face smudged with soot and a new dent on her shoulder armor. "What the hell?" I bent down and scooped up Calvin, spinning back to face my secret tunnel and hide.

But it was no longer there.

I stood there, stunned, cringing as the howling grew louder and closer, coordinating their attacks. "Open, damn you!" I cursed, slapping at the wall. "Please!"

That's when I heard Gunnar right around the corner, snarling savagely with his wife in hot pursuit. Shit. Falco didn't want to reveal her secrets with them so close. I took off at a dead sprint, motioning for Kára to get ahead of me. If my friends saw anyone, I wanted them to get a long hard look at Peter's ass,

Not Kára's ass—that was for my eyes only.

I stumbled at the abstract thought but pressed on.

Calvin licked at my arm, whining and wriggling happily, somehow able to see through my illusion when no one else had been able to. Or maybe he could smell me beneath it. Dogs trusted their sense of smell more than their eyesight. "You okay, boy?" I asked, wondering why they had let out such panicked barks if they hadn't been under duress.

Kára glanced over her shoulder at a fork in the halls, silently asking for my guidance. I took a gamble and pointed to our right—the quieter of the two. More howls echoed throughout the mansion, and I heard dragons roaring and blasting flames outside. Unfortunately, some of those roars also echoed, telling me some were also *inside* and on our trail. I briefly wondered what the hell they were blasting, but dismissed it since it wasn't me.

"I stepped on her tail and the other one tackled me," Kára muttered, rolling her shoulder where I had seen the fresh dent. "I gave them some jerky to calm them down, but that's when I saw Callie down the hall. She didn't see me, but she heard me. She has a blast first and ask questions later attitude that I don't appreciate."

I cursed. "You're sure she didn't see you?"

"Positive. I saw the back of her head and was already fleeing down an adjacent hallway before she turned. She didn't even look before flinging power at me. There was some kind of explosion. Sounded like an armoire of china crashed to the ground and then she began blasting away at it with fire, shouting about a failed Gateway. Falco's doing?" she asked.

"I sure as fuck hope so. Why didn't you meet me?" I demanded.

"You looked busy," she said in a suddenly stiff tone.

I frowned. "Wait. You *saw* me?" I asked, perplexed.

She nodded. "Spying on Othello and Death," she mumbled. "Let's just get out of here before your friends catch and decease us."

Calvin and Makayla chose that moment to begin howling in response to their brethren, joining in on the song of their people. "Fucking werewolves!" I snapped, trying to clamp Calvin's muzzle shut.

I heard an explosion of fabric from not far enough behind me, right as Kára darted down a new hallway to our right. "There he is!" Gunnar roared. "He has Calvin! I will fucking eat your heart, PETER!"

I almost tripped and fell in sheer terror, the bloodcurdling tone of his voice physically making my heart stop and my sphincter's sphincter clam permanently shut. At least he hadn't seen Kára.

Calvin yowled excitedly, wagging his tail at the sound of his father's voice, enjoying the fun new game.

I risked a glance back and immediately regretted it. Gunnar was in full Wulfric mode—a colossal, seven-foot-tall mountain of white fur, claws, and wickedly long teeth.

I backpedaled, trying to see if there was anything I could direct Falco to do to save my fucking life from my best friend. I silently admitted that I was both the world's best and worst Godfather.

Armoires exploded in my wake as the mansion began to scream. Couches, chairs, tables, and priceless vases flew across the hall, splintering and shattering as they bounced and cartwheeled into the werewolf's path.

Gunnar tore through them all like a bulldozer, his lone eye blazing with electric fire as he lifted his hammer behind his head and hurled it at me.

The stone wall beside him exploded, peppering him with blocks the size of my head. They clipped his hand, body, and jaw, and he didn't even fucking *blink*—even as his body was hammered down an adjacent hall. The smoking corridor behind me was blocked from floor to ceiling with ancient blocks of stone, but I didn't notice that all too much.

Because Mjolnir was still screaming towards my face, unimpeded by the brutal beating Gunnar had suffered. A hand gripped me by the shoulder and yanked me out of harm's way hard enough to send me sprawling on the floor, sending Calvin sliding along with me. I looked up to see Kára slide a very surprised Makayla my way before planting her feet and stabbing the air with her trident. Acting as a human shield for us, she took the force of Mjolnir—and she did it with one hand and a haunting, somewhat excited grin.

The two weapons collided with a dazzling explosion of blue electricity that sent a visible shockwave outwards, slamming me and the pups against the wall. Kára skidded into my lap, clutching a dented, damaged trident tipped with black soot. Mjolnir sat in the hallway at the epicenter of the blast, seemingly unaffected.

Wizard fire and werewolf claws tore through the rubble in the distance, and I heard monsters of all types congregating on the source of the mayhem.

Kára grunted. "Nailed it," she wheezed dazedly.

As I stared at the rubble, I saw a bloody, white-furred claw break through and I gasped, scanning the walls for Falco's escape route. "Come *on*," I growled, clutching the pups and Kára as best I could. Calvin and Makayla licked at my face happily, wagging their tails at this insane new game of flee and destroy that their godfather was playing with them and their dad. "Give us a tunnel, Falco," I begged.

Kára turned and wrapped us all in a clumsy hug, plopping her chin over my shoulder. "Where we're going, we don't need tunnels," she whispered. "Consider this me picking you up for our date," she said amidst the fire and explosions and screams.

I released the balled-up note in my fist. The extortion note for Gunnar's pups.

The world winked out between one moment and the next.

49

Blistering heat made me squint my eyes on reflex, taking a few moments for them to adjust. I let out a breath of relief to see that I'd managed to release the extortion note in time, rather than taking it with us to this tropical hell-adise.

Calvin and Makayla barked excitedly, jerking free of my grip to go smell all the new things—which was pretty much ash and sulfur as far as I could tell. I still held Kára in my arms and I was suddenly squeezing her tightly, kissing the top of her head as I laughed triumphantly.

No one had gotten injured on either side; Kára hadn't been forced to poke anyone and, if the pups' excitement was any indication, our party was healthy and whole. Luckily, the pups hadn't chosen to turn into mist during our flight or our plan would have been blown to shit.

True to my thoughts, Calvin and Makayla tackled us to the ground in an exhausted, jubilant pile, making me laugh even harder. Kára squirmed, twisting her body until her back was to my chest, freeing her hands for self-defense. Or so she thought. The pups struck like vipers, deftly dodging her hands to slither in and lick our faces happily, whining and yapping directly into our ear canals.

Thankfully, they saw through my illusion. It would have broken my heart had they shied away from my touch, fearing me as a stranger. I hadn't realized how much I'd missed them. How much I'd feared for them after leaving them to flee the mountains with Fenrir. They'd used some heavy, hardcore, still unexplained magic, and I'd been concerned about the fallout.

So, I let them have at my face, covering me in puppy slobber as I hugged Kára and tried to catch my breath. She gave up fighting and clutched my hands over her chest, squeezing them reassuringly to let me know she was okay after her lightning rod impersonation.

The pups lost interest in the lazy humans and hopped off us, pressing their noses to the ground and trotting away with boundless curiosity. I scooted back so that Kára's head rested in my lap. "You sure you're okay?" I asked. She had looked a little wild-eyed back at Falco.

She nodded slowly. "I took that like a champ, didn't I?" she mumbled. "Saved you guys."

I gently shook her, alarmed by the lethargic look in her eyes. "You better not die on me, Kára," I growled, wondering if Mjolnir's lightning had done some unseen damage. "Where does it hurt?" I demanded, ignoring the barking wolves.

"Die?" she murmured sleepily. "Been there, done that. Didn't stick. I'm just exhausted."

"You just deflected Mjolnir. I'm pretty sure that surviving is considered a win. It blew through at least two solid walls and I think a statue before you smacked it down."

She smiled happily, her eyes seeming to refocus. "Let me go, you big oaf."

"Nah," I said, deciding to wait a while longer until I was confident she wasn't slaphappy. She sighed in resignation, but it didn't look like her heart was in it—more for show. I took my first real look around, frowning. I stared up at a brimstone sky and shuddered involuntarily. It felt like only a few hours ago that I'd been astral projecting in Charon's boat.

We were on a rocky shore, facing an incline that extended to a canary-yellow boulder field in the near distance. A yellow and black mountain loomed over it—the source of the rockfalls.

I spotted Kára's trident lying beside her. It was dented and damaged, covered in soot, and one of the prongs was bent at a harsh angle, but it still looked serviceable. I saw her staring at it with a sad frown, and I promptly decided it was now safe—and safer for me—to let her go. Kára slowly sat up and I scooted back, giving her space. She turned around to face me, smiling faintly as she swept some loose strands of hair from her eyes.

Her cheeks sported several gashes and abrasions, but her eyes looked more alert. "What happened back there? Before the gauntlet escape," I clarified.

"I was looking through a hole in the wall when the wolves walked right up to it and began sniffing curiously. I didn't want to risk them giving me away, so I slipped out of a door Falco provided for me. I looked both ways, saw the coast was clear, and the pups seemed excited to see me, so I seized the opportunity. When I turned around, the door was gone and I accidentally stepped on Makayla's tail," she admitted with a wince.

Makayla had obviously forgotten all about it. That's a lovely thing about puppies.

The same could not be said about father wolves. Gunnar was going to destroy anything in his path to get the pups back.

I waved a hand at her concern. "You did the right thing. Just took me by surprise. I was watching Gunnar and Ashley when you must have stepped on her tail. They fled the room, looking hungry for murder."

She nodded, scanning our surroundings. "Welcome to Hell. The rest of the date is on your shoulders," she said. I instinctively tensed at her choice of words, wondering if Kára had overheard my talk with Pandora about shouldering burdens. Her face told me nothing. But it did remind me of something else she'd said. She'd caught me spying on Othello and Death.

"I heard Othello mention someone had been abducted in Kansas City, so it looks like Carl and Yahn succeeded," I said.

Kára nodded woodenly. "Good."

I debated saying anything else about Othello or Death, but I had the sneaking suspicion that nothing I could say would help me. Like an idiot, I pressed on. "Death is suspicious about Alaric coming back from the dead. He's also meeting with Odin tomorrow night. Might have something to do with the rogue Valkyrie everyone's talking about. How she met up with Quinn recently." Kára's face went slack. I lifted my palms reassuringly. "Relax. We've got more important things to worry about, and you're not the only one with Quinn stories. It just caught me off guard, so I kept listening to them. I wanted to make sure they weren't hunting you down." She nodded, not offering up an answer. I'd also hoped that mentioning Death would give her a chance to bring up what I'd seen on the astral plane.

Kára reached for her trident and used it as a crutch to climb to her feet.

I sighed, following suit. So much for conversation. It was time for us to get to work anyway. I wanted to spend as little time here as possible. Kára assessed our surroundings with a growing frown, sweeping her gaze from left to right. I glanced over her shoulder to see that we were on the shore of the River Styx, the black water eerily still. I smiled crookedly. Well, talk about the perfect location. Kára stiffened, staring over my shoulder. "Fuck."

I spun to see Calvin and Makayla about fifty yards away, and they were stalking...

Well, a dog much bigger than them that seemed to have just woken up from a nap, judging by the three massive yawns from its three massive heads. "Cerberus," I breathed.

He was the size of a two-story building. On fire. With people jumping out the windows. Although I was certain that was just his aura. Each head bore a slightly different expression of frustration and confusion as they locked onto Calvin and Makayla dancing back and forth as they crept closer. They began to bark now that their prey was awake.

I felt a wave of panic roar through me. They were picking a fight with the biggest monster in the Underworld. Gunnar was going to kill me. This was the worst location, not the best.

Before I could debate the wisdom in shouting at them, my alarm quickly faded as I saw their tails start to wag. I let out a loud sigh of relief, my knees wobbling, as Cerberus mirrored them, wagging his tail and panting eagerly at the two relatively tiny wolves hassling him.

Kára stepped up beside me, shaking her head in wonder. "He *never* does that," she breathed. Cerberus leaned down onto his front paws, sniffing at them curiously. They circled him warily, snuffling at the air.

And then they lunged forward and began nipping at his paws, hopping back when one of Cerberus' three heads lunged to nip back. It sounded like bear traps snapping closed, but his bites were not even remotely close enough to harm the pups.

They, on the other hand, had no qualms about sinking their teeth into the infamous three-headed guard dog's flesh. He reminded me of a pit breed, covered in slabs and slabs of muscle. His three sets of jaws were big and strong enough to crush boulders in a single chomp.

This was not a breed you brought home to your daughter. Unless you wanted her to take over the world with nail polish and violence.

Unfortunately, one of the heads caught sight of me and no longer looked as playful.

I waved at him with a nervous smile, reaching into my satchel in hopes that I had some jerky left. Thankfully, I found a bone instead. It looked suspiciously like a human femur, and I mentally cursed Carl on reflex for shoving secret bones into my magic satchel.

I reared back and hurled it at him, wincing as it hit the ground in a puff of sulfurous dust, causing the other two heads to sneeze violently. Calvin and Makayla suddenly erupted in frenzied barks, lunging for the bone and snapping their teeth at Cerberus. The massive dog lifted his three heads as high as possible, with bewildered looks on each. Calvin and Makayla stole the prize, each carrying an end between them as they trotted our way.

Cerberus watched them, cocking all three heads in a crestfallen reaction, seeming to wonder how the pups had dominated them so easily.

I let out a shaky sigh and turned to Kára. She settled the butt of her trident into the stony shore and nodded agreeably. "Well, that's a first," she admitted. She pointed at the wide river in front of us. "How's that for front row parking?" she asked with a grin.

"Great job," I said, keeping an eye on Cerberus in the event he changed his mind. "We should hurry. I don't want my boss seeing me or he might rope me in for a long shift," I muttered. I cupped my hands around my mouth. "Calvin, Makayla! Get over here!"

The two mist wolves picked up their pace, pretty much declaring this the best day of their lives if their tails were any sort of barometer. They dropped the femur at my feet proudly, as if I hadn't ever seen it before. I smiled, crouching down to ruffle Calvin's head. "Good job, guys. He's terrified. Your parents will be so proud." I scooped up the bone, hoping I hadn't known the poor bastard or anything, and rose to my feet before either wolf could nab it from me. Calvin and Makayla promptly sat, quivering with anticipation.

I glanced from left to right, making sure we were alone. There was always the chance of a wandering spirit or monster guard. Hell, some of those Candy Skulls were usually lurking.

Kára noticed my concern and waved a hand. "Most denizens of the Underworld avoid Valkyries like the plague. We're about as safe from spirits as we could possibly be."

I grimaced. "I'm more worried about management." But I saw no one. The River Styx stretched out before us, wide and calm like a lake. In the distance, tributaries of fire and liquid ice merged into one hellish stew of steam and raging waterfalls, but this spot was relatively calm. We were almost in a private cove of sorts, with rock walls blocking us off from anyone further downstream.

I murmured a prayer, hoping that this would appease Gunnar's fury.

Then I tossed the leg bone into the River Styx.

The mist wolves tore down the beach after it and leapt into the river without an iota of concern. Their bodies struck the black water and disappeared. I gasped in alarm as a bright light abruptly flashed throughout the Underworld, followed by twin thumps that felt like a giant living in the apartment below us had just banged his broom against the ceiling, yelling us to pipe down. The wolves bobbed up to the surface, paddling for all they were worth as they raced for the femur. I remained tense, waiting for an alarm, but nothing happened.

I turned to see Cerberus watching us curiously, but he was panting unconcernedly, not looking the least bit alarmed at the flash of light or the pounding sound. I turned to Kára, grinning hesitantly. "We did it—"

Her smile slipped as she glanced over my shoulder, staring off into the distance, not at the pups. She really needed to stop looking over my shoulder. I spun to see an ancient, definitely not seaworthy, canoe drifting around the corner. Charon, the Boatman, lazily paddled our way, drinking a beer with one hand and managing an oar in the other. Well, claws, not hands.

And by drinking, I meant taking a beer shower, pouring it on his face.

Worse, he had a passenger.

A forty-something looking woman with long, auburn colored hair sat on a bright green cushion at the rear of the boat. She had massive sunglasses covering half her face, and a silk parasol was wedged into the rotted wood of the canoe to give her some shade.

Shade from what, I had no idea. There was no sunlight here, of course.

She wore a toga—a bad sign, in my opinion—and she was taking healthy gulps from a frozen daiquiri or margarita. Judging by her exaggerated movements and loud singing—which I hadn't noticed over the splashing of the mist wolves—she was absolutely smashed.

"Kára, get the pups. We need to skedaddle."

Of course, Charon saw me, waved happily, and angled his boat our way. He instantly stopped rowing upon seeing the pups thrashing about in the water, almost dropping his oar. He simply stared at them, completely motionless for about five seconds. Then he slowly swiveled his attention to his drunken passenger, who was still singing and oblivious to her surroundings.

Charon feigned nonchalance by reaching into his lucky cooler for another beer, but his other claw made sharp shooing motions at me, silently urging us to get the ever-living fuck out of the Underworld. He had told me he would provide a distraction for when I brought the pups here. That plan obviously hadn't worked out like either of us had intended. His passenger suddenly noticed their lack of locomotion and stopped singing.

She sat up abruptly, swaying back and forth as her unsteady gaze zeroed in on me. Then she yanked her sunglasses off and squinted, triangulating my position via the three versions of me she no doubt saw.

I spun to Kára, who was still trying to encourage the wolves to join us. Instead of listening, they had begun paddling towards the canoe, drawing the drunken passenger's attention. Charon grimaced, sighed, and then began paddling his boat to shore, resignation on his face.

"We need to leave. Now!" I hissed at Kára.

"They don't listen!" she said. I sighed, running through a dozen cover stories we might try to slip past Her Drunkenness. Charon's boat scraped onto shore and he shook his head helplessly. Then he downed his beer, once again moisturizing his face with alcohol.

The drunk woman held up a hand, sensing my desire to bolt. "Wait, or I'll call for help!" she crowed. Then she pointed a finger in Charon's general direction. She had about a bajillion bracelets on, so it sounded like a prison gang clanking along in a forced march. "Oil my back!"

Charon rolled his eyes so that only I could see, but he obeyed, turning to face his passenger as she hunched forward to give him a better angle. "Yes, Lady Hera," he rasped, popping the cap off a bottle of suntanning oil.

I shared a significant look with Kára but she shrugged, offering no suggestions.

I sighed. The party was just getting started.

50

Hera unhooked the shoulder of her toga and let the fabric drop to her lap with the same flair of sexual appeal as a mother of eight dropping her rucksack-sized purse and coupon book on the register counter after herding her swarm of children around the store for the last two hours. She draped her arms over the side of the boat and hunched forward much as the Kraken would wrap his tentacles around a ship to capsize it—and in a poll of *who wore it best*, the Kraken won.

Kára actually gasped in horror, taking an involuntary step back. That being said, Hera had a mighty nice...coupon book, proving that there really was a god of plastic surgery on Mount Olympus.

The obvious dichotomy made my head spin. I studied her face, wondering why I'd initially thought she looked old. Upon closer inspection, she was downright ravishing, with nary a wrinkle on her face. But something about her eyes, posture, and soul-deep slovenliness made it impossible for me not to envision Miss Hannigan from the movie *Annie*.

And not just because she was roaring drunk. She simply had that defeated, last call look on her face, as if she'd lost one of her heels five drinks ago, and now she was down to her last cigarette, slouching as she scoped out the available gents at the bar with a squinty eye, ready to one-up her personal best in decades of poor life decisions.

Impossible as it was for me to believe, I actually felt a brief pang of sympathy for Zeus.

"To what do I owe this pleasure, Lady Hera?" I asked politely, discreetly signaling Kára to get the pups under control. They had waded back onto shore and were shaking off their fur and pawing at the aged canoe. They didn't seem any different than before their swim, and I began to fear that my ploy to make them invincible hadn't worked. Since I'd risked my friendship—and life—in the attempt to stick to my promise to Gunnar, I was going to be rightly furious if it hadn't worked.

And now I had this walking mugshot of a woman to deal with.

Kára didn't seem eager to get too close to Hera or Charon.

Hera eyed me askance with a dignified air as if she was price-checking a personal massager at the local dollar store. Kára coughed back a laugh, not trying very hard to hide her amusement.

"I imagine you want to see that walking infestation of pubic lice as much as I do or you wouldn't be down here," Hera drawled, squinting at me. I arched an eyebrow, surprised at her description and not entirely certain who she was talking about. "Zeus," she slurred, somehow turning it into two syllables. "My dear husband," she clarified dryly. "Why do you think I'm down here? It certainly isn't to see how disgustingly in love my brother is with his wife, Persephone. Love is for losers. Real happiness is in daiquiris."

Right...

"Oh. Well." I scratched at my head, trying to get a read on Charon. He continued to oil her back, refusing to look up at me. I eyed Kára's trident, comparing it to Charon's paddle spear, and I didn't like our odds. With Hera's open disdain for her husband, and remembering something Prometheus had casually said, I took a gamble. I needed a way to distract Hera, but maybe I could actually get something useful out of her in the process. A weapon powerful enough to take down a Titan. That could always come in handy. And I knew just the one to make Zeus' skin crawl—especially if I could get *his own wife* to give it to me.

Cronus' Scythe—the blade Zeus' daddy had used to castrate his own father, Uranus. It all came down to how drunk Hera really was. "I need to obtain a weapon. Borrow it, really," I said.

She leaned closer, almost dropping her sunglasses into the water as her elbow slipped over the side of the boat. I could have used her daiquiri as a level to hang a picture—it didn't even tilt one degree off center.

Because Hera was a hero with priorities.

She took a big gulp of fortification, smacking her lips after. She frowned at me, chewing over the word *weapon* as if it might have made sense three drinks ago. "Don't you have the Armory to play with?"

The pups finally grew bored with the drunken boaters ignoring them and trotted over to me. I let out a sigh of relief, calmly bending down to rest my hand on Calvin's back. Kára did the same with Makayla and touched her foot to mine, completing the link so that she could get us out of here if things went south.

I felt her watching my face, waiting for a signal. I studied Hera, deciding to keep pressing and see where this led. "I was hoping for something a little bit more...nostalgic."

She arched an eyebrow and then a wicked grin split across her face. "Oh, sweet Dionysus' nipples. You don't mean..." she trailed off as if not sure she dared to say it out loud. Or maybe she'd lost her train of thought.

"An heirloom. Some might even call it the key to your grandfather's family jewels."

She blanched, looking as if she was about to vomit. "Too far. *Way* too far."

I laughed nervously, shifting my weight. "I was just trying to make sure we were talking about the same thing. Your father's sickle. Cronus' scythe."

"Charon!" she bellowed, waving her arms dramatically and almost knocking him overboard. "Make some room on this boat! It's time to collect the CASTRATOR!" Her voice rocked through the Underworld, and even Cerberus hunkered low, letting out a triplet whine.

At least I now knew Hera and I were on the same page—and that she hated her husband.

Kára stared at me in disbelief. I would have settled for baptizing the pups in the River Styx and escaping with our lives, but to convince my enemy's wife to give me the blade used to kill her own grandfather? Hell yes. I was going to stir some shit up, all right. It was exactly what I needed to better my odds for that last move in our game.

Between one moment and the next, a gleaming cigarette boat idled throatily in the river and I gasped, blinking in astonishment. "Why the fuck do you ride a canoe when you can do this?"

He shrugged. "Well, I actually have a new boat that Quinn MacKenna gave me, but it failed inspections, so it's in the shop." I blinked. Quinn MacKenna. Again. Charon continued. "I am a simple man. I just wish to drink and float. Going over a hundred miles an hour makes the beer splash all over my face from the wind." He poured a beer on his mouth, splashing his face. "Much better to chill and savor the flavor. Better for the heart."

Kára looked baffled that his solution to spilled beer was...spilled beer. "We should probably hurry. We each have counterparts here who might have a lot of questions."

Charon spit into the water. "Fucking Anubis."

"My sweet brother, Hades," Hera added.

"Freya or Odin," Kára murmured uncomfortably.

I glanced at Calvin and Makayla who were wagging their tails. "Puppies wanna go for a...*ride?*" I asked, drawing out the question with overt enthusiasm.

They barked crazily, their tails wagging so hard they seemed to propel the pups up into the gleaming cigarette boat. I grinned at Kára, leaning forward. "Now *this* is a fucking date."

She smiled shyly, her green and blue eyes twinkling in the brimstone sunset of Hell, and my breath caught for a moment. Then she was laughing as she climbed up into the boat. I followed suit, shaking my head at the absurdity of going on a party cruise with my enemy's spiteful wife. Charon cracked open some beers and passed them around. "Hold onto your favorite body part." He eyed me and then Kára pointedly. "Your *own* favorite body part, not someone else's."

I scowled at him, and Kára burst out laughing, seeming to embrace the prospect of dashing our careful plans in favor of an unanticipated, impromptu adventure. She stood at the prow of the ship, reminding me of a vaunted figurehead on a pirate ship. I grinned back at her.

Charon cackled and floored it. I almost flew off the back of the boat exactly one-tenth of a second later, but Kára caught me by the shirt with one hand.

I opened my mouth to thank her, but the words froze on my tongue. Oceans of lava silhouetted her from behind and her eyes smoldered. She pulled me closer, fighting the roar of the wind ripping through the boat without any noticeable effort. Over the roar of the engines, I thought I heard Hera cackling.

Kára didn't pay her any attention as she pulled me close to her chest. She stared down at my lips; her eyes impossibly huge.

"Stay still," she whispered. Then she leaned forward, craning her neck, and pressed her lips against mine. She whimpered faintly upon contact and my toes curled as she slowly kissed my lips, only enough for me to feel the inside of her lips taste mine. Then she pulled back slightly.

"Your turn," she whispered breathlessly, trembling with fear and uncertainty and hope and—

I leaned close before she could flee and mimicked her kiss to the letter —a single, teasing, maddening taste of her mouth using only my lips. Then I just as slowly pulled back, my heart hammering in my chest and my scalp and neck tingling. She panted raggedly, sucking in her lower lip with a dreamy, faraway look in her eyes and a growing goofy grin on her face.

I knew my own smile was just as big as I struggled to think of anything beyond the taste of her mouth and the unknown catalyst that had caused the surprise kiss.

Without a word, she turned away and walked to the bow, seeming to float, her shoulders lighter. Her arms rose to catch the wind and she flung her head back, letting out a wild, carefree shout.

I stared transfixed as the boat screamed out of the River Styx and onto the lava waves. No matter how much the boat rocked, Kára remained unmoving, standing almost lazily as her eyes pierced the horizon, soaking up the future ahead. Calvin and Makayla stood on either side of her, hanging their heads out of the boat, panting and snapping at the air.

Hera arched an amused eyebrow at me, lifting her glasses with a finger. Then she cackled again before sipping on her frozen daiquiri. "Foolish boy. You remind me of Icarus."

I grunted and sat down. "Says the spinster hiding underground to avoid her husband."

That shut her up.

I let out a sigh, hanging my head. "Sorry. I've had a trying day. Your husband has pushed me to my limits."

She studied me from over the lip of her glass. "Try marrying him," she said crisply.

After a few minutes of tense silence, Calvin and Makayla hopped down from their perch and sidled up next to me like guard dogs. Hera eyed them nervously. "I saw what you did. It will have consequences, boy. My husband does not appreciate insubordination."

I met her eyes levelly. "Can't be insubordinate if I never worked for him."

"That's what they all say. At first."

"And did any of them come to Hell with a Valkyrie, dip their mist wolves in the River Styx, and ask an Olympian for the Castrator?" I asked her in a resolute tone. "An immovable object is about to meet an unstoppable force. Your husband is going down, Hera."

She took off her glasses and studied me with hesitant excitement. "Oh, I sure hope so, dear boy. I sure hope so." She put her glasses back on and took a deep breath, smiling at the pups. "I'll talk to Hades about them. He'll need to cool down a little first, so I recommend this trip stays short and sweet or he might react emotionally. You men never know how to keep your emotions in check," she chuckled, shaking her head.

"What are you doing down here?" I asked, ignoring her jibe. She wasn't wrong.

"Hiding from my husband, like you so eloquently stated. Hades granted me sanctuary after I put a little bug in Zeus' ear." I arched an eyebrow and she chuckled. "He means to kill me."

Zeus' original task echoed in my ears—how he wanted to kill someone very powerful. "Wait. *You're* the person he's trying to kill?" I hissed. What a fucking stroke of luck! I could have cried.

She frowned. "Of course. Who else?"

I kept my face calm as a new thought hit me. If that was true, why had he roped me into this? I wouldn't have cared at all. Of course, I couldn't tell Hera this fun fact. "Why?"

She shrugged. "I told him there was a traitor in his midst, and he became a tad paranoid. I think he wants to kill me for answers." She calmly sipped at her drink again, frowning to see that it was almost empty.

I pondered her words, wondering why Kára was still standing at the front of the boat rather than joining our conversation. "Who is the traitor?" I asked Hera, fearing it would be Aphrodite.

Hera shrugged disinterestedly. "I have no idea. We were having an argument and I wanted to hurt him, so I just pulled that beauty out of the hat." She smiled smugly. "Must have worked too well. He tried to get an audience with the Sisters of Fate, but they denied him. I love it when my husband doesn't get what he wants."

I stared at her, stunned. I didn't dare pick apart the irony of her last comment. Zeus had said the opposite about the Sisters of Fate. He...had bluffed. Which meant he didn't have all the cards he pretended he did. "Let me get this straight. You had an argument and set your husband, the Father of the Olympians, on the warpath against everyone, making him believe a made-up conspiracy theory that risks the world...all so you could win an argument." She pondered my words and then simply nodded. "What was the argument about?"

She frowned. "I can't recall. Nothing important." I stared at her in silence, unable to kickstart my brain. She sniffed at the look on my face. "It's what we women do," she snapped stubbornly. "Win arguments."

I leaned back against my seat, wanting to scream at the crazy drunk. "Lady, I don't even know where to begin with that comment."

She leaned forward aggressively. The mist wolves snarled protectively until she pulled back. "Did you expect me to just back down and lose the argument? He was wrong. I'm certain of it."

I closed my eyes and counted to ten. This lady was unbelievable. No wonder Zeus was insane. He might have already been insane, but she'd only added fuel to the fire. I opened my eyes and looked at her. "Let's shelve hindsight. It's too late to look back on the past and point fingers. I'm now stuck in a shitty situation, and these Titan Thorns are preventing me from defending myself. Can you get them off of me?"

Hera leaned closer, touching them with her free hand. She didn't set down her drink, of course. Oh, no. That would have been a party foul. She grimaced and pulled away, brushing off her fingers. "Only true love could remove those. Filthy thing."

I was unsure whether Hera had meant that true love was a filthy thing or if she'd been referring to the Titan Thorns. "Where are we going, exactly?" I asked, hoping she didn't answer with happy hour. "Where is Cronus' Scythe?"

"It hangs in Hades' office." Her smile grew darker. "As does his Helm of Darkness."

I felt a cool sweat pop up across my brow, especially when Charon muttered a curse behind me. "The Helm of Darkness," I repeated. "That makes the wearer invisible, right? One of the three gifts the brothers received: Hades got the Helm, Poseidon got his trident, and Zeus got his lightning bolt."

She nodded. "The Helm of Darkness isn't as helpful in a direct fight as the trident or bolt, but it could be an ace up your sleeve. Especially if you have Cronus' Scythe."

I thought over my previous plan and I soon felt a grin of my own creeping across my face. "Yeah. That might just do the trick, Lady Hera." Then I hesitated. "How are we going to convince Hades to let me borrow it? Zeus is his brother."

Hera waved a hand dismissively. "He hates his brother for locking him away down here. You'll soon learn that as much as everyone fears Zeus, they hate him even more."

"Hades will just lend me the Helm?"

She snorted. "Never in a million years. We're going to steal it."

I blinked. "You want me to *rob* Hades?"

She shot me a withering look. "You're planning on killing Zeus. What's a little breaking and entering? Don't let your balls fall off now, boy. Judging by that kiss, you only just hit puberty."

51

Charon cursed louder, obviously having overheard Hera's plan. "I should have stayed with Anubis today," he muttered. "Fucking Valkyries breaking the rules and now this shit."

I glanced back, no longer able to hold a rational conversation with Hera the Lush. "What?"

"As I said, Quinn MacKenna paid me a visit recently. Figured lightning can't strike the same place twice. I forgot that down here, the impossibilities are endless." I dismissed the Quinn comment, deciding that I had plenty to worry about without getting roped into her messes. Charon was staring at me with a puzzled frown. "Why didn't you say anything?"

I frowned, feeling like I'd missed something. "About what?"

"I agreed to do you a favor, but I failed. You didn't call me out on it. I want to know why."

I stared at him, knowing exactly what he was talking about. Making a distraction so I could safely dip the pups in the River Styx. I shrugged. "It didn't seem to matter. I got it done."

He cocked his head. Then he glanced at Hera. "Can you explain it to him?"

I stared at the two of them. "It's not a big deal."

Hera pursed her lips. "It is. If one says they will do you a favor, and then fails, they owe you a new favor of your choosing, no questions asked."

Kára slowly turned to stare at Hera in disbelief. I felt the same way.

"And if you want to get into Hades' office," Charon said, "you will need a big favor."

He was right. "How about we skip all the questions you know I have, and I simply tell you that I need you to get me the Scythe and the Helm?"

Charon smirked, his lips tugging at the twine as he spoke. Well, his voice invaded my mind much like a creaking door in the middle of the night made your heart explode. "A favor is a favor. Consider it done." He pointed his strange, blade-like oar up ahead. Kára frowned at it suddenly, her eyes widening. She must not have noticed it until now. "They're in a budget meeting at the office. It's right around the corner."

Hera gasped. "Zeus is *here*?" she hissed.

I almost leapt out of the boat on instinct. Charon gripped my arm, shaking his head. "Zeus never comes to the budget meetings. It's usually just Hades, Poseidon, and Anubis."

Hera narrowed her eyes. "That's funny, because Zeus always tells me he's going to the meetings. Even that they often run late, no matter how boring they are."

I winced. Yeah. I'd heard that line used before.

"That son of a bitch. We're doing this," she snarled.

Charon nodded. "It's about time the lightning struck somewhere else," he said, pulling out an iPhone. I didn't even have the mental energy to question how he had acquired it or how it was functional down here in the Underworld.

Or why a selfie stick fell out of his robes in his haste. Kára was grinning, having noticed the same thing. I shrugged.

"It just so happens that Anubis owes me a favor as well," Charon said with a grim smile, lifting the phone to his ear. "I'll be the proxy, using his favor to pay for your favor. This is going to be very, very fun..."

WE SHORED up on a beach behind a low hill, obscuring our vessel from a small, surprisingly modern office building on the edge of the River Styx. Charon had laid out the plan, so all Kára and I had to do was watch it unfold. Hera had assured me that she was aware of the consequences, and that she would obviously be their first suspect. She hadn't seemed to be overly concerned about it, so I'd finally relented. I watched as Anubis slipped out of the building, looking suspicious as all hell before sneaking off into a boulder field behind it.

I turned to Hera and gave her the thumbs up once I was certain Anubis was well hidden.

She withdrew a bedazzled phone and made a call, peeking around the edge of the hill to watch the building as she put it on speaker. A gruff, no-nonsense voice answered. "Hello, Hera."

"Don't tell her he's not here," a different man's voice hissed in the background. I rolled my eyes. Jesus.

The first speaker, presumably Hades, snapped something back at him, sounding as if he'd attempted to cover the phone with his hand. "What can I do for you, Hera?"

Hera looked as if their brotherly exchange had been all the additional fuel she needed to pull this off. "I don't want to alarm you, but Charon and I were just cruising by Cell Block F, and I wanted to make sure they had the proper...construction permits for this monstrosity."

I cocked my head curiously, glancing back at Charon. He shrugged, looking just as curious. He also looked alarmed at the location she'd mentioned.

"Cell Block F," Hades murmured, shuffling papers. "Wait. Temple Island?" he demanded in a louder, troubled voice. "What do you mean, construction permits? What did they build?"

Hera let out a dramatic breath. "Well, it seems to be a work in progress of Anubis and you having...relations." She paused, biting back a laugh. "I'll just say the dog isn't the one catching the frisbee and leave the rest to your imagination."

Hades roared in outrage. I stared at her, horrified.

Hera held the phone away as she laughed into her elbow. Luckily, Hades was too busy screaming at Poseidon to stop laughing that he hadn't heard her. I stared incredulously. Both at her story, and at the location mentioned. Temple Island. My parents had made a goddamned island? The last I'd seen them, they'd turned their little corner of Hell into a prosperous little mining operation, but a fucking island with construction capabilities?

I stared at Charon and he winced, nodding apologetically.

"I'm not even supposed to be down here," Hera continued once the shouting had died down, "so consider this an anonymous tip."

Hades grumbled something vaguely affirmative and then hung up. We watched from the safety of our cove as Hades and a large, handsome man with a beautiful trident raced out of the office building.

Hades was short and squat, looking like a professional strong man. He cupped his hands around his mouth and called out in a deep, baritone cry. "ANUBIS!" I hung my head in my lap, muttering under my breath. Kára fell over, covering her mouth to hide her laughter. It sounded like Hades was calling for his dog.

Poseidon waved him down, shouting something that caused Hades to stiffen. A darkening scowl covered his face as Poseidon no doubt told him how bad the optics would look if anyone caught Hades calling out for Anubis before he raced over to axe the apparent construction project featuring him and his dog-faced lover.

The two gods turned and raced towards a boat tied up to a nearby dock. Poseidon turned the ignition and the boat roared to life. They backed out at a respectable speed, and then took off at full throttle.

I watched their boat disappear around a distant bend before I turned to the boulder field. Anubis was leaning around a jagged spire, waiting for our signal. I waved at him to let him know the coast was clear.

He shot us a grim scowl and then loped over to the small office building. He reappeared moments later with a golden helmet tucked under one shoulder and a wicked scythe seemingly made of dark gray stone over the other. He flung them both onto the boat, more or less in my general direction, as if hoping to poke me with one of the pointy bits.

Calvin and Makayla snarled at him, leaping up onto the seats and gnashing their teeth at the man-sized jackal god of the dead. He stepped back with a wary frown, sniffing at the air as if attempting to make out what the hell the mist wolves actually were. He obviously knew they weren't regular werewolves. He took one look at their wet fur and rounded on me.

"Get the fuck out of here before I change my mind!" he snapped. "You owe me, Temple—"

Charon coughed, interrupting Anubis. "He does not." Calvin and Makayla flickered into pale mist for a moment and Anubis leapt back with a start. He curled his lips at them and then took off, racing back towards the boulder field.

I turned to my crew of thieves and shook my head. Hera and Kára burst out laughing. Calvin and Makayla wagged their tails happily, content to join in the revelry despite having no idea what it was about.

I shared a long look with Charon. "You should burn the boat and head over to another realm. Anubis will obviously vouch for you if he wants to save his own ass from Hades." I paused. "Heh-heh," I chuckled, considering the monument Hera had made up.

Kára shook her head, hiding her grin at my adolescent humor. Charon pondered my suggestion in silence, eyeing the golden helm and scythe thoughtfully. Finally, he looked back up at me. "I've never been one to run from consequences. I embrace them."

I studied the surprisingly philosophical boatman, nodding in understanding. Oddly, it echoed Pandora's sentiments that I was still trying to process. "That makes you both brave and honorable."

He shrugged. "It also makes me an alcoholic," he said, cracking open another beer and dumping it on his face.

I sighed. Well. That was something to consider. Pandora's advice might not be as helpful as I'd begun to believe. I turned to Kára. "We should probably get back."

She nodded, turning to Hera. She curtsied. "Someday, I will share this story with my Valkyries. I think they would get a real kick out of it."

Hera beamed happily. "Best wait until you two finish your job." Her eyes turned to me, suddenly looking remarkably sober, and eerily malicious. The phrase *Hell hath no fury like a woman scorned* came to mind. "We don't know how the story ends yet," she said in a clear, non-slurring voice. A powerful, commanding, completely in control voice.

52

Kára had escorted us back from the Underworld to her bar in East St. Louis. Thankfully, there wasn't an army of pissed off Valkyries waiting to bring her in for questioning or anything. She'd seemed amused by my concern. She had already called Carl and Yahn and they were on their way over.

Things had changed between us in the last few hours. She'd grown more distant and observing. But then she'd kissed me. And invited me to kiss her back.

Since then, nothing. Not a word. As if I'd imagined it.

At first, I'd thought that I had said something to upset her—or that someone else had. But, as time stretched on, I realized it didn't necessarily feel like I was in the doghouse.

Of course, I was still in trouble somehow—as men always were—but I couldn't place my finger on anything specific. Not knowing what else to do, I'd decided to give her some space.

I had plenty of my own problems to deal with. Namely, surviving my confrontation with my best friends soon. Surviving that, I would progress to the next tier of holy ass whoopings and go toe-to-toe with Zeus and his posse.

And without magic, all of that was going to be a very violent, one-

sided experience, and not in my favor. Even with my new scythe and leverage, I only felt like I'd mitigated some of my weaknesses but not that I'd
necessarily acquired a big shining weapon with an immediate impact
factor.

So, as all of this was going on, my mind was constantly scouring over
my visits with Aphrodite. The difficult conversation I needed to have with
Callie. Pandora's stern suggestions and reproachful critique of my moral
code. My recently dredged up, painful thoughts about lost love with
Othello.

And the intimidatingly beautiful, overly competent Valkyrie playing
sidekick for the inept wizard. Who went from hot and heavy to ice cold
quicker than you could say Valhalla.

To solve this conundrum, I sat at the bar, drinking straight from the
bottle as we waited for Carl and Yahn to arrive with their prisoners. They'd
been cagey about who they'd taken from Alucard, but they had confirmed
having Ryuu in their rear cargo storage—because they'd picked up Yahn's
jeep from his apartment. They'd duct taped Roofie Ruxpin to Ryuu's hands
as an abundance of shuriken because he was a ninja. There was every
possible chance that the ninja wasn't even aware he'd been abducted,
thinking only that he'd fallen asleep and was pleasantly dreaming. Or
having terrifying nightmares, as Yahn proclaimed.

Maybe I hadn't slept with it long enough. Or I was immune to the
nightmare factor.

I took a hefty pull from the bottle and gargled the scotch swill before
swallowing it. Calvin and Makayla glanced up at the bubbling sound,
skewering their godfather with judgy eyes.

Kára leaned her head out from around the corner, eyeing the bottle in
my hands. "That's disgusting."

I shrugged. "I was trying to see if I could numb all my taste buds at
once so I could tolerate another drink. It's not my fault this place has cheap
booze."

She gave me a flat stare. "We're in East St. Louis, not the Central West
End," she grumbled. "I cater to my clients. The top-seller is Jager Bombs." I
shuddered and she smirked.

I lifted the bottle. "This is cheaper than gasoline and tastes worse." I
took another swig of the swill and she chuckled, shaking her head.

"Pace yourself, hero. I think they just pulled up," she said, pumping a shotgun I hadn't noticed her carrying around.

I hopped off my stool. "Then why do you have a shotgun?" I demanded. "Have you had that this whole time?" I asked, eyeing her armor suspiciously.

"I told you I had one under the bar," she muttered. "And I'm carrying it in case I'm wrong and they're Cubs fans," she said in a solemn tone.

I grinned. "Nice."

A jeep was parked out front, as close to the door as it could get without driving it inside. Carl, wearing a long trench coat, sunglasses, and a ten-gallon cowboy hat—for some inexplicable reason—strolled in, dragging a ninja by his feet.

I repeated that statement in my head a few times, wondering if it would make more sense.

It didn't.

"I caught the ninja," he said, carelessly bumping Ryuu's head on the doorframe before dropping his feet. "You didn't mention he had a Shadow Skin."

I shrugged. "Life is all about new challenges."

Kára was scowling at the empty air suspiciously. "Show yourself, Yahn, or I start shooting."

Calvin and Makayla drifted into the room like specters, growling in warning. Yahn winked into view a few feet ahead of Carl, holding up his hands in surrender. He held a wrapped burger in each hand, and he was grinning at the mist wolves. They flickered back to their usual wolf forms, wagging their tails excitedly. "Hey, you two. I'm glad you're all right," he said kneeling before them and unwrapping the snacks.

Kára lowered her shotgun as Yahn tossed them each a burger and then straightened to his feet, brushing off his hands. He turned to me and then the pups. "You know, it's very concerning how easily we abducted our best friends' friends and children," he said, grimacing.

I frowned at the two of them. "Where are the Reds? I'm meeting the Horsemen in less than an hour. Leverage only works when you actually *have* leverage."

Yahn nodded, setting his lip. "We only have one Roofie Ruxpin, so trying to hold the Reds hostage puts us at a numbers disadvantage." I took a drink from the bottle and folded my arms, waiting. "I went to their place and saw them freaking the hell out," he said softly. "About *me*." The last sentence was barely a whisper, and he was no longer staring at me. He was staring into the middle distance, shaking his head. "I never knew how much Alucard and Tory cared about me until that moment. And...I couldn't do it."

I clenched my jaw, understanding his sentiment, but not appreciating his initiative. "I understand that, Yahn. Really. But do you think it was easy for me to take Gunnar's pups away from him?" I growled. "He immediately caught on and chased us through Chateau Falco. The look in his eye when he saw me fleeing with his pups," I rasped, visibly shaking, "broke my damned heart, Yahn. I've known Gunnar my entire life, and I still did it. To *protect* him from Zeus!" I roared, hurling the bottle against the targets for the hatchets.

Yahn didn't flinch as the bottle whipped past his head. Instead, he nodded calmly. "What you want is for the Horsemen to be rationally furious, not irrationally raging. Look at how they reacted to find me missing. If I'd then kidnapped the Reds, it would be too much for them to handle. They wouldn't listen to a word you said. Did you know they almost destroyed the entire dragon estate? Even Raego? If Death hadn't shown up to calm Alucard and Tory down, the Obsidian Son would be dead right now." He stepped forward, jutting out his jaw. "And you wanted me to add the Reds to that? It was a bad call. I made a different one."

Kára was suddenly between us, forcing me back in an unyielding shuffle until she had literally backed me up across the entire bar. The sheer ridiculousness of such a long walk snapped me out of my blinding rage. "If he fucked this up for me, I'll kill him," I snarled.

Kára gripped my chin in one hand and pressed her forehead against mine. Hard. "Okay."

I blinked, caught off guard by her agreeable tone.

"How do you want to do it? I can hold him down while you stab him, but we'll need to keep an eye on Carl in case he gets uppity," she murmured thoughtfully. "Might have to kill them both so no one talks," she said conversationally.

I blinked at her, confused. Wait. Was she really agreeing with me?

She finally leaned away but didn't step out of my personal space. "Feel better now?" she asked in an entirely different tone, her features softening slightly as she set her palm on my chest. "You just proved his point, by the way. And I just saved your dignity."

Then she turned her back on me and walked back towards Yahn. She didn't say a word. Instead, she stepped back behind the bar and poured herself a drink. The three of us watched her warily, wondering what Valkyrie sorcery she'd used to diffuse the situation.

53

I pondered her words. She...

Was right. I'd almost lost what little grip I had on my sanity when Yahn challenged my authority by doing something that I believed would put my friends in greater danger. I'd been so angry that I might have done something incredibly stupid if I'd had access to my magic.

Since I didn't, Yahn would have made very short work of me, humiliating me in such a way that neither of us would ever be able to forget.

In a way, it was exactly what Yahn warned would have happened to Alucard and Tory if he'd moved forward with abducting the Reds. They would have lost their minds, and they had no problem with using their powers at the moment.

I took a deep breath. "Thank you, Kára. Like a broken clock, you—"

I ducked as she flung a bottle of tequila at my head. It shattered on the wall behind me, crackling as it shorted out a neon sign. I grinned toothily, having anticipated it. She didn't even look back at me, but instead continued to pour another drink as if nothing had happened. "You're paying for the new sign," she said casually. Yahn stared at me, baffled.

I sighed and made my way over to him. "You were right. I was less right."

Yahn smirked faintly at my non-apology, but he still looked wary of the consequences he'd racked up in calling me out like he had. "Just to be clear, I almost took them anyway. I could have, but it felt counterintuitive to what you really wanted. To the outcome we need that will allow us all to walk away from this. It was not an emotional decision on my part."

I placed a hand on his shoulder, and he stiffened instinctively. "Your plan was better. I just didn't see it because I also didn't consider how much they cared about you. I knew it, based on talks with Alucard, but I considered the Reds a far greater prize. No offense to you, of course."

He nodded. "I understand. They're a family."

I smiled at him. "Apparently, you are as well. And that's why *you've* been promoted to Alucard's hostage."

Yahn nodded. "That's why I stuck the note she wrote to the windshield of their car before they left. Figured the note was vague enough to make them think Peter had taken me hostage. They definitely saw it, judging by how fast they took off for Chateau Falco."

I grunted, impressed. He really was a good strategist. "Perfect. Callie got hers?"

Carl nodded. "I used his own sword to pin it to her door," he said proudly. "I put some of his blood on it for authenticity."

Yahn winced guiltily.

I stared at Carl and then glanced at Ryuu, still sleeping on the floor just inside the doorway. The pups were guarding him, not looking very trusting. "Why was he bleeding?"

"He resisted a bit," Yahn said.

At the same time, Carl answered in an overenthusiastic tone, "It just fell right out of him." His tail twitched erratically behind him at the blatant lie—like a version of Pinocchio's nose.

Kára choked on her drink. I sighed. Ryuu looked none the worse for wear. "Fine. Gunnar should have his, too, so it looks like we're all set."

Yahn studied me for a few seconds. "I challenged you."

I chuckled. "I'm not a shifter, Yahn. I'm just a temperamental man, as infallible as anyone else, I would imagine. And it's in my best interest to not have another yes man working with me."

His shoulders finally relaxed. "Thanks, Nate."

I appraised him thoughtfully. "You've come a long way, Yahn. From sparkly leotards to badass womanizer. It's pretty incredible, actually."

He shrugged. "I still like to dance. I just don't flaunt it. I'm teaching the Reds salsa."

I grinned. "Good. We all need to hold onto our weirdness. Carl has his shoes—"

"My shoes are not weird," Carl hissed. Yahn smirked.

"And you have dance," I said, shrugging.

"What about you?" Yahn asked me, grinning curiously.

I thought about it for a moment. I smiled to myself, coming up with the answer quickly. Then I turned away, not answering. "How about some liquid courage, Kára? If you would be so kind."

She'd been watching us thoughtfully, analyzing our every word. Then she jerked her chin at the bar. Three glasses of tequila already sat in a row. She grinned, leaning against the back counter.

I motioned for Carl to join us and leaned down over my glass. "Okay. I'm going to meet with the Horsemen and see if I can convince them who I really am. If I can't, I'm immediately fleeing through a Gateway back to the Armory. If you don't hear back from me within one hour, meet me there," I said, reaching into my pocket to pull out a few of the Tiny Balls I had borrowed from Pandora. I held them out to Yahn. "You'll need these."

Yahn nodded, accepting the marbles as he considered my plan. He slipped them into his pocket. "Should we just go there now?" he asked.

I shook my head. "The Horsemen have access to the Armory—Callie has her own private entrance, as a matter of fact. I don't want to risk any of them accidentally running into you guys before I have a chance to talk to them—for better or worse. Wait an hour and head there."

Yahn cleared his throat. "Okay. Do you have a plan to convince the Horsemen not to kill you on sight? Because it can't be anywhere Zeus might see—like Chateau Falco, the place you picked on the note."

I shifted uncomfortably in my seat. "I was thinking Niflheim or the Armory—another reason I don't want you guys going there early. The real Peter couldn't get into the Armory, even if he had one of those," I said, pointing.

"That could work, but it doesn't buy you any time. Just privacy."

I nodded. "I think I'm going to have to go nuclear." Everyone looked at me anxiously. "I'm going to have to unleash the Temple charm," I said soberly. "It's a power I'm reluctant to use. There is no defense against—hey!" I snapped, glaring at Kára.

She was chugging straight from the bottle, shaking her head in the process.

Yahn reached out and set a glass marble on the bar top. I glanced down, frowning at the Tiny Ball. The word *Vaults* was etched into it. I looked over at him, confused. "Grimm Tech won't help either, unless you're suggesting we set up an ambush. Which isn't a terrible idea—"

"No," Yahn said. "*Vaults*, not *Vault*. Plural," he said, lifting it up for me to see. "It's to the Freak Bank, not Grimm Tech, although now I realize the glaring security flaw," he said, pursing his lips. "Anyway, I struck a deal with their Board. They permit me to make Tiny Balls that lead to their lobby in exchange for me making Tiny Balls to aid them in collecting outstanding debts." He shrugged. "Equal trade, and this way we don't have to deal with the security and logistics of shipping large quantities of gold."

I stared at him incredulously. Kára was staring at him, impressed. "And why does Grimm Tech need large quantities of gold on hand?"

Yahn frowned. "I'm a dragon. And it's always good to have a rainy-day fund on hand."

I stared at the ball, wondering why the bank was better than Niflheim. Then it hit me. "Their security floor," I breathed, stunned. "It's practically impenetrable."

Kára frowned. "How does impenetrable security help?" she asked, sounding concerned and suddenly not as impressed with Yahn's suggestion.

Yahn was grinning smugly. "It can supposedly break through any illusion. *Any* illusion. The only trust bankers believe in is their own institution," he said, alluding to a financial trust.

I clutched the Tiny Ball with an excited grin, recalling the last time I'd been there. It had revealed all sorts of crazy—even unknown—things about me and my friends. "If this works..." I whispered, "the Horsemen would see the real me."

Yahn folded his arms. "Only one way to find out, but you can use Niflheim as Plan B. This way could be more efficient and less violent. Think it will work?"

I wrapped an arm around him and tugged him close in a macho hug. "Toe-tah-lee."

He smirked. "I lost that accent—and the pudginess—years ago, Nate."

I sighed. He'd lost the exuberant cheer as well. Things like that happened after enough near-death experiences. "Yeah, I know. But we can't forget how we got here," I said, thinking back on Pandora's advice. "Life's about the journey, not the destination."

Kára watched me thoughtfully, and I wondered how open Pandora had been with her. If she'd given the Valkyrie the same advice.

"You should probably go, Confucius," Yahn said, glancing at his phone.

54

I stood near Ruin's tree on the front lawn of Chateau Falco, feeling naked and afraid. Exposed. I wasn't, because I wore one of the eyepatches I'd stolen from Grimm Tech. Still, my hands shook with both guilt and concern as I waited.

One by one, my Horsemen approached from different directions, eyeing each other and their surroundings suspiciously—likely wondering why the others were there. Because I'd told everyone to come alone and not flap their lips.

Alucard wore flip flops, swim trunks, an unbuttoned linen dress shirt, and large, Ray-Ban sunglasses. With his outfit and tanned skin, he looked like the boss of a drug cartel south of the border. The look of barely restrained violence in his posture only added to the image. Don Alucard was ready to hand out some Colombian neckties. Maybe the glasses were to somewhat mask the warning gleam in his eyes. He'd almost killed Raego.

Callie openly carried two katanas, her arms folded so that the blades crossed her chest like spikes. She wore the same style of clothes she'd had on at her picnic, but these were pristinely white. Maybe she had a bunch of the same outfits. Her face was utterly devoid of all human emotion. I was betting one of those blades belonged to Ryuu.

Gunnar carried Mjolnir loosely at his side, and he wore jeans and a white v-neck—probably so he could easily tuck his beard away when he was calmly pinning me down and ripping out my innards before Ashley called him to dinner. He wore a white eyepatch with a silver coin in the center, and that strip of leather made me decidedly uneasy for some reason.

With my Titan Thorns, I couldn't sense my Horsemen, and they couldn't sense me. But they could sense each other. They acknowledged their compatriots in silence, quickly realizing this was some kind of setup and not seeming particularly concerned about it. They'd all suffered abductions, so their suspicion of each other slowly faded as their eyes shifted to their surroundings. I flinched every time one of them swept a cold glare over me, even though I knew I was invisible.

I took a deep, reassuring breath, and then lowered my eyepatch to let it hang around my neck. "Long time no see," I said snidely, getting into the mindset of Peter for Gunnar's sake. The others had never met him. They tensed, spinning to glare at me with unbridled hatred. The fact that I—Peter, in their eyes—held their friends captive was the only reason they didn't immediately rip me in half. We all knew it. I patted my satchel. "I'm looking for Nate. He missed a meeting I requested, leaving this behind in his stead. You're going to help me open it if you want to see your loved ones again. I die, they die. Oh, and Alaric is watching," I said with a sneer, "so don't try anything funny. Let's go," I said, motioning for them to approach.

And, with balls of solid steel, I turned my back on them. I waited until I heard them draw close, barely managing to hide my anxiety. I brandished my hand theatrically, careful to show off my cuff like I was using it for magic, and I flicked Yahn's Tiny Ball down before me. A Gateway screamed to life and I leapt through.

Rather than wait for them to follow, I hurried forward until I stood just before the edge of the vast open space leading to the teller lines. Right here, I looked like Peter, but one step backwards and my illusion would be shattered. The bank was surprisingly empty for the middle of the day. I saw only one teller, and he was staring at me with open fear.

I opened my mouth to tell him not to even think of hitting an alarm when he promptly disappeared. I stiffened, my mouth clicking shut. I scanned the rest of the lobby, suddenly uneasy. Where was everyone? But my Horsemen calmly stepped through the Gateway.

Callie was the last through, and she slowly sheathed the swords over her back so the hilts poked out over each shoulder, making her look like Calliepool. Without a word, she turned around, gripped the edge of the fiery portal, and snapped it like a stick. The Gateway winked out with a gurgled *thump*, sending a shockwave of air outwards. Just as calmly, she turned back around and nodded to herself satisfactorily. I stared incredulously. I...hadn't known that was possible.

And it very likely should have incinerated all of us—or set off the alarms. Using the VIP access of Yahn's Tiny Ball must have granted us privileged access because the gargoyle sentries remained inert.

Although Callie's action had been pointless—the Gateway had been about to wink shut all on its own—it was a humbling display of power, and a psychological shot aimed directly at me. Whatever Peter thought he knew about magic, Callie could dance circles around. Peter was nothing but a gnat buzzing around her ears—and she was only *one* of the Horsemen he'd managed to piss off. The fact that he'd had to resort to abduction to get her here was the only way he could have bested her. And the outcome of that was yet to be determined.

Alucard and Gunnar had fanned out a few steps to scan their surroundings for potential ambushes or innocent bystanders. The grim set to their jaws told me they were equally wary about the lack of customers during lunch hour. Or lack of employees, for that matter.

"Consider this Switzerland. If any magic other than that Gateway goes off, these statues come to life and beat down *everyone*."

They stared at me in utter silence, their faces devoid of any reaction to my words.

I calmly took a step back, holding my breath.

The three of them lurched forward suddenly. Alucard ripped off his glasses and crushed them in his hand, staring at me in disbelief. I realized that his eyes were bloodshot.

Callie clutched at her chest, her legs wobbling unsteadily as her face contorted in confusion and pain. Guilt quickly overtook her emotions and her face paled—because she was here now for Ryuu, and hadn't shown up to Hermes' meeting about Nate, perhaps.

Gunnar dropped his hammer, making a small crater as it destroyed the tiles below. The glowing light around the hammer—crackling blue arcs of electricity—fizzled out and he stopped breathing.

"Nate?" Callie whispered, no longer a hardboiled wizard but a frightened woman.

"What the *hell* is this?" Gunnar demanded.

"Where. Is. Peter?" Alucard demanded in a strained rasp. "If you killed him, I will never forgive you," he said, aiming his rage at me. The real me. Nate Temple.

Did he not believe what he'd just seen?

"Yahn was never in danger," I told Alucard, lowering my eyes. "I didn't mean to abduct him, believe it or not. He gave me a birthday tackle through a Gateway."

Alucard stared at me, unable to make sense of my words.

"Your pups are safe, too, Gunnar. Better than safe, actually," I said, smiling at him. "They were running around like lunatics when I shared a drink with Yahn less than an hour ago," I continued, shrugging. I pointed at his hammer. "You almost killed me with that earlier." Gunnar stiffened, opening his mouth wordlessly.

"What about Ryuu?" Callie whispered, looking desperate.

I nodded with a compassionate smile. "He's fine. He was sleeping when I left to come here. I'm not even sure if he knows he was taken yet," I admitted. "I'm sorry, Callie," I said, watching her eyes swell up with tears.

She crashed to her knees, letting out a sob of both relief and pain. "How...*could* you?"

The accusation cut deeper than almost anything I'd ever felt. I hung my head in shame, accepting their anguish. I had no regrets over my plan —not in the slightest.

But that meant that I needed to accept the related consequences. To accept their blame without deflection. To keep their loved ones safe from Zeus—unlike Alice—I'd had to beat the god of lightning to the punch—to strike first, so to speak. And I'd had to make it believable.

"To keep them all safe, believe it or not. And to give you plausible deniability. Zeus was planning to do exactly what I did to you. Because he's been running around town wearing my face, trapping me in the guise of Peter and Carl in the guise of Alaric. He's the one who took Alice," I whispered, gritting my teeth. "She wasn't as lucky as your loved ones. She got taken by a real monster. In your case, a monster saved your loved ones. If I'd approached you in any way other than this cloak and dagger scenario, Zeus had assassins watching you. All of you."

Tense silence answered me. But I didn't miss the troubled looks they shot each other to hear about Alice and the assassins. I wasn't naive. I didn't expect a parade. I'd walked into this knowing that this was the best-case scenario.

Trust had been broken. Their pain would not be brushed under the rug, even after my explanation. Their leader had struck them each in the heart, knowing the swiftest and surest way to shut them down. And it had worked, all in less than a single day. That thought would fester in the backs of their minds every time they looked at me in the coming days.

"He speaks the truth," Kára said, stepping out from behind them. The Horsemen jolted in alarm, crouching warily. I flinched. What the fuck? What was Kára doing here?

55

Thankfully, Yahn stepped up beside her, nodding. Alucard gasped like someone had physically ripped his soul from his mouth. "We were never in danger. Well, Gunnar almost killed Nate, I heard," he said calmly. "Other than that, not even a scratch." He glanced at me with a guilty shrug, pointing a thumb at Kára. "She asked about the risk to innocent bystanders and I realized that I hadn't even considered the customers or employees," he said. He glanced over my shoulder. "They're now in a private meeting to give us some privacy. Once I was confident these three had seen through the illusion, I had the manager disable the alarms, so you can use magic again. The anti-illusion field always stays on, which is probably a good thing right now," he said, assessing the somber faces.

It was my turn to shake my head in anger. But...I was also proud of Kára's initiative. Pandora had said my actions had unintended consequences—that no matter what I did, others would take their own initiatives and risks, especially to keep me safe.

I smiled at them gratefully. "Thanks."

They shrugged it off, keeping their eyes on the silent Horsemen.

I eyed Kára. "Mind stepping over here?" I asked her, suddenly realizing that the security here might reveal her true identity. That I could find out who she truly was—

"Not a chance," she said sweetly. And I understood the reason she was about as far away from the security measures as possible—specifically so as *not* to reveal her secrets.

I frowned, shooting Gunnar an imploring look as if to say *see what I've had to work with?*

He didn't respond. He just stared at me. Then he averted his gaze and I felt the knife twist. I hung my head, bearing that added weight.

I turned to Yahn. "At least tell me you didn't leave Carl in charge."

Yahn smirked. "I left the pups in charge, of course."

Gunnar tensed, shooting Yahn a sharp look. The younger dragon stood firm, not wilting under the alpha werewolf's glare.

Callie finally climbed to her feet, settling her glare on Kára. She turned back to me with a thoughtful frown. But only for the briefest of moments. "Someone needs to explain. Now. Is Peter truly free or was that another stunt you pulled to terrify us? And why can't I sense you?" she demanded, appraising me up and down.

Her feelings for Ryuu were glaringly obvious. On the other hand, I picked up on a different type of anxiety from her that almost made me smile. She didn't know how to tell me about Ryuu, not wanting to hurt my feelings. Even now. After what I'd just done to hurt hers.

That...was incredibly touching.

Like a floodgate, the other Horsemen took my silence as an invitation. Gunnar and Alucard were suddenly shouting over each other, demanding answers to all kinds of questions, their voices echoing and competing for dominance in the large open space.

I held up a hand, silencing them. When they'd quieted down, I turned to Yahn. I didn't even bother directing my question to Kára, knowing she would do as she pleased, regardless. "Can you head back and keep an eye on everyone?"

Kára preened satisfactorily, smirking discreetly so as not to draw ire from the Horsemen.

Yahn nodded, ignoring the arguing shouts from Gunnar about how he better bring the pups here right the fuck now. Alucard silently watched

Yahn toss a Tiny Ball on the ground and hop through the Gateway. Despite being so concerned, he hadn't said a single word to Yahn.

Perhaps his own rage had surprised him. Scared him, even.

They turned back to me and I gathered my thoughts. Then I began to explain the situation, including pretty much everything. I even mentioned how my Titan Thorns were to be removed, pointedly not looking in Callie's direction. I told them about Kára helping me, and how I'd been abducted by Zeus after we broke out Fenrir, and then kept prisoner and tortured for the last week. For Kára's benefit, I even mentioned my dreams with Quinn and how they'd been oddly realistic. How she had somehow helped me save Pan's life...

Kára had grown thoughtful at that, but she didn't look even remotely guilty.

In short, I was more honest than necessary, even sharing irrelevant information like my discovery of the Underground Railroad hub. I didn't mention the secret passageways, specifically, but that was because Falco's secrets were for Master Temple, and blabbing about hidden tunnels defeated the whole point of having them.

My Horsemen had sat down on the floor, looking like their legs needed the break. Gunnar shook his head woodenly. "It's all tying back to the beginning," he murmured, gesturing at my current Peter disguise. "When the dragons came to town with Alaric Slate."

I nodded. "We've all been played by the Olympians. By Zeus. Especially you guys. He's a sick, twisted, clever man. I have to give him that. But here is the important bit—and the reason for my secrecy." They focused on me; their eyes boring into mine like drill bits. "You cannot let on that you know any of this. I didn't kidnap everyone just to get your attention. I need Zeus to see you furious, emotionally wrecked, and focused like a laser on Peter. He needs to know you are broken and malleable. His hubris is his greatest weakness. I need you to do this for Alice. And me. And your loved ones—who are now safe from his reach, thanks to me."

They slowly looked up at my self-congratulatory comment, narrowing their eyes reflexively.

"I knew this would hurt you, but I valued knowing that your loved ones would not become the next Alice over the pain of knowing that I had to hurt you to make them safe. I'll carry that guilt to my grave," I whispered somberly. "But I would do it again in a heartbeat. That's part of the job, Horsemen."

The bank grew silent. Painfully silent. It wasn't long before they were giving stiff, begrudging nods. They even studied each other, verifying that they were in agreement—which brought a faint smile to my face.

We were a family. A unit. My recent actions had brought them together through shared pain. I hated that, but sometimes it was the best way. To remind everyone what was at stake.

This wasn't a LARP or book club. This was a war council. We were Horsemen.

We had to be made of sterner stuff. Our bonds had to be stronger than blind duty.

Our bonds had to be chains around our hearts.

And...I'd given them that. I'd shown them their vulnerabilities in a contained environment to let them know how bad things could get. Now that they'd survived that, what else did they have to fear? Just like...

I glanced over at Kára to see her dual-colored eyes smoldering in silent, vehement approval.

I'd done the same thing to my Horsemen as her blood ritual had done to Carl and Yahn.

"We have spilled first blood, so now we have nothing left to fear," I said, plagiarizing her speech. "We have tasted the worst already, and we have overcome it. Together. Now, there is nothing we cannot do, my brothers and sister," I said, meeting each of their eyes.

Surprisingly, they climbed to their feet, nodding determinedly. Specters of pain still lurked in the depths of their eyes, but they were not strong enough to hold my Horsemen back. It was just another burden to pile onto our shoulders.

And none of their knees buckled. I felt pride growing in my chest. Pride for them, not pride for me. It was better than I could have hoped for, to be honest.

"Go along with whatever Zeus asks of you. I don't know, exactly, how his plan will play out, but you need to be convincing if Hermes shows up with an ask."

"How do you know he will?" Alucard asked, speaking for the first time in a while.

I grimaced. "Oh, he definitely will. I've come to know him very well." I met their eyes, showing them my resolve. I turned to Callie. "Whoever shows up, get a good read on them. You know how to play people well. Convince them by manipulating their personality type. If you need to show a little aversion to authority or capitalize on your worry for your abducted loved ones, do it. The rest of you, follow her lead."

Callie turned to her brothers, nodding firmly. "I can do that." They nodded back.

"Peter is working for him—whether willingly or not, I don't know. You can tell us apart by my Sensates," I said, showing off my wrists and then pointing at my necklace. "He doesn't have them. Again, Callie will read the social cues and act accordingly. We will cross paths tomorrow night."

"What if he asks something of us that disrupts your plans?" Gunnar asked.

I smiled. "I don't have plans. I have dice and a board that I think can be utilized for any situation. I'll let you know when to break character." I took a deep breath. "Horsemen, prepare for war. Tonight, we downsize the Greek Pantheon. Tonight, we let every other pantheon in the world know we're here to stay. Tonight, the world will meet the new Horsemen—the Dread Four."

The three of them smiled wickedly, nodding at our new name.

Gunnar frowned. "We won't have long. He said he will have Peter with him tonight and that we can extract our vengeance then."

I gritted my teeth. "Oh, really?" I asked in a cold tone.

He nodded. "You're sure my pups are safe?"

I smiled. "They are the safest people in the world right now. I took them *swimming*."

He gasped, falling to his knees. "You mad bastard," he rasped. "You did it." Callie and Alucard shared a thoughtful look.

"That's what I do, man. Now get a hold of yourself. The Dread Four do not get sappy."

56

Kára had seized on a momentary lull and stormed over to Gunnar, brandishing her trident at him while pointing at his hammer with a scowl. He stared at her in surprise and I saw Alucard smirking in amusement, making his way over and looking like he was shoving popcorn in his mouth. I pulled Callie aside while Gunnar was taking one for the team.

"Can we talk?" I asked. She nodded, joining me near one of the sentinel statues.

"How did you know to take him?" she asked before I'd had a chance to open my mouth. "How did you know—"

"What he meant to you?" I asked gently.

She tensed, shaking her head stubbornly. "No. I don't know. It's—"

"Complicated."

She grew still, eyeing me sidelong as if anticipating a trap. Alucard had been pulled into Kára's vortex and earned himself a stinging cheek and a burning ear for trying to touch her trident. Gunnar was scratching his head with a bewildered look on his face as Kára continued to fume at the poor men. Callie briefly flicked her attention to Kára, as if the Bat Symbol of Emasculation had caught her attention, but she declined the call and focused back on me. I kept my face blank, giving her nothing. Give Callie an inch and she'd take a mile.

"Yes. Very complicated," she finally admitted. I didn't comfort her, because that would only have been patronizing. She didn't need me to hold her hand. She needed to accept this on her own. Much like... Aphrodite had been trying to teach me.

If I told her how she felt, she might rely on that as the foundation of any potential future relationship with Ryuu. Even the perfect house, if built on a cracked foundation, would crumble. I wasn't going to give her a cracked foundation. Mainly because I didn't have a solid foundation for my own house yet.

"He's a stand-up guy, from what I've seen," I said gently.

"Who is she?" Callie asked absently, not meeting my eyes. I smiled, glancing over at Kára. She was holding her palm out and Gunnar was miserly counting out cash into her palm. For some reason, Alucard had been roped into the apparent debt repayment, and was reaching back for his own wallet with a shell-shocked look on his face.

"My bartender," I muttered dryly, aiming for some levity.

Callie turned to me with a slow, mischievous smile. "I wasn't asking about Kára..." she said slyly, watching my face. "I was asking about your *complication*." She tapped her lips thoughtfully at my sudden flinch. "Maybe they are one and the same," she mused, seeing something in my eyes that corroborated her suspicion. "You don't know who Kára really is, after all," she suggested, eyeing the sentinels that broke illusions. "Or else you wouldn't have asked her to walk over here and stand beside you."

I narrowed my eyes at her for good measure.

Now that I thought about it, no one had crossed the line to reveal themselves. I bit back my paranoia that one of the guests here could be a spy—not who they were pretending to be. That was my life, now. Being suspicious of everyone would only serve to stay my hand, preventing me from action. I would just have to take the necessary precautions and hope.

I sighed. "To be honest, Callie, I don't know. That's part of the fun, I guess."

She turned to face me. "No. You know." Although her words could have come across as jealousy or envy, her eyes were oddly compassionate.

I shrugged. "If I do, I'm too dense to tell myself the truth," I admitted. She arched an eyebrow dubiously. I decided to go straight for the jugular to see how she reacted since she didn't know about my spying on her talk with Ryuu. "I'm serious, Callie. I love a lot of people in different ways. You, for example. We could have been great together. Sure, we have our differences. Who doesn't? We could've worked them out, though, and had a great time in the process."

She smiled sadly, nodding. "I agree."

"So, why didn't we?" I pressed.

She grew still, staring off at nothing. "I...don't know. It never felt like the right time."

"Later," I agreed. "I'm thinking it was too easy. Or maybe our timing was just off. Or maybe we were both wrong. The point is, I love you, Callie. But there is a very strong doubt deep within me. I don't know why or what it means, but it's there. A gut feeling."

"You sound like Aphrodite," she muttered.

I flinched, slowly turning to look at her. "You've spoken with Aphrodite?" I asked. The goddess had told me she would talk to Callie, but I hadn't expected her to pounce on her newest prey so soon. All things considered, I should have.

She nodded. "She kept encouraging me—in unacceptable ways—to question my heart."

I chose my next words very carefully, feeling a sickening sensation in my gut. "Did you, by any chance, have your doubts *before* Aphrodite came to you?"

She nodded without hesitation. "Yes. Otherwise I would have stabbed her in the heart for trying to manipulate me."

I let out a sigh of relief, my paranoia doused. "Yeah. Me, too."

She cocked her head at something in my tone and studied me with a suspicious frown. "You...*liar!*" she burst out with a cackle, swatting me in the shoulder. Then she doubled over, laughing. "You totally fell for her *come hither*, didn't you?"

I folded my arms, my ears burning. "It's not funny. I was vulnerable and we didn't do—"

She laughed even harder.

"No. Listen, Callie. I was her prisoner—"

She roared with laughter at that, struggling to breathe. "In her kinky sex dungeon! You idiot!"

I narrowed my eyes. "Okay, fine. I might have led her on. For strategic reasons."

She could barely breathe, she was laughing so hard.

"No one takes me seriously, and I'm getting sick and tired of it," I complained.

After a while, she finally wrapped me up in a hug and kissed me on the forehead. "How about this. If we find out that Aphrodite fucked me like she fucked you..." her eyes twinkled in amusement as if fishing for evidence, "we will save each other for a rainy day."

I sighed, pressing my head against hers. Her comment removed the last vestige of doubt from my mind—not that I'd had any left at this point. "And we come full circle," I whispered.

She pulled away, frowning at my somber tone. "What?"

"*Later*," I explained. "It's always *later* with us. I think that's kind of the point." And Kára had taught me that later could mean something much more positive.

Callie considered my words, her smile fading. "Yeah. I guess you're right."

After a few minutes, she nudged me with her hip. "Tell me about that bartender, loverboy."

I shook my head, forcing myself not to look towards Kára. "That really was a slip of the tongue."

"Exactly," she said, grinning brightly.

I rolled my eyes. "If she was the one, these cuffs would have fallen off," I said, showing her my Titan Thorns. Callie frowned vexedly, inspecting them and the hasty tape job marring some of the runes. She winced, almost as if recognizing the symbols, but she didn't comment on them. I knew she would have said something had she known anything beneficial to share. It was simply the face of someone seeing the Omegabet and knowing the underlying dangers. I'd had that face often enough in recent days. I continued on, "Kára really likes me, and I won't deny that I really like her, too. But she has a lot of secrets." Callie flashed me a stern look and I chuckled. "I'm not making excuses or being hypocritical, I'm just pointing out facts. I'm sick and tired of being blindsided by those I let close to me. I want raw, unfiltered honesty."

"Is that your love language?" she asked. "Aphrodite asked me about mine."

I shook my head. "Physical touch."

She turned to me. She stared at me. Then she laughed at me. "You are such a *guy*!" she hissed, swatting me in the shoulder again.

I shrugged, smiling shamelessly. "I am a proud member of the Man Club, and I've memorized our Code. United, we are unstoppable. I stand ready to serve."

She grunted, risking a glance towards Kára—who was now pacing back and forth before Gunnar and Alucard like a drill sergeant. The two men stood at attention, nodding stiffly. Callie turned back to me with an approving sniff as if to indicate how superior her side was. I scowled at the weak-kneed recruits besmirching our grand reputation. I'd have to make a call to management to revoke their cards.

"What was your love language?" I asked.

"It was a tie," she said, shifting her weight shyly. "Acts of service and quality time."

I nodded thoughtfully. "Ryuu seems like he'd be good at those."

Callie smiled wistfully. "He is, even though I didn't notice it at first."

"How long have you known him anyway?"

"Not long enough to justify my feelings," she admitted. "Maybe I'm wrong. Maybe we're both wrong. Who knows?"

"Well, if we're both wrong, neither one of us has to tell anyone about it. And this way, you can't say I told you so."

"You're so childish, and Ryuu is so much more mature. I guess I'm glad I'm leaving you."

"Good luck with that. You can't leave me. The floor is lava," I said, pointing at the ground.

She rolled her eyes, capitulating with a warm smile. "It's always winning with you."

"I have it on good authority, that winning arguments is the key to a happy relationship."

"Oh?" She asked, sounding amused. "Aphrodite tell you that?"

I shook my head. "Hera. I've never seen a woman hate her husband so much. It was endearing. She also said love is for losers."

She shuddered. "Sounds like a real piece of work."

I nodded. "She's a lush. Reminds me of Miss Hannigan in Annie." Callie laughed, shaking her head. "Hey, on a serious note. Do you know why Carl was wearing a cowboy hat when he brought Ryuu back?" I asked, unable to imagine the stoic ninja wearing such a getup.

Unless...he was a cowboy ninja.

Callie laughed. "It belongs to Xylo. He likes hats. Says they help him fit in." She frowned at me. "I was wondering why Xylo was so agitated earlier. Why did Carl take *that*?" she asked with a bewildered look on her face.

"Some answers can be worse than the questions, Callie. I think twice before asking Carl anything these days. Apologize to Xylo for me. I'll get it back." I thought about it. "You know what? How about I just write you a check for damages. Carl can be possessive."

She chuckled. "Just forget about it." She pointed at Gunnar and Alucard, who were standing around unsupervised. I was surprised Kára hadn't sent them to polish her armor. Speaking of...

"She left through a Gateway about five minutes ago," Callie answered the look on my face. "Looked like the inside of a bar. Need a ride?" she asked, gesturing at my Titan Thorns.

I nodded, realizing Kára had used my last Tiny Ball to go to her bar. Why hadn't she waited? "Please. Mind dropping me off at Buddy Hatchet? Unless you don't know where that is," I said with a frustrated frown.

"Oh, I scoped it out," she said in an overly neutral tone. When I frowned at her, her cheeks colored and she punched me in the shoulder. "Heard you were a local there and I had one too many glasses of wine one night," she said defensively.

I nodded, keeping my face blank. "Nothing happened, Callie," I reassured her. "I didn't—" I froze. Except something *had* happened with me and Kára. *Before* I'd spoken with Callie. I shot her a miserable look. "I kissed her this morning—"

Callie pressed a finger to my lips, smiling with a heartfelt smile. "It's okay, Nate. The fact that you even told me says a lot. And the fact that it was only this morning means even more. You had already made up your mind by then. And...I had too, technically. We just hadn't compared notes yet," she said reassuringly.

I nodded gratefully. She shifted her weight, looking mildly impatient. I narrowed my eyes. "So...how long has it been since your last confession, Miss Penrose?" I asked, mockingly.

Her cheeks flushed a deep red and she shook her head firmly. "How about that Gateway?" she blurted, ripping a hole in reality about six inches away from me, making me leap back. "There. It leads to a nearby alley since I never actually had the stones to go inside," she muttered. "Well, I didn't trust my self-restraint, to be accurate."

I stared at it in silence for a few moments.

"Did you have something else on your mind?" she asked.

I nodded. "Someone needs to end the bank meeting."

Silence answered me. Callie must have expected a different comment.

I hopped through. "Goodbye, Callie. I'll give Ryuu a very inappropriate hug for you and tell him how much you cried—"

"You wouldn't," she hissed, clenching her fists.

I grinned and she looked skyward, letting out a frustrated breath. "You're impossible."

"I prefer incorrigible," I replied.

The Gateway winked shut. I was still grinning as I spun in a slow circle, searching for Buddy Hatchet. I sucked in a breath, panicking. The front door had been kicked in and the window was smashed. The tires of Yahn's jeep had even been slashed.

I was already running, reaching into my satchel on instinct.

57

I cursed myself for poking fun at Callie and causing her to shut the Gateway in a huff. She could have helped me here—

I cut off, shaking my head. No. She couldn't be seen with me. That was the damned point.

So much for Kára's vaunted security. Then again, she hadn't been here to turn it on.

I sucked in a breath, wondering where she was. Callie had seen her come here only minutes ago. I saw no blood or broken bodies lying on the floor, and I didn't smell any gun residue in the air. The pups weren't barking either. Was this a random break-in? The bar was silent. No one was on the street to call the police. Which, in all honesty, I probably didn't want anyway.

They might not know how to handle a cowboy lizard man, a blonde Wonder Woman, an unconscious ninja, and two puppies who turned to mist when they felt threatened. Rather than loitering outside a crime scene and getting the cops called on me, I slipped inside as silently as possible in the event the building wasn't as empty as it seemed.

I came to a halt, curling my lip.

Peter sat at the bar, sipping a glass of scotch. I stared at him, clenching my jaw. He glanced over at me with a warm smile. He was idly toying with a familiar bracelet—the one that gave him ridiculous levels of power. It made him into a wizard, for all intents and purposes. What he lacked in skill and experience, he made up for in raw power. A second glass sat next to him.

"Join me, old pal," he said, nudging the extra glass. "We haven't had one of our Round Table discussions in...oh, a *while* now," he said darkly. A pale, bumpy, zippered scar crossed his throat from where Raego had allegedly killed him. I made a mental note to always lean in favor of decapitation in the future. The added mess was worth it.

I made no move to join him. Where was everyone? Had Peter caught them or had they escaped? Where was Kára? I didn't bother asking how Peter knew it was me. Zeus had woken him up. It had probably been the second thing he'd heard, right after *come with me if you want to live!*

Or maybe the third, right after *I'll impale you on this live lightning bolt if you disobey me.*

But I did have a few questions. And I needed to stall him. I knew I didn't stand a chance against his magic, and if I reached for anything in my satchel I'd only be handing that weapon over to him on a platter.

"How did you find me?" I asked, frowning. Kára's bar was not a well-known holdover for magic and intrigue. Then again, Callie had known about the place. And she'd sent me here. Telling me that Kára had just come here. But...I hadn't seen Kára leave.

I shuddered, forcing back the paranoia. That was a dark, winding path to take.

"Ares and Apollo warned me about my imposter," Peter said, name-dropping the gods as if they were old friends who summered together in the Hamptons. I rolled my eyes at his lack of tact—how blasé he acted about letting the information slip, as if this were some client Christmas party and Peter had used the *special starch* to iron his networking underwear. "They demanded to know if I was behind the recent kidnappings. Framing me...that hurts, Nate. That really hurts," he said with mock sadness. "I assured them that you always thought with your heart, and that you must be behind it."

I waited. "That didn't answer my question."

"I kept tabs on the dragon's apartment after his abduction at your company. Saw him pick up the jeep earlier. Apollo tracked it here." I bit my tongue. Damn it. Yahn had used his own jeep. At least I knew Apollo and Ares were back in play.

"And where are your masters, Ares and Apollo? You never could do anything without stronger men backing you. Hate to tell you that those two little manbitches only eat their peanut butter and jelly sandwiches if Zeus cuts off the crusts, first—"

Peter burst out laughing, glancing over my shoulder.

I spun and was instantly served with one of my own recent favorite meals.

Ares' big beefy knuckle sandwich hit me on the chin, knocking me out cold.

I woke up with a groan, my chin aching and my skull pounding. I was in a storage room. Judging by the kegs of beer, I assumed we were still at Buddy Hatchet. I was chained down to a sturdy wooden table, the metal links wrapped around my chest at least three times. Overkill since I had no magic. Two electric bulbs hung from an unfinished ceiling, and a lone window on the far wall told me that night had fallen.

Shit.

How long had I been unconscious? What about my meeting with Zeus? I had to be at that meeting to have even a hope at saving Alice.

A groan beside me caused me to flinch reflexively. I glanced over to see Kára chained down beside me on a second wooden table. My eyes bugged out of my head. No...

How had Peter gotten the drop on a fucking Valkyrie—

"A little pigeon came pecking around for you," Ares said, chuckling at his little Valkyrie joke as he pointed at Kára. Right. I'd forgotten about that asshole. "Tweet, tweet," he said, flapping his elbows in a clumsy attempt at the chicken dance.

Kára strained against her chains, rocking her whole table a few inches to the side, cursing up a storm. She still wore her armor, but it wasn't doing her any good. She shot me a frantic look, and I knew it wasn't fear for her own safety. She was terrified of what these clowns would do to me—right beside her. In her mind, she'd failed. She knew how these types worked.

She would be used as leverage against me. And that alone was enough to break her. I could see it.

I'd been tortured for a week. I knew the look of someone who had a chink in their armor. I'd spent days patching mine up, and making sure Carl stayed strong. Kára was tough, physically, but her heart...

Was vulnerable.

She shrieked, arching her back and making the chains actually groan and creak. But they didn't break. She panted harshly, settling back down on the table, her eyes diamonds of hate.

Ares chuckled. "Perhaps not a pigeon, but an eagle!" he chuckled.

She sneered at him, spitting on his boots. "Face me like a man, or was your sister right? How you can only get hard for the helpless—"

Ares snarled and then snapped one of her fingers. Apollo laughed. I roared, bucking against my chains, cursing incoherently.

"Come take a turn, Hermes!" Ares bellowed over our animalistic thrashing. "She's all warmed up, and she has a *mouth* on her!"

Apollo stepped out of the shadows where he must have been leaning against a wall, pretending to check all his Insta comments. I sneered at him. "I bet you touch yourself to pictures of sunrises," I said sweetly, "racing to see which one of you can rise the fastest."

Kára burst out laughing. Apollo's face darkened and he stiffly turned to Ares. "Hermes should stay out front. We don't need his illusion faltering and the cops getting calls about the break-in. Otherwise we won't have time for our fun." He obviously had no interest in Kára, but the look he cast my way told me he was practically salivating for a turn.

Ares grunted and stepped back from Kára, making way for Peter to step forward. He hefted a very long kitchen knife in his hands as he made his way to the space between Kára and me. He turned to settle his glare my way.

"Why?" he demanded. I struggled against my restraints, trying not to look at Kára before it broke my own resolve. She was gritting her teeth against the pain of her broken finger, but I knew she could ride out physical agony. The question was how much could she handle psychologically?

I had no idea what Peter was referring to, so I answered the situation in general—why I was resisting a partnership with the Olympians. "Zeus is a prick. And these two are textbook codependents with daddy issues."

Apollo smacked me across the jaw, loosening a tooth. "Answer his questions so we can move on to my turn," he growled hungrily.

I had warm romantic thoughts of Cronus' Scythe in my satchel, and what I would do to Apollo with it. The Castrator was going to earn another nickname for each new generation of Olympian I neutered. The Pickle Sickle. No. The Dicksickle.

"No," Peter snarled furiously. "Why did you let Raego kill me?" His words were clear, concise, and clipped. "I saw the look in your eyes right before everything went black. You sanctioned my death." He tapped his throat where the wicked scar glistened with pale skin. To be honest, I wasn't sure how he hadn't died. "You did *this*," he whispered.

I sighed, shaking my head. "Well, you're welcome for botching it, dickwad."

Peter's face purpled and he opened his mouth—

"We don't give a shit about your childhood trauma," Ares warned. "You have a job to do, little human. It's the only reason we woke you up. Get on with it so my brother can have a private word with the bastard."

I grunted, shooting Peter a sly look. "Don't mind him, Peter. He's just mad I fucked his sister better than he could." Ares snarled but Apollo forced him back.

58

Peter discreetly masked a reflex grin—a little of my old friend shining through—at my mockery of Ares. I didn't fall for it or anything, but it earned him a little honesty. "You were not yourself, Peter. You wouldn't listen to reason. I tried everything."

He shut down. "No!" he snarled, livid. "You had *everything*! Magic and money and friends, but you destroy everything you love, Nate. Your friends, even your lovers. Take Othello! Once you had your fun with her, you let her fall to the trash pile. Couldn't risk mixing a peasant into the royal Temple bloodline," he snarled bitterly.

My heart stopped and my blood instantly boiled as my earlier nostalgia over Othello loomed into my mind's eye in Dolby Digital Surround Sound. And how she was now happily enveloped in the arms of another man —Death.

My heart *raged*, sending torrents of lava-hot blood through my veins like a broken dam.

"That's not true! I loved Othello! It just didn't work out between us!" I roared.

Peter scoffed, thumbing his knife angrily. He smirked at Kára, who glared back. "And how does that make you feel, sweetheart?" he teased.

"Looks like you're just a shiny toy for the local billionaire, too." She fought at her chains, snarling like a wet cat.

I panted harshly, my throat raw, as I stared at the cruel, satisfied look Peter was giving Kára.

He was more of a monster than ever before. His time encased in stone had only served as a Petri dish for his madness to reproduce and spread into every cell of his body. I caught him absently checking his bracelet as if to make sure it was still there. He loved that power more than anything he'd ever loved before it.

Ares and Apollo watched Peter with approving grins, unable to deny his success. Since it resulted in watching me squirm, they seemed content to let it play out a little longer before getting their own hands dirty again.

Peter was looming over Kára, waving the knife back and forth before her eyes, speaking in low, threatening tones. Kára, for her part, looked calmer than before. The only win for us was stalling, so she was letting Peter have his fun—especially if it meant he wasn't cutting into me.

Maybe there was something to be said about absolute power corrupting absolutely.

Peter and Indie had both been ravaged by their first taste of power.

Neither had been born with magic, and forcing magic onto them had resulted in epic disaster.

Just like the gods sitting too long in power, with no checks or limits to their desires. They had also become corrupted by it. The Carnage, as Aphrodite had warned me.

Someone really needed to do something about that. Someone really needed to protect the Regulars of this world—from contracting power that would corrupt them, and from narcissistic gods who still flaunted their Letterman's jackets, demanding the worship they'd once received.

That was what Zeus wanted. He wanted adoration. By force, if necessary.

Because he was a monster. Many of the gods were monsters. They infected each other with their penchant for unlimited greed.

The Regulars needed a champion. A monster of their own. But a monster with a heart. He could be the peoples' monster. Their advocate.

Their Horseman.

No. The Four Horsemen were foretold to eradicate the souls of men from the Earth during the End Days. That was the opposite of what I wanted.

The Dread Four, on the other hand...

Well, we were a second team of Horsemen, and we didn't yet have a mission statement. Perhaps we could be the Horsemen...to the *gods*. To eradicate *their* numbers and let *them* taste fear for the first time in centuries. The gods would rally, banding together out of necessity. I couldn't do it all by myself. Gunnar had killed a god. Callie had killed Dracula. Alucard had...

Well, he'd done quite a bit of suntanning. But I'd seen him in action. He could probably kill a god if he put his back into it. The only thing that had held him back was a fear of becoming a monster. This would be a happy compromise. Be the right kind of monster.

The Dread Four's conscience, perhaps. Absolution seemed to marry that role well.

Callie was the tactician—giving our enemies Despair.

Gunnar was the force—giving our enemies the Justice they truly deserved.

And I was the Catalyst—giving the Regulars Hope for better days. I was willing to make the calls no one else would—but that didn't mean I was always right. I needed them as much as they needed me. Plus...

Hello, Temple here. Of course, I would be in charge.

Another concerning thought was how Zeus wanted my Horsemen for himself. Perhaps he knew exactly what kind of danger we represented, and that was why he wanted us on his side. So he could aim us at all the *other* gods—not his. That was a Zeus tactic for sure.

But none of it mattered unless I broke free. I was currently tied to a table, unable to access my Horseman's Mask. This point was verified by the fact that no one in the room had shat themselves.

"What are you smiling about?" Peter demanded, snapping me out of my thoughts. I hadn't known I was smiling. I looked up to find him staring at my Titan Thorns with a look of horror.

I glanced down and blinked. They had cracked. A sharp, jagged line marred the once solid surface, bisecting one of the strange runes. They hadn't broken entirely, but they had cracked. And I could sense some of my power leaking through to me.

I sucked in some of the power and shuddered in relief as Apollo and Ares began to shout at each other. I tried throwing my magic at them, but nothing happened. I could feel it trickling into me, but I couldn't do anything with it.

Realizing this, my jailers calmed down, laughing uneasily and demanding answers from Peter in harsh, dangerous tones. Kára was staring at me with a hopeful look but I shook my head.

Why had they broken? I'd been thinking about my Horsemen destroying the pantheons, not love. I hadn't even said any of that out loud, which Aphrodite had said was necessary.

I hadn't said any names—

I froze.

Othello. I'd said her name. I'd said *I loved Othello.*

Even as I thought it, I knew it was the truth. But the cuffs had only cracked.

"I love Othello," I whispered, putting my heart into it, wondering if it hadn't worked because I'd used the past tense with Peter.

Kára cocked her head, looking confused. "What are you doing?" she whispered while the others were grilling Peter for answers. "Did it work?"

I shook my head miserably, wondering why it had only partially worked. Knowing this truth only made my situation suckier, because I kept imagining the romance I'd seen between her and Death. That was the cruel part—the whole unconditional part of unconditional love. Even knowing she was happy with Death, I still knew I loved her.

It didn't matter if they reciprocated. That was called a condition.

Love sucked sometimes.

Part of me felt dead inside.

Apollo stepped up to me, cutting off my view of Kára. He scowled down at me. "We don't have time to play any more games. Father wants us on the mountain soon."

Ares snarled angrily. "Who gives a fuck what the old man wants?"

I blinked, surprised. Was there a fracture in the family business? Even bigger than I had previously thought? Peter looked just as startled, likely realizing that he was now the middle manager in the untenable position of standing between his boss and his boss' petulant children.

Ah, Corporate America. How I love thee.

Apollo got right up in Ares' face. "If we aren't there in time, all this would have been for nothing, and our chance will be lost. The Titan Thorns fucking cracked, you moron. What happens if they break all the way?"

Ares grunted. "We need to get Pandora's Box!" he argued. "Otherwise, this *will* be a waste."

I glanced over at them, their argument percolating in my mind. It was time to figuratively streak through the middle of the family picnic, scarring generations of Olympians for good.

"I gave it to your sister, you idiots. Why do you think I fucked with your head so hard? I needed you out of the picture. Aphrodite promised to break me out of my cell if I got her the box. It's hard to say no to a woman who can do the things she can." I shrugged shamelessly. "Plus, it earns me a seat at the table when she overthrows your father."

The two brothers stared at me, looking terrified and furious all at the same time.

"That's impossible!" Ares roared, stomping my way. "Our plan was—"

Apollo clasped a hand around Ares mouth, jerking him to a halt as he shot me a frantic look. Then he shook his head at Ares. So, there really was a coup in process. Hera's crazy ass mind games against Zeus had been true. Huh. Vindictive spinster for the win.

"You can hate me all you want," I said, splitting my gaze between them, "but it looks like we might just be on the same side. Your dad wants to use me, and I'm not a fan of that. Your sister roped you into helping her overthrow your father. I'm guessing she's the brains of the operation, which makes sense, since she recruited me as well."

The words made my own heart ice over. She'd been helping me. I'd genuinely believed her about the Titan Thorns and the inner workings of my own heart. I understood her desire to boot Zeus from his perch, but how could she work with these two ass clowns? Her theory on the manacles hadn't exactly panned out either. Had she played me?

Regardless, I was going to capitalize the shit out of the situation. I managed to worm my fingers into my pocket without them noticing—they were too absorbed in a hushed argument. I masked my surprise at finding my pocket was not empty.

The gods turned back to me. "She did break him out," Ares said, thinking out loud.

Apollo shook his head adamantly. "She would have told us."

"Well, we don't have fucking time for a crossword puzzle," Ares snapped. "We need to make a decision now before one is made for us. Either way, we need to be on that mountain."

I nodded. "Tick. Tock."

"You are not going to let Temple side with you," Peter warned, his fists crackling with energy. "He is mine. He will not win this time. Not again!"

I glanced at Peter, frowning compassionately. "Oh, Peter. You know they're just using you, right? Like Alaric tried to do." His face darkened, but he didn't interrupt me. "You're not part of the family. Even with that bracelet, you're just a wizard. They are gods," I said gently, so he didn't think I was being cruel.

For the second time in my life, I sanctioned Peter's death with a handful of words, not even having to lift a finger.

"I'll get you something better than your bracelet if you get me out of here in ten seconds. We'll never have to see each other again. Just get me out of here."

Chaos ensued as Ares and Apollo stormed forward—heading straight for me.

No doubt to take me to the mountain before Peter did something stupid.

I might not have needed to lift a finger to sentence Peter to death, but I was willing to do it for two angry gods. I awkwardly extracted my fingers from my pocket and threw a Tiny Ball in front of Ares and Apollo.

A Gateway roared to life between us and they crashed through it, unable to halt their momentum. I heard screams and roars and explosions through the Gateway, followed by dark, wicked, malevolent laughter.

It was like a chocolate fondue fountain for my ears.

The Gateway winked shut to reveal Peter on the other side of where the Gateway had appeared. His face was haunted at whatever he had seen. "What did you just do?" he whispered.

"What happens in Niflheim stays in Niflheim," I said with a bright grin.

Because I'd pocketed a Niflheim Tiny Ball, thinking I would need it to confront my Horsemen.

From the sounds of it, Fenrir and Loki had set up camp again.

And Nate Temple had been their UberEats driver, giving them Ares and Apollo.

I stared at Peter. "Now, where were we…"

59

Peter stared at me for a few long moments. "That won't go over well. They'll return shortly, and you'll wish you hadn't done that."

I scoffed. "Oh, they won't be returning as the same men," I laughed bitterly. "I meant what I said. You're more screwed than I am—whether they return or not. I'll get you enough power to protect yourself and run. We don't have to be friends, but I can save your life. This time."

Peter studied me warily, and then calmly walked over to Kára. "You know, it's funny," he said, picking up a long, thin knife. "You didn't start talking until they began hurting the girl."

I snarled, railing against my chains as he slowly sliced his knife across her exposed abdomen. She groaned, gritting her teeth. I railed against my chains harder, hoping to snap the manacles loose by deepening the crack. Other than that, I was useless. Even though I could feel magic trickling into me, I could do nothing with it.

And that was so much worse—my mind screaming at me to do a dozen different spells, not understanding why it wasn't working when I was holding the tools of our salvation.

"Do you have anything to say, sweetheart?" Peter cooed, brushing a lock of hair from her face and wiping off a bead of sweat with his thumb. "You'll be too busy moaning to form a proper sentence here in a few minutes," he promised, and then he dragged the blade down her cheek. She screamed, suddenly babbling in a foreign language.

I was too busy struggling against my chains to bother listening. I had to find a way out!

Peter leaned close, tapping a finger against her breastplate. "How about we peel this off and see how tough a Valkyrie is without her armor? All those lovely tender bits beneath the candy shell." But it had been a misdirect, because he abruptly snapped one of her fingers with a startlingly loud pop, laughing over her screams.

I raged, panting and straining, my manacles cutting into my wrists as I tried to physically force the crack deeper. Peter was unbuckling her armor, but he paused to frown at her chest. "It's a shame you had to scratch this stupid emblem on there. Would have been worth more when I sold it later. Who draws a fucking pile of blocks on such elegant armor?"

"Lighthouse," I snarled angrily. "It's a fucking *lighthouse.*" He ignored me.

I struggled and fought as I heard him finish unclipping her armor. I hadn't realized that it was physically attached since I'd seen her make it vanish and reappear with a thought. Maybe it had to be physically strapped on before she could do any of that. Peter wasn't all that bright, because he'd forgotten she was chained down to the table.

She began laughing at him. "You fucking moron. Forgot about the massive chains in your way?" she taunted. "Sitting here and spilling my blood only guarantees your own death when the Olympians return. They said Hermes was outside. You can bet your ass he won't believe *we* sent them away," she grinned, eyeing Peter's bracelet. "I wonder who Hermes will blame..."

Peter paused, looming over her. "Maybe Zeus is aware of their games and gave me my own set of marching orders," he said without a flicker of concern. "Orders that supersede theirs."

I stared in horror. Shit. That...was not good.

Kára spat in his face and he backhanded her with his fist, snapping her head to the side. He lifted his knuckles to find a splash of her blood. He frowned, and then wiped it off on the front of her armor.

"And you seem to have forgotten that I'm a wizard," he muttered. He lifted his palm and Kára instantly flattened to the table as if glued to it.

Peter began to whistle as he bent down to insert a key into a lock I hadn't seen. The chains came loose and Peter calmly hefted off her armor, whistling while he worked. He dropped the chest piece to the ground with a metallic clang, and then began reassembling the chains, all while Kára struggled to breathe, as she was pressed so tightly against the table.

I stared down at the discarded armor, at her own blood painting the crude lighthouse. It was hopeless. I couldn't get out of my restraints and I couldn't tap into my magic.

Kára screamed at him in a violent string of guttural words I did not recognize as he finished resetting her restraints. Then he cut her again, forcing her to choose between her cursing and screaming. He paused long enough for her to catch her breath in a ragged pant. "You always were a scared little man, Peter," she snarled. "Nothing but a terrified little *Sooka*."

I frowned, something about her statement catching my attention, although I couldn't place it.

Peter was silent, but I couldn't peel my eyes away from the blood lazily filling in the lines of the lighthouse. "Well, whatever you just said, I heard you say my name, so I'm betting it wasn't nice. What language was that? German?" Peter asked absently.

Kára suddenly went quiet.

That was what had caught my attention. She had spoken a different language again. The last word had been familiar. *Sooka*. And she'd rolled her *R*'s perfectly...

"Russian," I whispered, frowning to myself as I stared at the bloody lighthouse. Because I'd translated her words in my mind. Kára...had known Peter?

"What was that, dear?" Peter asked, glancing back at me. "Did you have something to say?"

"She was speaking Russian," I murmured, "and she called you a *sooka*. A bitch."

I heard another finger bone snap and Kára screamed. "Is that true, Valkyrie? Did you call me a bitch?" he snarled, snapping another finger. "You have six more fingers. How about we stick with your theme and play a little Russian roulette?"

I flinched at his threat, but not just in fear. Something else...a casino?

Roulette? Kára had clamped her lips shut, refusing to talk and give him the satisfaction of a response.

"I'm not going to shoot you, but I am thinking of a number between one and six. Guess right and I'll let you choose which finger I break next," he said, laughing at his own ingenuity.

My heart was racing, and I couldn't stop staring at the lighthouse. "A lighthouse," I mumbled, forcing my sluggish brain to action. The scrolls in the Armory! Pandora had said they were from Alexandria. A hint to a riddle. But what riddle?

"Oh, great," Peter muttered. "He's delirious, Kára. You're being too quiet for him and he's falling asleep. Let's try the big knife. See if that will wake him up." I jolted, looking up right as he stabbed her in the side with a wider blade. I snarled as he twisted it, panting heavily. Kára grunted, her eyes bulging. But she did not scream. Instead, her head lolled to the side and she stared at me, a tear falling from her blue eye and spilling down her cheek.

Peter left the blade in her side and placed his hands on his lower back, stretching. "This is hard work. I need a drink." In my peripheral vision, I watched as Peter strolled over to a table against the wall and twisted the top off a bottle of water.

I couldn't peel my eyes away from Kára. An apology resided deep within her dual-colored eyes. An unnecessary one.

"Kára," I whispered, blinking through my own misty eyes as pieces of a puzzle began clicking into place—even though they formed a maddening picture that made little sense. "You rolled your R's," I whispered.

She stared back at me with a suddenly panicked look on her face.

"That's the *Alexandrian* lighthouse on your armor," I whispered. "Pharos."

More pieces clicked into place, expanding the picture to make more sense—in an impossible way. I recalled hearing Othello and Death's conversation from earlier. How frustrated Othello had been about her failure to locate me.

My eyes widened. "*She's* not the best hacker in the world," I breathed. "*You* are."

Peter shouted something at us but it was just white noise.

More tears spilled from Kára's eyes and her lips quivered, not acknowl-edging Peter's frantic shouting either.

"You..." I whispered, blinking through tears. "You are *Othello*..." I breathed.

Peter was suddenly back, and he stabbed her in the arm, shouting angrily. Kára didn't flinch from the blow or break eye contact with me, and I knew that my words had hurt her far worse than Peter's blade.

"And I love you," I whispered, "Othello, Kára...what's in a name, anyway?"

She closed her eyes, her composure shattering before my eyes, her mental armor destroyed. "I love you too, Pharos," she sobbed. Something she'd never said to me before.

And...it lit a fucking *fire* in my soul. The impotent magic swirling within me screamed and roared like an oncoming tornado, destroying everything in its wake, scraping my insides raw, and obliterating the mental tower I'd built to hide my heart's greatest desire from myself—like Aphrodite had told me.

I *had* known it all along. Othello had always been in my heart. That fire had just gone to ground, waiting. Because it had been born in silence.

Peter raised his blade high overhead. "That's it. I'm sick and tired of you two ignoring me."

The blade came down, but Othello didn't react, refusing to break eye contact with me.

A sharp cracking sound echoed in the storage room like a gunshot, and Peter suddenly cried out as something struck his hands, snapping bones and sending his knife flying.

The Titan Thorns, now nothing more than broken hunks of metal, dropped to the concrete floor. They'd broken the moment I'd voiced my love.

Peter fell to the ground with a scream, clutching a bloody stump. "You son of a bitch! You cut off my goddamned hand!" he shrieked.

I sat up from my table, ripping off the chains with my bare hands. Molten hot metal hissed and screamed as it flew across the room in a shower of sparks.

I stumbled over to Kára, and her chains exploded, zipping past me without harm—but peppering Peter, judging by his screams. I scooped her up in my arms and blinked through tears as I stared down at her. I felt like sand beneath a wave, the topical and inane parts of my soul washing out to sea, leaving only the firmest, oldest sand and bedrock behind. The foundation.

She was badly wounded. Maybe fatally.

"Othello," I breathed, unable to make sense of it all. She still looked like my Valkyrie, Kára. Ever since Othello had died, she'd been in a romantic relationship with Death. But I was now certain that the woman I'd seen with Death at Chateau Falco had been a double. She'd claimed not to be the world's best hacker.

Othello would never say that.

And she hadn't known Peter, but Kára had. The double had needed to use a memory shard to recall who Peter was. And then Death had interrupted Kára's conversation with Freya outside Yggdrasil when I'd been astral spying. He had not wanted the goddess—or me—to hear something.

"Pharos," Kára breathed through a faint bloody smile. A single drop of blood fell from her finger as I crouched down to collect her chest piece. The ruby drop splashed over the lighthouse, filling in the rest of the crude lines.

Kára had...etched my name—Pharos—into her armor.

A permanent reminder, right over her heart, of what mattered right now. The worlds could wait for *later*, but Pharos had mattered right *now*. She'd been willing to turn in her trident and wings to see me safe. To possibly give up her soul.

Her eyes fluttered closed as I gently pressed my lips to her forehead and ripped open a Gateway of fiery sparks behind me. I could feel her pulse, but only barely. Rather than use my hands to collect her armor, I remembered I could now use my magic. I scooped it up on a tendril of air, letting it float at my side. Spotting my satchel on the table, I picked that up, too.

Peter was screaming something at me, clutching his stump with a manic look in his eyes.

I paused to stare at him. He grunted, staring back at me. "Nate," he whispered, eyeing me from head-to-toe. My illusion must have broken.

"Yup."

Then I drew upon my magic and sent a blade of icy air at his remaining hand, slicing it off at the wrist as well. Blood spurted as he screamed in horror. He pressed the stumps against his thighs, screaming incoherently. I used a tendril of air to round up his hands and let them float at my side where he could see them. One of them still had the bracelet because I'd inadvertently severed it too high on Peter's wrist.

Whoops.

"It was really nice seeing you again, Peter. We'll have to do it again some time. Thanks for helping me find her. I don't know what I would have done without your helping hands."

Then I stepped through the Gateway, carrying my Valkyrie across the threshold and into my Armory where I knew I could keep her safe.

Her armor, my satchel, and Peter's severed helping hands followed in my wake.

As did Peter's desperate pleas.

The Gateway closed. Not open for mercy.

60

I entered the Armory to find Pandora frozen in place, staring at me with a mixture of relief and horror at my cargo. Prometheus leapt to his feet, his fists crackling with fire as he stepped between me and Pandora in a wary stance.

He saw Kára in my arms and reached out for her.

I snarled protectively and blasted him away with a thought, the air suddenly crackling with my raw magic, smelling like burnt ozone. The Titan blew through the solid stone wall and crashed into a distant room with a muttered curse. Dust hovered in the gloomy hole, and the Armory was utterly silent. "Hey, Nipple," the Titan's voice grumbled from within the darkness. "Thought you might be Zeus," he said, coughing. "Congrats on getting rid of your illusion."

I blinked. My illusion was gone. Right.

Pandora stared at me holding Kára and her composure cracked. "Oh, Nate," she whispered sadly. Kára whimpered in delirious pain and Pandora let out a sharp sob of relief. I clenched my jaw as Kára's cry hit me on a molecular level, my knees buckling and almost giving out. But I straightened them and set my shoulders determinedly. "About that hot tub..." I growled.

"Of course," she whispered. "Follow me."

I sensed other bodies in the room but I didn't bother looking at them. "Put the hands on the mantle. Don't touch the bracelet with your skin," I added, dropping the hands on the ground with a bloody splat. Then I was carrying Kára after Pandora.

Pandora set a brisk pace—as fast as possible without actually running. My strides soon caught me up to her, urging her to go faster. "You're covered in blood. Is it yours, or hers?" she asked as the door came into view.

"Yes."

She tugged open the doors and I slipped into the balmy room, pausing before the hot tub.

Pandora dry-washed her hands anxiously, watching me. "Go on, my host. I'll stand guard."

"Her armor," I rasped.

"It will not be harmed," Pandora assured me. "Just step in—"

"She will need it when she wakes," I said, using my magic to hold Kára in midair so I could let go—even though not a single fiber of my being wanted to break contact with her.

I kicked off my shoes and began tearing off my own clothes, staring at Kára's chest to make sure her breathing did not change. As I kept my eyes on her and undressed myself, I used my magic to unclasp the rest of her armor while dropping the piece with the lighthouse etching. Dozens of tendrils of air lashed out of me like tentacles. The pieces fell from her body under their deft touch, but I caught them all with cushions of air before they struck the ground.

"Mustn't scratch them," I murmured as I tugged off my socks and poured more magic tendrils into the mix, carefully unstrapping harnesses, unlatching buckles, and setting them all in an orderly pile without breaking eye contact with Kára's chest. There had to be a hundred fingers of air blowing about the room, now.

Pandora gawked, her hair whipping around from the frenzy of air stripping Kára down to her skin, until all that remained was her warskirt.

"She won't want to fight in wet clothes," I murmured, slipping out of the last of my clothes.

I used tendrils of air to carefully unbraid her hair as dozens more worked in concert to remove the last stitches of fabric from my Valkyrie.

My breath caught to see her hovering in the air like a warrior princess.

My hundred loving fingers of magic held her; she was safer than she had ever been, now, even though her numerous wounds spilled fresh blood onto the ground below her. I scooped her up in my arms, holding her close as I climbed up the steps towards the magical healing waters.

I hastily but cautiously descended through a wall of steam, staring at Kára's lips and smiling anxiously as I carried her into the water, holding her close to my chest. She sighed as the water touched her toes, but as the water splashed over her wounds, she curled up against me with sharp whimpers and gasps of pain. I clutched her tighter until she stopped flinching and began to relax. Then I held her out to float before me, with only my hands supporting her, as I lowered myself until my eyes were just above water level and only inches from her most severe wound.

The hole in her side.

I stared, transfixed, as the flesh knitted closed. Within moments, it was finished, and I felt her body relax in my hands, floating on the pool's surface. I drew closer, pressing my lips against the healed flesh of her ribcage and bit back a sob of relief. Her breathing was steadier as I rose up from the water, staring down at her.

My eyes swept over every inch of her body, every rise and valley, searching for wounds and making sure every last one had been healed by the water. Her long blonde hair fanned out behind her, the blood washed away as if it had never been. Her chest rose and fell without pain and her breathing was steady. Her fingers were no longer swollen and broken. Tears fell down my cheeks and I smiled at her.

"My Valkyrie," I whispered. "You. Are. *Mine*."

Kára looked...pure.

Peaceful.

Safe.

I let out a shuddering breath, hanging my head.

"All will be well, my host," Pandora murmured from behind me. I glanced back to see her leaning her forearms on the lip of the pool, staring at Kára with an adoring smile. "You finally found her," she whispered happily.

I nodded. "She found me first."

"Let me put her to bed. You have work to do tonight." She straightened, holding a thick robe out. "Well, don't just stand there. Bring her over here," she chastised in a stern tone.

I grunted. "Yes, ma'am."

With my magic back under my control, we made short work of drying her off and getting the robe into place. I carried her to one of the Armory's private bedrooms and tucked her into bed under a pile of furs, smiling as she breathed peacefully, recovering. I didn't know how long she would sleep, but I knew the first thing she'd want to do would be to fight. No matter what anyone told her. They would be wise not to stand in an angry Valkyrie's way.

And I agreed with her. I wanted her to fight by my side.

I had no right to ask her to do otherwise. And I knew her loyalty was unparalleled. On the other hand, she wouldn't put up with any of my idiocy either. The perfect balance.

"I will not be able to slow time, but she will be safe," Pandora said. I shot her a questioning look and she nodded. "Even with what you have planned, she will be safe," she repeated in a firmer, resolute tone.

"Can you get my satchel for me? I left it in the hot tub room. And have someone clean off her armor. She will need it," I repeated. "She didn't have her trident..." I said, frowning.

Pandora nodded. "She left it here, Nate. Do not worry." She left the room, and the only sound was Kára's breathing.

I gestured with my hand and the fireplace ignited. I tied it off so that it would burn out once Kára left the room. A piece of me to keep her warm while she slept. Pandora returned and handed me the satchel. I pulled out a pen and paper, jotting down a quick note.

Find me.—Pharos.

I set it down on the side table and then placed one of Hermes' golden coins on top. She would know what to do.

I had no time to wait for her. A little girl's life might be on the line.

And my Horsemen would be gathering. It was time for war. And to kill a couple of gods. If I was lucky, I might have already thinned the ranks with my special delivery to Niflheim. But I wasn't banking on it.

"Before you leave, you need to see Yahn," Pandora said guardedly. "I will tell him you're coming," she said. "Say your goodbyes."

I nodded, kneeling down beside the bed and resting my chin on the furs. Kára's face was visible over the edge, burrowing her chin under the blankets with a faint moan. Her lips were slightly parted as she dozed. Some of her hair hung down over her cheek.

I used a light tendril of magic to carefully shift it back, smiling to myself. My magic had returned, and now that I knew Kára was safe, I was only just beginning to comprehend the significance of that, and how it would affect my initial plan. Kára had done that for me.

But she'd done something much more important.

"You gave me my heart back," I whispered. "Sleep, my dear Valkyrie. When you wake, we will celebrate in a shower of ichor."

It was a promise I intended to keep.

61

Yahn stood in the hallway, waiting for me. His nose was a shattered ruin and he had two black eyes to match. Being a shifter, I knew they would heal fairly soon.

"She's okay, Yahn. Just resting," he sagged, letting out a loud breath of relief. "What happened? Where did you all go?" I asked him, straightening my satchel over my shoulder and gesturing for him to walk with me back to the main area.

"I tried to stop her," he said, in a stuffy tone, pointing at his broken nose. "Kára returned from the Vaults and freaked out about two seconds later, screaming at me to get everyone to the Armory. I threw down a Tiny Ball and she grabbed the pups by the scruffs of their necks and leapt through the moment the Gateway opened. The rest of us made it through just as someone blew down the door to the bar. Luckily, our Gateway winked shut before they pursued."

"She came back for me," I mused, smiling.

Yahn grunted. "After breaking my face for trying to stop her, yes." I smirked absently, nodding. I spotted a freshly cleaned smear on the floor and cringed. Someone had already cleaned up the trail of Kára's blood. "Kára knew you'd return to the bar and that you would be helpless without your magic." He eyed my bare wrists with a smirk. "Prometheus said that was no longer an issue," he said, dryly.

I winced. "He made a sudden movement," I muttered. Yahn chuckled. "He was laughing about it. Kára didn't even have confidence in all of us to defend ourselves, so she knew you'd be taken. She went back to try and intercept you."

"I'd be dead if she hadn't." I looked over at him, dipping my chin. "Thank you for letting my Valkyrie clobber you, Yahn."

He nodded. "Sure. I just kind of took it, for all intents and purposes. She headbutted Carl when he threatened to go with her. Knocked him out cold," he said, shaking his head.

My eyebrows almost climbed off my head. "You're shitting me. She knocked out an Elder?"

Yahn nodded. "Toe-tah-lee," he said. "I've never seen Carl so proud. He's bragging about it."

I shook my head. "Of course."

"Who was it?" he asked curiously. "Who was she so concerned about? Zeus?"

I shook my head. "Ares and Apollo. Hermes was supposedly standing guard, but I never saw him. Peter was there, too, working with them. They were his hands."

Yahn struggled to process that as we entered the main area to find Prometheus, Pandora, and Carl—in his stupid cowboy hat—waiting for me. No one spoke.

"She's fine. Resting," I said.

They let out a collective sigh of relief. I saw Peter's hands in a flower vase and smiled proudly. It was on a table all by itself, the fingers resembling a bouquet. The bracelet rested safely at the base of the vase. Yahn grimaced at it, now that it had a name.

I scanned the room with a frown. "Where are Calvin and Makayla?" I asked, realizing that the pups were nowhere in sight, and they hadn't tackled me with puppy kisses upon arrival.

Instead of answering, Yahn pointed at a couch facing away from me— the one I'd slept on with Kára. I frowned and took a few steps closer, unable to see them from my angle. I tensed when I saw that the side table was a pile of splinters. Then I saw two gangly, tow-headed, pre-teen strangers snoring silently, sprawled out on the couch beneath a pile of blankets, their hands and feet poking out like two pairs of starfish. Ryuu knelt before the couch, looking concerned. He met my gaze for a brief moment, nodded, and then resumed his watch of the kids. One boy. One girl.

The hair on the back of my neck rose—and not because the ninja was awake and unrestrained. I slowly turned to Yahn. "What. Happened?"

He swallowed nervously at the edge to my voice. "Calvin and Makayla started playing tug of war with Roofie Ruxpin. They began flickering back and forth into mist like strobe lights, and suddenly two kids crashed to the ground, unconscious."

I stared at them, imagining Gunnar's hammer crunching my face bones. "Are they hurt?"

"Not that I can tell. Calvin fell into the table and broke it with his face, but he must be a lot luckier than me because it didn't break his nose. Didn't even get a scratch. Crazy, right?"

I nodded jerkily. "Yeah. Crazy," I said, feeling a little wild-eyed. Because I hadn't told them about taking the pups to the River Styx. The fewer who knew, the better. The River Styx had worked.

"They are healthy," Pandora assured me.

I grimaced, wondering what to do with this new wrinkle. Calvin and Makayla were no longer mist wolves. Was that a result of the cursed teddy bear or their dip in the River Styx? And what would happen when they woke? They would, undoubtedly, freak the fuck out to realize they no longer had paws yet still liked to sniff butts.

There was only one man for the job. I turned to Cowboy Carl. "I need you to—" I cut off abruptly, staring at his wrists in disbelief. His Titan Thorns were gone. I pointed. "The *hell* is that all about?" I demanded.

He stared down at his wrists with a frown. "I was hoping you could explain. They...exploded shortly before you arrived."

I frowned. "That's about when mine broke free," I mused. "Did you fall in love or anything while I was gone?"

He shook his head. "I do not believe so..." he said, eyeing the crew. "Did I accidentally love on any of you?"

Yahn stared at him. "You...don't love on someone and forget it."

Carl took off his hat, seeming to frown. "I do not understand how to love."

Pandora turned to me. "Perhaps your manacles were linked? Elders do not love, per se."

Rather than take offense, Carl nodded eagerly, looking relieved. "We mate, serve, and protect our spawn."

I let out a sigh. "Well, that's great. This is even better now that you have your powers back," I said, because Elders had mental abilities that were unparalleled. To be blunt, I wasn't even sure what he was capable of. "I need you to stay here and watch over everyone. Especially them," I said, pointing at the sleeping kids. "When they wake up, it's going to be weird. And *you* are my weird guy."

He hesitated for only a moment, looking disappointed he wouldn't participate in the fight on Olympus, but he saw the necessity of someone guarding the Armory and the pups—kids.

If I failed...Zeus and his cronies would come knocking next. With or without me.

"Yes, Master Temple. If they annoy me, I will put the dogs to sleep."

Yahn waved his hands dramatically, axing the idea. "You can't *say* that, Carl. It means something totally different with dogs."

He cocked his head. "If they annoy me, I can...*make* them sleep?" he asked in a slow, questioning tone, watching Yahn's face for an affirmative nod.

I stepped closer, locking eyes with the Elder. "You have the strongest mind here, and I need to know that they are okay. Physically, they're safe, but what they've gone through..." I said, staring at the two pre-teens. "If anything happened to them, I would die. Before Gunnar and Ashley even had a chance to kill me. I think I might just stop breathing if that happened," I said.

Prometheus watched me thoughtfully, looking surprised. Pandora elbowed him followed by a stern glare. He grunted, turning to study the Elder.

Carl nodded. "Yes, Master Temple. Of course."

"It would make sense if he serves you," Prometheus said, still staring at Carl and his bare wrists. "Elders bond to their masters. If you were cuffed, he would be as well. Locking him up with manacles that require true love

to break would not work on an Elder, because they do not love like we do."
I frowned thoughtfully. Prometheus saw my confusion and sighed. "It
would be like me making manacles that will not break unless you learn to
fly. The magic won't permit impossible requirements. It's hopeless, so there
is no magic to fuel the spell."

I stared at him, blinking. "Wow. That actually...makes complete sense,"
I said. "You're not just a pretty face, Prometheus."

He narrowed his eyes. "You're welcome, by the way."

I turned to Ryuu and Yahn. "Carl is in charge."

"I want to go with you," they said in unison.

"Carl is in charge until Kára wakes up. After that, it's up to her. She
knows my plans and I trust her judgment. Carl and Kára are the only two
who know where I'm fighting, so you have to win one of them over."

Ryuu gritted his teeth. "I work for Callie, not you."

I met his gaze levelly, biting back my instinctive response. "I get that,
Ryuu. Truly. But up there," I said, pointing at the ceiling in a figurative
manner, "you're just leverage. Even as badass as you are. Leverage to be
used against Callie—which is why I took you off the board in the first
place. To make her safer. And stronger. She trusts me. Get in line."

Ryuu took several deep breaths, looking frustrated. Finally, he lowered
his eyes in a bow. "You are correct, but I cannot think straight knowing she
is in danger," he admitted.

I nodded, placing a hand on his shoulder. "Which is why you're going
to convince Carl and Kára to let you play. And then you're going to go
shopping," I said, gesturing dramatically at the Armory. His eyes widened
and he gasped, turning to look at me. "I don't like liabilities. Become an
asset. But first, prove your heart," I said, tapping his chest with a finger.
"Convince Kára or Carl." He nodded eagerly, staring out at the various
hallways with a hungry look. "And this is just a loan," I told him, smiling.

I turned to Yahn. "You've already proven your heart and capabilities,
Yahn. What I want you to think about is whether or not you're willing to
leave Carl as the only guard for Gunnar's kids. This is not a guilt trip. You
need to genuinely think on it. I trust your judgment."

He nodded, glancing over at the sleeping Calvin and Makayla. "I think
it would be best if I gather my research on Roofie Ruxpin. Find out what

might have caused them to change so suddenly. I'll see if I can find anything on Niflheim while I'm at it."

I motioned to Pandora and Prometheus. "A few words in private before I leave," I said.

"Wait. Isn't Pandora going to be here to keep the Armory safe? It won't just be Carl," Yahn said, frowning.

Pandora smile sadly. "I will be...otherwise occupied." Then she was walking towards the balcony with Prometheus.

I turned to Yahn and nodded solemnly. "I trust your judgment," I said, gesturing at the Armory in general. "There is no good answer. Welcome to Team Temple."

And I turned away, heading towards Prometheus and Pandora. I pulled the ancient box out of my satchel and tapped it with a fingernail as I met Pandora's determined look. "It is time, Pandora. I'm sorry."

She nodded stiffly. "So be it, my host. Luck," she said with a faint smile.

I shook my head, gripping her chin gently. "No, Pandora. Not luck. *Hope*. Luck is fickle, but Hope will never let you down."

I needed to hurry, because I was pretty sure I might already be late. There hadn't been an exact time on my invitation to the End of the World Party.

62

I 'd wrapped up a few last-minute errands. Having my magic allowed me to accomplish quite a bit in ten minutes, thanks to Gateways.

I hefted my satchel and then checked my neck. I wore two neck-laces, now. My Horseman's coin and my Sensate necklace. My Horsemen would remember the distinguishing factor of the Sensate so as to tell me apart from any potential doppelgänger—like Zeus.

It was also a reminder of Yahn's efforts. A part of him was in this fight. I wouldn't be here without his help. I'd considered bringing Carl's cowboy hat for the same reason, but it looked to weigh fifty pounds and it wasn't my color. I'd look like a cowboy FBI agent in this suit.

No one would take me seriously.

I glanced up at the night sky with a sigh, reaching into my satchel to check—for the hundredth time—that I still had Pandora's Box on me. I felt like I had a neon sign over my head, telling everyone I held it. Kind of like when you took a significant amount of cash from the bank and suddenly felt like every single person who saw you was on the verge of mugging you, even though the cute old lady in the walker had no idea what day it was, let alone that you had a wad of cash in your pocket.

I drummed my finger on the box. "Let's do this, Pandora." I murmured, feeling a warm, reassuring touch on my finger. Then, I put my mean face on. "Do or die, Hope. Do or die."

I flipped Hermes' golden coin, and a Gateway whispered into existence before me, much different than my own. There was no ring of sparks, for one thing. Just a faint shimmer in the air like a heat haze off concrete. I also couldn't see through it to the other side. I took a deep breath, hoping Hermes' coin wouldn't send me to the bottom of the ocean or some craziness. I wasn't entirely sure where Hermes stood on the trust spectrum. He'd supposedly been guarding Buddy Hatchet while Kára and I were restrained by Ares and Apollo, but he sure hadn't been much of an asset to his team.

I pushed the thought from my mind, waited a few moments in order to firmly establish that I was fashionably late, and then stepped through, ready for anything.

The first thing I noticed were the clouds. They were black and pregnant, both above and below the familiar pavilion. Flickers of distant red lightning occasionally illuminated them, followed by faraway thunder. Zeus hadn't been kidding about the storm he'd predicted. I was cold, calm, and detached. I was ready to play, even though I knew the other players would have just as many—if not more—surprises to spring on me.

Probably on each other as well.

I'd appeared on the Temple Crest, just like Hermes had told me. It was still stained with Apollo and Ares' golden ichor. I intended to spill more Olympian blood this night.

I was doubly glad to find that I didn't instantly bump into Zeus or his henchmen.

I turned to see the rest of my Dread Four, wearing the same clothes from earlier, standing to my left. Their eyes instantly shot to the Sensate necklace I wore, and then they let out a collective sigh of relief, but masked their emotions quickly. I discreetly shook my head to remind them to keep up the ruse. Now was not the time to get too close to me. Nor was it time to tip their hand. This fight was going to be a long one.

I turned the opposite direction to find Zeus waiting. He had a jovial smile on his face. But those eyes...

They told a darker story. I could see them calculating the positions of the various pieces on the game board as he shook the dice cup, thinking. He didn't look surprised to see me without my Titan Thorns, but he did look annoyed about it.

Probably because of the tattletale kneeling in front of him. Peter's face was pale, and I could tell it was taking everything he had to remain conscious. Poor guy. I was disappointed to see his stumps had been cauterized. If I hadn't warned them about my telltale Sensates, my Horsemen might have thought that was me kneeling before Zeus and that I'd lost my freaking hands. No wonder they'd looked so relieved to see me. Especially if Zeus had also chosen to wear my face for them. Even I would have been confused at that.

Zeus shifted his gaze towards my Horsemen and I saw a flicker of electricity in his eyes. The threat was obvious—play along or die.

I didn't react to the threat. Instead, I shifted my attention back to Peter and smiled.

"Deja vu," I mused. "So weird. Reminds me of the time you betrayed me to work for Alaric Slate." I glanced up at Zeus, gauging his reaction. Because he'd chosen to disguise Carl as Alaric Slate. Had he done so to make Peter's breakout more impactful, or had he been taunting me about his possible past involvement with Alaric? I'd probably find out tonight.

Zeus stared at me, smiling politely. "I am so glad that you made it, Temple. I just heard the most troubling news from your Horsemen. That this man," he said, pointing at Peter, "abducted several of your friends." So, we were playacting. I'd bite.

"He's pretty much the worst," I agreed. "I had to teach him to keep his hands to himself, which is ironic since that involved taking them away from him," I chuckled harshly.

Zeus' face remained perfect calm, but those eyes...

They were warning me to keep the theatrics going. I was fine with that. I was more relieved to learn that my Horsemen had successfully deceived him—that he didn't know we'd already met up and that I'd come clean. Or so Zeus wanted me to think. That was pretty much how this whole night was going to go, so I steeled my resolve and numbed my surprise factor with mental novocaine. Otherwise, I'd be too paranoid to move.

"I'm sure—as a gesture of goodwill—the Horsemen would appreciate you *handing*," I paused to smile at Peter, emphasizing the word, "him over to their custody." Peter narrowed his eyes at me, but he did not speak. Party pooper.

I noticed Aphrodite standing off to the side, looking remarkably nervous. I knew she'd been working with Ares and Apollo to get Pandora's Box. But that could mean many things—good or bad—for Team Temple. She eyed my suit thoughtfully and I blinked, suddenly feeling like I was wearing a bear trap. Shit. What had that meant? Zeus followed my attention and clenched his jaw. "I too know something of betrayal, but I think we've come to an understanding," he said.

She nodded stiffly at her father, refusing to meet my eyes. I could feel the plot thickening.

Zeus smiled. "I must applaud you on incapacitating this criminal," Zeus said. "It bodes well on our future partnership. Loyalty is vital."

I nodded. "Cool. Why isn't he walking past me yet? The Horsemen are right there," I reminded him, pointing at my crew behind me.

"Maybe he needs a hand," Alucard drawled, lifting his sunglasses as if to get a closer look.

Zeus pursed his lips. "I have a few questions for him and then he is all yours. It seems my sons are missing, and I believe he might know where they are. Hermes is looking for them as we speak. Once he returns, the criminal is all yours." Peter's eyes widened in surprise, but he didn't make a sound. Maybe Zeus had magically gagged him.

I shook my head at Zeus' words, grinning. "Oh, I'm sure they'll be here any minute..."

Aphrodite looked up sharply and Zeus' smile slipped for a second. I pressed my advance.

"I spoke with Hera, believe it or not. Boy, is she a talker," I said, shaking my head and stepping away from the center of the pavilion. I didn't want a Gateway to rip me in half. I continued walking until I could keep everyone in sight without giving myself whiplash. I set my hands on my hips, staring up at the stormy black sky, shaking my head at the distant flashes of red lightning, reminded of my time on the astral plane. "This is so beautiful. The red on black. I *swear* I've seen it before..."

I felt Zeus glaring daggers at me. "Oh?" he asked. "Did my wife—"

"How about we just cut the shit, Zeus," I said, turning to face him. "You're going to give me the girl back. Then we can discuss our *partnership*." I spat as if the word tasted foul.

He stared at me. "Do you mean Alice?" he asked, frowning. "You brought her here yourself. To keep her safe," he said in a faux puzzled tone. He turned to Aphrodite.

She waved a hand, and Alice was suddenly standing between her and Zeus. She wore a cute little yellow dress with her usual white tights and glossy black shoes. And...there wasn't a scratch on her. Alice blinked, momentarily confused at her surroundings, and then she saw me. Her eyes lit up with excitement. "Nate! You're back!" she squealed. "Look!" she giggled excitedly. "Freya helped me make a magic purse so I can be just like you!" she said. A bright blue shoulder purse suddenly appeared at her hip. She patted it lovingly.

I forced my knees not to buckle upon seeing her safe and in good spirits. I didn't even care that she'd disrespected me by calling my satchel a purse. "It's beautiful, Alice. I'm so glad you're safe," I said, gritting my teeth at my overwhelming sense of panic to have her so close yet so far from my arms where I could guarantee her safety. Zeus had found his secret weapon in Alice, but who was his target? Was it Hera, like his wife thought?

The Horsemen watched, their faces blank. Well, occasionally, Callie would glance over at Peter with a glare. Gunnar and Alucard followed suit, sporadically, taking their cues from her.

Zeus placed a hand on Alice's shoulder in a gentle manner, but the threat was plain. Alice smiled up at him. "Safe?" she asked, turning to me with a faint frown. "Safe from whom?"

Thinking quickly on my feet, I pointed at Peter. "He was abducting people I care about—"

She clutched her dress and swiftly shuffled forward to kick Peter with the fury of an angry little girl, surprising the hell out of him as her pointy little shoes struck his kidney with princess power. He groaned, recoiling, but he didn't budge from his spot. His mouth remained closed as well, basically confirming my suspicion. He was restrained somehow. Alice sniffed. "Bully."

Zeus arched an amused eyebrow. "Good job, Alice. He is a terrible,

terrible man," he said, squeezing her shoulder and meeting my stare with a kind, grandfatherly smile. I narrowed my eyes, imagining a steamroller driving over him.

Alice frowned, reading my face. "Are you mad at me?" she asked in a soft, scared voice. I shook my head reassuringly, but she was staring at me with her chin cocked just so, and I knew she was using her budding Seer powers. She hadn't bought my answer. She gasped abruptly. "Oh! Don't be scared. I've kept your Catalyst book safe. It's in my magic purse," she said, sounding on the verge of tears as she reached inside to pull out a tattered book. My heart stopped. The Catalyst book.

Zeus calmly reached over her shoulder and plucked it from her grip with a hungry grin. "Finally," he breathed, a look of rapture on his face as he smiled down at the book.

"Hey!" she snapped, kicking him in the ankles. "Give it back, you big bully! That's mine!"

He cursed in surprise. "Move even a finger from that spot, or utter another syllable, and I will end your miserable existence, you wretched creature," he snarled, his eyes suddenly crackling with electricity. Alice froze. "You can't count the number of times I almost threw you off the cliff to cease your endless babbling," he muttered. "This makes it all worth it," he said, smiling at the deadly book.

Alice hung her head, her shoulders shrinking. Then they began to tremble.

She sniffled...

And that tiny little sound from my tiny little girl almost kicked off the Apocalypse. I almost blew my plan to hell right then when I saw him hurt my little girl's feelings.

This is how the world ends. Not with a bang, but with a sniffle.

Zeus met my eyes, brandishing the book with a grin, completely aloof to the result of his harsh words. "This will be of great help in the upcoming war. Knowing how the Catalyst ticks."

He would use it against me somehow, was what he meant.

"The book you found in Fae," he mused. "The book that got her parents killed. The book about the Omegabet and the Catalyst."

I stared at him, wondering exactly what the book was. How dangerous it was. The thing was, no one truly knew. No one alive, anyway. Because the only way to pass it on was for the previous owner to die—

My eyes danced sharply to Alice, who was perfectly hale. I glanced back at the book, licking my lips uneasily. I sensed magical cahoots, all of a sudden.

"One step closer and I'll burn it to ashes," Zeus warned, eyeing me and my Horsemen. "You need it just as much as me, Temple. That much I know. Right, Alice?" she nodded stiffly, still sniffling. I held my hand out to stall my Horsemen.

Gunnar growled loud enough for everyone to hear. "I'm here for my kids. That scumbag will pay for what he's done," he snarled, glaring at Peter. The others echoed their agreement.

Something was wrong here. Alice should have died—or been on the way to it—once handing the book over to Zeus.

"Let's make a deal, old man." I lifted Pandora's Box from my satchel and there was a collective intake of breath from all sides.

Zeus frowned suspiciously, and then licked his lips, no longer trying to hide his interest—his ravenous thirst for power. "She's inside?" I nodded. "I will not be handing over my leverage, Temple," he said, dryly, lifting the Catalyst book. "With this, I can *make* you do what I want."

I shook my head. "Keep the book. Give me Alice."

Zeus grunted. "Why? A vile slip of a girl for Pandora and her Armory? That's foolish."

I shrugged. "Think about it, Zeus. All the scary stories you've heard about me...the stories that keep you awake at night. I did all of those things *without* the Armory." I gave him a cool smile. "I don't need the trinkets within to be the Catalyst."

He considered this for a moment. "One condition," he said, crouching down and beckoning Alice close. She shied away from him, careful not to move her feet due to his threat.

"Touch her and the Omega War starts *now*," I warned him.

He scoffed. "I need a quick favor, is all. I will not touch her. Consider it rent for her visit. I had to send Hermes to buy crayons just to get her to shut up for more than five minutes."

I hesitated. "Alice?" I asked.

She nodded nervously, putting on a brave face. She flashed me a shaking thumbs up.

He was close enough to kill her already. I had no leverage. "Fine," I growled.

"Come here, child," Zeus said, smiling like a snake. I slipped my hand into my satchel, ready for anything. Alice approached, her little shoes tapping on the marble stone and her dress bouncing with each hesitant step. Zeus bent down and murmured into Alice's ear.

I held my breath. Alice slowly turned to look at Aphrodite. Then she glanced at me. I gave her a reassuring nod. Alice turned to Zeus. "I can see that your daughter is loyal," she said.

I frowned, momentarily confused. Zeus let out a breath of relief and it hit me.

According to his wife, Zeus had never visited the Sisters of Fate. In their absence, he'd needed someone else to verify who he could and couldn't trust. And Alice had taken my nod in an entirely different way. He hadn't just wanted the Catalyst book. Damn.

She was his lie detector. His traitor detector, put more accurately. Seers could do that.

Aphrodite smiled, but I'd seen her flicker of hesitation upon Alice's statement. I let it slide.

Alice...the little stinker, had just lied to Zeus. What in the ever-loving fuck was going on? Whatever game she was playing, he would kill her the moment Aphrodite made the wrong move. I needed to make my trade. Now. Nothing could get in the way of—

Two bodies suddenly slammed into the pavilion, sliding across the marble, an audible smear emanating from the Temple Crest. Everyone jumped. I cursed to see Apollo and Ares groaning and whimpering, relegated to bloody, partially mauled slabs of shame. Mist drifted off their clothes like dry ice.

Of all the goddamned luck. Loki couldn't have used the coin I'd given him sooner? He'd been more than happy to add some mischief to the mix when I'd confronted him before coming here. I'd wanted to make sure Apollo and Ares really were out of the picture, and to take them off Loki's hands if he had indeed been the one who so warmly welcomed them when I'd sent them through the Niflheim Gateway.

Because he'd warned me about inter-pantheon drama. So, imagine my surprise when he seemed more than eager to broker peace by giving them back to their father in more or less one piece. Piece for peace. He'd thought that hilarious, of course.

His timing could have been better. It definitely couldn't have been worse.

63

Zeus narrowed his eyes at his sons with a scowl. "Incompetent pieces of shit," he growled. Wow. With a dad like that...

"The box for the girl," I repeated hurriedly, capitalizing on his lack of compassion.

Zeus studied me suspiciously. Then he shrugged. "I can't say they didn't deserve a little payback," he admitted unconcernedly. "And if the two of them couldn't get the best of you while you were shackled and tied to a table, they deserved what you gave them."

Right. That. "I left them alive as a show of goodwill."

He smirked. "Or a stroke of cruelty." I shrugged noncommittally, wanting nothing more than to get Alice over here. I held out the box. He studied my face, looking for deceit. Finally, he nodded. "Bring it over."

"No. I'll give it to Aphrodite. You now know you can trust her, and I know she would never hurt a little girl. It's fair. I've learned to always trust the boobs of the operation."

He glanced at Aphrodite with a warning glare and finally nodded. I stepped around the pile of pain that had been Ares and Apollo, and approached Aphrodite.

"Is this a good idea, Nate?" Alucard asked.

I glanced back at him. "I would do anything to protect a child, Alucard. *Anything*. Even if it hurt my friends and those I care about. Even if it hurt me."

He stared back, taking my words to heart—about Yahn. Even though he wasn't a child, Alucard obviously saw him as a son of sorts. He finally nodded. Gunnar and Callie watched calmly, their faces giving away nothing. But their eyes were easy to read.

Aphrodite licked her lips nervously—just as anxious as me, which was what I was counting on—as I handed her the box. She knew Alice had lied about her loyalties and that she was on borrowed time. I met her eyes and calmly backed away. Zeus shoved Alice dismissively. The frightened little girl sprinted towards me, her little shoes *tap-tap-tapping* the whole way. I knelt down, holding my arms out, my heart hammering in my chest as I stared at her tear-stained cheeks, my heart breaking.

She wrapped me up in a hug and I rose to my feet, clutching her tightly to my chest as I backed away. "It's okay, Alice. Dad's got you," I whispered, my hands shaking.

She burrowed her face into my neck and whispered the scariest thing I'd ever heard, because it was entirely unexpected.

"It's just a coloring book," she breathed. "Tell him to look at page three. Unicorns are my favorite." And then she *giggled*, making it sound like a laugh of relief rather than humor.

"You are so brave," I whispered back, warily eyeing the Catalyst book in Zeus' hand.

"I knew it wasn't really you when he came to collect me," she whispered. "Freya did too. I told her to trust me."

I almost lost my footing as I continued backing up closer to my crew. "Why?" I hissed.

"To keep you safe, silly," she whispered. "We couldn't fight him because Kára was out looking for your heart, and that was super important. And if he hurt Freya, the pups would be hurt. Did they wake up yet?"

My heart was about to explode from this little girl's capacity for throwing mind-bombs.

"They're not pups anymore, if that's what you mean."

"Good. Makayla will need a part of your heart, but it's a part you can share, and she doesn't need it yet." My skin pebbled, not knowing if she was being literal or not. "When justice comes, submit to your sentence." I flinched involuntarily. I suddenly wanted to get this fortune teller from hell about as far from my ears as possible.

Zeus was frowning because Aphrodite hadn't moved. "Okay, Alice," I whispered. Then I set her down between me and the Horsemen, keeping her behind me as I turned back to Zeus. Aphrodite was staring down at the box in her hands with a dreamy smile on her face that even I found chilling.

I heard a faint whisper of sound behind me, followed by a reassuring swat on my ass. My eyes bulged and I glanced back to see only an empty spot where Alice had been. My Horsemen looked just as startled to see Alice suddenly disappear, but I shook my head reassuringly, biting back a grin at the familiar scent lingering in the air.

Kára.

"Hand it over, daughter," Zeus warned. "Or have you forgotten who has Hephaestus?"

She slowly looked up at him, cocking her head with an amused frown. "And will that matter when I open this box and watch your flesh peeled from your bones?"

He narrowed his eyes warily. *Damn it, Aphrodite*, I thought to myself.

"You see, Father, I think I've reached that age in a young woman's life where she needs to spread her wings. You know what I mean. That special day when you wake up and just know that today is the day your father dies," she said, smiling sweetly. "Because you just love him too much to let him keep on living," she said deadpan.

Right. The girl was crazy. Check. I knew she hated her father, but this was reckless. And she was going to ruin everything.

"Be very, *very* careful, daughter. My patience has limits."

"You are destroying our legacy," she seethed. "You are a monster. And I will not stand for it. I care more about my *own* family. My loving husband and his daughter, Pandora. *Our* daughter. Your warmongering is over." She stared down at the box wistfully. "I can feel her inside. The power," she breathed, her eyes dilating.

Zeus snarled. He spun to me, looking for Alice. He blinked to see her gone.

And that's when—in a single moment—I saw a man's mind break.

A father's heart shatter.

A king's crown fall.

I laughed. Hard. I couldn't help it. He jerked his attention to me, his eyes crackling with electricity. "I didn't even plan this one," I admitted. "You did this to yourself, you sick bastard."

The crimson lightning and peals of thunder drew alarmingly closer, and the wind began to whip at my hair. "What is the meaning of this, Temple?" He patted the book in his hands warningly. "I thought we had an understanding."

I grinned, raising my voice to be heard over the approaching storm. "I'm not very good at understanding. Oh, and before I forget, Alice wanted me to tell you something before she left. Page three is her favorite," I said, pointing at the Catalyst book—his only leverage.

He flipped open the aged book, and a single item slowly floated to the ground. A black feather with a red orb at the tip. I didn't need the feather to call Grimm. It was merely a hint. A little love note from a truly frightening little girl. A *Seer*.

"Grimm," I breathed, grinning like a lunatic as I felt the tides of fortune change.

"Come to me."

My Riders stepped up beside me, staring up at the skies with wicked grins. My unicorn appeared in the sky, silhouetted against the crimson glow of the black clouds so that he resembled a solar eclipse with a ring of pulsing ruby light around his majestic form.

I had to admit. He looked elegant and noble and—

"Hidey Ho, motherfuckers!" Grimm's voice boomed from the clouds above us. "Check this out. I can shoot freaking rainbows from my freaking *head!*"

And a nimbus of dark power bloomed around his horn, screaming like the souls of the damned, even as his horn began to crackle with white light inside the orb of evil.

"TASTE THE PAIN-BOW!" Grimm screamed.

And a rainbow consisting of seven shades of sin burst out of his horn, shrieking down in a hateful stream of grays and blacks like a charcoal painting of misfortune. It slammed into the ground, missing Zeus by about a foot as he leapt to safety.

Lightning immediately crackled in the sky—much closer than before—silhouetting Grimm from behind. I clasped my hand over my Horseman's Mask as I stared up at my unicorn. One of the ruby bolts writhed to life, reaching out to my unicorn like a tentacle. It latched onto his horn and exploded in a red flare that made me wince. Zeus burst out laughing, sitting on the ground and pointing his finger at where Grimm had been flying.

A moment later, Grimm slammed down onto the pavilion, flipping up his tail and dropping a deuce. Right on top of Ares and Apollo. He met Zeus' eyes as he shook his coat and feathers with a motor boating sound. "That loosened my bowels a little, thunder-snatch."

Zeus' blast hadn't incinerated him because he was now covered in diamond armor the color of inky obsidian. I grinned from ear-to-ear, relieved that my last-ditch attempt to protect him had worked. My Mask had saved him.

Peter was suddenly standing, his eyes wide and terrified as he pointed his stumps at his mouth, looking as if he was trying to shout but unable to open his lips. Being unable to move from his designated spot, Grimm's painbow blast had caused him to have a little potty accident.

Zeus climbed to his feet with a snarl. He shot a look at Aphrodite as if begging her help now that they were completely outclassed, relying on Stockholm syndrome to save him.

Pandora's Box sat on the marble. Aphrodite was struggling to her hands and knees, groaning. She looked as if she couldn't hear anything, but she saw the box and sucked in a breath.

Zeus lunged for it with a triumphant shout, obviously more concerned with power than his daughter's injuries.

He clutched it to his chest with an evil grin, turning to me. "We've both played our games, Temple, and you played better than I anticipated, but we both knew it would come down to this," he said, tapping the box.

I chuckled unconcernedly. "Unless it's empty," I said, turning my back on him. I lifted my finger high above my head, rotating my hand in a circling motion to signify that it was time to wrap it up. "I'm starving. Anyone want pizza?" I asked my Riders.

"I was holding out for a gyro," a familiar, disembodied voice purred, making the other Horsemen jump. "But I'll settle for you, Pharos." And her unseen fingers brushed my cheek as her scent filled my nostrils again.

"Kára?" Callie hissed incredulously, her eyes darting left and right in an attempt to locate the invisible Valkyrie.

"What do you mean?" Zeus demanded from behind me.

"Alice is safe," Kára said. "But I have something to do before we leave."

My three Horsemen stared at me, looking about ready to explode with questions. "Don't look at me," I said with a grin. "The girl does what she wants. I'm just along for the ride."

"You wouldn't dare bring me an empty box!" Zeus shouted. I sighed, annoyed, and turned back to him. "I can feel her power within," he argued. "It's undeniable. Aphrodite, get your husband out here. I put him in Temple's old cell. He will verify that his daughter is inside the box or he will die sobbing at your feet."

Aphrodite flinched—apparently able to hear, after all—her eyes widening in alarm. Despite hating her father, she obviously loved her husband more. She stumbled to her feet, and all but fell down the steps leading to the cells. I narrowed my eyes, wondering if this was a favorable or problematic development. I was saved from this moral conundrum by a surprising visual.

Out of nowhere, Peter grunted with three sizable holes suddenly appearing in his stomach as Kára hit him from behind with her trident. Although we couldn't see her, I knew the holes were her weapon's barbs poking out of his gut. And then Peter was flying across the ground, his feet dragging behind him as if propelled by a moving truck. He slammed into a marble column with a sickening—definitely lethal—sound and Kára flickered into view, lifting the Helm of Darkness from her head. I felt a pang of anxiety to see she hadn't used the eyepatch I'd left her, but it was overridden by my relief to see her back in action. I stared at her now gleaming golden armor, grinning proudly at the evil man she had just murdered as the thunder and lightning flickered across the hellish skies behind her.

That picture fit her perfectly, and would forever be imprinted upon my mind.

My Valkyrie.

Grimm neighed. "She's so badass. Never argue with her. Ever," he warned.

Kára let out a huff. "That was *empowering*." She set her boot on Peter's back and yanked her trident out. Then she glanced from Zeus to us, brushing a few loose strands of hair back with a gauntleted hand. Alucard made an approving sound and I elbowed him in the gut, knocking the wind out of him on reflex. Gunnar smiled absently, clenching Mjolnir tightly.

"ENOUGH!" Zeus roared. He lowered his attention to the box in his hands. But I could see the flicker of fear and doubt in his eyes, wondering if it was a trap or empty.

"All right. Pay attention, everyone," I said in a low tone, motioning Grimm and my Horsemen to huddle around me. "You're about to see a man look into the abyss," I said, watching Kára jog our way.

"What do you mean?" Callie asked. "Why would you give him the box?"

I ignored her question, keeping my eyes on Zeus. "And the abyss is about to fight back," I said, licking my lips as Zeus reached down to touch the lid of Pandora's Box. "I can practically taste the fear in the air already."

"I'm here," Kára said—as if in answer to my comment—as she skidded to a halt beside me. She reached down to briefly squeeze my hand affectionately, but she didn't peel her eyes away from Zeus. "Did you do it?" she asked.

I nodded. "Yup."

"He's going to shit."

"Wait. How do you know what I did?" I asked, frowning. I hadn't told her.

She shrugged. "Alice is a talker. Apparently, she's been learning quite a bit from Freya," she said with a proud smile.

"Anyone else about done with the cryptic lovers?" Alucard grumbled, annoyed. "Because I want to hit something. Now."

I blindly pointed at Ares and Apollo, whispering so only we could hear, although the storm pretty much covered any eavesdropping. "Good. Because they're faking it. Empty bottles of Ambrosia in their hands. Heals them right back up. Any minute now."

Callie snarled, subtly angling herself to face the new threat.

Grimm chuckled. "Now I feel bad," he said, laughing even harder as he pawed at the ground with his hooves, igniting a line of white fire. He obviously didn't feel bad for defecating on them, but it was the thought that counted.

"What were you two talking about?" Gunnar pressed. "What did you do?"

"Just watch. You should probably put on your Masks. There might be fallout..."

64

Z eus grinned like a madman as he stared down at Pandora's Box.

I grinned like a madman as I drew deep on my magic, creating a thick, milky mist to suddenly flood the pavilion. Zeus was too busy to notice, but my Horsemen watched me curiously.

"When you see them get up," I said, pointing at Ares and Apollo, "I need you to howl as loud as you can, Gunnar. I want you to make your vocal chords hurt. Howl for Calvin and Makayla."

He grinned wickedly. "I take it they're scared of wolves?"

"They weren't a few hours ago, but they spent some time in your old vacation spot."

He chuckled. "They'll think the mist is from Niflheim," he said, nodding his approval.

"If they don't scream it, I need one of you guys to do it. Loud enough for Zeus to hear."

They nodded.

"And put your damned Masks on!" I snapped. I gripped Kára around the waist and pulled her close, giving her a real kiss for the first time in entirely too long.

She melted into it as the mist swirled around us and my Horsemen put on their Masks. I cut the kiss short and pressed my forehead against hers. "I'm glad you're here for this."

She grinned. "Ditto," she breathed.

Then we pulled away at the same time, glancing back to see my Horsemen staring back at me. I grinned wolfishly. "They're all growed up," I said, proudly, as if I was dropping my kids off at their first semester of college.

Despair stared back at me, wearing a white Mask of raw crystal. From the waist down, she was merely a thick haze of white, glittering mist, seeming to stretch across the entire pavilion thanks to my magically born fog. When she moved her upper body, she left a trail of vapor, as if she was a ghost.

Justice was a towering white wolf, easily eight-feet-tall even though he was slightly hunched forward. His golden mask had reformed to fit his canine face, making me think of those old plague doctor masks with the long beaks. His paws sported long black diamond claws.

Absolution hovered above a scorched circle on the ground. He gleamed with emerald light, his skin also resembling quartz. Claws of pure flame hung from his fingers like whips, and I could feel their heat from five feet away.

"Ahh, shit!" Grimm neighed, clopping all four hooves excitedly. "It's *happening!*" he said, whipping his head anxiously.

I dipped my chin at them. "Make your legend, Riders." I lifted a hand to point behind them. Through the mist, Ares and Apollo were climbing to their feet, looking alarmed to be surrounded by their aversion to mist. Gunnar howled, and they both jumped in terror, jerking their attention left and right as they swatted at the fog frantically.

"NIFLHEIM!" Apollo screamed. "Why is it so dark—"

Ares shook him violently, pointing at the three Horsemen staring them down. "This ain't Niflheim," he growled. "Get your shit together." He drew a flaming sword and doubled in size, and I saw at least two dozen *other* forms rising up from the mist.

Apollo glared furiously, but his eyes told me he was biting back his fear —not that it had gone away entirely. He began to glow, powering up—

Absolution tackled him in midair, looking like Green Lantern, and the two of them flew out into the sky, sinking into the black clouds. Blooms of golden and then green light within made the clouds sizzle before reforming and I blinked. "Wow." A green and golden knot of light suddenly screamed overhead, the two of them zipping back across the pavilion just to scare the hell out of me, obviously.

"They, uh, learn pretty quick," Kára commented, sounding impressed but crouching slightly in fear of another flyby. "And now we're surrounded," she said, gripping her trident tightly.

She was right. Ares' army surrounded us. It began to rain, splattering down over us and our new enemies, making their heads glisten like fresh blood when illuminated by the crimson lightning.

Great sheets of rain abruptly slammed down upon us as Zeus turned up the dial, making it hard to see clearly, and hammering away at the mist I'd created. It had served its purpose anyway. I shoved Kára to the side, urging her closer to Zeus. "Let's give them room."

Despair stepped forward, wielding a spear of light in her hands. "They are just skeletons," she said calmly, her voice cracking across the pavilion like thunder. "And bones *break*."

She aimed her spear forward and the skeletons simply exploded into dust.

Ares snarled, slamming his fiery sword down into the ground.

This time, *hundreds* of skeletons rose up from the mist, and these all wore armor and wielded gleaming weapons. Luckily, they focused on Gunnar and Callie—Justice and Despair.

Justice reached down and grabbed one of the new skeletons, ripping it in half with a roar. His massive tail wagged, beating at the mist and almost clotheslining me before we escaped its radius of lethality.

We raced towards Zeus as the sounds of battle rose to a fervor behind us.

We were just in time to see Zeus practically rip the lid off Pandora's Box with a manic grin.

The look of victory and wonder slipped from his face as he realized he'd fallen for the old Trojan Horse shenanigan.

Embers and sparks erupted from within like a volcano had belched in the god of lightning's open mouth. His beard caught fire and he screamed, dropping the box.

But not before a Titan jumped out and punched him in the face with a fist of magma. Not even the torrential rain was enough to put out the flames. Zeus fell to the ground with a roar of pain, surprise, and outrage to see his old foe, Prometheus, play jack-in-the-box rather than Pandora, like he'd...

Heh. Like he'd *hoped.*

Kára turned to me with a feral grin, the rain plastering her hair to her scalp and accentuating the sharp lines of her face. "Prometheus," she shouted over the storm. "I thought—"

"But wait...there's *more*..." I shouted back, pointing.

She turned to see Zeus flat on his back, flinging his hands forward and snarling, even as the flesh of his cheeks burned and sizzled from the splash of lava. Lightning bolts struck a dripping shield of hardened magma Prometheus now held, knocking him back enough to give Zeus time to stumble to his feet.

And only just in time to miss the wicked stone scythe that slammed into the ground where he'd been lying prostrate. A small slip of a girl—half the size of the weapon—snarled like a panther. Pandora, and she had one of Yahn's eyepatches hanging around her neck rather than the Helm of Darkness I'd told her to use.

I narrowed my eyes at Kára and the Helm of Darkness she held under the crook of her arm.

She smiled back innocently. "It was her idea, not mine. I was unconscious, if you recall. I found this sitting next to my armor when I woke up."

I grunted, shaking my head. Invisible was invisible. Despite the comical size difference between Pandora and her blade, she yanked it from the ground and spun it in a dizzying blur, like it was a martial arts tournament, screaming as she deflected about a hundred sporadic blasts of lightning from Zeus's hands.

Pandora abruptly sidestepped and swung Cronus' Scythe like a baseball bat, goring Zeus across the stomach as his blasts tore into the space where she'd been standing a second before.

Prometheus skidded beneath the blurring scythe feet first like he was going for a slide tackle, but he abruptly rose up with a molten lava uppercut to Zeus' chin that sent him flying with an explosion of embers and sparks.

Zeus hovered high overhead, clutching his stomach. Ichor and lava dripped down to splash onto the pavilion as he hurled more blasts of lightning down upon Pandora and Prometheus—who now couldn't reach him and were forced to play defense. Prometheus lifted his hands above his head and a ceiling of molten rock suddenly formed to protect him and Pandora. Rain exploded into steam upon contact, but it didn't faze either of them. Prometheus was glaring at Zeus. "Coward!" he spat. A glob of lava struck the ground rather than saliva, and his eyes swirled with molten stone rather than light. He was tapping heavily into his Beast, Ignus, risking everything for this fight.

I began hurling balls of fire at Zeus as I ran, closing the distance.

Zeus cursed, spun, and fled the mountain, aiming for open air.

I slid to a halt beside Prometheus and Pandora, staring at Zeus as he flew a safe distance away, holding his arms out wide. The black clouds began to swirl around him, the crimson lightning screaming as it grew, piling on top of itself. Zeus' eyes glowed like stars and I knew he was about to blow up the entire goddamned mountain.

I snatched the scythe from Pandora and glared out at the god of lightning. Grimm trotted up behind me, following suit with his own death stare.

Alucard and Apollo sporadically screamed across the skies like fiery comets, disrupting Zeus' efforts, his lightning winking out or stabbing down into the empty sky rather than the mountain. Buying us time. I wondered if Alucard was doing it on purpose. Knowing him, probably.

I glanced back at Pandora. "Aphrodite ran to get Hephaestus," I said, pointing. "Your dad needs you. I've got this."

She smiled, wiping golden ichor from her cheeks. "I know you do, Hope." She roped her arm around Kára, pulling her close. "Our knight in shining armor."

Kára's smile slipped. "Wait—"

Pandora grinned. "My *platonic* knight," she assured her. Kára nodded, appeased. Then Pandora was running towards the prison cells. She must have slapped on her eyepatch halfway down the stairs, because she disappeared between one step and the next.

"Go, Prometheus," I said, turning back to the Titan as Zeus' lightning

winked out a few more times at a particularly blinding flurry of golden
flashes from Alucard and Apollo. I continued wiping water from my eyes
as the rain hammered down on us. "Keep her safe. I don't really know
which side Aphrodite might fall on. Or Hephaestus, for that matter. It's
family versus family, at this point."

"Looks like grandpa needs to step in," he agreed, shooting Zeus a dark
glare. He flung his rock shelter to the side. "You make him suffer, Nipple.
He's earned it."

I nodded. "I will."

He departed, leaving Kára and me to stare out at Zeus and his third
attempt at the crimson lightning. "How about a second date?" I asked Kára,
keeping my eyes on Zeus.

"Oh, yes. I wore this just for you," she said with a grin.

I turned to Grimm. "Room for two?" He eyed Kára thoughtfully. "As
long as she doesn't have a sensitive stomach."

Kára rolled her eyes. "I have my own ride, pony. Try to keep up."

She flared her wings out and Grimm grunted dismissively. "Show off.
But *you* don't have anyone to ride you—" He cut off abruptly and Kára
burst out laughing. I grinned at my unicorn, arching an eyebrow.

"Well, Grimm," she said, chuckling, "when a Valkyrie really loves a
Horseman—"

"I get it," he said grumpily. "And now you made this weird. Put up or
shut up."

She slapped the Helm of Darkness on and abruptly disappeared. I
couldn't sense a thing. I instinctively reached out with my hand and
managed to briefly touch the mountains of Heaven before she swatted my
hand away. "Stop!" she snapped, laughing.

I grumbled. "Fine. Let's go wrangle up a god, pardners," I growled in
my best Clint Eastwood rasp, wishing I'd taken Carl's cowboy hat, after all.
I climbed atop Grimm and held on for dear life.

"Yeehaw!" Grimm squealed, taking us to the skies with a sickening
lurch.

"We've got him on the run, now!" Kára screamed in an Old West drawl
—probably pointing, but that was extremely unhelpful with her being
invisible.

Zeus took one look at Grimm racing towards him, and he promptly turned and bolted away. I relished the irony of Zeus being pursued by the last thing he'd put in Pandora's Box. Hope.

The god of lightning fled.

And the Horseman followed.

To hunt down a varmint or something.

65

I batted away my tenth bolt of inbound lightning, swearing angrily. "Your horn is a goddamned lightning rod," I shouted through the wind. "You need to get out of here!"

"Did you grow wings that I'm not seeing?" Grimm yelled back.

I slapped the Mask of Hope onto my face, and bone spines erupted from my back as a wave of black diamond grit suddenly rolled over my flesh, encasing me in armor much like Grimm wore. I glanced down to see my satchel was now affixed to my waist as part of my armor. It looked like—

I glared at my Horseman's fanny pack, cursing the world in general. Whatever. I was still cool. Zeus' lightning might not kill us with the protective armor, but it would still hurt like hell and slow us down, letting him get away. And two targets were better than one.

"Keep your distance," I shouted. "This thing isn't at a full charge, but maybe I can juice it up with some of these lightning bolts," I growled.

Grimm cursed as I slapped him on the ass and leapt off his back in a perfect backflip.

"Is that a fanny pack?" Grimm hooted, roaring with laughter. I ignored him, focusing on my majestic acrobatics—

I was struck by a bolt of crimson lightning exactly one second later, and my perfect backflip morphed into a starfish suffering a seizure. My arms and legs shot wide and I gasped as...

Raw *power* fused through me, thickening my diamond skin and heightening my senses even more than usual. I shuddered as the last of the tremors subsided, realizing that it hadn't actually *hurt*. It had made me spasm involuntarily, but it had also *jumpstarted* my Mask.

I saw Zeus frozen in mid-flight, staring at me in stark disbelief.

I pointed a single claw at him and roared.

Grimm neighed as lightning narrowly missed him, silhouetting him in the clouds above. He aimed his horn and shot a black painbow down on Zeus, his wings unfurling in a cape of black feathers. The red tips made his matching colors transform him into the apparent monster causing the storm around us.

I drew my power and flung a whip of black lightning at a nearby crimson bolt from Zeus. It froze in place as my whip wrapped around it. I tucked my wings back and swung, using the frozen lightning like Tarzan used tree branches—to swing through the jungle of clouds.

At the apex, I released my whip and unfurled my bone spine wings, catching air. Despite having minimal feathers and being designed for combat, they served perfectly well as real wings because a membrane of dark magic hung between each spine. Zeus hurled a dozen more bolts at me and Grimm, and I chose my favorite, flinging my black lightning whip at it.

Again, the crimson bolt froze upon contact, and I repeated the process, swinging towards the god faster and faster, as I gained a rhythm of the undulating motions.

"I'm Miles Morales!" I cackled, feeling like the newest Spiderman—the kid who sported black and red threads and wicked sneaks.

Zeus began to panic, focusing more on his own escape than sucker punching me in the air, since that was now pointless. He was only giving me monkey bars to play on. Silly god.

Rather than rely on my wings for speed—because I had no conscious idea of how to use them in a specific way since they had always kind of worked on a subconscious level—I hurled more whips at the same clouds Zeus used and found I was able to use them just as well as the crimson fingers of electricity.

Maybe my Catalyst trick had let me tap into Zeus' power and it had nothing to do with my Horseman skin at all. As a Catalyst, I'd learned that I seemed to suck up powers as I confronted them, able to tap into them as needed.

So, even though Zeus stopped hurling as many bolts, I closed the distance quickly, thanks to Grimm's blasts of painbows herding Zeus directly into my trajectory.

The Horseman and his unicorn hounded the petty god.

And I heard Kára laughing gleefully, the sound booming like thunder across the skies. An unseen force struck Zeus in a professional tackle, and the lightning bolt he'd been preparing went limp and flaccid.

He cartwheeled through the air for a moment, struggling to make sense of things and find a purchase to latch onto with his own whips of lightning.

Which was when I kicked him in the back of the head, and then latched onto him in a tight hug, wrapping my wings around him so he couldn't throw out any more whips.

We sunk into the black clouds below with Grimm and—hopefully— Kára in hot pursuit, plummeting like rocks. I laughed into Zeus' ears like a maniac.

"You never should have opened that box, godling," I snarled, sinking my claws into his ribs.

To hold him tighter, of course. He gasped and screamed, begging for us to renegotiate, promising me the sun and moon, demanding me to release him, crying that I would need him.

The sounds rolled off me like water on a duck's back.

I did not need this...*wretched creature*—as he'd called Alice.

The world did not need this vile varmint either and I was the new Sheriff in these here parts, so it was my job to be the long arm of the law.

I couldn't think of any other Western tropes, although I tried.

We broke cloud cover and I winced in surprise at the perfectly blue sky with pristine white clouds above us. A gleaming city of glass and blindingly white marble raced towards us—surprisingly small, but no less elegant for it.

Olympus was fucking *beautiful*.

And I was aiming straight for the Acropolis.

We tore through the roof—courtesy of Zeus' face—and slammed into a statue of, well...

One could say Zeus was taken down by his own ego.

His face slammed into the seated statue of himself, head butting his own head and snapping the marble god's dome clean off—like he'd attempted to tackle his reflection in the mirror, but with a less humorous or harmless outcome.

For him.

The marble head crashed to the ground out of sight, and I managed to ride the Olympian down his own chest and lap like a skateboard, leaving a golden smear of ichor from throat to groin before I kick flipped his battered body down to the ground and landed in a perfect superhero pose, my knee grinding into Zeus' back. I hopped away guardedly, staring at my makeshift skateboard.

Zeus lay nearly still—trembling and whimpering in a pool of his own golden ichor.

Fun fact. Worship service was in, because we weren't alone.

I flared out my wings and reached into my fanny pack of doom, like a badass.

66

Odin and Freya stood on one side, blaspheming by merely existing in this place. They were terrified of my fanny pack, judging by the horrified looks on their faces.

I saw Loki and Fenrir loitering out front, peering through the open concept entrance of the Acropolis. As big as the building was, it wasn't quite large enough to house the wolf, so they remained outside. Loki waved at me jovially.

Hera stood beside her brothers Poseidon and Hades. Hermes stood a few paces back, smirking at my fanny pack. Poseidon gripped his trident, Hades gripped a tall pitchfork, Hermes held his caduceus, and Hera gripped...

A frozen daiquiri. She took a loud slurp, smirking at me from over her glass. "Sanctuary daiquiri," she said in answer to my silent question. Her eyes shifted to her groaning husband and I could practically hear her purring louder. "I'm in mourning. Preemptively. And I drink when I'm stressed. And when I'm relaxed. And when I'm celebrating."

I nodded very slowly, wondering who I'd need to take out first and how willing Fenrir was to help with a little demolition rehab of the Acropolis.

The Horseman of Death stood between the two factions, holding his scythe but he wasn't wearing his Mask. Instead, he looked like a charming, handsome, older gent—a lawyer to settle a property line dispute between two neighboring families after a shared oil field had been discovered.

Not knowing what else to do, I whipped out Cronus' Scythe from my fanny pack.

The gods took one look at the blade and stiffened, their eyes widening in fear. Well, Hera took another lil' sip of her frozen adult beverage. Part of me really wanted to hang out with her more.

Death maintained his calm. "So, *that's* where it went," he said slowly. "I assumed as much as soon as Hades told me of the theft." He shot a glance at Hera, but she pretended not to notice. She obviously hadn't ratted on me. "And Pandora?"

No one had asked about Zeus, although his brothers were staring at him with stern frowns.

"She's around," I said in a mischievous tone, letting them worry that she might be *around* the corner—a lot closer than they would like.

Death nodded. "Thank you for arresting him," he said, indicating Zeus.

Hades shot a look at Hermes and then nodded affirmatively. "He has indeed lost himself to the Carnage. I had to see it for myself to believe it."

Hera rolled her eyes and snorted.

Poseidon thumped the butt of his trident onto the marble floor and dipped his chin. "Thank you for bringing him to justice, Master Temple."

Odin and Freya were noticeably silent, assessing the situation. Zeus was now sobbing, and I realized he had managed to climb to his knees to kneel before me.

I considered the situation very carefully. I had already done so several times in my most hopeful dreams and thoughts, asking myself what the conclusion to this scenario should entail.

"Lords and Ladies of Olympus, I accept your kind invitation as a guest." They grimaced but nodded. "We have not been formally introduced. I am Nate Temple, the Horseman of Hope," I said confidently. Again, they nodded, obviously well aware. "This man threatened to use one small child to get to another small child. That is unforgivable."

"We agree, Master Temple," Poseidon said, choosing to use my formal title again.

Hades nodded. "We will lock him away—in Tartarus, if we must. Let him spend eternity with the Titans."

I lifted Cronus' Scythe and they all flinched. I studied it in silence, nodding absently. "Time," I mused thoughtfully. "The problem with your suggestion, Lord Hades, is that it lets a morally *bankrupt* man believe he has anything left to *spend*. Time is the most valuable commodity, as you well know. To let this man have the dignity of spending time *anywhere* is a crime. And..." I turned to appraise the broken, bleeding god before me. "A Horseman needs to make an example. Not just for you, but for the world. For the other pantheons," I said, shifting my attention to Odin and Freya. "They need to know that karma has a name. They need to know that Zeus should have never opened Pandora's Box. And he never should have let Hope escape, for I was his undoing."

Death held up a calming hand, knowing me well enough to pump the brakes early. "You are correct, of course, Nate. But think about this. He has allies. Putting another target on your back by executing him will not help your cause."

I cocked my head, glancing back at him. "Execution?" I asked slowly, tasting the word and finding it lacking. I shook my head. "No, not that." They visibly relaxed. "This is an *exhibition*."

And I swung the scythe, decapitating the god of lightning as easily as if he were a reed in a field at harvest. His head bounced, coming to a rest at my feet. His eyes blinked. I watched until the electricity finally winked out of the old boy. Hera had set down her drink and was slow clapping with a cigarette hanging from her lips. I had no idea when the lush had lit up, but smoke 'em if you got 'em, sister.

"Now he is unplugged," I said, which was funny. Kára's disembodied laugh backed me up, startling the fuck out of everyone present. Hera coughed out a cloud of smoke, cackling. Poseidon and Hades shot her disapproving frowns, but Hermes was biting his knuckles to stifle his own laughter. Probably at my joke, not Hera's hacking.

I calmly withdrew Gungnir from my fanny pack of devastation. Odin gasped, taking a step back as his eyes reflexively shot towards Fenrir. The wolf growled hungrily, warningly. Zeus' soul zapped into the yellow Devourer on the tip of Gungnir with an audible gulping sound.

I slowly turned to the gods, holding Gungnir in one hand and Cronus' Scythe in the other.

Odin eyed Gungnir anxiously and I met his eyes without any indication of my intent.

Hades looked displeased that I had stolen his brother's soul.

It had been risky to reveal Gungnir, but I had needed to take Zeus' soul before Hades had an opportunity to gain any measure of power over the situation. I had needed to keep everyone on their toes—especially Odin.

Hera was puffing contentedly on her cigarette, and had picked up her drink again. She lifted it in cheers to me, shooting a smug look at Zeus' head.

My decision to utilize Gungnir's Devourer, yet not hand it over to him, served to let the Olympians know that I was also not beholden to Odin— and that I would not give him any measure of power over their own pantheon. Or the hulking threat to Odin's life looming just outside the Acropolis, who was still growling audibly.

The Olympians nodded satisfactorily.

Odin, on the other hand, had the benefit of having witnessed me killing the Father of the Olympians and hefting a scythe that could make short work out of any of them. It would even make short work of the Titans. And I wasn't handing that over either.

I held blades to both throats, proving my impartiality.

Death nodded with silent pride. He and I had a long talk coming, but I didn't have time right now. He might not be so happy, then.

I scooped up Zeus' head with a tendril of magic—because *ick*, and my hands were full. I spotted Grimm chatting with Fenrir and Loki out front near a grove of trees. Loki took a drink from a flask, eyeing the contents with a pleased grin. I saw a young woman's silhouette slipping through the grove of trees and Loki lifting the flask to her with a mischievous grin.

Had Loki already found a way to score some local hooch? Judging by how much better he looked than he had earlier tonight when I'd arranged for him to dump Ares and Apollo on the mountain, I was betting he was sipping Ambrosia.

The god of mischief was a Rockstar. Hermes met my eyes and winked conspiratorially.

I grunted. Make that *two* gods of mischief.

"I assume there is a mutually unfavorable truce?" I asked Odin, jerking my chin towards Fenrir. He nodded. "Good. Let's all step outside," I said. "There are...*things* to discuss."

The gaggle of gods—both pantheons—shared significant looks with each other before following my suggestion, herded forward by Death. I took my Mask off and rolled my shoulders. With a thought, the coin was back around my neck, and I was in a posh suit, courtesy of Aphrodite.

"Rawrr," Kára purred in my ear, swatting me on the ass as I took my first step.

Freya glanced back at the sound of the slap, frowning. I grinned sheepishly and smiled.

She followed the others outside. "Be ready," I told Kára.

"For?" She whispered.

Watching the array of gods, I sighed, shrugging my shoulders. "I'm a Horseman, not a therapist."

She chuckled darkly. "Noted."

I slipped the two big ass polearms into my fanny pack of—

Damn.

It was gone since I had switched back to normal clothes. It had kind of been growing on me. With a sigh, I slipped the weapons into my satchel, freeing up my hands for things to come.

67

I leaned against a pillar, spending a few moments locking eyes with each god. I'd already announced a new truce for the duration of our meeting, just to be sure Fenrir followed the rules. Still, he licked his lips hungrily, eyeing Odin like a slab of raw beef.

Odin set his jaw, refusing to look at his nemesis. Loki watched in wry amusement, still tipping his flask back and looking healthier by the minute. He lifted it to Hermes. "Thanks, cousin. Just what I needed after Niflheim."

Hermes smirked back. "No problem. I'm thinking we all need to learn to work together these days. Family being what it is, and all."

Loki snorted. "Dude. My dad and son want to *kill* each other," he agreed, grinning.

Hermes eyed the severed head at my feet and pursed his lips. He didn't look upset, but he did look...thoughtful. He finally lifted his eyes to mine. "We are without a god of war, and we will need someone to guide us when the time comes."

"The Omega War," I said, grimacing. "Ares might not be dead. Yet. But let's proceed as if he is. I would bet my everything on that horse crossing the finish line first."

The Olympians nodded and, judging by the looks in their eyes, I had no doubts that they would take care of the Ares job for me if I asked.

"We would agree to fight behind you," Hermes pressed.

I grunted. "And how would that work?"

"We could each swear on caduceus," he suggested. "It symbolizes negotiation."

I didn't answer him immediately. Instead, I turned to Loki. "Mind giving me a drink? I feel a slight headache coming on."

Loki closed the flask and tossed it to me. I caught it and unstoppered it. I took a quick drink and let out a contented sigh. Then I held it out to my side. "And one for my homey," I said, tipping it.

Before a drop of Ambrosia spilled, the flask simply disappeared.

The gods stiffened abruptly, falling silent. Kára took a loud drink, making sure everyone knew she was there. I felt the flask hit my hand and accepted it. The gods gasped to see it reappear in my hand again, and I sensed Kára silently shifting to my other side before she became a target. Hades glared, knowing exactly what was happening, but that hadn't been my point. Death had outed me about the scythe, so Hades already knew I had his Helm.

Tensions rose as everyone suddenly wondered *who* the hell my invisible friend was. I knew who they *thought* it was, which was my intention —Pandora.

Instead of addressing the little drama I'd created, I eyed the grove of trees. "What are those?"

"Olive trees," Hermes said, smirking at the tension I'd caused.

I nodded. "Okay."

I lifted my hand and one of the trees screamed as I ripped it to shreds, imploding it in on itself, tearing up the earth in the process. The gods cursed and huddled into two camps—Asgardian and Olympian. I ignored them, knowing Kára would keep an eye on them as I worked.

I compacted the tree, twisting it in on itself further until it became the size of a staff. I tapped into my Fae magic, weaving the power into my creation in order to remove the weight of the tree so that the staff was light enough to carry.

Finished, I snapped my fingers. The newly formed staff zipped into my outstretched hand. The pale wood hummed in my grip, but it wasn't complete like I had hoped. I looked up at the gathered faces and nodded.

I reached down and dipped my fingers in the pool of ichor from Zeus' severed head and wiped it on my new staff. The ichor absorbed into the wood like water to a sponge, creating golden veins in the wood that resembled arcs of electricity.

"Give me some of your essence," I commanded. "Something that symbolizes you, specifically. Doesn't have to be blood. Just something to signify your agreement."

"Our agreement to what, exactly?" Hermes asked, obviously the spokesman.

"An Olive branch," I said. "A symbol of peace, not negotiation. Because you all need to really understand something," I said, leaning forward, "this is *not* a negotiation. This is an ultimatum."

They nodded soberly.

"Did you need to destroy the whole tree?" Hera asked, frowning at the torn earth.

"Yes. There can be no peace without war and destruction."

It might say something that they didn't bother arguing with me. Even Fenrir and Loki joined in. Fenrir licked it. Loki shrugged and pricked his finger, dabbing the blood on the surface. It instantly soaked into the wood, forming a strange symbol. I handed him back his flask and he took a sip, marveling as the wound on his hand closed. Odin and Freya approached at the same time, sliced each other's palms with daggers, and then gripped the wood. Runes burned into the wood as if they'd branded the staff with a hot iron.

The Olympians followed suit, their offerings sinking into the wood and either leaving behind a symbol or an aesthetic addition. Black water from River Styx from Hades turned the entire staff black. Water from the darkest depths of the ocean from Poseidon left behind a trident symbol. Hera... well, she poured some of her Daiquiri on it. Since it left behind a hazy symbol, I shrugged in acceptance. Hermes spit on it and the staff felt even lighter than before. I glanced down to see a pair of wings etched into the base.

Grimm hit it with a tiny black painbow that scared the shit out of everyone since he hadn't warned us. Fenrir burst out laughing.

Death approached but I pulled the staff away with a polite shake of my head. "This is between my Dread Four and the gods, not you and yours." He studied me thoughtfully, no doubt wondering if it had been a slight—a storm on the horizon between us. It wasn't, but it didn't hurt to keep him on his toes. For now. I wasn't upset with him, but I was kind of upset with him. In my youth, I would have been furious with him for deceiving me.

But with the wisdom of a century of chaos packed into less than a decade, I was merely perturbed. So, my silence was a figurative *get off my lawn*. I reached into my satchel and lifted Gungnir back out. Fenrir's ears perked up nervously and Odin grew still, looking like he'd heard the first broken bottle in a seedy bar and sensed that fists were about to fly freely.

With my magic, I plucked the Devourer—the gem now crackling blue and gold with the addition of Zeus' soul—out of the blade and held it above the tip of my new olive branch staff. The black wood stretched and grew, encasing the Devourer in a protective hold and firmly embedding it in the wood.

I nodded satisfactorily and then flung the staff into the air near my side. Kára—still invisible—caught it, and the staff disappeared. Odin gaped in disbelief, sputtering incoherently. Freya gripped his arm forcefully and shook her head. He visibly calmed, but his eye was murderous.

"Thanks," I murmured, hefting Gungnir and turning to Odin and Fenrir. The spear was still ridiculously powerful—perhaps even strong enough to kill Fenrir—but it no longer held his beloved Devourer. It was nothing personal, I'd just needed one, and I'd needed something symbolic from Odin for what I intended next. Something to show Fenrir his devotion.

"Your feud ends now. At least until this Omega War is over. And that means a promise from both of you. None of this *as long as he doesn't try to kill me* garbage. In fact, you two are now allies, and I demand that you work to help each other. The same way Odin would fight to save his wife and Fenrir to save Loki. You're family. Start acting like it or you'll end up like Zeus." The Olympians studied me thoughtfully. "If one of you dies suspiciously, I kill the other. Period," I said. "I'll save the investigation for after the funeral pyre."

Fenrir studied me somberly. Finally, he spoke. "I will not kill Odin. I will fight by his side as a respected brother through the Omega War."

Odin slowly turned to look at him, looking taken aback. Freya was biting her lip hopefully. "And beyond, if he can abide it." He glanced up at me. "That last part was because you have impressed me, Catalyst. Keep doing that."

Loki grunted, lifting his flask. "Damn."

Odin nodded, eyeing Fenrir with a faint smile. "I will not kill Fenrir. I will fight by his side as a respected brother through the Omega War. And beyond, if *he* can abide it," he added with a smile.

Then, the two dipped their heads at each other, and the tension swamping the grove dissipated. Almost as if by magic.

I handed Gungnir to Odin. "Thank you, Dean," I said, emphasizing the name he'd carried for most of my life—as my butler. He smiled warmly, appreciating it. "I'll find you a new Devourer. This was a...necessary gesture," I said, my eyes flicking towards Fenrir meaningfully. Both of them nodded, understanding my meaning. Remembering Alice's strange advice —and Freya's warning to Kára about quitting her Valkyrie job, I added one more bit. "I submit to the judgment of Asgardian Court," I said, taking a shot in the dark.

Freya's jaw dropped and Odin grunted. "How did you—"

"What is this?" Hermes snapped, suddenly anxious.

I held out a hand. "It has nothing to do with this," I said. "It is a personal matter. Right?"

Fenrir sat down, cocking his head thoughtfully.

Odin met my eyes with his one, his eyepatch reflecting the light. He looked truly baffled. "Yes. It is a personal matter. Nothing to do with...this," he gestured vaguely.

Freya cleared her throat. "Kára must also stand for her crime," she said sternly.

I folded my arms. "Dear?" I called out with a smirk, glancing to the empty space beside me.

Kára appeared, lowering Hades' Helm of Darkness from her head. The gods stirred in a chorus of gasps. Hades openly cursed, glaring at his helmet. "I knew it!"

Poseidon frowned. "I thought it was Pandora!"

"That's what you get for thinking," Grimm drawled.

Hermes smirked at Kára, nodding his approval. Kára held the helm out to Hades and dipped her head. "Thank you for letting me borrow it, and I promise not to talk about the statue on Temple Island."

Hades froze in the act of accepting his helm, and shot her a horrified look. Then he accepted it with a respectful dip of his chin. "Of course, Valkyrie. My pleasure." The look he shot towards Hera, on the other hand, promised later words. She shrugged, sipping her daiquiri.

Kára was clever. She'd just forced Hades into agreeing it had been a loaner or she would tell the world about his love of dogs—alluding to the totally fictitious statue of him...embracing Anubis.

Kára had helmet braid, but it still looked cute as she turned to face her boss, Freya. "I will submit to your judgment."

Freya pursed her lips, not pleased by the ruse that Kára had been here the whole time—a witness to her humility.

"When?" I asked warily.

Odin and Freya shared a long look. "A month?" Odin asked his wife.

Freya narrowed her eyes. "No. Now."

Odin sighed reluctantly. "As you wish, my wife." He settled his glare on me. "You have left a vacancy in Asgard. You murdered Thor. My son. Then you kept Mjolnir—a powerful symbol to Asgard. That cannot go unpunished."

I nodded, waiting.

"Although he deserved it, I cannot ignore such a crime. Thor had duties and responsibilities, and now those are being neglected. Since your fellow Horseman holds Mjolnir, and he only killed Thor with the assistance of your power, Asgard holds you accountable."

"That is fair."

"For your crime, you will take Thor's seat. Not as a god, but as a member of our war council." He eyed the Olympians and pursed his lips. "Given the circumstances, that shouldn't be a problem."

I considered it. Finally, I nodded. "I accept this sentence."

Freya cleared her throat, facing Kára. "You have failed in your duties as a Valkyrie. You neglected your duties to arrest Loki and Fenrir, and abandoned your post for a war involving a different pantheon," she said. Obviously, she was talking about this whole shit show.

Kára nodded, pursing her lips. "And I would do it again."

Freya narrowed her eyes. "I warned you that abandoning your role as a Valkyrie would cost you your soul."

"You did," Kára said stiffly.

Freya watched her student in silence for at least a full minute. "You are stricken from the ranks of the Valkyrie army."

Kára stared at her, but she looked more confused than defiant. "Not stripped of my wings..."

Freya shook her head. "No. But you are ill-suited for the military unit. I therefore require that you work for the war council. Each member has their own Valkyrie guard to protect them in the interests of Asgard."

Kára gasped. I stared incredulously. Alice was definitely getting some new crayons. For sure.

Freya was obviously forcing herself to remain composed, but I saw the smile warring to break through her stern countenance. "You will serve as Master Temple's Valkyrie guard until one or both of you die."

Kára sucked in a breath, trembling excitedly. "I agree," she whispered.

Freya dipped her chin. "Do not fail me a second time. Justice will not be so lenient."

She nodded hurriedly. "Yes, Freya."

Odin cleared his throat. "Then justice has been served."

Well. Wasn't that something. Not wanting to stretch my luck, I shook my head meaningfully at Kára. She nodded, flexing her fingers at her sides in a restless manner as she clamped her lips tight, lowering her gaze in a somewhat meek pose.

I'd humbled both Fenrir and Odin, and shocked the hell out of Asgard's power couple. Alice had told me that Freya knew all about Zeus impersonating me, so she had to know I'd uncovered this startling gift from the little Seer. In fact...maybe this was an offering. For saving Alice. Freya had found a way to both punish and reward the both of us.

I knew I had liked Freya for a reason.

The Olympians were staring at the two of us with open grins, blowing our cover. I squinted at them, but they just smiled wider.

I let out a breath, squaring to face the Olympians. "I guess I'll be your king, since you asked so nicely."

"General," Hermes corrected, frowning.

"Sure. That, too," I said, accepting both titles. "Oh, and pay up," I said, holding out my palm. I'd almost forgotten our bet.

A slow smile stretched across his cheeks. "Gladly."

He pressed four golden coins into my palm. I was actually surprised, because technically, the four he'd already given me could have arguably been my winnings. I didn't turn them down, though. Winning a bet against Hermes was worthy of a myth in and of itself.

I pocketed the coins and addressed the gods. "I did this, not out of cruelty or for my own vanity. This was a lesson for the world. I am the Catalyst. I am the Horseman of Hope. Me and my Riders—Despair, Justice, and Absolution—are not here to deliver the souls of mortals to the afterlife at the End of Days." I felt Death staring at me so intently that he was practically licking his lips. "My Riders are here to deliver the souls of broken gods to the afterlife. We are the godkillers, and karma is our blade. It's time for you to remember at whose pleasure you serve. The people worship you in exchange for your *protection*, not your arrogance and vanity. In case any of you do not understand this, I will send one of my siblings to discuss it with you. The Dread Four will ride, and a god shall die."

They shuddered, their faces pale. Finally, they nodded.

Surprisingly, they looked...hopeful. Even though I had killed their relative, they looked relieved that someone was here to act as a check to their power. Unless they were playing me.

Death gave me a very discreet smile and a proud nod. "The scythe suits you," he mused.

I smiled back, scooping up Zeus' head. "It's growing on me. The three of us need to have a nice, long chat. Bring your girlfriend. I feel like I don't know her very well," I said dryly, referring to the fraud Othello with the memory shard necklace. "Even though you've been dating her for years, now."

Death nodded knowingly. "Of course. Whenever you wish."

Kára leaned forward. "Before anger gets the best of you, remember the result of his ruse," she murmured, meeting my eyes. "The ends might justify the means," she said with a coy smile, gesturing at her body. "He might be my second favorite person in the world right now," she said, smiling at the Horseman.

I sighed in resignation. She wasn't wrong, but good freaking god. He deserved a slap on the wrist or something, right?

I mounted Grimm, preparing to leave. Poseidon stepped forward, lifting his trident. Grimm lunged, setting the tip of his now-glowing horn against the god's chest. "Easy, pal. You'd look really funny with a rainbow through your heart."

Poseidon nodded stiffly and backed up. "When will you return?" he asked, looking up at me.

I surveyed the city, noticing people—gods—milling about a safe distance away, obviously watching us and wondering who had destroyed their Acropolis. One look at Fenrir gave them an easy suspect and sent them scurrying.

"Hopefully soon. And under more benevolent conditions. Just so you know, I won't be coming alone until I have assurances you can keep your crew in line." I jerked my chin at the growing crowd. "Tell them the truth— along with the explanation I gave you. If I hear even a whiff of you attempting to spin this, I will be back sooner than you think, and under much different conditions. With more associates by my side. We have peace," I said, jerking my chin towards the hole in the ground where the olive tree had been. "The Dread Four will swear on it as well, or you may consider today's agreement nullified."

They nodded. "Yes, Master Temple."

I studied Zeus' brothers. "For what it is worth, Lords Poseidon and Hades...I am sorry for your loss. I had hoped Zeus could stand beside me in the upcoming War. He wanted to do so, but only if I and mine had collars around our necks. That is no way to win a war. Still, I dream of better days, stronger families, and greater empathy."

They looked taken aback for a few moments. Then they dipped their heads. "Apology accepted, Master Temple. To be fair, the Titans may have done worse to him."

I smiled. "You saw through my tough guy demeanor. Damn."

Ghosts of smiles split their faces for the first time, and they dipped their chins, looking thoughtful.

Death grinned and bowed.

Hera rolled her eyes. "Bye, husband. And good fucking riddance." She turned, weaving her way towards the city. I arched an eyebrow at Hades and Poseidon and they nodded in resignation.

"Hop on, Kára. We're not finished."

68

I decided to fly us back rather than making a Gateway or using one of Hermes' coins. I had no idea what I would find on the pavilion, and appearing directly in the center of the fight could be bad for my health. Unfortunately, Zeus had kicked up a doozy of a storm, and Grimm's horn seemed to attract the errant bolts now that they had no god to command them. After a few minutes of deflecting attacks, I realized it was not going to be a relaxing, celebratory flight with my newly-minted Valkyrie bodyguard pressed up against my back.

So, with a grimace, I slammed Zeus' head onto the tip of Grimm's horn. "Sorry, man."

Amazingly, it worked—much to Grimm's annoyance. The bolts no longer sought us out. "This is so humiliating."

Kára rested her chin on my shoulder as Grimm flew through the skies. The lightning—no longer hunting us down—was a peaceful light show of reds against black clouds. The thunder rumbled across the skies, and I smiled. It was oddly peaceful and serene, this chaos. I thought about my time on the astral plane, how I'd often found myself in a black world with red lightning in the distance. Had I somehow known it would end here? Had I seen the future somehow?

"So, *boss*," Kára murmured playfully, "what are the rules for workplace romance?" she asked, squeezing my waist.

"Not while I'm driving," I grumbled, even though her hug had been seemingly innocent. She laughed.

"How did you know?" she asked.

"Something Alice said. And I've come to trust her. She made it sound important. That we need to agree to their judgment. It made my skin crawl at the time, but I'll be damned if she wasn't right," I admitted.

Kára kissed my neck briefly and fell silent. "I'm still trying to process everything. I already thought the world had turned crazy," she whispered. "But never in a million years did I expect that. I thought she was going to knock my feet out from under me, taking you away," she whispered, her voice strained and on the verge of cracking.

I squeezed her hand reassuringly. "You might guard me, but I also guard you, Kára. No one is taking you from me. We gave up too much to get here."

She nodded. "Thank you. I needed to hear you say it." She grew silent and it felt right. Nothing needed to be said. Just being near each other was a soothing balm on my soul. "Alice told me some things, too. When I took her back to the Armory." Kára sounded pensive, but also...excited.

Before I could pepper her on it, the mountain spread out before us. And it was surprisingly calm. I nudged Grimm faster, not knowing if that meant a good or bad outcome for my Riders. We landed on the misty pavilion, disturbing the white blanket of fog so that it drifted up above our heads, briefly obscuring us. It no longer rained here, and the thunder and lightning were slowly rolling away, leaving behind only the black clouds and distant flashes of ruby light.

Zeus' head rose up out of the fog first and I heard Apollo shout. "Zeus lives! Father lives!"

Grimm snorted and slowly advanced, letting out a dark chuckle as he emerged from the fog with Zeus' head on his horn. "Don't get ahead of yourself, sunshine. I ain't yer daddy."

Startled gasps answered him as it became apparent that Zeus was just a severed head.

I hopped down from Grimm's back and held out a hand to help Kára down. We swept our eyes over the pavilion, searching for dangers. Thankfully, my Horsemen lived. They'd taken off their Masks and stood in a row before a very battered and embarrassed Ares and Apollo. I saw Pandora and a man I did not know standing before a kneeling Aphrodite a few paces apart from her brothers.

Prometheus was sitting on the lip of the mountain, hanging his legs over the edge of the world. I frowned, leaning low to whisper to Kára. "Can you give me minute?"

She nodded, assessing the Titan. "Of course." She trotted over to my friends, pulverized and shattered bones crunching under her boots. I smiled, shaking my head. Then I approached him.

Prometheus was shaking his head and muttering under his breath as I approached. He was smoking a cigar, the familiar smell making me smile as it brought back distant memories of my father. He had loved his cigars.

"How you holding up?" I asked, squatting down beside him, breathing in the sweet smoke.

He glanced at me with a tired smile, clenching the cigar between his teeth. He pulled it out. "Fucking family, am I right, Nipple?" He turned to look behind me, instantly spotting Zeus' head—still wedged on Grimm's horn—and smiled warmly, looking as if a great weight had been lifted off his shoulders. He took a celebratory puff and blew it up into the air. Then he appraised Kára, who was speaking with Callie in a soft, silent, tense conversation. "You don't do anything in half-measures," he said, chuckling. "Cigar?" he asked, offering me...

A Gurkha Black Dragon.

I froze, staring at him. That was why the smoke had been familiar. I'd chalked it up as cigar smoke in general. But he was smoking the *exact* cigar my father favored above all. Another thought came to mind, making my skin pebble. The Pandora Protocol had included another warning. I could still see the word flashing on the screen of the security feed from my parents' murder:

Titan.

"No way," I whispered, plopping down onto my rear as I accepted the offered cigar with shaking hands. "That was about you," I said, stunned.

"I don't know if you're aware," Prometheus said uncomfortably, "but your parents kept a secret or two."

I grunted. "Understatement."

He frowned, looking relieved that his comment hadn't set me off. "Oh. You mean they didn't tell you about any of this?" he asked, gesturing at the pavilion. I shook my head. "That's just bad parenting," he muttered, frowning in disapproval.

I stared at him in disbelief. Was he being serious right now, or was he kidding around.

"Small world, Nipple. Small world," he said pensively. "Your parents gave me a glimmer of hope years ago, appearing atop my mountain at night to tell me a few...unsettling things. I didn't believe them at the time, of course. Thirty-something years went by until their words came true," he muttered unhappily. "They didn't outright tell me that my glimmer of hope would literally end up chained beside me. That was why I got so panicked when you didn't free me," he admitted guiltily. "I thought I'd missed my moment." He grew silent, pondering his meeting with my parents. "Their claims were more general, but the highlights were the same," he said, gesturing at the aftermath of the fight I had mostly missed here on the pavilion. He pointed his chin at the others. "That should go well. You've got a few minutes before they need you, if your parents were right about that, too. I think. It was a while ago," he admitted, sounding doubtful of his mental recall.

I stared at him, baffled. Finally, I let out a sigh, giving up. "I'm feeling lucky today, so I'll take that gamble. It's not every day you win a bet against Hermes."

Prometheus snorted. "Damn Temples," he muttered. "Right again."

I grunted, letting the comment go. Just another crazy revelation on top of the mountain of secrets my parents kept. "Now you know how I feel," I grumbled. He opened his palm, and Ignus appeared. The little matchstick man lit the tip of my cigar with a high five. Prometheus was careful to keep the Beast in his hand, looking as attentive as a mother hen.

"Is that safe?" I asked. "I thought this mountain was covered in runes to trap Beasts?"

Prometheus nodded. "As long as he doesn't hop down onto the ground, he's fine. It was the combination of my shackles and the mountain that prevented me from even that much freedom."

I'd actually thought we were on a different mountain than where I'd first met Prometheus. I frowned. Maybe there were other peaks on the opposite side of the prison cells. Ignus sauntered up to the edge of Prometheus' fingers and fidgeted with his pants.

I frowned. "Um. What is he doing—"

A line of fiery sparks suddenly arced out of Ignus' waist, looking like a sparkler on the Fourth of July. I blinked. The Beast...was taking a piss. The little shit was taking a piss off the edge of the world.

Prometheus sighed. "I'm sorry. He's usually better behaved," he grumbled. "Little rebellious after being cooped up for so long."

Ignus angled his stream to strike the pavilion and wrote *Zeus* on the marble, scorching it into the surface. Then he began swinging his hips from left to right to scratch through it. Finally, his fiery shower petered out.

Heh.

I shook my head, puffing on my cigar. "Well. He's not wrong," I admitted.

"It's probably time for you to go sort that out. You can trust Callie, whatever *that* means," he said, obviously passing on information from my parents.

I studied the Titan in silence. Then I patted him on the shoulder. I rose to my feet, dipping my chin at him and Ignus. "I'll talk to you soon."

He grunted noncommittally.

I sighed, and made my way over to the others. Halfway there, I dropped the cigar and ground it out under my heel, having lost my interest in the nostalgic cigar after Prometheus' words.

I stepped up beside my Riders, smiling. "Everyone all right?" I asked, checking them over with quick pats and visual cues.

Gunnar rolled his eye, smiling. "Stop mothering us, Nate. It was fun," he said. Alucard was grinning smugly, seeming to be holding a staring contest with Apollo—who was obviously annoyed and definitely not reciprocating.

Callie smiled. "No problems, and it *was* fun," she agreed, smiling at Gunnar. "We made a great team, right Ares?" she teased.

The god of war grimaced, not meeting her gaze.

I turned to Pandora and the man at her side. "Lord Hephaestus, I presume?" I asked, making my way over.

The tall, burly man nodded. "You must be the Master Temple my daughter keeps raving about. Sorry, I've been a little out of touch with current events," he said, rubbing at his wrists. The pale flesh told me he'd been in cuffs for quite some time. Much longer than me.

Pandora beamed at me. "Nice staff."

"Watch it," Kára warned, smirking. "Paperwork's signed but I haven't driven it off the lot yet."

Pandora laughed delightedly. I studied Aphrodite. "Well, you got your wish," I said, gesturing at Zeus' head. Grimm seemed to be playing peek-aboo with Ignus, ducking Zeus' head below the mist and then popping up sporadically. I shook my head, wondering why the mist hadn't left.

I glanced at Callie, sensing her magic in the air. She winked at me, jerking her eyes towards Apollo and Ares, who kept watching the mist nervously, flinching and shying away from it. Callie was keeping the mist up to make them anxious—causing them *despair*.

I was proud of her. I smirked, nodding back.

"You helped me right a wrong," Aphrodite said calmly, drawing my attention back. "Thank you."

Hephaestus pointed at Aphrodite's wrists. "I slapped some new Titan Thorns on—and the key is not love, like the ones you wore. Pandora implied—very strongly—that I needed *your* permission to deal with *my* wife," he said, casting a heavy glare my way to show me what he thought about that.

Pandora rolled her eyes. "Father," she said, rolling her eyes and drawing out the word in an embarrassed tone. A faint smile tugged at the edge of his lips at his dad win.

I nodded thoughtfully, studying Aphrodite. "Can you give me a few minutes, Lord Hephaestus? There is a lot more to the situation than meets the eye, and I would hate to make a hasty, emotional decision. Tempers are high tonight."

He straightened at my respectful tone. "As you wish...Master Temple," he added, sounding appreciative and thoughtful.

I smiled, dipping my chin. "Thank you." I made my way back to my Horsemen. I quickly caught them up on my adventures on Olympus, showing them the new staff. They each nodded, agreeing unanimously. Then they bonded their essence to the staff—all of them chose their blood. Each left a strange symbol burned into the wood, in a vertical column from top to bottom.

The four of us turned to Ares and Apollo, who had heard everything I'd said and now looked absolutely horrified. Stunned silent. To hear they'd been ostracized...had broken them. They'd truly never believed that such a punishment could happen to men like them. Which was the whole point of the Dread Four. We were all about educating the gods, one soul at a time. Within heartbeats, they began pleading and begging for their lives —suddenly finding themselves in the position of mortals before gods.

Where their lives were actually in the betting pool and the dice had come up snake eyes.

Gunnar calmly stared at them, his lone eye cold and pure.

I restated my thought. Not Gunnar...

The eye of *Justice* studied the pitiful wretches before him, and he meted out their sentence. He turned to Alucard and Callie and drew a line across his throat. "I've already killed a god, so they are yours if you want to claim them. Nate and I can handle it, if you do not want to," he said in a neutral tone, not passing shame or judgment on either choice. I nodded my agreement.

Alucard stepped up to Apollo...

Callie stepped up to Ares...

And...they did their jobs. They didn't smile. But there was no forgiveness or mercy either. I knew the gods deserved their fates, but it was still hard to watch two men beg and cry, unarmed, as they faced a demise they'd never thought possible. Dying in battle was very different than sitting on a cold rock and looking your executioner in the eyes.

Kára set her hand on my lower back supportively. She did not flinch or turn away.

The pleas ceased, and Aphrodite let out a sharp breath.

Their souls zipped up into my staff's Devourer, crackling with red and bright white light for a moment, making the Devourer look like a rainbow. Then it dimmed.

Callie and Alucard shared a meaningful look and then turned to me. They nodded. There was no pride in the act, but satisfaction in the consequences. No one else would suffer their cruelty.

69

I made my way over to Aphrodite and met Hephaestus' eyes. I didn't blink. "Thank you."

He sighed. "They deserved worse," he said in a low whisper. "Much worse."

I nodded my agreement, staring into Aphrodite's terrified eyes.

I remembered everything she had done for me. Every little smile and tear we'd shared in our magical moments together. I remembered the feel of her flesh against mine. How her fingers had so carefully painted the Omegabet all over my skin. How she'd gotten me a suit. I remembered...

All the unconditional love she'd shown me.

She'd helped me fight back the carnage and find Kára. And she'd done all that so I could help her save Pandora, her husband's daughter. Aphrodite's words came to my mind in a soft whisper.

You inspired me to be a better step-mother to Pandora. I learned that love isn't about blood. I refuse to let Zeus break the child worse than he already has. She was conceived in a placenta of guilt and shame and horror, born in a womb of embers and sparks from Hephaestus' forge. Hephaestus did not put hope inside the box for mankind—he put hope inside the box for her. To protect Pandora from herself. Hope was to be her knight in shining armor...and look who is now the Horseman of Hope. You, and only you, can save her.

"You should know that she did all this for you—even more than for her hatred for her father. You," I said, looking at Pandora and Hephaestus, "were the catalyst that finally pushed her to act rather than remain silent. If Ares and Apollo hadn't been working for her, they would've been working for Zeus. Either way, we would have fought them. And ended them. They would have likely died fighting, but dead all the same."

Pandora smiled sadly and Hephaestus looked torn, wrapping a protective arm around his daughter as he stared at his wife.

"The crimes they committed were not at my request," Aphrodite said, lifting her chin proudly. "I did the only thing I could to try and harness their cruelty to a better purpose. I merely distracted them with trying to steal Pandora's Box before Zeus could. So that I could reunite my husband and his daughter. I accept your judgment." She glanced at me. Then Kára. Then Callie. "I can die with pride. I have accomplished more in the past week than the last millennia. Remember the good times," she told us.

I didn't let her comment sway my decision. I'd already made it. Now it was time to see where the others stood.

I glanced at Kára. "Well, she changed my life." Kára smiled, nodding her agreement.

"Me, too," Callie said. "I could...take her for a while. I know a safe place."

Aphrodite pursed her lips. "I would prefer a clean death."

Callie shook her head. "I was not implying torture. I think you might have more to teach me. Maybe some things I could teach you. About family. Perhaps love should not die this night."

Her words hung heavy in the air, and we all turned to Hephaestus, her husband.

He nodded. "That could work." He stared at his wife for a long while, looking torn. "I will need time to think on you, wife. I do not know if I trust you any longer. Perhaps, over time, I could try."

Pandora nodded, clutching her father's hand. "*We* could try," she said, smiling at her stepmother.

A single tear fell from Aphrodite's eye and she nodded, unable to voice her feelings. Then she let go, hanging her head to her chest. And she wept.

Kára smiled sadly, clutching at my hand. I squeezed back, patting it comfortingly.

With that settled, Callie set about arranging transport to Solomon's Temple, speaking with Hephaestus and Pandora in low tones. I didn't voice my thoughts that her secret castle had a direct connection to my Armory—since we leased the space from Callie. But Pandora's smile—and her sudden earnest proposal that Hephaestus should stay with her in the Armory—brought a smile to my face. I agreed. It was impossible to say no to Pandora when she smiled in that way.

And I was her knight in shining armor. I wasn't *allowed* to say no. There were rules.

"Sap," Kára teased, resting her head on my shoulder. I smiled, staring out over the edge of the mountain. The storm had dissipated quickly, emitting stubborn flashes in the distance, but no rain or lightning on the mountain.

"He left," I said, indicating the spot where Prometheus had been sitting. Pandora was frowning sadly, crestfallen.

Kára frowned. "Why?"

I sighed. "I'm not sure. I hope he's okay." My Riders stepped up beside me, staring out at the fading storm. "A new one is coming," I told them.

They nodded.

"We'll be waiting," Gunnar said. After a few moments, I felt him staring at me like a creeper. "We've been talking..." I glanced over at him, arching an eyebrow. I steadied my resolve, not sure if I liked the sound of his introduction. "We want you two to come to family movie night," he said in a rush, his eye darting from me to Kára. He let a breath out in a rush, and relaxed his shoulders.

Alucard and Callie were grinning over his shoulder, amused at his discomfort.

I chuckled. "Okay. That wasn't so bad, was it?"

Gunnar eyed Kára. "She makes me nervous," he said.

Kára beamed. "Do we need to have another talk?" she asked softly.

Gunnar shook his head, parroted by Alucard.

Callie studied Kára thoughtfully. "I think we need to have a talk. Whatever Valkyrie mind games you played on them works like a charm," she said, grinning.

Gunnar's phone suddenly belted out the *level-up* mushroom sound from the original Super Mario Brothers Game, and I burst out laughing. He fumbled with it, silencing it.

He glanced down at his phone with an embarrassed frown. "Ashley's probably wondering where I am."

Alucard grunted. "Was there a curfew on saving the world?" he asked, sounding amused.

Gunnar shook his head uneasily, shifting from foot-to-foot. "I might have told her I was getting groceries..."

Callie cursed, throwing her hands up. "I'm done. See you morons later. Where's Ryuu? I don't want him catching whatever idiocy Gunnar's sick with."

Kára hooted with laughter, clutching at her knees. "You're a dead man, Gunnar."

His face grew sickly. "It was the first thing I thought of," he mumbled.

I leaned closer, motioning for my Horsemen to huddle close. "We did a good thing tonight," I told them. "And we did it for our families. Our *family*," I amended. "I can guarantee they are more worried about you than you are about them."

I lifted my arm and ripped open a massive Gateway to the Armory. Our friends stood on the other side. Yahn let out a shout of joy to see Alucard. Ryuu didn't bother waiting, and leapt right through to rush to Callie's side, gripping her face tightly and pressing his forehead to hers.

And...I winced.

Ashley had apparently found her way into the Armory.

Carl waved his huge cowboy hat at us. "It's okay. I called her the moment they woke up. Surprise!" he said, nodding satisfactorily. Alice was standing on her tiptoes, grinning broadly.

Gunnar actually jumped in alarm to see his wife glaring at him. She planted her fists on her hips. "*Groceries?*" she roared. Carl's jubilant grin faded abruptly, and he cocked his head.

Alice grasped his claw and patted it reassuringly, still craning her neck to get a better look at Gunnar. Carl looked down at her for a moment, and then he promptly picked her up and set her atop a table so she could get a better view. She grinned and gave him a peck on the cheek. Carl's eyes widened and he froze, seeming unable to move.

But wait. If Ashley was in the Armory, then that meant...

I saw two beautiful blonde preteens shifting from foot-to-foot awkwardly, hiding behind...their mother. And I suddenly realized what Alice had been so intent upon seeing.

Calvin had pale, almost transparent, icy blue eyes, a strong jaw, and broad shoulders. He was a gangly scarecrow, but his bone structure made me wonder if he might wind up bigger than his father.

Makayla was a tall, pale-haired specter. Her prominent cheekbones and sharp jawline foretold some of the haunting beauty of the Norwegian heritage, and her eyes were a rich, vibrant blue.

My godchildren stared at their father with fear, desperately seeking his approval.

Gunnar fell to his knees and all the air left his lungs. He gripped Mjolnir as if it was the only thing rooting him to the ground.

Ashley's ire evaporated and her composure crumpled. "Come see your children, you foolish man," she croaked, tears spilling down her cheeks. Gunnar exploded through the Gateway from a kneeling position, sliding back onto his knees to wrap up the two beautiful children in his big beefy arms.

And then he cried.

Hard. His shoulders shook violently, and he had to have kissed their heads a hundred times each in a matter of seconds.

Although they had drastically changed their physical forms, and were noticeably self-conscious about it—as if fearing their parents love was somehow rooted in how they had once physically looked—they had known each other on a much deeper level than anything so topical.

That was the thing about wolves. Their definition for pack went far beyond *looks*. They could *feel* each other, smell each other. Their unity had nothing to do with the kids suddenly being humans—just like Freya had assured me. On the other hand, they were not seven-years-old like we had expected. Even still, the four Randulfs *knew* each other on the most important level, and were soon hugging each other like long-lost family rather than newly-found family. They were a dog pile of arms, limbs, and love.

Sure, it was confusing and everyone had questions and concerns, but they would face all that together as a pack—as a family.

I let out a sigh, my own eyes misting at the raw passion filling the Armory.

I glanced back to see Callie stepping through a new Gateway with Ryuu and Aphrodite. The three of them turned and smiled at me before it winked shut.

Pandora had stepped through into the Armory with Hephaestus, and was eagerly tugging him by the arm to show her daddy her first apartment. He flinched to see Carl suddenly sniffing him, but he handled it well. Especially when Alice grabbed his other hand.

I glanced at Kára, smiling. To hear such sounds in the Armory...

The sounds of *family*.

I'd been a bachelor for entirely too long. The chorus of family was what I really wanted.

Before she could say anything, I scooped Kára up in my arms, sweeping her off her feet.

And then I carried her across my threshold, grinning at her laughter.

I told Carl to make sure everyone had rooms inside Chateau Falco, and then I made a second Gateway to a different place entirely.

I let it wink shut before anyone could pester or follow us, and the torches in the Sanctorum flared to life. I smiled at Kára and set her down.

"This is my cave—"

She shoved me down into the concave bed of furs and pillows set below ground level, already stripping off her armor. "We're not talking. For a while," she said, her dual-colored eyes smoldering.

I grinned, tugging at my own clothes. It wasn't until I'd gotten my jacket off that I realized she'd spoken in Russian.

She slipped under the covers and curled up next to me. My heart thundered in my chest, reminding me of something. I closed my eyes and touched my chest with my thumb and forefinger.

Kára gasped beside me. "What is *that*?"

I opened my eyes to see the glowing pearl Aphrodite had shown me. "It's yours. I'm tired of carrying it around. You left it there a long time ago."

She blinked at me, her pupils big and dreamy. "I...don't understand," she breathed.

I propped myself up on my elbow and leaned over her. "Do you trust me?" I asked, smiling.

She nodded. "Yes."

I held the pearl over her heart and let go. It sunk into her body, disappearing from sight. She gasped, staring at me with a growing smile. "Oh, Nate," she whispered. "It's *you*," she said, touching her chest with an awed look on her face.

I smiled. "It's my heart's greatest desire. You."

She bit her lip, staring up at me...

And then we had wild crazy monkey sex.

Yeah.

It was pretty awesome.

And that was all I had to say about that. The rest of the world could just wait patiently until the wizard and the Valkyrie opted to leave their cave.

70

W e sat before the fireplace in the Sanctorum—the most uncomfortable double date ever.

Death and Othello—the woman with the memory shard —sat on the couch across from Kára and me. The two of us wore robes from the mansion. I'd made a Gateway to grab some essentials from Chateau Falco's kitchens and my bedroom so that we could stay nested here in our secluded paradise, away from the drama of my friends and the problems of the world.

Those were for later.

This conversation was all I cared about right now.

Death studied Kára with a pleased smile before turning to me. "I will try to start at the beginning," he said, leaning forward.

I nodded, waiting. Kára pressed up against me and pulled my hand into her lap, squeezing it tightly with both of hers. She seemed just as nervous as me.

"Recall the time we first met," Death began. "In the bar. You were dealing with the Academy Justices, angels, and Nephilim—who had used a Blood Debt on you to strip you of your magic. Your friends had all left town and you were all alone. Until Othello came to your aid. At the time, you did not know the Academy had taken her nephew in an attempt to blackmail her to betray you and turn you over. They wanted the Armory."

Kára trembled, her lips parting at the memory. I nodded, shuddering. "I remember."

"You used my Mask to defeat them, managing to pull off a win by the skin of your teeth, I might add. But...Othello died. You were able to bring her back, but you did so in a sloppy manner. To be fair, you shouldn't have been able to do it at *all*, even with my Mask. This was why my brothers took note and asked you to become a Horseman. This is why all of Heaven and Hell took note. You...seemed to have a natural, although unrefined, affinity. But we already had Four Horsemen."

I nodded. "You helped me fix Othello, saying I could bring her back to life, but only if I gave up my wizard's magic," I whispered.

Kára rested her cheek against my shoulder. "And that sacrifice—for me —saved my *soul*," she whispered. "You gave up your most cherished possession to save me," she sobbed softly.

Death nodded. "That sacrifice was goddamned fucking *powerful*, Nate. Almost destroyed my Mask," he said, shaking his head. "It set off a chain reaction of unanticipated consequences like a domino. I had to seek outside help to contain it."

I felt numb. Not with anger, but with disbelief. Here were three people who had shouldered impossible burdens for me, not saying a word about this for *years*.

I leaned forward, studying Othello beside Death. She wilted under my scrutiny. I remembered all the times I'd seen her since her rebirth. How she'd always been flirting with me, teasing me—even in front of her new boyfriend, Death. I'd had talks with her, conversations that only the real Othello would have been able to participate in. I eyed the memory shard necklace she wore with a pensive frown. That was how she'd accomplished it. "The memory shard grants you access to the real Othello's memories," I mused. She nodded. "So, who are you, really? A skinwalker of some kind?"

She shook her head. "We've known each other for years," she said, smiling at Kára. "We were hackers together. Anichka was my boss."

I frowned, turning to Kára. "Anichka?" I asked, confused.

She winced. "That is a name I gave up long ago, Nate. It has nothing to do with this, but I'll tell you all about it later. I promise."

I nodded thoughtfully. I'd had a different name from my earlier childhood in Fae—Wylde—so I couldn't blame her. We definitely had a lot of catching up to do, but it could wait. I turned back to the new Othello. "Okay, so you worked together as hackers."

She nodded. "I knew how she felt about you, Nate. She never stopped talking about her Pharos. She often said she was a ship lost at sea, searching for the lighthouse to bring her home." Kára blushed, lowering her eyes. I squeezed her hand lovingly, my heart swelling at the cute little story. "Hemingway came to me and told me the situation. That Othello had died and needed my help. Her soul was too powerful—now filled to bursting with your wizard's magic—to fit into her old body. It needed to be broken up until it had time to adapt to the power. He asked if I would take her body for my own." She smiled guiltily. "It was an upgrade, thank god."

Kára chuckled, rolling her eyes.

I stared at her memory shard, stunned. "So, all this time, you wore her body and the memory shard to...split her up, and her soul was sent into Kára's body," I whispered, shaking my head.

Death nodded, sliding back into the conversation. "That is the reason for her green and blue eyes. It is often a mark of someone with great powers beneath the surface. Yet, even with all of these safety measures in place, her soul was *still* too powerful. Your magic was tearing her apart from the inside. So...I had to help her get a job to alleviate the pressure."

"Freya," I whispered. "You lied to Freya so Kára could become a Valkyrie—a powerful, resilient, immortal body."

He nodded. "Odin—your nosy butler, at the time—instantly knew something was up. How I was now dating Othello after she died, and how his wife gained a new Valkyrie with an unknown past. To keep the secret—and to assure him it was in your best interests—he demanded that Kára swear an oath to watch over his wife, Asgard and, most importantly, *you*." The Sanctorum grew silent as they waited for me to pick up the pieces of my brain scattered across the floor.

"Which, of course, was not a problem," Kára murmured warmly at my side.

"Why not just *tell* me all of this?" I asked.

Death grunted. "You were dating Indie at the time," he said, "but that wasn't the deciding factor. If you learned of this without accepting in your heart how much Othello truly meant to you—on your own—both women would have instantly died. Permanently. Not just their bodies, but their very *souls*."

My eyes widened.

Death nodded. "That was how powerful your sacrifice of magic was when you decided to give it up for her. It was the first domino that symbolized how much she truly meant to you. It was an act of true love, although your mind had not consciously realized it. As such, the true consequences could not be shared until you fully realized how much this woman meant to you."

Othello leaned forward, fingering her memory shard. "It's why I was always flirting with you in front of Death. To try to trick you into falling for her again. Anything to save my friend's soul."

I leaned back into the couch, shaking my head. Kára slowly extracted herself and made as if to leave and give me space. I grabbed her hand and pulled her back down to the couch. "You're not going anywhere, Kára," I said softly. "I only just got you back."

She sighed, melting into my arms. "I thought you were upset," she whispered.

"Just overwhelmed, Kára." I glanced up at Death and Othello. "Thank you. For everything. For bringing my eagle back to her perch," I said with a warm smile, recalling Aphrodite's subtle hint about the woman I secretly loved.

Death nodded. "I would apologize, but...I'm not sorry, brother," he finally said. "Through this, you have also given me the chance to love," he whispered, turning to smile at Othello. "I...cannot think of a greater gift. Thank you, Hope."

Othello smiled, nodding her agreement and clutching his hand tightly.

And just like that, the world became a brighter place.

"True love conquers all," I said. Everyone nodded, mumbling their agreement. "Now get the hell out of here so I can love all over my girl."

They left, laughing, and Kára wasted no time climbing onto my lap. Her dual-colored eyes glittered brighter than the gems set into the ceiling of the Sanctorum as she straddled me, wrapping her arms around my neck. "My Pharos..."

I smiled, leaning closer. "I'm not calling you Othello anymore," I whispered. "It makes me think of Death, but Kára makes me think of *life*."

"Kára sounds better on your lips," she agreed in a whisper.

"Tastes better, too," I agreed, licking my lips.

And that was the beginning of the story on how we broke an antique couch that was at least a few hundred years old. Twice.

But the second time was her fault.

DON'T FORGET! VIP's get early access to all sorts of Temple-Verse goodies, including signed copies, private giveaways, and advance notice of future projects. AND A FREE NOVELLA! Click the image or join here: www.shaynesilvers.com/l/219800

Nate Temple will return...

Turn the page to read a sample of **UNCHAINED** *- Feathers and Fire Series Book 1, or* **BUY ONLINE (FREE with Kindle Unlimited subscription).** *Callie Penrose is a wizard in Kansas City, MO who hunts monsters for the Vatican. She meets Nate Temple, and things devolve from there...*

(Note: Callie appears in the TempleVerse after Nate's book 6, TINY GODS...Full chronology of all books in the TempleVerse shown on the 'Books by Shayne Silvers' page)

TRY: UNCHAINED (FEATHERS AND FIRE #1)

The rain pelted my hair, plastering loose strands of it to my forehead as I panted, eyes darting from tree to tree, terrified of each shifting branch, splash of water, and whistle of wind slipping through the nightscape around us. But... I was somewhat *excited*, too.

Somewhat.

"Easy, girl. All will be well," the big man creeping just ahead of me, murmured.

"You said we were going to get ice cream!" I hissed at him, failing to compose myself, but careful to keep my voice low and my eyes alert. "I'm not ready for this!" I had been trained to fight, with my hands, with weapons, and with my magic. But I had never taken an active role in a hunt before. I'd always been the getaway driver for my mentor.

The man grunted, grey eyes scanning the trees as he slipped through the tall grass. "And did we not get ice cream before coming here? Because I think I see some in your hair."

"You know what I mean, Roland. You tricked me." I checked the tips of my loose hair, saw nothing, and scowled at his back.

"The Lord does not give us a greater burden than we can shoulder."

I muttered dark things under my breath, wiping the water from my eyes. Again. My new shirt was going to be ruined. Silk never fared well in the rain. My choice of shoes wasn't much better. Boots, yes, but distressed, *fashionable* boots. Not work boots designed for the rain and mud. Definitely not monster hunting boots for our evening excursion through one of Kansas City's wooded parks. I realized I was forcibly distracting myself, keeping my mind busy with mundane thoughts to avoid my very real anxiety. Because whenever I grew nervous, an imagined nightmare always—

A church looming before me. Rain pouring down. Night sky and a glowing moon overhead. I was all alone. Crying on the cold, stone steps, an infant in a cardboard box—

I forced the nightmare away, breathing heavily. "You know I hate it when you talk like that," I whispered to him, trying to regain my composure. I wasn't angry with him, but was growing increasingly uncomfortable with our situation after my brief flashback of fear.

"Doesn't mean it shouldn't be said," he said kindly. "I think we're close. Be alert. Remember your training. Banish your fears. I am here. And the Lord is here. He always is."

So, he had noticed my sudden anxiety. "Maybe I should just go back to the car. I know I've trained, but I really don't think—"

A shape of fur, fangs, and claws launched from the shadows towards me, cutting off my words as it snarled, thirsty for my blood.

And my nightmare slipped back into my thoughts like a veiled assassin, a wraith hoping to hold me still for the monster to eat. I froze, unable to move. Twin sticks of power abruptly erupted into being in my clenched fists, but my fear swamped me with that stupid nightmare, the sticks held at my side, useless to save me.

Right before the beast's claws reached me, it grunted as something batted it from the air, sending it flying sideways. It struck a tree with another grunt and an angry whine of pain.

I fell to my knees right into a puddle, arms shaking, breathing fast.

My sticks crackled in the rain like live cattle prods, except their entire length was the electrical section — at least to anyone other than me. I could hold them without pain.

Magic was a part of me, coursing through my veins whether I wanted it or not, and Roland had spent many years teaching me how to master it. But I had never been able to fully master the nightmare inside me, and in moments of fear, it always won, overriding my training.

The fact that I had resorted to weapons — like the ones he had trained me with — rather than a burst of flame, was startling. It was good in the fact that my body's reflexes knew enough to call up a defense even without my direct command, but bad in the fact that it was the worst form of defense for the situation presented. I could have very easily done as Roland did, and hurt it from a distance. But I hadn't. Because of my stupid block.

Roland placed a calloused palm on my shoulder, and I flinched. "Easy, see? I am here." But he did frown at my choice of weapons, the reprimand silent but loud in my mind. I let out a shaky breath, forcing my fear back down. It was all in my head, but still, it wasn't easy. Fear could be like that.

I focused on Roland's implied lesson. Close combat weapons — even magically-powered ones — were for last resorts. I averted my eyes in very real shame. I knew these things. He didn't even need to tell me them. But when that damned nightmare caught hold of me, all my training went out the window. It haunted me like a shadow, waiting for moments just like this, as if trying to kill me. A form of psychological suicide? But it was why I constantly refused to join Roland on his hunts. He knew about it. And although he was trying to help me overcome that fear, he never pressed too hard.

Rain continued to sizzle as it struck my batons. I didn't let them go, using them as a totem to build my confidence back up. I slowly lifted my eyes to nod at him as I climbed back to my feet.

That's when I saw the second set of eyes in the shadows, right before they flew out of the darkness towards Roland's back. I threw one of my batons and missed, but that pretty much let Roland know that an unfriendly was behind him. Either that or I had just failed to murder my mentor at point-blank range. He whirled to confront the monster, expecting another aerial assault as he unleashed a ball of fire that splashed over the tree at chest height, washing the trunk in blue flames. But this monster was tricky. It hadn't planned on tackling Roland, but had merely jumped out of the darkness to get closer, no doubt learning from its fallen comrade, who still lay unmoving against the tree behind me.

His coat shone like midnight clouds with hints of lightning flashing in the depths of thick, wiry fur. The coat of dew dotting his fur reflected the moonlight, giving him a faint sheen as if covered in fresh oil. He was tall, easily hip height at the shoulder, and barrel chested, his rump much leaner than the rest of his body. He — I assumed male from the long, thick mane around his neck — had a very long snout, much longer and wider than any werewolf I had ever seen. Amazingly, and beyond my control, I realized he was beautiful.

But most of the natural world's lethal hunters were beautiful.

He landed in a wet puddle a pace in front of Roland, juked to the right, and then to the left, racing past the big man, biting into his hamstrings on his way by.

A wash of anger rolled over me at seeing my mentor injured, dousing my fear, and I swung my baton down as hard as I could. It struck the beast in the rump as it tried to dart back to cover — a typical wolf tactic. My blow singed his hair and shattered bone. The creature collapsed into a puddle of mud with a yelp, instinctively snapping his jaws over his shoulder to bite whatever had hit him.

I let him. But mostly out of dumb luck as I heard Roland hiss in pain, falling to the ground.

The monster's jaws clamped around my baton, and there was an immediate explosion of teeth and blood that sent him flying several feet away into the tall brush, yipping, screaming, and staggering. Before he slipped out of sight, I noticed that his lower jaw was simply *gone*, from the contact of his saliva on my electrified magical batons. Then he managed to limp into the woods with more pitiful yowls, but I had no mind to chase him. Roland — that titan of a man, my mentor — was hurt. I could smell copper in the air, and knew we had to get out of here. Fast. Because we had anticipated only one of the monsters. But there had been two of them, and they hadn't been the run-of-the-mill werewolves we had been warned about. If there were two, perhaps there were more. And they were evidently the prehistoric cousin of any werewolf I had ever seen or read about.

Roland hissed again as he stared down at his leg, growling with both pain and anger. My eyes darted back to the first monster, wary of another attack. It *almost* looked like a werewolf, but bigger. Much bigger. He didn't move, but I saw he was breathing. He had a notch in his right ear and a jagged scar on his long snout. Part of me wanted to go over to him and torture him. Slowly. Use his pain to finally drown my nightmare, my fear. The fear that had caused Roland's injury. My lack of inner-strength had not only put me in danger, but had hurt my mentor, my friend.

I shivered, forcing the thought away. That was *cold*. Not me. Sure, I was no stranger to fighting, but that had always been in a ring. Practicing. Sparring. Never life or death.

But I suddenly realized something very dark about myself in the chill, rainy night. Although I was terrified, I felt a deep ocean of anger manifest inside me, wanting only to dispense justice as I saw fit. To use that rage to battle my own demons. As if feeding one would starve the other, reminding me of the Cherokee Indian Legend Roland had once told me.

An old Cherokee man was teaching his grandson about life. "A fight is going on inside me," he told the boy. "It is a terrible fight between two wolves. One is evil — he is anger, envy, sorrow, regret, greed, arrogance, self-pity, guilt, resentment, inferiority, lies, false pride, superiority, and ego." After a few moments to make sure he had the boy's undivided attention, he continued.

"The other wolf is good — he is joy, peace, love, hope, serenity, humility, kindness, benevolence, empathy, generosity, truth, compassion, and faith. The same fight is going on inside of you, boy, and inside of every other person, too."

The grandson thought about this for a few minutes before replying. "Which wolf will win?"

The old Cherokee man simply said, "The one you feed, boy. The one you feed..."

And I felt like feeding one of my wolves today, by killing this one...

Get the full book ONLINE! http://www.shaynesilvers.com/l/38952

Turn the page to read a sample of **WHISKEY GINGER** *- Phantom Queen Diaries Book 1, or* **BUY ONLINE.** *Quinn MacKenna is a black magic arms dealer from Boston, and her bark is almost as bad as her bite.*

TRY: WHISKEY GINGER (PHANTOM QUEEN DIARIES # 1)

The pasty guitarist hunched forward, thrust a rolled-up wad of paper deep into one nostril, and snorted a line of blood crystals —frozen hemoglobin that I'd smuggled over in a refrigerated canister—with the uncanny grace of a drug addict. He sat back, fangs gleaming, and pawed at his nose. "That's some bodacious shit. Hey, bros," he said, glancing at his fellow band members, "come hit this shit before it melts."

He fetched one of the backstage passes hanging nearby, pried the plastic badge from its lanyard, and used it to split up the crystals, murmuring something in an accent that reminded me of California. Not *the* California, but you know, Cali-foh-nia—the land of beaches, babes, and bros. I retrieved a toothpick from my pocket and punched it through its thin wrapper. "So," I asked no one in particular, "now that ye have the product, who's payin'?"

Another band member stepped out of the shadows to my left, and I don't mean that figuratively, either—the fucker literally stepped out of the shadows. I scowled at him, but hid my surprise, nonchalantly rolling the toothpick from one side of my mouth to the other.

The rest of the band gathered around the dressing room table, following the guitarist's lead by preparing their own snorting utensils—tattered magazine covers, mostly. Typically, you'd do this sort of thing with a dollar-bill, maybe even a Benjamin if you were flush. But fangers like this lot couldn't touch cash directly—in God We Trust and all that. Of course, I didn't really understand why sucking blood the old-fashioned way had suddenly gone out of style. More of a rush, maybe?

"It lasts longer," the vampire next to me explained, catching my mildly curious expression. "It's especially good for shows and stuff. Makes us look, like, less—"

"Creepy?" I offered, my Irish brogue lilting just enough to make it a question.

"Pale," he finished, frowning.

I shrugged. "Listen, I've got places to be," I said, holding out my hand.

"I'm sure you do," he replied, smiling. "Tell you what, why don't you, like, hang around for a bit? Once that wears off," he dipped his head toward the bloody powder smeared across the table's surface, "we may need a pick-me-up." He rested his hand on my arm and our gazes locked.

I blinked, realized what he was trying to pull, and rolled my eyes. His widened in surprise, then shock as I yanked out my toothpick and shoved it through his hand.

"Motherfuck—"

"I want what we agreed on," I declared. "Now. No tricks."

The rest of the band saw what happened and rose faster than I could blink. They circled me, their grins feral...they might have even seemed intimidating if it weren't for the fact that they each had a case of the sniffles —I had to work extra hard not to think about what it felt like to have someone else's blood dripping down my nasal cavity.

I held up a hand.

"Can I ask ye gentlemen a question before we get started?" I asked. "Do ye even *have* what I asked for?"

Two of the band members exchanged looks and shrugged. The guitarist, however, glanced back towards the dressing room, where a brown paper bag sat next to a case full of makeup. He caught me looking and bared his teeth, his fangs stretching until it looked like it would be uncomfortable for him to close his mouth without piercing his own lip.

"Follow-up question," I said, eyeing the vampire I'd stabbed as he gingerly withdrew the toothpick from his hand and flung it across the room with a snarl. "Do ye do each other's make-up? Since, ye know, ye can't use mirrors?"

I was genuinely curious.

The guitarist grunted. "Mike, we have to go on soon."

"Wait a minute. Mike?" I turned to the snarling vampire with a frown. "What happened to *The Vampire Prospero*?" I glanced at the numerous fliers in the dressing room, most of which depicted the band members wading through blood, with Mike in the lead, each one titled *The Vampire Prospero* in *Rocky Horror Picture Show* font. Come to think of it...Mike did look a little like Tim Curry in all that leather and lace.

I was about to comment on the resemblance when Mike spoke up, "Alright, change of plans, bros. We're gonna drain this bitch before the show. We'll look totally—"

"Creepy?" I offered, again.

"Kill her."

Get the full book ONLINE! http://www.shaynesilvers.com/l/206897

(Note: Full chronology of all books in the TempleVerse shown on the 'BOOKS BY SHAYNE SILVERS' page.)

MAKE A DIFFERENCE

Reviews are the most powerful tools in my arsenal when it comes to getting attention for my books. Much as I'd like to, I don't have the financial muscle of a New York publisher.

But I do have something much more powerful and effective than that, and it's something that those publishers would kill to get their hands on.

A committed and loyal bunch of readers.

Honest reviews of my books help bring them to the attention of other readers.

If you've enjoyed this book, I would be very grateful if you could spend just five minutes leaving a review on my book's Amazon page.

Thank you very much in advance.

ACKNOWLEDGMENTS

Team Temple and the Den of Freaks on Facebook have become family to me. I couldn't do it without die-hard readers like them.

I would also like to thank you, the reader. I hope you enjoyed reading *CARNAGE* as much as I enjoyed writing it. Be sure to check out the two crossover series in the Temple Verse: The **Feathers and Fire Series** and the **Phantom Queen Diaries**.

And last, but definitely not least, I thank my wife, Lexy. Without your support, none of this would have been possible.

ABOUT SHAYNE SILVERS

Shayne is a man of mystery and power, whose power is exceeded only by his mystery...

He currently writes the Amazon Bestselling **Nate Temple** Series, which features a foul-mouthed wizard from St. Louis. He rides a bloodthirsty unicorn, drinks with Achilles, and is pals with the Four Horsemen.

He also writes the Amazon Bestselling **Feathers and Fire** Series—a second series in the TempleVerse. The story follows a rookie spell-slinger named Callie Penrose who works for the Vatican in Kansas City. Her problem? Hell seems to know more about her past than she does.

He coauthors **The Phantom Queen Diaries**—a third series set in The TempleVerse—with Cameron O'Connell. The story follows Quinn MacKenna, a mouthy black magic arms dealer in Boston. All she wants? A round-trip ticket to the Fae realm...and maybe a drink on the house.

He also writes the **Shade of Devil Series**, which tells the story of Sorin Ambrogio—the world's FIRST vampire. He was put into a magical slumber by a Native American Medicine Man when the Americas were first discovered by Europeans. Sorin wakes up after five-hundred years to learn that his protege, Dracula, stole his reputation and that no one has ever even heard of Sorin Ambrogio. The streets of New York City will run with blood as Sorin reclaims his legend.

Shayne holds two high-ranking black belts, and can be found writing in a coffee shop, cackling madly into his computer screen while pounding shots of espresso. He's hard at work on the newest books in the Temple-Verse—You can find updates on new releases or chronological reading order on the next page, his website, or any of his social media accounts. **Follow him online for all sorts of groovy goodies, giveaways, and new release updates:**

Get Down with Shayne Online
www.shaynesilvers.com
info@shaynesilvers.com

f facebook.com/shaynesilversfanpage

a amazon.com/author/shaynesilvers

BB bookbub.com/profile/shayne-silvers

O instagram.com/shaynesilversofficial

y twitter.com/shaynesilvers

g goodreads.com/ShayneSilvers

BOOKS BY SHAYNE SILVERS

CHRONOLOGY: All stories in the TempleVerse are shown in chronological order on the following page

NATE TEMPLE SERIES

(Main series in the TempleVerse)

by Shayne Silvers

FAIRY TALE - FREE prequel novella #0 for my subscribers

OBSIDIAN SON

BLOOD DEBTS

GRIMM

SILVER TONGUE

BEAST MASTER

BEERLYMPIAN (Novella #5.5 in the 'LAST CALL' anthology)

TINY GODS

DADDY DUTY (Novella #6.5)

WILD SIDE

WAR HAMMER

NINE SOULS

HORSEMAN

LEGEND

KNIGHTMARE

ASCENSION

CARNAGE

FEATHERS AND FIRE SERIES

(Also set in the TempleVerse)

by Shayne Silvers

UNCHAINED

RAGE

WHISPERS

ANGEL'S ROAR

MOTHERLUCKER (Novella #4.5 in the 'LAST CALL' anthology)

SINNER

BLACK SHEEP

GODLESS

ANGHELLIC

PHANTOM QUEEN DIARIES

(Also set in the TempleVerse)

by Cameron O'Connell & Shayne Silvers

COLLINS (Prequel novella #0 in the 'LAST CALL' anthology)

WHISKEY GINGER

COSMOPOLITAN

OLD FASHIONED

MOTHERLUCKER (Novella #3.5 in the 'LAST CALL' anthology)

DARK AND STORMY

MOSCOW MULE

WITCHES BREW

SALTY DOG

SEA BREEZE

HURRICANE

BRIMSTONE KISS

CHRONOLOGICAL ORDER: TEMPLE VERSE

FAIRY TALE (TEMPLE PREQUEL)

OBSIDIAN SON (TEMPLE 1)

BLOOD DEBTS (TEMPLE 2)

HURRICANE (PHANTOM...9)

BRIMSTONE KISS (PHANTOM...10)

CARNAGE (TEMPLE 14)

ANGHELLIC (FEATHERS...8)

SHADE OF DEVIL SERIES

(Not part of the TempleVerse)

by Shayne Silvers

DEVIL'S DREAM

DEVIL'S CRY

DEVIL'S BLOOD

Printed in Great Britain
by Amazon